THE DOOMSDAY MEDALLION

Sixteenth-century French prophet Nostradamus predicted the Great Fire of London, Napoleon's conquest, Hitler's rule, and the atomic bomb. Can the VanOps team keep the old seer's secrets out of blood-stained hands?

Aikido black belt Maddy Marshall is celebrating the completion of her black ops training when news of a military takeover in the South China Sea shocks the world because it was predicted by a sixteen-year-old French student. When intel chatter spells danger to Avril, the young seer, VanOps Director Bowman assigns Marshall and her twin brother, Will Argones, to protect the girl.

Emotions between the siblings are running hot due to their aunt's recent stroke, which has reminded them of the childhood accident that scarred both his chin and her heart. Tensions ratchet higher when they arrive at Avril's home to find the instant social media star has been kidnapped, leaving them with only clenched fists and cryptic clues that lead to a mysterious formula encoded on an etched-bronze medallion.

While Taiwan fears an invasion that will set off an apocalyptic chain of events, Marshall and Argones race through medieval French towns, Italian cathedrals, and ancient Greek temples attempting to find Avril before their enemies use the girl to discover the Holy Grail of military intelligence. If the team fails, they won't need a crystal ball to know millions of innocent souls will be destined to join Nostradamus in the afterlife.

The Doomsday Medallion is an electrifying, globe-trotting thriller that delves into humankind's timeless fascination with prophecy and illuminates the mesmerizing and dangerous potential of a weaponized oracle.

ALSO BY AVANTI CENTRAE

The VanOps Series:

The Lost Power - VanOps #1
Solstice Shadows - VanOps #2

PRAISE FOR THE DOOMSDAY MEDALLION

Honorable Mention — Southern California Book Festival

"With a jaw-dropping, rewarding twist at the end, every mystery, crime, and thriller fan should read Doomsday Medallion." —*San Francisco Book Review*

"An epic and bewitching mashup of historical suspense and political thriller. Perfect for fans of Steve Berry and James Rollins." —BestThrillers.com

"Masterful. A perfect blend of roller-coaster thrill ride and historical revelation." —David S. Brody, bestselling author of *Cabal of the Westford Knight*

"An action-packed, high-stakes journey through ancient European landmarks in search of a secret so powerful it can explain the past and predict the future." —Al Pessin, multi-award-winning author of the Task Force Epsilon thrillers, *Sandblast, Blowback,* and *Shock Wave.*

"Centrae is a master of the page-turner. It wouldn't surprise me if Nostradamus himself predicted *The Doomsday Medallion* would be a bestseller." —Rob Samborn, author of *The Prisoner of Paradise*

"One of the best thrillers of the year." —Rick Treon, author of *Divided States,* a 2021 Best Thriller Book Awards finalist

"Sizzles with suspense!" —Elena Taylor, award-winning, bestselling author of *All We Buried*

THE DOOMSDAY MEDALLION

A VANOPS THRILLER

AVANTI CENTRAE

THUNDER
CREEK
PRESS

GENRE: THRILLER/SUSPENSE

THE DOOMSDAY MEDALLION
Copyright © 2021 by Avanti Centrae
Cover Design by David Ter-Avanesyan/Ter33Design
All cover art copyright © 2021
Edited by Andrea Robinson

Hardcover ISBN: 978-1-7349662-9-9
Paperback ISBN: 978-1-7349662-8-2
eBook ISBN: 978-1-7349662-7-5

Library of Congress Control Number: 2021920021

First Hardcover Publication: March 8, 2022

Printed by Ingram in the USA.

Published by Thunder Creek Press: **http://www.thundercreekpress.com**
Grass Valley, California

For my "other mother," Kathleen T. Schaefer

And for all those who love their traditional, and untraditional,
moms

"If you know the enemy and know yourself, you need not fear the result of a hundred battles."

—*The Art of War,* Sun Tzu

Ripped from recent headlines:

"ALMOST 40 CHINESE WARPLANES BREACH TAIWAN
STRAIT MEDIAN LINE; TAIWAN PRESIDENT CALLS IT A
'THREAT OF FORCE.'"

— CNN, September 21, 2020

"Beijing's strategy isn't just based on undermining Taiwan's
resistance; it's also a gamble on how the U.S. will approach the cross-
strait issue."

— Daniel Russel, former top State Department official, Sept. 8, 2020

"U.S. VP HARRIS SAYS CHINA INTIMIDATES TO BACK
SOUTH CHINA SEA CLAIMS."

— Reuters, August 24, 2021

PROLOGUE

PRESENT DAY

SALON-DE-PROVENCE, FRANCE

JANUARY 13, 1:45 P.M.

Disguised as a hunchbacked old man using a cane, the Watcher followed her down the narrow street called Rue Nostradamus. The raven-haired sixteen-year-old with a scarred face and her middle-aged au pair moved with purpose, their soles clacking like bones on the ancient cobblestones. He'd been waiting for them at the café near the intersection, where a handful of metal patio tables still clutched last night's frost.

Per his choice, only one young operative accompanied him on the potential kidnapping mission, a short, pit bull of a man named Raphael. Unhappily camouflaged as a woman, Raphael had followed the pair of females from the train station while updating the Watcher on their progress through a discreet high-tech bone-conducting microphone.

Moving further down the alley, he braced himself and the cane against the cold afternoon wind. As he hobbled past a battered blue barn door with rusty hinges, Avril, the girl, stopped and glanced back.

Does she know we're following her? he wondered.

He kept shuffling toward her, eyes downcast so she wouldn't notice his one glass eye. She turned her attention to the square plaque next to the entrance of Nostradamus's former abode. From prior visits, the man knew the sign announced that the famous prophet had been the guest of royalty during his lifetime and had left behind an impressive legacy of prophecies that fervent believers pored over whenever dramatic world events occurred.

The girl's hips swayed as she and the au pair entered the Musée Nostradamus. There were signs that the building was once beautiful— its tan brick walls held the remains of stucco, and the second-floor windows were laid out in an intriguing diagonal. But the modern touches, like the black metal and glass door, made it lovely no longer.

Taking shelter in a deep doorway next to the faded blue barn door, the Watcher leaned his cane against the wall and pulled out a pack of American cigarettes, the likes of which had added layers of gravel to his voice over the years. He spoke in French. "They are in the museum."

"I am around the corner." The operative's voice was low and rough, the sound of death rustling dry leaves in the night.

The deep voice made for an interesting contrast to Raphael's disguise, which had the man squirming the second he saw the navy skirt, flats, a fine wool coat, and flashy silver hoop earrings.

The Watcher took a single cigarette from the pack and, cupping his hand around the tip to ward off the wind, lit it with his gold lighter. "Good, wait there."

"We should take her today and find out what she knows."

He inhaled the smoke and considered the suggestion. His foreign patron had given him carte blanche. And it *was* tempting. But he'd been after this prize for most of his adult life and had learned to wait and observe. He'd earned his nickname.

"The time isn't right," he replied.

"But you believe she has the formula that Nostradamus used to see into the future."

For a moment, staring at the glowing tip of his smoke, he saw far into the past, recalling one of the bearded man's prophecies. On the first evening of July in 1566, Nostradamus, renowned physician, astrologer, and herbalist, had told his secretary, "You will not find me alive at sunrise." The prophet died the next day.

Based on mountains of research, the Watcher was convinced that Nostradamus had not only predicted his own death, but also hid the formula he used for his trances in a sealed box bequeathed to his daughter. Although the world's superpowers had been searching for decades to find the formula as a way to gain military supremacy, it remained hidden in the shadows of time.

"I have a hunch, only," the Watcher said, pulling on his smoke. "We have no facts yet that the girl has the box. It hasn't been seen in 450 years. And if she does have it, it's unlikely she'd be here, looking at wax mannequins."

"Why is she here then?"

Of late, the girl seemed fascinated with the seer. "I think she's learning what she can of Nostradamus. Research."

"If she does have it, though, it's worth a bonus for us, right?"

That was exactly why Raphael was here. Money. A generous, retire-to-the-Greek-islands financial reward. But for the Watcher, the funds paled next to the influence he would wield by having the ability to tell the future. He'd been obsessed with all things Nostradamus since before he joined the army. The United States had shown interest in the prophet in the 1970s after a new biography hinted that the seer had documented his secrets in a formula, but had dropped their search after a lack of immediate success. He smiled to himself; he'd played no small part in dissuading them to move on by eliminating the operative who'd been hot on the trail.

Such fools the Americans were. He knew the value of patience. And the potential prize of prophecy.

His benefactor was also well aware of the value of knowing the future. According to his sponsor, scientists had made strides with getting test subjects into trance states using sound and light machines, but the prophetic results were inconsistent. They needed precision, bullets-produced-to-spec-level consistency. From reading between the lines on recent encrypted phone calls, the Watcher didn't need a fortune-teller to tell him war was in the wind. The forthcoming military campaign would be won or lost based on how the US responded to his patron's first move.

Inside the museum, the girl wandered past the glass door, hands behind her back as she studied a wall-sized arcane diagram, similar to those drawn by Leonardo da Vinci. The Watcher had examined those images for decades, looking for hidden meanings. He'd never found any.

He took a final drag on his cigarette, dropped the butt, and ground it into the stone cobbles with the heel of his boot until no spark remained.

"Yes," he finally answered Raphael. "That's why we have her under surveillance. We *will* snatch her when the time is right."

CHAPTER 1

Maddy sped down the ski chute, kicking up clouds of chalky snow with every turn. Her twin brother, Will Argones, had wagered that he could beat her to the bottom of Alpine Meadows Ski Resort's most dangerous run—a double black diamond.

She yelled back at him. "Catch me if you can!"

They'd grown up here in the Lake Tahoe region, and had made a day trip from Napa to celebrate the completion of her covert operations training. She'd been wanting to get AJ, her adopted son, on the slopes, too, and it was a good day for it.

The sky was the type of deep cerulean blue she'd only seen on crystal-clear days in the mountains, and it had snowed last night, a good six inches of fresh powder on a base that had been building since late November. The air smelled crisp and full of pine. The green limbs of the tall Jeffrey pines and fir trees were covered in brilliant white. It was a scene right out of a snow globe. She'd almost made the Olympic ski team once, and was in her element.

Loose snow ran up her body and across her face, blurring her vision. They called skiing on powder "snorkeling" for good reason. She whooshed around a tree and then dropped over a gnarly cliff tall enough that it sent her stomach lurching.

Problem was, Will and her boyfriend, Bear, were both good skiers, and she and Will had competed against each other on every mountain in the region. She ground her skis into the snow, digging for purchase.

There was something about coming up here that always brought out a nasty sibling rivalry between the two of them. Maybe it was seeing the icy turn where her mom had been killed when they were six. Or perhaps it was driving by the house they lived in throughout high school, until Dad had moved down to the Napa Valley to pursue his winemaking dreams—before his untimely death.

Ghosts. There were ghosts here.

They'd even lost two good friends in the same deadly avalanche at Kirkwood. Tom and Sara. Both had been expert snowboarders. After the accident, Maddy had developed a keen fear of the rolling snow-based tidal waves, but the gang had convinced her conditions were not ripe for a rush of snow today.

She glanced over her shoulder. Will's dark, wavy hair was dusted in white, and his bright snow jacket showed off his tan face. Dark sunglasses covered his eyes above a strong nose. He was gaining on her. She was tall, but his legs were longer. Bear, her sweet lover who kept hinting at having babies that she wasn't ready to make, was a good twenty feet back.

Turning on imaginary afterburners, she got even more aggressive with her turns. Her long dark hair, somewhat restrained under a black cabbie hat, whipped as she jackknifed down the mountain. Her thighs began to burn. All that black ops training had gotten her in shape for shooting a semiautomatic while rolling under a moving car, but she was out of skiing shape. They were only about halfway down the Keyhole, the steepest slope Alpine Meadows had to offer.

A series of low moguls appeared and she crouched low, hitting the first one with enough velocity that she sailed over the next two bumps and landed smoothly. Over the years, she had learned to meditate with her eyes open, calling it *listening* because focusing on sounds helped her achieve that special mental state sought after by mystics, weekend yogis, and trained warriors. Wanting every advantage in this race, she tuned into the sounds around her. Her skis *shooshed*, a chunk of snow fell off a nearby tree with a *thunk*, and wind whistled in the pines. The clean scent of the fir trees became more pronounced and visual details around her sharpened.

Will flew by on her left, flashing her a Cheshire-cat smile. Distracted, her ski caught an edge and she nearly wiped out. Years of training meant she didn't fall, but her momentum took a hit. She was only human, but the mistake irritated her.

Will held the lead now.

Clenching her teeth, she barreled down the fifty-five-degree slope. Will had seemed especially bitter today when they'd driven by the corner where Mom's car had lost control. Tensions between them had been running high since Aunt Carole had a stroke last week; even though the prognosis was good, it was clear their childless aunt could no longer live alone in Danville. Will thought Aunt Carole should live with him and his cat on his live-aboard boat, while Maddy figured she and Bear were the better option, as Will was not exactly a chef. Bella, their sister, who was still steaming mad that the twins couldn't discuss their work with her, had told Will that Aunt Carole didn't belong with either of them, and that she and her husband, with their "more stable life," would be the best choice.

Maddy thought the rift between Will and her over their mother's death had closed, but with the Aunt Carole situation, tensions had flared. The morning of their mom's demise, Maddy had woken from a dream screaming that their mother was going to die. No one believed her. Now, Will was pressuring her to control her dreams to predict how to save their aunt from other health issues. With escalating annoyance, Maddy tried to tell him that type of intervention was impossible.

Since Mom's car accident, Maddy had dreamed only a handful of other prophetic visions. None of them good.

It seemed like in many ways time had frayed that day. There was life with Mom, and life after. Hardly a day went by when Maddy didn't long to see her mother's face again. Where was her spirit now?

On the slopes, Maddy was closing fast on Will. Good, because the bottom of the run was rapidly approaching. She used the last strength in her thighs to propel herself forward.

They turned a corner in the run, neck and neck. Tall as skeletal giants, snow-covered pine trees flashed by on either side. A wide, four-foot-tall mogul caught her off guard, coming up fast. Will approached from the right, she from the left.

They both flew high into the air, and collided, like tangled, wingless birds.

CHAPTER 2

Inside her bedroom, Avril put her leopard gecko, Fleck, into her pocket as she cleaned out his aquarium. Once a month, she took everything out and did a deep clean, and today was that day. The rest of the room needed cleaning too. Maybe tomorrow.

She worked swiftly, and as she scrubbed and threw out the old substrate made of aspen shavings, she thought about the men who had been pursuing her.

"I think someone has been following me," she told Fleck.

Fleck didn't answer, so she pulled him out of her pocket and looked at him. His eyelids blinked. She had only one good friend at her new school, and had found talking with her pet to be rather fun. Sometimes she made up his responses in what she imagined was a dry male lizard tone.

Now he said, "That's kind of scary. Why would someone shadow you?"

"I don't know," she said, admiring his wide head and beautiful spotting. "That's the problem."

"Have you told Monique or your grandfather?"

She shook her head. "No. I'm not certain that's what's going on."

"Tell me what you saw."

"A few weeks ago, when Monique and I were at the Nostradamus Museum, there was this creepy guy following us. He had one glass eye and used a cane."

"An old man with a cane? Sounds innocent to me."

"I know. That's the problem!"

"Any other evidence?"

"A few times I've thought a dark sedan was following me, or parked down the street."

"I see. Hardly rock-solid proof." He twitched his tail. "Have any of those special mealworms today?"

"I do. Let's get you settled first."

She put him back in her loose shirt pocket and went about getting his environment set up. First, she checked that the heat pad, just in half the enclosure, was warm to the touch. Then, she added new shavings, a fresh water dish—this one with little geckos painted on the sides—two partial logs, and a small cardboard box for climbing and hiding.

Once his home was arranged, she lovingly removed him from her pocket and set him inside. "There you go, buddy."

He waddled onto a half log and twitched his plump tail expectantly.

The window rattled in the wind, putting her on edge.

She took a mealworm from the pouch and put it into a plastic bag with a powder calcium/vitamin D3 supplement. Shaking the bag fiercely, she worked out some of her angst, and then dropped the covered worm on top of the cardboard box. Fleck moved over and started maneuvering it into his mouth with his tongue.

Putting the lid atop his enclosure, she stared at her black desk and the computer there. It was time to make her next prediction.

Sitting down, she pulled up TikTok, her favorite social media video site, and checked her number of followers. They grew by the day. Soon, one of her forecasts was going to hit the bullseye, and then she'd be hugely popular. That would be nice, especially at school.

Maybe it would be today's prophecy. She had a feeling about it.

Using a brush, she attempted to tame her long, dark-wavy hair, and then caught herself. It didn't matter what she looked like. Due to the ugly scars that covered her face and neck, she videoed Fleck instead of herself,

She set up the video camera so that it would capture her handsome avatar in her arms, with his adorable eyes looking out at the world.

Fleck was done eating. She picked him up, began to record the video, and spoke the prophecy in her own voice.

CHAPTER 3

After dinner at the vineyard, Will sat gingerly on the couch in front of the woodstove and put his feet up on the coffee table. His whole body felt bruised from the collision at Alpine Meadows.

His twin sister, Maddy, and her boyfriend, Bear, were cuddling on the oversized leather armchair. Bear wore his usual jeans and white T-shirt, but had taken his black boots off. Maddy wore gray sweatpants and a green long-sleeved V-neck sweatshirt. She glowered at Will around the ice pack on her new black eye. "Really? Feet on the furniture?"

Screw her. His tired legs wanted to relax.

He motioned her away. "It's my house, too."

Reaching for his silver, harp-shaped harmonica, he plucked it from its tooled-leather case, then put his lips to the gold-plated mouthpiece, and began to blow a mournful tune. After being struck by lightning, he'd developed a talent for playing the instrument and had treated himself to a high-end Suzuki SCT-128 professional 16-hole Tremolo Chromatic. The music soothed his jagged nerves.

After a time, he put the harmonica down. He stroked the scar on his chin, thinking about the accident that took his mother. Tahoe always made him feel morbid.

Maddy's face had softened as he played. She turned to watch AJ roughhouse with the golden retriever he called Damien, his red hair bright against the dog's yellow fur. The kid's ears were almost as big as the dog's.

She said, "I admit you did a wonderful job getting rid of Dad's eighties décor. I'm more impressed by the new security, though."

Bear jumped in, his southern drawl more pronounced after a long day of skiing. "I'm impressed, too, Argones. The security camera system alone must have set you back some serious cash."

Will's chest warmed with pride. "Maddy wanted the place safe for AJ. Sensors sound an alarm if a trespasser comes within even a quarter mile of the house."

Bear crunched an ice cube from his glass. "Didn't you tell me the infrared system puffs out fog screens and some sort of nasty-smelling gas?"

"Yepper," Will replied. "That gas will disable an intruder."

Bear, who had a better sense of smell than the rest of them, scrunched up his nose in distaste.

"And if that doesn't stop them, the Burglar Blaster will shower them with pepper spray."

Bear nodded his appreciation. "Did you name that?"

Will declined to answer.

Maddy tossed her dark ponytail over her shoulder. "I'm glad you finally listened to me and put in the self-contained panic room. Didn't you tell me it has something like eighteen-inch-thick steel walls?"

He tucked the harmonica back in its case. "I did. And it does."

Damien walked over and put his head on Maddy's knee. She patted the pup on the head, and scratched under his chin. The dog's tail thumped madly, nearly knocking Bear's sweet tea off the coffee table. The interaction made Will miss his cat, Paolo, who was back in DC on his live-aboard boat.

"And no keys," Maddy continued. "I misplaced the keys to my loft in the city once. The biometric recognition software is very handy."

Of course she'd appreciate the software. At heart, his sister was a computer geek.

As she rubbed the dog's chest, the matching ruby-red lorandite rings on her hands gleamed in the firelight. After years of aikido martial arts practice that had begun when they were in high school, he understood that she'd learned to perceive the life force of opponents, as well as her own energy. Leveraging that black-belt talent, she could now channel ball lightning through the rare, highly superconductive material she wore on her fingers. At one time, they'd had large shards of lorandite. Now, all that remained were two dime-sized chunks, which she wore as rings on the middle fingers of both hands.

He would have never believed her skills if he hadn't seen them firsthand, and if she hadn't saved his life on more than one gut-wrenching occasion. He'd researched the hell out of the lightning phenomenon, trying to figure out exactly how it worked, and had a solid physics theory based on zero-point energy.

With such small pieces to work with, he'd wondered how much energy she could channel. Yesterday afternoon, after she'd flown in from Washington DC, she'd taken a walk in the vineyard, and he'd gone with her to find out.

Amidst the leafless vines of the vineyard, he'd set up an uncarved orange pumpkin, leftover from Halloween, as a target between rows.

"Move it a little to the left," she'd ordered.

He complied, and got out of the way, returning to her side.

She turned her rings so the lorandite touched her skin, took a few deep breaths and pointed her index and middle finger as if her hands were guns. A blue flash left her hands and the carroty ball went flying backward through the plants.

"Not bad," he said. "What's your range?"

"About the length of a house on a damp day like today. Set it up again for me and let's test it."

He trudged down the row of grapes, centered the squash, and walked back about a hundred feet until he stood behind her.

She'd told him her process was to quiet her mind, and move energy out through her heart and into her hands, through the mineral, which focused the energy. He was dying to learn more about exactly how she did it, but every time he asked, they argued. Instead, he figured he should shut up and watch.

Again, she focused. A blue ray carved sightless new eyes on the face of the squash.

"Nice work. Let's go back fifty feet," he suggested.

This time, though, the ray went no more than three quarters of the way to the pumpkin before it just petered out. He decided that although she was throwing less lightning than when she'd had larger chunks of lorandite, she had more accuracy, at least at her range.

For kicks, he'd thrown one of his knives at the squash. He couldn't hit it either. At that distance, they'd both need a cold and heavy semiautomatic to blow the pumpkin to smithereens.

Not wanting to disturb the silence of a winter afternoon with gunfire, they'd returned to the newly renovated house.

"It was a fun remodel," Will said, returning his attention to the conversation. "I'm glad Director Bowman let me work remotely for a few months so I could oversee it."

"You were able to visit Aunt Carole, too, while I was learning to jump out of planes."

"Hey, that reminds me. I found something strange that I want to show you."

As he jumped up and headed down the hall to his bedroom, their VanOps teammate Jags and her girlfriend, Deana, walked into the living room bearing aromatic dessert plates. The helpful pair had kept an eye on AJ at the ski lodge while the experts skied the challenging runs, and now had made pie. Will nabbed the postcard from the top of his dresser and brought it back, wanting some of the delicious-smelling cinnamon-infused apple delight.

He interrupted a kiss between Maddy and Bear.

"Break it up you two."

Bear glared at him. "You need a girlfriend. What do you want to show us?"

"I found a postcard in Aunt Carole's house. I think it's from Mom. But when was she in Italy?"

The whole situation with Aunt Carole was tearing him up inside. She reminded him so much of Mom and had been his primary source of memories about their mother as they'd grown up. It was hard to see her in a hospital gown. She looked so frail. He knew that it would be difficult for him to keep Aunt Carole with his globe-trotting lifestyle, but it didn't stop Will from *wanting* to take care of her. She was the last link he had to Mom.

He handed the postcard to Maddy, who stopped eating her steaming pie to look at the grim image of a reclining skeleton above two Greek words: *gnōthi sauton.*

"That's not just strange, it's downright disturbing." Maddy handed the image to Bear. "What do you and your history fascination make of it?"

Bear put his fork down. He examined the image and turned the postcard over. "It's a picture of the 'Memento Mori' mosaic from excavations in the convent of San Gregorio. Now in the National Museum's Baths of Diocletian in Rome."

She elbowed Bear in the side. "I can see that." She turned to Will. "Can you read the Greek?"

"It's a Greek motto for 'know thyself.'" He'd had to look up the rest, but wasn't going to admit that. "Combined with the image, it's supposed to convey the famous warning: *Respice post te; hominem te esse memento; memento mori.*"

"'Memento' sounds like 'memory' or 'remember.' Or a keepsake. Translate for us ignorant Neanderthals, please," Bear said.

Will smiled, glad to make Bear squirm a little with his gift for languages, since Bear outgunned him in most other categories. "Look behind; remember that you are mortal; remember death."

"I guess that's supposed to make us appreciate being alive, but . . ." Maddy trailed off, turning the card over. "You really think it's from Mom?"

"Look at the handwriting. And the signature."

He watched Maddy's wheels spin the same way his had when he'd grabbed Aunt Carole's glasses from her dresser and had seen the writing side of the postcard tucked into a corner of the mirror.

Will turned to Jags and Deana. "Tasty pie."

While most of them wore baggy après-ski sweatpants and sweatshirts, Jags, as always, looked like the LA model she'd been before joining the NSA and then VanOps. Her sleek loungewear fell in smooth lines and her short black hair managed to look stylish even after wearing a hat all day.

"Thanks," Jags replied with a smirk. She tilted her head to her partner. "Deana made it."

"Mary Louise Marshall," Maddy interrupted. "And it looks like her handwriting all right."

AJ walked over. "Can I see it?"

"Sure." Maddy handed the faded postcard to AJ and ruffled his carrot top with affection. She glanced up at Will. "Why was Mom in Italy?"

"I have no idea. No date on it either."

The existence of the card bothered Will. He'd been trained by VanOps to take advantage of his natural tendency to spot anomalies, as they often signaled potential danger. When he wasn't on a mission, he was part of the Red Team, poking holes in the plans of other operations. This postcard shouldn't exist. But what did they really know of their mother's life before she had birthed them?

Maddy wiped her mouth with a napkin. "We should ask Aunt Carole when she's feeling better."

A lump formed in his throat. If their aunt died, all ties to his mother would be lost. "Or maybe you could have a dream about it."

Maddy shot him the evil eye.

"Hate to interrupt the family reunion," Jags said, finishing a last bite of crust while she looked at her phone. "But here's an interesting news alert."

Bear ran a hand over the stubble of his blond buzz cut. Once a marine, always a marine. "Oh?"

"China just invaded one of Taiwan's outlying islands. And a sixteen-year-old female civilian in France predicted it."

CHAPTER 4

7:57 P.M.

Maddy was glad for the subject change that halted the nascent argument with her brother. "What do you mean a sixteen-year-old girl predicted a Chinese invasion?"

"That's all I know. The world is shocked and there will be a news conference in a half hour," Jags replied, with her usual perfect smile. "It's still early morning in France."

Jags's name was understandably short for Jarmilla Agiashvili. Of Georgian descent, she was a thin, black-haired woman with blue eyes, and a personality that emanated a mix of strength and femininity. She and Deana had joined them in Napa to help celebrate the completion of Maddy's covert ops training.

"Huh. Think she really predicted it? Maybe she got intel from a boyfriend, or . . ." Maddy paused, collecting her thoughts, and twirled a lorandite ring around her finger. "Or somehow hacked the People's Liberation Army?"

It felt strange for her to be doubting the girl, after experiencing her own premonitory dreams. She glared at Will again. His snide comment about calling up a dream to find out why Mom was in Italy was a perfect example of how he never listened to her. Sibling tensions aside, could the sixteen-year-old have a similar talent?

"Doubtful," Jags replied. "*We* have trouble hacking them. Plus, this island was not on our radar as being threatened."

Maddy's left index finger twitched as she adjusted the ice pack on her bruised eye. She was lucky an errant ski hitting her face was the only casualty from crashing into Will atop that mogul. She'd rolled twice before slamming into a pine.

Will's eyes narrowed, accentuating his long eyelashes. "Doesn't Doyle have family in Taiwan?"

Maddy swallowed, remembering Doyle's brother Quinn, who had died on a mission with them about a year ago. Both siblings were members of a hidden group that she also belonged to—an ancient sect of royal spies that had been established by her father's forbears.

"I think you're right." She looked up and away. "I think his grandparents live there."

Before they could turn on the news, Jags's phone buzzed the special signal that meant Director Bowman wanted them on a secure video feed ASAP. Maddy's skin prickled with excitement.

Jags turned to Deana. "Can you watch AJ for a minute while we head downstairs?"

Deana's red hair had more blonde tones than AJ's firebrick-red mop. She nodded, her blue eyes conveying understanding. She repeatedly told them she liked watching the boy, and had done so on the slopes earlier after he'd gotten worn out on the bunny hill. AJ gave them all a quick glance and went back to playing with the dog.

Maddy's heart bloomed. Although her life with VanOps was not suburban soccer-mom style, he'd adapted to it like a champ. She sure loved that kid.

Jags stood and led the way to the secret staircase that had been installed behind the wall of the guest bathroom shower. Maddy followed Bear, noticing that his limp from Afghanistan was more obvious after skiing all day. She reached out and gave his hand a quick squeeze, wondering if he would ever tell her what had happened that day.

Five minutes later, the VanOps team was downstairs in what Will had dubbed Command Room West. The director had allowed them to work part-time from Napa Valley if they footed the bill for installation of the encryption technology that allowed secure communications. Not wanting to raise AJ in Washington DC, Maddy had agreed to the expense, grateful she'd been able to afford it after the software company that she used to work for had gone public.

"Sorry to interrupt your celebration, gang, but we have a developing situation," Director Alfred Bowman said.

Maddy focused on the bank of oversized computer monitors that seamlessly rendered the director's image. He was a sharp-eyed, gray-haired African American man who currently wore a white shirt with rolled-up sleeves and a striped purple tie. He'd recently grown a beard, now neatly trimmed, and she thought it looked good on him. His tone was deep, but his words were machine-gun fast.

"Related to Taiwan?" Maddy asked.

"Indirectly, yes. Other members of our intelligence services and armed forces are meeting right now to discuss how to counter China's surprising takeover of the primary Pratas Island, also known as Dongsha Island. But our mission lies in France."

Bear's wide shoulders tensed. "First, could you tell us how close are they to Taiwan, sir?"

Maddy liked that Bear always got formal with the director.

"Pratas Island is in the north section of the South China Sea, Bear, roughly halfway between Hong Kong and Taiwan. About 275 miles southeast of Taiwan, but still too close for comfort. The island, airport, and nearby wildlife atoll have been disputed for years."

"Sir, were there casualties?"

"Our satellite feeds showed heavy fighting. The island held about five hundred Taiwanese marines. They were hunkered down in bunkers, but . . ." He trailed off, his voice somber and slower than usual. "The People's Liberation Army, or PLA, came with a swarm of tanks."

A muscle in Bear's jaw began to twitch.

This didn't look good for Taiwan. And was worrying for Doyle's family.

Jags asked, "How can we help?"

"Have you seen the news that a young girl in France predicted this attack when Pratas wasn't even on our bloody radar?"

"We did, yes."

"We have some signals intelligence that indicates her life may be in danger from a foreign power interested in her prediction capabilities."

Maddy brushed a lock of hair behind her ears. "She's the real deal then?"

The director turned his dark eyes her way. "That's part of what I need you to find out."

Will crossed his arms. "Why are we interested in a fortune-teller?"

"If she's consistently accurate, her skills would not be in that ballpark, Will. A little history here might help." Bowman sat back in his chair and steepled his fingers. "Before VanOps existed, our country had a team in the seventies that was formed to keep pace with the Russians. The STARGATE project studied out-of-body experiences, remote viewing, killing from a distance, and experimenting with drugs like LSD. Trying to weaponize parapsychology."

Maddy and Bear exchanged a glance. She'd had no idea.

The director continued. "When STARGATE was exposed in the press, and shown to be a failure, the public demanded its head. However, obscure threats remained. VanOps was formed when STARGATE was disbanded; the program just became a deeper shade of black. Funding had to go through more backdoor channels."

"How does this history relate, sir?" Bear asked.

"One of the STARGATE projects was a mission codenamed 'Hourglass' that took place in the town where the French girl lives with her grandfather. It's the only connection I could find. I'll send you the file. Read it on the plane."

Maddy nodded, her mind abuzz with questions.

Jags asked, "Our mission is to protect the girl?"

"You're going to provide support for the team from here in DC, Jags. Or you can work from the vineyard. Your leg hasn't been cleared for combat and there will be a lot of research required to get to the bottom of this."

Did her lower lip just tremble? Maddy thought. No, Jags never got emotional.

Jags executed a stiff, mock salute. "Happy to help, sir."

"I knew you'd be thrilled. But yes, our mission is to protect the girl. See who wants her and why. I doubt she can predict the future, but find out, and if she can, we need to keep any secrets in her pretty little head out of the hands of our enemies. Our intel indicates someone thinks she's for real. Reporters are outside her house right now going mad."

"Do we have support from the locals?" Will asked.

"French police will assign two men. I fear it won't be enough. That's where you come in. Spying is in your blood, after all."

The comment caught Maddy off guard. What does he mean? She thought, *He must be referring to the crazy Spanish side of our family and my membership in the sect, officially named the Order of the Invisible Flame.*

That gave Maddy an idea. "Will we have any support from the Order?"

Bowman smiled. "Actually, yes. I've been in touch with the master and Doyle has volunteered, given his family in Taiwan."

Good. The master had an ancient library and a global team trained in espionage at his disposal. Those resources might come in handy. Will often called the Order a secret sect of stately spies because it was comprised of members descended from old Spanish royalty. Maddy had a scar on her shoulder, more like a trophy, to prove her membership. Will, though, had been unable to pass the esoteric tests required for membership, and had soured on the group.

"I'm glad Doyle will be able to help," Maddy said, even as Will frowned.

"Me too," the director said. "If we can find out what the People's Liberation Army is planning next, it would save a lot of bloodshed."

Maddy felt excited and nervous to be assigned to a mission so soon. She'd thought she might have to wade through a sea of boring cyber desk work first. She'd joined VanOps to make a difference. To help make the world a better place. Keep it safe.

AJ would also need to be kept safe. Deana was able to telework in her role as a VanOps analyst, and earlier they'd discussed her interest in keeping an eye on the boy and getting him to school when Maddy was on a mission.

Then Maddy realized they'd need to leave Aunt Carole under Bella's care while they were gone, which would prove Bella's point that she and Will left town too often to care for their aunt. Maddy's heart sank, yet her fingers itched to get her hands on the reports from, what had he called it, Codename Hourglass?

"We understand, sir," Bear said.

"Good. Now, Jags, can you start doing some digging while the others catch the next flight to France?"

"Of course."

"Thank you. The rest of you, get moving. I'll be in touch."

CHAPTER 5

Thanks to the short notice in getting a flight out of Travis Air Force Base, Will found himself sitting in the very rear of the C-17 cargo plane, stuck in the row nearest to the toilet. His narrow seat was drafty, cold, and noisy. But at least they were able to bring their weapons along for the ride.

The belly of the beast was filled with backward-facing rows of cadets so young it made Will remember his college days. He found it curious the wide plane had a line of red, webbed seats along the fuselage wall, as well as rows laid out in the more traditional horizontal arrangement, which faced the tail for safety. Maddy and Bear were near the wing, sitting next to one another, probably holding hands. He rolled his eyes, ignoring the little voice that said he should just get over missing Maria and find a girlfriend. The lovebirds had half the Hourglass files; he had the other. At least he had the row to himself so he could study the paperwork without worrying about breaking security protocol.

Given the disco-era date on the files, he shouldn't have been surprised that they were typed, but he was. The formal font lent an oddly impersonal and almost spooky atmosphere to the reports, as if they were from another planet, instead of simply from another time.

Three reports. He skimmed them first, to get an overview.

Each had a similar header and footer containing a time and date, the name of the operative, the location referenced, and a two-line summary.

Two files were from an operative named Leo. They'd been sent from Saint-Rémy, France, and spanned twenty-four months in the late seventies. He set those aside.

The first report was from an analyst and described the background for the mission.

Throughout mankind's history, religious figures claimed spiritual experiences outside of their bodies. Shamans flew with eagles. Priests convened with the spirits. More recently, an engineer found a way to float above his body on command. Such out-of-body experiences are rich with intelligence potential, and we began to research quantum physics to explain and harvest what we can from the phenomenon.

The words "quantum physics" grabbed Will's attention like a stage hook. Although an engineer, he'd found an interest in physics during college. His breath quickened and he skipped down the page.

Time is defined as a measurement of energy in motion, but for motion to occur, it must take place inside a pattern of vibration, or a frame of reference, at a specific location. If energy isn't contained, there's limitless force. We call this an absolute state, or "The Absolute."

That last bit sounded like the Newtonian concept of absolute time and absolute space, or the zero-point energy that he suspected Maddy harnessed to throw ball lightning. When Will had lived in Brazil, he'd enjoyed discussing those concepts with a friend over a glass or two of wine on the stern of his boat.

The ancient world was insistent that man should "Know Thyself" as a prerequisite to a fulfilling life. Modern psychology agrees, and we've also found that the most objective perception of self can be discovered through altered states, where one directly perceives the hologram of the Absolute.

What the hell was the hologram of the Absolute? That didn't make sense. Eventually the analyst got to the information more relevant to their mission.

Intelligence coming out of Moscow indicates the Russians are gaining the upper hand when it comes to using out-of-body experiences to gather intel, what we're now calling "remote viewing." They have one particular individual who is consistently able to enter a trance state without the usual sound machines and who produces visions related to a specific longitude/latitude coordinate. We have two subjects who provide similar material. They have proven more accurate than initially suspected. For instance, a tip from one led to the recovery of a lost military plane in Central America, earning additional funding for the program. Also, remote killing experiments are underway by both superpowers to determine if a heart can be stopped from a distance using mind power alone.

Whoa! Talk about a creepy weapon.

However, a new biography of Nostradamus has hypothesized that the famed prophet used an herbal formula to induce the state of mind necessary to see the future. The biography was based on letters that were sent to his astrological clients between 1556 and 1565. He was an herbalist and physician who helped heal victims of the Black Plague and published hundreds of prophecies, many of which have arguably come true. Obtaining that formula would be the holy grail of military advancements, and would leapfrog us ahead in the race with the Russians. We have reason to believe they, the Chinese, East Indians, and Iranians are all interested in discovering the formula. If the enemy is able to reliably forecast the future, no number of nuclear missiles or technological enhancements will be able to make up for that competitive advantage. It would be 'game over.'

Will looked out the window at the pinpricks of light on the ground far below. He scratched at his stubble, wanting a shave. He'd heard of Nostradamus, of course, but hadn't thought about him in years. Decades, really. He'd been in his teens when the twin towers fell in New York. He remembered the gut-wrenching horror of watching the planes fly into the buildings on television, and he also recalled hearing that Nostradamus had predicted the attack. When his friends blathered on about what a marvelous prediction it was, Will had shown them that the four-line verses, also known as quatrains, attributed to Nostradamus couldn't have been written by him. Steel, for instance, was not around in the mid-sixteenth century.

Will didn't believe a word of what Nostradamus had written. The medieval fraudster was a con man, a hustler, and a horoscope teller of the worst kind. Will had been surprised to find so-called physicians at the time, including Nostradamus, studied *astrology*, which was a vat of hogwash. As bad as leeches. The man sure had been famous during his lifetime, though. Kings and queens had asked Nostradamus to provide detailed horoscopes for their newborn children. Will shook his head in disgust and kept reading.

Leadership has chosen an operative, codenamed Leo, to infiltrate the town where the descendants of Nostradamus still thrive. Leo's mission is simple: find the formula before the other world powers, and bring it home to America.

The report was familiar in its structure. When he wasn't on field missions, Will wrote similar assessments. And yet a shiver ran down his spine—he'd had no idea that the CIA had been involved in such esoteric pursuits. LSD experimentation he could understand in a twisted sort of way, for crowd control, or as a truth serum, but explorations of consciousness, remote viewing, killing, and herbal formulas seemed far-fetched for a government agency.

Still, if other governments were looking into the same thing, there must have been good reason. There would be data to back it up. And some level of success to warrant the funds, even if it was black-box funding.

He thought back to some of Maddy's predictions, which came in dreams. Before their mother and grandmother had died in that car accident, Maddy had woken up screaming. She'd practically begged their mom not to take him to that birthday party. He, on the other hand, had been a petulant child, demanding they go celebrate. It had been an expensive mistake, costing him a broken arm, his grandmother, who always smelled of lavender, and his beloved mother, as well as leaving him with a scar on his chin.

More recently, Maddy had a dream about his wife, the night before Maria was killed. His gut clenched and he turned his thoughts to yet another dream Maddy had that had saved his bacon in Egypt. As an engineer and scientist, he didn't like to think about such things. Yet, the undeniable conclusion was that Maddy's dreams had reliably predicted the future, at least a handful of times.

They were just too random. If only she could dream on demand. Control them. At least let him run some experiments to test if they could be regulated. But every time he brought it up, she crossed her arms and stubbornly refused to even discuss it.

He knew that science was just scratching the surface of the mind's ability. If sound combinations were being used by the CIA as far back as the 1970s to explore consciousness, what tech was being used today to delve into that final frontier? He knew of at least one example. Headbands could be purchased off the internet to provide biofeedback for people wanting to learn to meditate. Maddy was forever going on about the wonders of meditation, and had even bought him a headband device for Christmas. He'd researched the brainwave pattern the device encouraged, and had been fascinated to find mystics, monks, and meditators all exhibited a slowing of thinking beta brain waves along with an expansion of dreamy alpha and theta waves.

It just wasn't his thing though. He'd used the headband once and promptly stored it, forgetting about it. He had to admit, though, the tech was cool.

He made a mental note to ask Jags to research the latest scientific discoveries related to herbs that might induce visions. Maybe Nostradamus did have some type of herbal formula.

Turning his attention back to the pages, Will examined the first report from Leo.

I believe that at least one foreign power is also present here in Saint-Rémy, where I've settled to attempt an infiltration of Nostradamus's family. I took a walk yesterday by a set of monuments near the sea. While I was engaged in reading about the Trojan War on the monument next to one called the 'Arc,' I spied a man watching me.

Will turned the page, wondering what else Leo had reported about the man, but there was no other data.

The next report provided detailed background on Nostradamus, abbreviated as N.

In his time, N's name was a household word throughout France, Italy, Austria, Germany, Spain, and England. Born in a house in Saint-Rémy on Rue de Viguier, today the road is named Rue Hoche. A post-WWII marble plaque is installed above the doorway. His coat of arms has two eagle heads and two wheels that could be herbs or suns. According to his own words, N gave his eldest daughter two walnut coffers that contained 'clothes, rings and jewels' and no one else was 'permitted to see or look at that which will be (found) therein.' The walnut boxes have not been seen in centuries, but would have been the perfect vehicle to pass down the formula to his progeny. It's my aim to see if the coffers exist.

N published a booklet in 1555 called The Treatise of Cosmetics and Jams. *'After my having spent the greater part of my youthful years . . . in pharmacy, and in the knowledge and understanding of medicinal herbs, I moved through a number of lands and countries from 1521 to 1529, constantly in search of the understanding and knowledge of the sources and origins of plants and other medicinal herbs—(exploring) medicine's very frontiers.' N was intimately familiar with herbs, and has numerous recipes for common maladies in the Treatise.*

Will's curiosity was now piqued. He had to admit their mission was intriguing. The girl, Avril, lived in the same town where Nostradamus had once resided. Could she have stumbled across the old wizard's formula? Was it possible 'N' really had foretold the future, at least enough of it to earn a sort of influencer status in his lifetime?

Will's skeptical nature reasserted itself. Nah, it was probably all a bunch of hooey, and the girl likely had a boyfriend in the Chinese Army.

But if it was all smoke and mirrors, why was a foreign power interested in the girl?

CHAPTER 6

MARSEILLE, FRANCE
7:30 A.M.

In the grim early morning light, Henri Seymore, the man also known as the Watcher, used his fist to hammer on the door of the motel room where he'd left Raphael several nights before. They'd come back to Marseille so that Seymore could make an appearance at his cover job, and had left another of his men to watch Avril at her grandfather's home in Saint-Rémy.

He sighed. He was tired of his job at the library, even if his national reputation as an expert on Nostradamus did work well to bait anyone interested in the prophet.

When there was no answer, Seymore again pounded on the door.

"I'm sleeping," complained Raphael.

A stiff wind blew up the collar of Seymore's jacket. "Not any longer. Open up."

There was a sound like bare feet shuffling across tile. A bleary-eyed Raphael swung the door open before lumbering back to the bed, where he collapsed. "What on earth is so important?"

Seymore shoved an espresso into the short man's hand. "Drink. We have work to do."

Raphael tried a sip. "What work?"

Seymore sat down in the desk chair with his latte. "Avril made a prediction last night that came true."

Raphael raised his thin eyebrows. "Now you have my attention."

"I thought that might do it. She predicted that China would invade the Pratas Islands and news of the invasion broke two hours later. I've been on and off the phone with our boss all night. He said there's no way the girl should have known that was coming."

Raphael took another sip of the espresso. "That's impressive. We were right. She either has a gift or is in possession of the old prophet's formula."

"I agree." Seymore smiled, feeling like a kid about to unwrap a birthday present. "That's why we are going to kidnap her this afternoon."

Raphael's eyes lit with excitement and he sat up straight. "At last! Following her around got boring weeks ago."

Seymore ran his hand over his bald head. "Ha. You think you're ready for action? I've been on this trail for decades. This is the best lead I've had since before you were born."

Raphael's eyes narrowed in what Seymore took as skepticism, but it was the truth. He was getting older, and at one time, he'd just wanted to get the money from this job and retire before the grim reaper came calling. With five million Swiss francs, he could escape to a balmy Greek island and a fine villa. He'd long fantasized about meeting a widow who knew how to make spanakopita, his favorite.

But now that the game was afoot, Seymore was thinking bigger picture. He wanted modern-day kings and queens to bow to his knowledge; he wished to hold the world in the palm of his hand as Nostradamus once had. Women and riches would flock to him.

Raphael put his empty paper cup on the table next to the bed and squared his shoulders. "We taking the green van?"

"Yes, but we need equipment."

"Okay." Raphael stood. "I need a quick shower."

Seymore popped a cigarette from its case and lit it with his gold lighter. "That's fine, but don't linger. Our orders are to move heaven and earth to kidnap the girl and learn how she predicted the invasion."

CHAPTER 7

A s they walked off the plane, Maddy's stomach growled loud enough that Bear looked at her.

She rubbed her belly. "I know we need to get to Saint-Rémy ASAP, but I'm starving."

It had taken them fifteen hours to get from Travis Air Force Base to Paris with a layover in Atlanta, then another hour and a half to get to Marseille in a propeller-based twelve-seat mini-plane. She hadn't been aware the Air Force had such small planes. Bear told her it was a C-23A Sherpa, which meant nothing to her.

"I'm hungry too," Will agreed.

"Let's grab one of those fancy French sandwiches for lunch and eat in the rental car on the way," Bear suggested, in a tone indicating that it wasn't up for discussion.

Thirty minutes later, they were speeding north through the fallow French countryside in a comfortable BMW X5 SUV, Bear driving and her in the backseat while Will rode shotgun in the front passenger seat.

"Will, have you heard anything from Bella about Aunt Carole?" Maddy asked around a bite of turkey on flaky croissant.

Will glanced at her over his shoulder. "No. Have you?"

"She hasn't spoken to me in a year. I figured she'd be updating you."

"She's also mad at me."

Maddy blew out a breath. "At least the two of you are speaking."

"If you can call it that. She raked me over the coals for not telling her about my job and insisted that I'd make a lousy caretaker for Aunt Carole."

Maddy thought Bella right on the last count, but held her tongue. For now.

Bear interrupted. "Argones, what did you learn from the three reports you read?"

It bothered her when Bear played peacekeeper between her and Will.

Her twin removed a crumb from his overly expensive button-down shirt. "The first report summarized why they sent an operative named Leo here to Saint-Rémy. A fresh biography, with new firsthand material, had come out about Nostradamus and speculated that he used an herbal formula to see his prophetic visions."

"I know about Nostradamus," Bear replied. "He was hounded by royalty during his lifetime for his predictions and horoscopes. But he had some kind of formula? We saw a reference to that in our report, but didn't know what it meant."

"No one knows." Will paused and rubbed his stubble. "Leo thought it likely that if there was one, Nostradamus hid it in a walnut box, and gave it to his daughter. The contents of that box were secret and the box disappeared, never to be seen again."

"Just my kind of mystery," Bear drawled.

"A mystery about history," Will said. Then he turned to Maddy. "The background report on the CIA's para-operation went into a lot of detail about remote viewing and even remote killing."

Other than the comment the director had made on their initial briefing, Maddy had never heard of the latter. "Remote killing?"

"They were trying to kill people from a distance by stopping their hearts."

Maddy's sandwich suddenly tasted like sawdust. "Eww, learn anything else?"

"Leo thought he was being followed by a foreign operative, and . . ." Will trailed off and looked out the window, thinking. "There was some history about Nostradamus, and how he was a doctor and herbalist. He traveled extensively and wrote a treatise that included more everyday formulas."

"Got it." Maddy sipped her water. "Of course, your skeptical brain probably thinks Nostradamus's prophecies were all false."

"The thought had crossed my mind," Will said dryly. "Although I finally got around to believing in your talent."

"Only after I saved your life." Maddy wished her premonitory dreams had never come true. Only that one dream about Will had been useful.

"Speaking of, when are you going to try that experiment I devised?"

The air in the car immediately felt icy. She imagined frost forming on the windows.

She lowered her voice in warning. "The one where I meditate before bed on what I want to dream about?"

"Yes."

Maddy crossed her arms. "I'm not."

"C'mon. I know you can bring them on if you try."

Bear interrupted the argument. "Our reports must've picked up where yours left off."

Will gave Maddy a final glare. "What happened next in the life and times of Leo the formula-hunting spy?"

Will's wisecracking irritated Maddy. "Stop."

"All right. Tell me."

"Okay," Maddy said. "The fourth report introduced an unidentified antagonist, and discussed his efforts to beat the US to the formula. Now that we know he had a recipe to see the future, it makes sense foreign powers would be after it."

"Russians? Chinese?" Will asked.

"Leo didn't know."

"I see. Then what?"

"In the fifth report, Leo made progress befriending some of Nostradamus's family, but had an unplanned love child."

Will scowled. "Things never end well for unplanned children of spies."

Maddy nodded. She and Bear should stick with just AJ. Another kid would complicate everything. "Probably true here as well. Leo thought the operative was onto him."

Will sipped his root beer. "Not looking good for Leo."

"Right. It gets worse. Leo thinks he's hot on the trail of the formula, but gets orders to vacate France and head back to the States. The CIA thinks Mission Hourglass is going nowhere. With someone on Leo's trail, and heads rolling up the chain due to bad publicity, he had to bail and leave the love child behind."

"Wow, he had to disappear? Without the kid?"

Her left index finger began to twitch. "Yes. It's all very sad."

Maddy could only imagine the heartbreak of leaving a child behind forever. She met Bear's blue eyes in the rearview mirror. On the plane he'd again joked about making a baby with her. Her biological clock had been ticking with her last boyfriend, but the second hand seemed to have stopped since she'd taken on the role with VanOps. How would a baby affect her work? She'd had a tough enough time leaving AJ at the vineyard in Napa last night, even with Jags and Deana there to get him to school.

"And that's the last report?" Will asked.

"Yes." Maddy finished her croissant and wiped her mouth. "Well, sort of. There was also a file on Avril."

"What was in that one?"

Maddy glanced out the window. On her left, an icy, white-capped lake spread for miles, sending a chill through her bones. "Not a lot, but the analysts didn't have much time to pull it together. She has over five thousand TikTok followers. Her father died about a year ago. She's been living with her grandfather and an au pair in Saint-Rémy since her dad's death. They lived in Paris before he died."

"Anything suspicious about his death?"

"Small engine plane went down while he was on business in Dubai."

"Could have been sabotage; I'll ask Jags to research it." Will paused. "That's all we have to go on, huh?"

"It's more than we usually get, Argones," Bear said.

"Just seems pretty weak," Will replied. "We've got some razor-thin files from a failed forty-year-old mission, and a sixteen-year-old girl who could've just gotten lucky."

"Somebody's gunning for her, though."

Bear's comment shut Will up, at least for the time being. Maddy looked out the window at the bare winter countryside. A dark-green van sped past the SUV. Who were they up against this time?

About an hour later, the team drove past Avril's home. The place was swarming with reporters. With all the TV station vans, there was no place to park. Will piloted the car to the nearest parking spot, several blocks away, and they walked quickly back to the aged stone building.

An older Black man wearing a bloodred beret stood in a courtyard at the front of the house, gesticulating at the reporters. Several had shoved microphones in his face. Although Maddy didn't speak French, his message was clear. "Get out of here!"

There were no rolling cameras that might compromise their mission by capturing their faces. She turned to the men. "C'mon. Let's make a friend."

She beelined for the reporter closest to the gesturing man, trusting Will and Bear would get the idea. Mimicking, she used her arms to signal that the reporters needed to back up. Once Bear cracked his knuckles, it didn't take them long to retreat.

The instant Will had an opening, he began conversing with the older man in French. Was the fellow Avril's grandfather? Maddy caught the name, Sébastien.

While her brother worked his magic, she and Bear continued to hold the tide of reporters at bay.

At one point, Sébastien yanked the beret off his silver hair and thumped Will in the chest with it. Will got animated as well. Both voices rose for an instant, and then shifted.

Finally, Will strode toward her, his long legs enabling him to quickly cross the courtyard. "The kid isn't here."

"Where is she?" Maddy asked.

"Downtown. About five minutes away."

CHAPTER 8

SAINT-RÉMY-DE-PROVENCE, FRANCE
2:19 P.M.

At the market, Avril was on high alert. As she'd told Fleck, she'd sensed men following her for weeks, and after the invasion by the press corps this morning, her level of paranoia had spiked off the charts.

She was used to scanning for danger. As a Black teenager with a scarred face, Avril rarely relaxed in public; classmates made fun of her and strangers often reacted with wide eyes and an open mouth when they saw the markings on her left jaw and down her neck. She'd endured jeers, taunts, and sidelong glances her entire life. Twice she'd been beaten by schoolmates and once she'd been slapped by a stranger for the imaginary offense of sitting on a bus.

Even so, today she was more anxious than usual.

Perhaps she shouldn't have come to the market with her au pair, Monique, but Avril had wanted to get out of the limelight. An army of reporters had descended before the sun had risen. Her grandfather had tried to send them away with wildly waving arms and loud swearing, but many of them lingered, like bloodhounds on a scent, their cold breath filling the small front yard with starbursts of fog. She'd watched from the second-story window after awakening to the news that her prediction for the Pratas Islands had proven accurate. Should she be elated at her success or horrified that the PLA had taken the islands with heavy casualties?

She cupped one hand around her hot latte, putting the other hand in her pocket to warm Fleck, and looked out the window of the café, across and just down the street from the small market where Monique shopped for baguettes, a chicken, and vegetables for soup. Rain fell from a leaden sky. Five minutes ago, Avril had tucked her leather satchel under her canary-yellow rain slicker, slipped out the market's back door, raised her hood against the rain, and walked around the block and into the back entrance of the coffee shop. She wanted both a latte and to keep an eye on the black sedan that had pulled up outside. Perhaps she should have told Monique, but the blonde au pair was engaged in a flirtatious conversation with one of the town's schoolteachers and Avril hadn't wanted to interrupt the hormonal small talk.

The drink smelled good. She took a tentative sip of the hot milked coffee. It felt like it took a full layer of skin off her tongue.

Movement in the street caught her attention. A dark-green van skidded to a halt in front of the market. The van's back doors yawned open and three men in military fatigues and black balaclavas leaped from the depths, rifles at the ready. Just then, Monique and the school teacher stepped out of the market's front door, heads swiveling like weather vanes. One of the military men shot the balding teacher in the forehead with a pistol. The schoolteacher slumped to the wet pavement, dead.

The shooter ran over and grabbed Monique by both arms. She opened her mouth wide in a primal scream, but inside the café, the sound was muffled by the howling wind, rain, and the gloved hand that smothered her face.

Monique struggled in the men's arms, and nearby shoppers scattered like sand in a windstorm.

Unsure what to do, Avril stood frozen behind the plate glass window. One of the masked men began to stalk in her direction.

CHAPTER 9

2:22 P.M.

Will jumped out of the SUV and ran toward the commotion in front of the market. As soon as Bear had driven the car into the narrow streets of the medieval town's center, chaos had broken out a block ahead.

Two rifle-toting men wearing black balaclavas were manhandling a short blonde woman toward the cavernous mouth of a dark-green van, while a third stood guard from inside the vehicle's belly. Another was walking through the rain toward a coffee shop, scanning the area.

Pedestrians were rapidly fleeing the scene. A young man on a motorbike, wearing a jacket with the logo of the nearby market, lost control as he came around a corner. He dropped the motorcycle on its side, skidded to a stop, scrambled to his feet, and ran the other way. The body of a balding man lay next to an overturned cart that had been full of apples and winter squash.

Will swore.

They had to be here after the girl. The kidnapping was already underway.

Where is she? In the van already?

Will ducked behind a black sedan. The attackers were well armed. His team's only advantage was surprise. He glanced back to Bear, who nodded.

With that approval, Will let two knives fly into the wind. Since realizing he needed to learn to protect himself, he'd discovered that he had a talent for knives and was more accurate with them than with his sidearm at this distance. A silver blade bounced off the back of one of the assailants who had a grip on the woman, and when the fellow turned, a bullet from Bear struck him in the chest. The gunman grunted and fell backward into the van. He was likely wearing a Kevlar vest or body armor.

The assailant that had been scouting near the coffee shop rushed back to the van and hopped inside, guns blazing.

From a dark corner of the get-away vehicle, a masked guard let loose a round of automatic gunfire as Will's other knife caught him in the throat. The man got one hand to his neck before keeling over atop a dark pile. Was that Avril?

To Will's right, Maddy took aim with her lorandite-enhanced hands, but hit the top of the van, which sat about fifty feet away. Her next beam of energy, however, hit an attacker with a jolt of blue lightning between the shoulder blades. The enemy pitched forward into the cargo area, letting go of the blonde, who immediately dropped to the ground behind the van.

The driver gunned the engine. The vehicle's wheels spun on the wet pavement, caught purchase, and ripped off down the street, back doors flapping shut.

The black sedan Will was using for cover quickly pulled away from the scene. Bear ran for the fallen motorbike.

Will sprinted for the woman huddled on the road. She was curled into a ball, her head in her hands. He wanted to see if she was injured, and talk with her if he could, before the local police arrived.

Will peeled her hands away from her face. In French he asked, "The girl, Avril. Do you know her?"

The woman's eyes held a dazed expression. She nodded slightly.

"Was she taken? Was she in the van?"

"I think so!" She began to wail.

Bear righted the motorcycle. He jumped on the seat and revved the engine. Maddy vaulted up behind him.

They took off after the van. Crazy fools. Did they really think they'd be able to catch the kidnappers and get the girl back?

CHAPTER 10

2:26 P.M.

Maddy grabbed on to Bear's waist with her left hand and held tight as he spun the rear wheel of the small motorcycle, turning the back end of the bike 180 degrees before it caught traction and leaped forward like a sprinter off the blocks. She pulled her sidearm from her waist harness, wondering about the attacker she'd zapped with a quick jolt of lightning. Her intention hadn't been to kill— she'd meant only to have him let go of the woman. As much as her peaceful-warrior ways put her at odds with her coworkers, she continued to wish the man no harm. She also hoped no bystander had noticed what she'd done.

The dark-green van had a good head start. It barreled down the commercial street lined with tall gray trees, whose limbs looked like clawed hands reaching toward the darkened sky.

Bear accelerated and Maddy gripped the bike with her thighs to steady herself in case she could get a shot off. The interior of the vehicle had been fuzzy and shadowed, but she had seen a single darker mound toward the back before Will's knife speared the guard's throat. That dark spot was likely Avril, and Maddy would have to be careful not to hit the girl.

However, she had no good shot. Not that she was a fan of firearms. She preferred hand-to-hand combat, where she could feel and sense the opponent's energy using aikido.

Her other weapon was the lorandite rings she'd had made and wore on each hand, and which she'd used to zap the attacker a minute ago.

After being cut and polished, the red rocks looked like substantial rubies and were set in platinum. She and Will had bickered for weeks over how they focused energy—she'd noted they worked better with a degree of static electricity in the air, as she told him how she had to quiet her mind and move energy from her heart out through her hands. He'd described zero-point energy and a bunch of physics gobbledygook she didn't understand, and eventually she threw up her hands to stop the arguing because, honestly, she didn't care how it worked. All she knew was that with larger chunks of the superconductive material available to her in the past, after much practice, she'd been able to generate substantial balls of lightning by focusing the energy in her hands through the otherworldly material. With these pebbles, the lightning was smaller, but narrow, more like a laser beam.

Besides the slight size of the lorandite, the other problem she had was a twitch in her left index finger, which had caused her to miss her first 'shot' at the attacker near the back of the van. The annoying tic had started a year or so ago after a close call with a lightning bolt, and although the doctors assured her it was nothing to worry about, it could affect her aim. The spasm came on at random times, not often, but frequently enough that she was not eager to use the lorandite.

Bottom line, she preferred her opponents to be up close and personal where she could take advantage of her martial arts skills.

The quintessentially French street speeding by reminded her of the California towns near where she'd done her lorandite target practice in the vineyard: downtown Napa, or maybe Calistoga. The off-white buildings had green or light-blue shutters and the occasional wrought-iron balcony.

After passing a narrow alley on the right, they entered an area filled with outdoor patios and galleries.

She held close to Bear, glad he was taking the brunt of the rain. Her pulse thrummed in time with the bike's engine. Adrenaline hummed through her veins. The chase was exhilarating.

Ahead, the road split into a Y just in front of an ancient building with a neoclassical Greek façade. The van veered left and was momentarily slowed by a powder-blue transit bus. A pistol appeared out of the kidnapper's passenger-side window, and the bus weaved violently back and forth before crashing into patio tables under the crimson awnings of a restaurant.

In front of them, a bicyclist wearing an earthy tweed jacket flew over his handlebars and landed in the street beside the bus. Maddy cringed with empathy as they sped by.

The van tipped up on two smoking wheels as it made a sharp left turn onto a one-way alley, going the wrong way. Making the same turn, Bear gunned it again. The alley, named Rue Nostradamus, was narrow and Maddy prayed that another car wouldn't come from the opposite direction.

Maddy's heart raced as they threaded the needle down the thin alley. She got a single shot off toward the back of the van, but they were still too far apart for the speeding bullet to do any good.

At a T in the road, the van skidded around the right turn.

Just as it did, a small cherry-red car turned onto the street and headed directly for them. Maddy clenched her teeth. The driver didn't slow. *Does he not see us?*

From behind a wall fountain on the right, a pedestrian lost in the world of his phone jumped out in front of them. Caught between the red car and the pedestrian, Bear had no choice but to brake hard.

Their motorbike's wheels seized up. It skidded before slamming into the side of the fountain, and Maddy was thrown into the air.

Thousands of aikido practice sessions took hold and her body formed itself into a ball as she came back to earth. She rolled, hand-to-forearm-to-shoulder and came up on her feet panting, grateful there was no pine tree nearby. Bear lay on his back, a dazed look on his face. He shook his head, rolled over, and slowly sat up, holding his knee.

The dark-green van sped around another corner and out of sight.

Maddy swore out loud.

Avril was gone.

CHAPTER 11

2:27 P.M.

Will bent over the sobbing blonde woman and put a hand on her shoulder. "Are you okay?"

She shrugged off his touch.

He tried again, asking the same question. Since telling him she thought Avril was in the back of the van, she'd done nothing but huddle into herself and cry.

Unsure what to do, Will looked around. The wet street was deserted. Rain fell fast and thick, making overlapping circular patterns in the puddles. Sirens were converging on the scene. He wanted to at least get the woman out of the rain.

Bending down next to her, he said in French, "I'm here to help. Let's get you into the shelter of the doorway."

When he received no response, Will put his hands under her arms and gently tugged up. She resisted at first, and then got to one knee. Her ruined eye makeup gave her the appearance of a scared raccoon, and her blonde hair was plastered to her head. He tried making eye contact, but her smudged eyes locked onto something behind him.

He glanced back. She was looking at the hole in the forehead of the man by the fruit cart.

Her mouth, framed by pink lipstick, dropped open and she began to howl.

His hesitation falling away, he pulled her to her feet. When she tried to rush to the dead man, he picked her up and carried her away from the carnage. She struggled like a snared animal for the first twenty paces before going limp.

He was about to stop in a doorway when he spied their rental BMW. The doors were wide open and wet, but it would be a safe spot and he wouldn't have to carry her again. Trotting the last few paces, he placed her in the backseat as gently as he could, where she curled up into a ball and continued to sob.

Shutting the passenger doors, he got into the driver's seat, turned on the car for warmth, and waited for the police to arrive. He wasn't looking forward to their questions.

CHAPTER 12

2:45 P.M.

After Maddy and Bear tumbled off the requisitioned motorbike, they hailed a taxi and returned to the market area, where they found Will talking with authorities while a distraught blonde woman sobbed in the back of the large BMW.

Once she was sure the scene was secure, Maddy found the market's owner and got his contact information so VanOps could reimburse him for the damaged motorbike.

As the annoying police interviews dragged on, Maddy yearned to break free. Poor Avril was being driven away by trained gunmen and the local cops wanted to know how they happened upon the scene and why they had weapons. It had taken three phone calls back to DC before they were released.

Hours later, in the sitting room of Avril's home, they faced the wrath of a purple-faced grandparent. The pipe-smoking Black man, who had introduced himself as Sébastien when they'd met him earlier that day, had eyes full of fury. Maddy was glad she didn't speak French and it was Will on the hook to deliver the bad news that they'd failed to keep his granddaughter safe.

Sébastien also glared at the blonde woman. French words tumbled from his mouth, and fell like unrecognized pebbles to the wood floor. The sole word Maddy recognized was "Monique," but she could tell from the body language that he was upset and wanted answers.

Trusting that Will would translate the conversation for her later, Maddy excused herself to the restroom. The rainy day had turned to night and the narrow windows reflected only darkness as she headed down the unlit hallway.

As she arrived at the water closet, she decided to explore while the others were arguing. It might take days for Sébastien to open up to them, which meant it was a good time to tag-team. Aunt Carole told them Mom had always said, "Two heads are better than one." Wishing she had more memories of their youth, Maddy turned on the bathroom light, shut the door, and headed up a set of narrow stairs. The house was old, the rooms small. Maddy guessed Avril's room would be upstairs.

At the top of the stairs, rooms appeared to the left and right. She turned on a penlight, which revealed the room to the left as that of a teenaged girl—the rock-star posters were a dead giveaway. Maddy smiled wryly, recalling her own room when she was a teenager. But unlike this one, hers was always neat. The room in front of her was a mess. Clothes were strewn atop the bed, and piles of charcoal sketches hid the black corner desk. Lace curtains didn't do much to stop the draft that came through the single-pane window.

A lump formed in Maddy's throat. Where was Avril sleeping tonight? Was she even resting, or . . . Maddy didn't want to think about the more likely scenarios.

Knowing she didn't have much time, Maddy visually swept the room. A naked phone charging cord announced its missing device. Some sort of pet, perhaps a lizard based on the logs and heat lamp, was either hiding or missing from its dry aquarium. A small glass held the remnants of orange juice. Maddy's heart hammered. She had to get back downstairs.

A hairbrush on the desk gave Maddy an idea. After collecting a clump of black, tangled hair, she tucked it into a clean tissue, wishing for a sealable evidence bag. Then she shoved the packet into her front backpack pocket. Perhaps the girl's DNA would be useful.

The pile of clothes gave up no clues. A half-eaten pretzel lay on the floor.

Maddy threw back the sheets. There. A silver laptop gleamed in the beam from her penlight. She snatched the computer up and threw it in her backpack. The pack went back on her shoulders and she rushed downstairs as quietly as she could.

She slipped into the bathroom, quickly did her business, and flushed. After washing her hands, she stepped into the living room. Bear, who also didn't speak French, stood with his arms crossed, clearly bored.

At least Bear hadn't been too badly hurt when their borrowed motorbike crashed into the fountain. Always a history geek, he'd smiled through his pain when he read the plaque on the wall next to the landmark fountain, announcing that its bust of Nostradamus was made in 1859 to honor the famous prophet. She just hoped Nostradamus had looked better when he was alive.

Bear limped across the room to join her by the hallway.

He whispered in her ear. "That fall banged up my knee. You okay?"

"I'm fine."

"Good. Now that you're an official operative, I know I shouldn't worry about you, but I do."

She confirmed the others were busy before answering. "No need. But thanks."

"I'm jonesing to get out of here."

They both glanced at Will, still in the thick of conversation. Sébastien touched his lower lip for a second and glanced sidelong at Maddy before continuing his argument.

"Me too," she replied softly. "The trail is getting colder by the minute."

CHAPTER 13

6:37 P.M.

Will said again, "No, we were not involved in Avril's kidnapping."

The silver-haired man wagged his pipe at Will. "How do I know that? You show up from nowhere, and, poof, she disappears. Where is she?"

Will wondered if Sébastien had been born in Africa. He had a thick South African accent.

"I don't know!" Exasperation seeped into Will's tone. "We want to help you find her."

"Why should I believe you? Who are you people?" Sébastien made a gesture that took in Maddy and Bear. The two were standing in the doorway, likely commiserating since they didn't speak French.

Will took a deep breath, attempting to control his rising blood pressure. It had been a long day. "We work for the American government. I can't tell you more."

The lines on Sébastien's scowling face deepened. "Oh, as if *that* is supposed to instill trust? You Americans. Always pushing your ideas around." He waved a hand at Will. "Bah! I was betrayed by one of you."

Will sat back in his chair, hoping the relaxed body language cue would get through. "Who? What happened?"

"My wife, Avril's grandmother. That's who."

"Where is she now?"

The forehead lines on the older man's face smoothed, and he seemed to deflate. "She drowned herself in the sea. Lung cancer."

Will exhaled slowly. "I'm sorry."

Sébastien puffed on his pipe, oblivious to the irony. "I'm better off without her. But Avril . . ." He paused. "It's been hardest on her. My daughter never understood why her mother drowned herself, and ended up with the bottle as her best friend. She accidentally set fire to their apartment curtains one night when Avril was a child, and Avril not only lost her mother, but still bears the scars on her face and neck."

"I see."

"You don't see, boy." Sébastien glared at Will. "You're too young."

On top of all the recent fighting with Maddy about her dreams and their mom, this was too much. Will's reserve broke. He sat forward in his chair, furious. "You have no idea what I've lived through."

A spark of curiosity lit the old man's eyes. "No? Tell me then. What devils have you slain?"

Will spat out the words. "My mother died when I was six. And my wife . . . my pregnant wife . . . and my father were gunned down in front of me."

Monique covered her mouth.

Will felt his face flush red and he stood to go.

Sébastien extended his hand, palm out. "Wait."

Will turned, and the silver-haired man searched his eyes for a long moment. Will's pulse hammered in his temples.

After a few beats, Sébastien motioned for Will to return to his seat. "Sit down." The old man sighed and put a hand on his chest. "I see we share a broken heart. If you can help me find Avril, perhaps we can keep my old ticker from cracking to pieces."

Will inhaled deeply and sat down. He took a minute to gather himself in the present. "Yes. I would like to help you find your granddaughter. And Monique saw that we tried to stop the kidnapping. She can vouch for us."

Sébastien turned to Monique. "Could you bring us some wine and cheese please, before telling us what you saw today?"

"Of course."

The au pair disappeared through a dark-paneled door.

"What do you need to know?" Sébastien asked.

The conversation had taken a dramatic turn. Will thought quickly about how to take advantage. "Tell me more about Avril."

"She's smart, she is," Sébastien said, his face alight with pride. "She's excelled in school even without a mother."

"What subjects does she like?"

"Math, computers, science, English. She does well in them all, but those are her favorites."

"How did she come to live with you?"

"Her father died in a plane crash. He'd been raising Avril in Paris, near his work, but when he died, I wanted her to come here."

Will nodded to keep the words flowing. "When did she start making predictions?"

"I don't know."

Monique walked into the living room carrying a bottle of red wine under her arm, a handful of stemmed glasses, and a cheese plate. She looked more attractive without blood on her face. Will jumped up to help her.

"Thank you," she said, releasing her hold on the wine bottle. "I can answer that question," she said after Sébastien nodded his approval.

Monique motioned for Maddy and Bear to sit on the sofa, before setting the cheese plate on the glass-topped table that sat in front of the couch. "She started making predictions on TikTok a few months ago."

Will popped a cheese cube in his mouth. It tasted good and sharp. "Did any of her other predictions come true?"

Monique handed out the glasses and filled them with wine. "No, I don't think so."

"Does she have a boyfriend or any friends in Asia?"

Monique and Sébastien shook their heads.

"Any military connections?"

Both murmured no.

Will sipped the wine. She'd chosen a full-bodied red with aromas of black currant, plums, and an earthy undertone. "I like your wine choice. A Bordeaux?"

She nodded, and smiled shyly.

"I have to ask this. I'm sorry. What did you see today?"

Monique's smile faded and her wine glass started to tremble. Putting her glass down, she hugged herself. Her lower lip shook. "I . . ." she trailed off and closed her eyes.

Will gave her space, unsure what else to do.

After a long minute of chewing her lower lip, Monique began to speak. Her eyes remained closed while the words tumbled out. "I saw a bundle in the back under blankets. It must have been Avril. She'd stepped outside while I finished buying bread. We were looking for her when they . . ." Gasping, she put her head in her hands. Rallying after a breath, she added, "Anyway. There were also two men in a nearby sedan. Just watching. The bald one wore sunglasses, strange in the rain. He took them off for an instant and I saw he had one glass eye. For some reason, he looked familiar."

"Familiar how?"

"I saw someone who looked like him when Avril and I visited the Nostradamus Museum."

"Thank you," Will said softly.

Will hadn't remembered a sedan. Wait—he'd taken cover behind a black one.

"Was the sedan you saw black?"

Her eyes opened, brimmed with tears. "It was."

He groaned. Had the enemy been that close? At least it was good intel. Maybe the man had been following the women, or maybe they were bystanders at the market. At least the glass eye was a lead. "Any idea why Avril started making predictions?"

Monique dabbed her eyes and glanced sideways at him as if she appreciated the change in subject. "Like her grandmother, she's fascinated by Nostradamus, especially after getting that walnut coffer. We'd recently traveled to Montpellier to see where he studied."

Remembering the Hourglass file, Will made a mental note to ask more about the walnut box, but now he looked at Sébastien. "What does she mean, like her grandmother?"

Sébastien blew a ring with his pipe smoke. "My wife was a historian, researching Nostradamus for a book she was writing. She even interviewed Avril's father's mother and the two became friends."

"Why would she interview Avril's paternal grandmother?"

"Because the woman was a direct descendant of Nostradamus."

CHAPTER 14

Maddy leaned into Bear on the uncomfortable hotel couch cushions, nearly asleep. She was exhausted, her internal sense of day and night all out of sync. The plane ride to France had given her time for a meditation and some sleep, but jet lag erased both hours ago.

After arriving at the hotel, which was located just down the street from Sébastien's home, they'd shipped the hair sample off to HQS and ordered room service.

As Will debriefed them about his interview with Avril's family, he made a remark that made her wonder what time it was back home. What would AJ and Aunt Carole be up to right now? Was it earlier in the day, or later?

Wait, what did Will just say?

She asked, "You're telling us Avril is a descendant of Nostradamus?"

"Yes, that's exactly what I'm saying."

"Whoa," Bear drawled. "That adds an interesting wrinkle."

"I'm not even done recounting the conversation with Monique and Sébastien."

"I can't figure out how we missed that in her file. Glad I found some of her hair for DNA testing." Maddy waved him on. "By all means, please continue."

"Perhaps it wasn't in her file. They said they're ultra-private about her lineage. Anyway, Avril received some sort of walnut box from her father as part of her inheritance."

"Dad kicks off, she gets a box?" Bear asked.

"Right. But neither Monique nor Sébastien knew what was in the box. Avril never told them."

Bear chewed on an ice cube leftover from his ice tea. "I remember one of the Leo reports said to keep an eye out for a walnut box, as the old prophet's formula might be inside it. What did the girl do with it?"

"Monique said Avril became obsessed after she opened it and took it with her everywhere. She eventually talked Monique into doing some day trips for research."

"Where to?" Bear asked.

"Montpellier, where Nostradamus went to medical school, and then Salon-de-Provence, where he lived later in life with his wife. Oh, Monique sent a video of that trip. Let me pull it up."

Will plucked his phone from his front shirt pocket and Bear leaned in. Maddy yawned and kicked aside the backpack at her feet so she could see too.

It was a short video, mostly of Avril walking on a wide, verdant lawn in front of a limestone building. *The girl has gorgeous long black hair and sways her hips.*

"When did she start making predictions on TikTok?" Maddy asked.

"Sometime after she got the box," Will replied. "Oh, and get this. She made some other prediction about an apocalypse in an ice cave to the reporters this morning."

Bear scratched his chin. "That's a curious follow-up to the Taiwan invasion."

Maddy glared at Will. "Maybe she can't control her predictions either."

"I thought it was strange too," Will said, ignoring her comment.

"What about a formula?" Maddy pressed.

"Didn't get very far on that."

"Why not?" Maddy asked. She knew her tone sounded critical, but was too tired to care. "That was the most important part."

Will turned on her. "Well, excuse me. Sorry, I got info about Avril's lineage, past movements, other predictions, and a walnut coffer that may hold the answers we need. What the hell did you find?"

Maddy reached into the backpack at her feet and held the laptop up triumphantly. "I found her brain."

Will reached in his back pocket and held up a piece of paper. "I got her phone number."

Bear turned to Will. "Did either the grandfather or au pair say anything about a formula?"

Will's glance at Maddy held daggers. "No, I didn't ask. I think it would've been in that walnut box, though. *If* such a thing exists, and I still think it's a big if, my money is on a pharmacological formula based on plants."

Maddy growled, "Mine is on using a meditative technique."

Bear stood up and put his hands out to each twin. "Y'all stop it."

Maddy sat back on the couch, face burning from the reprimand.

Bear looked back and forth at them, shaking his head. "You both need to learn to stay calm and keep your eyes on the prize. There's an innocent girl out there who needs our help. Let's try calling Jags again and see if she was able to dig up any camera footage of the kidnapping."

CHAPTER 15

9:23 P.M.

Will leaned forward in his chair to better hear the encrypted call Bear had just initiated with Jags to see if any closed-circuit TV cameras could shed light on the girl's kidnapping. He hoped his security measures at the vineyard were holding up and that Jags, Deana, and AJ were all safe.

Their coworker answered on the third ring. "You guys okay? The director and I were briefed on the Marseille shootout."

"Yeah, we're all dandy," Bear answered. "Just a little banged up. Except the girl, Avril. The au pair, Monique, thought she saw the kid in the back of the van as it sped away. Lucky we showed up and she didn't get kidnapped, too."

"Local police weren't so excited you were there shooting up the town. I've been doing some damage control, but that's their problem. Learn anything else from your debrief?"

"Monique saw a glass eye on a familiar man in a dark sedan."

"I'll get to work on that. Will check the databases."

"Were you able to track the van?"

"Not yet. I've been viewing satellite footage, and locally installed security cameras, but nothing has clicked yet."

"Thanks, Jags. Will got a few other tidbits from interviewing the grandfather and au pair."

"Do tell."

While Bear recounted the scraps learned about Nostradamus, and as Maddy hacked into Avril's laptop, Will thought about the kidnapped girl. She seemed like a smart kid who'd had a tough time of it. She'd lost her mom young, then her dad, and now was in the hands of a powerful group that clearly would not hesitate to hurt her if it served their goals. His gut twisted, thinking about where she might be tonight. Was she being raped? Tortured? Every cell of his body wanted to help her.

When there was a lull in the conversation, Will asked, "Jags, have you been able to research who might be behind this kidnapping?"

"By looking at all the state and nonstate actors who we have psy-spy intel on, I've narrowed the field to Russia, China, and Israel."

It took Will a minute to realize 'psy-spy' was an abbreviation for psychic spying, which was probably her shorthand for operations involving parapsychology.

"But isn't Israel an ally?" he asked.

"Usually yes."

That gave Will pause. "How about any herbs that might be used for trance states or telling the future?"

"Not much there. Lots of studies on healing applications, everything from migraines to tummy aches, but I've found no research on prophetic uses."

Will sighed. "Forgot to tell you, I was able to get Avril's phone number." He read off the digits. "Can you put a tap on the GPS location?"

"Sure thing, cowboy. I'll also try to touch base with our man in Russia. See if he knows anything."

Will used to think Jags was flirting with him when she called him pet names. He'd eventually realized that was just Jags. She was an ornery one.

With their man in Russia, he figured she was talking about Pyotr, a Russian operative who had turned into a mole, albeit reluctantly. Although, Will understood the man's tongue-less mother had recently been rescued from an unpleasant situation and was in US custody. That success might make Pyotr more helpful.

Bear rang off with Jags and turned to Maddy. "Find out anything on the laptop?"

Maddy stifled a yawn. "Sébastien wasn't kidding about Avril being into computers. The kid is an AI geek."

"Remind me what AI is."

Maddy frowned at Bear for an instant and then put on her polite face. "Artificial intelligence."

"I know you're a geek, darlin'. How can you tell she's one too?"

Maddy smiled. "She has some machine-learning programs on here and some frameworks and tools, as well. TensorFlow, Caffe, PyTorch, CNTK. That sort of thing."

"Okay, stop with the tech porn. Find out anything about Nostradamus?"

"Yes. She's been researching him. Her web search history is full of hits."

"Anything good?"

"He wrote something called *The Treatise of Cosmetics and Jams* in 1555."

"How exactly is mascara and peach jam relevant?" Will said, even though it sounded familiar.

She gave him a look that said she was about ready to stab him with one of his own knives. "Unfortunately, Avril highlighted a quote that works well for your herbs argument. It's about Nostradamus traveling the world seeking knowledge about herbal medicine."

Will smiled, recalling now that one of the Hourglass files had mentioned that treatise. "Herbs. I knew it!"

"Yeah, well, could be coincidence."

"My ass."

"Children," Bear interrupted with his no-nonsense warning tone. He turned to Maddy. "You look exhausted. Are you up for calling the master tonight to see when Doyle is going to join us?"

"The master texted me while you were chatting with Jags. Doyle is on the way."

Maybe it was because Will had failed the initiation tests at the Jerusalem Testing Society. Or maybe it was because he was loyal to VanOps. Perhaps it was because he'd seen Doyle's brother die a horrible death that nearly took Will's life too. Either way, he wasn't looking forward to Doyle's arrival. Nor was he happy about relying on help from the ancient sect.

"Sounds good." Bear touched Maddy's shoulder. "Let's get some shut-eye."

Maddy nodded and closed the laptop lid.

Will stood to brush his teeth.

An explosion rattled the windows and knocked him back onto his chair.

CHAPTER 16

9:41 P.M.

The explosion jolted Maddy off the couch. The bone-chilling thud had come an instant before the windows rattled.

Fearing the worst for Avril's family, Maddy shoved the laptop into her backpack, slung it over her shoulders, and ran out the door of the hotel room.

Skipping the elevator, she jumped down the stairs four and five at a time. She rounded a corner of the stairwell and smacked into the same boy who'd brought their room service an hour ago. The food on his tray flew into the wall with a crash.

"Sorry!" she yelled and kept going.

Soon she was at the exit door, which opened to an alley on the side of the hotel. The air smelled of smoke. She sprinted left through the lane, and then right onto a thoroughfare. Down the street, flames dominated the night, their eerie red and yellow fingers licking at bare-limbed trees and nearby structures.

She zigged around wide-eyed pedestrians fleeing the scene, and zagged around clusters of social-media-inclined onlookers who were already filming the madness. There were no sirens or flashing lights.

As she neared ground zero, her heart dropped. As she'd feared, it was the house they'd left only an hour or so before. The entire structure was ablaze. *How can I get in there to see if Monique or Sébastien is alive?*

Spying a garden hose at the neighbor's house, she ran to it, ripped her backpack and shirt off and doused the blouse and her entire body with water. It was a cold night, and goosebumps broke out across her flesh. She wrapped the shirt around her mouth and nose and ran into the building.

"Maddy, wait!"

She ignored Will and shouldered her way through the doorframe and into the inferno. Smoke and flames were everywhere. She knew she'd only be able to stay for seconds.

Sébastien lay facedown on the floor of the living room, his pants on fire. She rolled him over and saw his chest move. Eyes burning, she pulled a curtain off the window and used it to smother the fire on his legs. Then Will was there, and the two of them pulled Avril's grandfather out through the front door and onto the lawn.

Maddy's heart pounded as she ripped the now-dry cloth off her face and knelt to feel for a pulse. Faint, but there. Same with Sébastien's breathing. His eyes fluttered open for a second, and then closed again.

Will kneeled across from Sébastien and pointed at her left leg. "Your pants leg is on fire."

She jumped up and used the neighbor's hose to douse her leg. It didn't seem to have damaged her flesh, or she was too amped up to feel it. She put her shirt back on.

Bear ran up, out of breath. "Are you okay?"

"Yes, but I didn't see Monique. We have to go back in there."

"Maddy, no!"

As if to punctuate his words, the upper story of the house collapsed, sending burning embers flying through the night sky like fireflies.

Maddy clenched her jaw and pounded her palm on her thigh. If Monique had been alive before, she wasn't now.

Sirens sounded in the distance.

Bear grabbed her sleeve. "C'mon, Maddy, we need to go."

She looked over at Will and the body in the courtyard. "What about Sébastien?"

"I'm sure an ambulance will be here soon."

"He could die in the meantime."

"We've done all we can here, and we sure don't need the cops interviewing us again. We might become suspects."

She knew Bear was right, but it still made her angry. "The real criminals might be lurking about."

"Fine. But let's watch from the shadows across the street."

Throwing the hose to the ground, she ran to Will and slapped him on the shoulder. "Let's go." Then she tossed her backpack on and glanced at Sébastien, frowning while she sent him a burst of healing energy.

When Bear's urgent head motions could no longer be ignored, they crossed the street and stood with a group of onlookers in the shadow of an old clothes shop.

"Poor Monique," Will said.

"Yeah, and another blow to Avril," Maddy answered. She thought about the girl whose life had been turned upside down. A brief memory surfaced. Her father's face had drained of color when he answered the phone call from the sheriff on the cold morning when her mother had died. She didn't want to think about that.

Within two minutes, the French police arrived in a swirl of red and blue lights.

Bear said, "Time to move on."

As they walked quickly down the street, a cold wind dried the last beads of sweat off her body, leaving her chilled to the bone.

"Don't think we should head back to our hotel," Bear said. "After this morning's kidnapping, that explosion had to be intentional."

"Odds are slim it was an accident," Will agreed. "Think they might be on our trail, too?"

Her brother always saw the world through trouble-tinted glasses, but in this case, she had to admit she shared his concern.

"It's possible. I saw a dive hotel about a half-mile east. Let's head there and grab our luggage after we catch our breath."

They blended with the thinning crowd. Through chattering teeth, Maddy wondered again who they were up against. And why had the enemy felt the need to burn Avril's house down and kill Monique in the process?

CHAPTER 17

Tuning into a local news channel, Seymore eagerly leaned forward on his comfortable Italian leather couch to observe the burning fire. A curvaceous female with straight brown hair and red lipstick reported while the home burned in the background.

"An unexplained explosion occurred just minutes ago in downtown Saint-Rémy. First responders are on the scene now, working to save the lives of the inhabitants."

Sirens wailed in the background and the camera shifted to an ambulance as it screeched to a halt in front of the burning residence. Firefighters had hoses trained like fountains on the structure, and smoke billowed high into the night.

The reporter added, "Investigators are waiting until the fire is out to explore the cause."

The Watcher knew what had caused the explosion. C4.

He lit another unfiltered American cigarette and then rolled the lighter around his fingers, his heart rate quickening with pleasure. They had not yet reported on the lives of Sébastien Chirac and Monique Le Guillou—he hoped Raphael had succeeded in eliminating the pair. The odds were remote, but Monique might be able to identify them, and the old man knew more than he should.

The fiasco of losing the au pair and the girl at the market still made him hot. Seymore had been watching them from the sedan nearby while his men did their work. Both women had gone into the market. All had been going according to plan until that team of operatives showed up. He realized later that one of them had even used the back of his car for cover.

Still, he had wanted to eliminate Avril's grandfather for decades, and the man calling the shots had finally agreed.

While not being the leader of this arrangement chafed, at least their agreement had been profitable. The commas in his bank account gave him much pleasure, for both the comforts they afforded and the knowledge that he'd never be poor again. He'd grown up in Roubaix, a city in northern France on the Belgian border. His father had died in the Second Great War, leaving his mother with six hungry mouths to feed after long days in the textile mill. She tried her best, bless her soul, but had been killed in an industrial accident and they'd all been roughly deposited into the French child protection system. Two of his younger siblings had been adopted, but he was eleven when Mother died and had suffered through several abusive foster homes.

He'd never forget the sneers of his classmates as they made fun of the patches on his clothes and the pathetic sandwiches he brought for lunch. Likewise, the straps used in the beatings handed out by his new "fathers" had left indelible marks on his sense of self. Books had become his best friends.

At seventeen, he'd run away and joined the army, where his fascination with Nostradamus had truly begun. After finding a paperback of prophecies in a used bookstore in Baden-Baden, Germany, he had been enthralled. It was at a like-minded convention a year later where he'd met the man who would change his life.

The prophecy that had convinced his patron of the accuracy of the seer was about the French Revolution. Nostradamus had written it as a quatrain, which was published in 1558:

By night will come through the forest of Reines
A married couple, by a devious route
Herne, the white stone, the black monk in grey, Into Varennes

The elected Cap(et?). The result will be tempest, fire, blood – and cutting off.

It still made Seymore shiver, the prediction of King Louis XVI's and Marie Antoinette's attempted escape on June 20, 1791. The royal couple wore hoods, slipped out a side door of the Palace of the Tuileries, got into a horse-drawn coach, and were guillotined about a year and a half later. The king was descended from Hugh Capet, king of the Franks from 987 to 996. The precision of the prophecy, in Seymore's mind, was obvious.

Over drinks, Seymore and his patron had discussed not only that prophecy but also Nostradamus's predictions of the death of Henry II, the Great Fire of London, Napoleon's conquest, the discoveries of Louis Pasteur, Hitler's rule, and Charles de Gaulle's reign. The latter prediction had even named the future French president: *A man named de Gaulle is a three-time leader.*

Seymore and his patron had bonded over their belief that Nostradamus was the most accurate prophet ever to have lived. His new friend saw the potential military applications if that ability could be harnessed. Using his benefactor's cash, drive, and connections, they'd embarked upon a decades-long quest to uncover the prophet's formula.

But now, he had begun to wonder if he could eliminate his backer and keep the prize for himself. Betrayal was always tricky, but not impossible.

Interrupting his musings, the curvaceous female solemnly announced that the blonde au pair had died in the explosion.

Between drags of his cigarette, Seymore smiled, watching the flames on the television burn away the sins of the past. He hoped it would warn off the team who'd interrupted his plans at the market. But if they wouldn't leave, he'd take care of them, also.

It was all in play now, and nothing could be left to chance. That's why the general had initiated a military tracking request on the girl's cell phone. They'd find her soon.

CHAPTER 18

SAINT-RÉMY-DE-PROVENCE, FRANCE
10:15 P.M.

Avril dropped the phone onto the carpet, as if it had suddenly become red hot. She stared at the device in horror, one hand to her mouth. Had the brown-haired news announcer just said that Monique was dead?

The reporter droned on, while flames leaped high into the night behind her. This was too much. First the attempted kidnapping at the market, now an explosion at her grandfather's house. And Monique, killed? Avril sucked in a breath. This was beyond awful. Her head was spinning, but she thought she'd heard her grandfather at least was alive and being rushed to the hospital.

She picked up the phone and stared intently at the screen, trying to control her rapid breathing. The news channel switched to another story and Avril swiped the app closed, and then turned it off to save battery power. Throwing the device onto the couch, she put her head in her hands and sobbed.

Monique!

Avril's gut lurched as she mentally replayed moments they'd shared over the years. Monique helping with homework at the dining room table at their flat in Paris. Monique sipping a glass of red wine while preparing a roast for the oven. Monique's hands covered in flour as she baked bread.

After Avril's mother disappeared, Monique had held that maternal role. She'd been cook and confidante, and would be deeply missed.

Feeling guilty about her prediction, which resulted in Monique's death, Avril screamed at the untimely loss and beat at the couch cushions until she was exhausted.

Eventually, a new thought crossed her mind and she opened her eyes. Was she safe here?

After the murder at the market, she'd dropped her latte and had run out the back of the coffee shop. Keeping to alleys, she'd jogged away from the market and the sound of gunshots. Once she was in a quieter part of town, she slowed to a walk and realized she shouldn't go home. After a few more blocks she turned left and began to head for Giselle's house. Avril's only friend here in Saint-Rémy was out of town this week with her family. Because she was lizard-sitting for Giselle's brother, Avril knew where the house key was hidden.

Upon arrival, she'd used her phone's flashlight to enter the home's back door because it was far past the time when she usually came over to feed the lizard. Once inside, she'd been glued to the news on her phone, watching the unfolding coverage of the market shootout. The reporters had danced around who had stopped the kidnapping of Monique, and Avril wondered if it was the police or another agency. When she learned that Monique had escaped, tension had fled from her body and she'd eaten a cheese sandwich and taken a short nap while considering her next move. She'd been about to head home when she thought to check the news again.

She pulled the gecko out of her pocket. "Fleck, Monique is dead."

"Oh no! Really?"

"That's what they said on TV."

"That's so sad. I loved her and the scraps she fed me. Is Grandfather alive?"

"I think so. But I'm scared."

The gecko flicked his tail. "You think the men that have been following us killed her?"

"Don't you?"

"Who else would do it?"

"Exactly. I'm glad we are on the same page."

The gecko bobbed his head. "I don't think we should go home."

"Me neither. Those men could still be watching."

Fleck looked around. "Are we at Giselle's house?"

"We are."

"I hope we are safe. Can I visit her brother's lizard?"

Avril stood and began to walk down the hall, again using the light from her smartphone. "Sure."

She'd been inside Thomas's bedroom many times to see his pet lizard before she and Giselle did homework. While the girls studied, Fleck often visited with Minerva, the black and gray African fat-tail gecko. Avril took a deep breath and pushed into the room. It looked the same as when she'd been here yesterday. The bed was neatly made and Minerva blinked at the light.

Avril and Fleck walked over to Minerva's vivarium.

Fleck said, "Hi Minerva. Can I spend the night with you?"

Avril made Minerva's voice higher than Fleck's. "Hello, Fleck. Nice to see you. Of course, you can stay here. Maybe your person will give us some treats."

Removing the lid to the lizard enclosure, Avril placed Fleck inside next to his friend. The crickets were in a cabinet below. She fed a few to the geckos. "Enjoy. I need to figure out what to do next."

After replacing the lid, she left, walked down the short hall, and entered Giselle's bedroom, hoping to find a spare phone charger. It took a minute of digging, but Avril eventually found what she needed underneath a fluffy pink pillow. She hesitated to turn her phone back on, though. What if they could trace her? She should use it only if she had to.

The cushion was atop a messy bed, full of comforters and other bolsters. Even though they'd never had a sleepover, Giselle wouldn't care if Avril slept here. She tumbled onto the bed, wanting a few hours' sleep. It was possible the men had seen her come here to feed Minerva over the last few days. She decided it wasn't safe.

Somewhere out of town would be better. With her father and Monique gone, Avril could take care of herself. At least until her grandfather got out of the hospital. She'd call him tomorrow using an antique pay phone in another town. Fleck would be fine with Minerva.

She'd been meaning to go to the library in Marseille to research Nostradamus with France's famous expert. What was his name? Henri Seymore.

In the morning, she'd catch an early train.

CHAPTER 19

JANUARY 27, 7:22 A.M.

Will pulled the blanket over his head and grunted.

"Wake up, Will. C'mon."

It took a minute for Maddy's insistent words to pull him out of the familiar nightmare. The bad dream had begun after surviving the car crash in which Mom died and it always involved enduring a never-ending free fall through a pitch-black void. Sitting up on the threadbare couch, he rubbed his eyes and grunted. Where was Bear?

Maddy's green eyes held concern. "You okay?"

He nodded.

"You were twitching. Nightmare?"

"Yes." His throat felt dry. "Any coffee here?"

"That's actually why I woke you. Doyle will be here soon."

It was going to be one of those days. First the old nightmare. Now Doyle's arrival. "Remind me again why we have to deal with him?"

Maddy's eyes narrowed, preparing to spar. "It wasn't really our choice. If you recall, our *boss*, Director Bowman, arranged to get his help."

"I just don't think we need him."

"No? His brother—"

The knock at the door interrupted her. She scowled at Will as she moved across the small, cramped space to answer. Bear had chosen a nasty little hotel to hide out in.

She paused at the door. "Who is it?"

"Hey, baby, let us in. I found a stray dog."

Ah, so Bear had gone to meet Doyle.

As soon as the two men walked in, the space felt overcrowded. At least they had beverages and a bag. Will hoped for food.

After handing Maddy a steaming cup, Bear held one out to Will. "You look like you could use a double shot of espresso this morning, Argones."

"Thanks. I'm fine."

"Nice to see you again, William."

Doyle's Irish accent was as thick as his brother's had been. They'd met at Quinn's funeral in Donegal, Ireland, at which point Will was astounded that two men could look so much alike and not be twins. They both shared rugged features with wide craggy eyebrows and high cheekbones that suggested their Asian heritage. Doyle sported one of those strange Samurai-like man-buns on the top of his head. Women probably found the guy handsome.

Quinn was the first and only operative that Will knew who had perished on a mission. He hoped no one died on this operation.

"Good to see you too," Will lied. "Have any breakfast in that bag?"

"I surely do."

Doyle broke out croissants, fruit cups, pads of butter, and hardboiled eggs.

Will applied butter to a flaky roll and took a large bite. It was quite good. Maybe the day wouldn't be a complete loss.

When they were all settled between the couch and chairs, Doyle said, "I'm glad to be here. My grandparents are in Taiwan and I'm worried. The master thinks China could invade at any moment."

"Sorry about your family," Bear responded. "We're thrilled to have you, but no information yet links our mission directly to what's going on there."

"I understand it's a long shot, but I'll do anything to help. Let me show you the latest developments."

"Sure."

While Will helped himself to another mouth-watering croissant, Doyle pulled up a video. "This was yesterday, after the PLA invaded the islands."

The phone showed a packed urban street with thousands sitting in front of factories and office buildings, chanting loudly. They held signs and other items in their hands.

"What are they saying?" Maddy asked.

"It's the equivalent of 'We hate China,' 'No working for tyrants,' and 'We'll fight to the death.'"

Looking closer, Will saw nearly every sit-in protestor carried a knife, baseball bat, or other homemade weapon.

"That's my grandmother there with the long-bladed kitchen knife. She normally manages a team in a semiconductor factory and is nearing retirement."

Will put the croissant down because he suddenly couldn't swallow. An old woman willing to risk her life by taking on People's Liberation Army tanks. Dear god.

Bear asked, "Where's the Taiwanese military?"

"Guarding the beaches. But they're woefully outnumbered. Only the threat of US intervention has kept China out of Taiwan in the past."

Based on the grim set of Doyle's jaw, Will could tell the Irishman was trying to keep his emotions from showing. However, Doyle's eyes betrayed his feelings. Those deep brown irises looked haunted, as if he'd already lost his entire family.

Maddy put a hand on Doyle's. "We'll do our best."

The man shuddered once and turned the phone face down. "Anyway, the master sends his regards, and of course, words of wisdom."

"What's the advice this time?" Maddy asked.

"Stay present. Only the timeless part of yourself can see the future."

Curious contradiction, Will thought. *Maybe the master doesn't know what he's talking about. Some days I'm glad I didn't pass the tests at that order he runs.*

Bear and Maddy nodded sagely. Will figured they didn't know what the master was talking about any more than he did.

"As you know, the Order maintains quite the library, with some contents as old as the pyramids," Doyle continued, and then waved a hand. "At Ms. Maddy's request, I searched the contents for Nostradamus-related info and chatted with the master before I departed."

Bear set down his coffee. Or had the man managed to source his favored iced tea? "Find anything useful?"

"Ay, well, lots of background. Nostradamus was a physician and healer. He traveled eight years studying herbs. Mostly Italy, Greece, and Turkey."

Will grinned at Maddy and mouthed "herbs."

She dismissed his comment with a wave of her hand.

Doyle sipped his latte. "The master believes that Nostradamus experienced a psychic awakening during this time."

The word "psychic" made Will nearly break out in hives. Before he could scoff out loud, Maddy looked at Will with a raised eyebrow and an "I told you so" look.

Doyle added, "It's said that the prophet would spend hours in his study at night, meditating in front of a bowl filled with water and herbs."

Will looked pointedly at Maddy. "Herbs?"

"Meditating?" she fired back.

"Yes." Doyle looked back and forth between them before moving on. "The old prophet had six kids from a second wife. In 1555, he published the first section of a three-part book intended to hold a thousand, mostly French, quatrains. Those four-line poems make up his famous prophecies."

Bear scratched at the tree-like lightning scars on his arm. "What do you mean *mostly* French?"

"He lived during the Inquisition. It was not a good time to do anything, shall we say, even remotely witchy."

They all nodded in understanding. Will shuddered, thinking of some of the torture instruments he'd seen in museums.

Doyle added, "He devised a method of hiding his meanings by using word games like anagrams, and a mix of other languages, such as Italian, Greek, Latin, and Provençal."

Bear ran his hand through his short hair. "Any examples?"

"Yes. I remember two. Rapis for Paris and Elvas for Savole, or Savoy."

"I see," Bear said.

"He died at the age of sixty-two, after foretelling his own demise."

Although the information clicked with the reports from Leo, Will still felt that an herbal formula must have been the seer's ticket to fame, *if* there was actually any recipe to find.

Before he could start up the argument again with Maddy, Bear's phone rang.

"Bear here." He listened for a second. "Hi, Jags. Doyle just arrived and has been giving us some background. Putting you on speaker."

Jags's throaty voice purred. "Sorry to interrupt the history lesson. I've picked up a signal for Avril's phone in Marseille."

CHAPTER 20

OLD PORT OF MARSEILLE, FRANCE
8:30 A.M.

The tang of fish and saltwater hung heavy in the air as Maddy walked next to Bear along the quay. Even though they'd hustled after getting Jags's intel, it had still taken precious time for them to drive from Saint-Rémy to Marseille, and then they had to find a place to park. She'd ground her teeth in frustration the entire trip, wishing for wings. Where was Avril? What had the girl been forced to endure the night before?

The morning boardwalk was already packed with throngs of winter tourists even though it was an overcast day with a bitter breeze coming off the Mediterranean. Did no one work anymore? Christmas had come and gone and spring break was a gleam in the eyes of most wage slaves. Yet it was so crowded.

Maddy's hands felt clammy. The stakes were high and they were in the danger zone with a lot of innocent people around. It would be a truly poor place for a shootout.

Bear's steady presence next to her helped keep her piano-wire tight nerves from snapping. He was a solid man with a good heart.

As if sensing her thoughts, he glanced over and smiled. "You're gonna be fine."

"Hope so."

He grabbed her hand and they continued walking. Just another set of love-struck tourists. She fantasized for a moment about a holiday on one of the yachts anchored in the harbor. Would she rather sail on that large catamaran, or motor on the ostentatious eighty-foot *Playboy*-esque Hugh Hefner love palace, complete with hot tub on the back deck? Tough choice. She and Bear kept trying to plan a getaway; it just never panned out. Work.

That brought her mind back to the task at hand. Jags had provided coordinates to the harbor, but nothing more specific. Finding the kidnappers had sounded easy enough back at the hotel. Here she had no idea how to narrow the field.

The sightseers trundled by in miniature open-air cars pulled by a blue faux-train engine. Cars, trucks, and vans sped along the cobblestone street that circled the harbor. Not one van was dark green. The gelato shops and delis did a brisk business.

Using the high-tech microphone custom fit to her molars, Maddy pressed a button in her pocket to engage the receiver and subvocalized to her brother, who was currently patrolling the other side of the harbor. "Will, see any green vans over there?"

"No. You?"

"Nothing."

They walked past the swimming society, a soap museum, and a drug store. To their right, a vendor hawked rides on a jet ski. Maddy picked up a stray piece of trash and deposited it in a can.

If finding Avril from her phone proved a bust, Maddy wanted to head over to the library and meet with a local Nostradamus expert Bear had found on the internet. It sounded like this Henri Seymore had studied Nostradamus for decades.

Exiting one of the piers, a muscled man with a black patch on his left eye and a thin mustache crossed their path.

Could the patch be hiding a glass eye? Earlier, they'd discussed the possibility that Monique had been killed because she knew something, which lent credence to the theory that the men she'd seen in the black sedan had been with the kidnappers.

Bear caught Maddy's gaze and she nodded, agreeing they should follow the man with the patch. Perhaps he'd lead them to the hideout where Avril was being kept. Crossing the street, they shadowed from a distance.

Maddy stopped to look at a menu posted at the entrance of a restaurant. "Will. We have a nibble."

"Oh?"

"Currently following."

"We'll circle your way."

She wondered if their quarry was the same man with a glass eye that Monique had seen. Maddy pursed her lips. No time to mourn Monique, but maybe her clue would help them find Avril.

Like a fish on a line, they let the man with the patch have some room. He continued to walk with the crowd, about sixty feet in front of Maddy and Bear.

She was about to ask Bear a question when muscle-man reached out, quick as a viper, and snatched a purple purse from an older woman. The thief bolted away, and turned a corner.

Maddy yelled, "Hey!" and took off in hot pursuit.

She ran to the corner. He was ahead, running up a hill. There was no crowd on the side street, just parked cars with curbed wheels and buildings with their metal doors shuttered. She pushed on, lungs beginning to burn. What would he do next? Her sensei at the dojo was working with her to see one step ahead in a fight. They practiced often, and so far, she'd failed every time.

The thief turned a corner. When she arrived, he was nowhere in sight, but a single garage-door-sized shutter was rolling down. She dove under it and found herself in a dry dock warehouse that smelled of grease and was filled with beached ships. Cranes held boats in the air and pneumatic air guns made hissing sounds.

Boots slapped on concrete one row of boats over. Heart racing, she pursued him up the aisle, running parallel to his flight.

Reaching deep into her reserves of strength, she cut through a narrow passage between two ships and caught up to him. Aikido was all about using an opponent's energy as a weapon to bring a situation back to a peaceful state, so she reached out and pushed him in the upper back while tripping one of his feet.

He flew forward, dropping the purse as his chin hit the concrete. While he was dazed, she grabbed his right hand and twisted it behind him in a *yonkyo* pinning technique that used a wrist pressure point to ensure compliance. For good measure, she knelt on his arm. No need to use her lorandite.

He shook his head, grunted, and tried to throw her off. She pressed harder on the wrist point and he stopped struggling.

When she was sure he wasn't going to move, she communicated her location to the team, eager to have their help to see if she'd landed a big fish or a minnow.

CHAPTER 21

Anxious to see who Maddy had captured, Will entered the warehouse out of breath and cursing his Irish partner, who'd left him in the dust as soon as they'd received Maddy's communication.

He followed the sound of voices up a broad aisle and found a small group of workmen huddled around Maddy and a mustached man she had pinned on the floor. Bear and Doyle were there already. A purple purse and its contents were spilled underneath a ship's keel.

Bear stood with crossed arms. "We'll take him to the authorities."

One of the workers put his hands on his hips and responded in French, "What is going on here?"

From the physical posturing, Will gathered the language gap was Grand Canyon-sized. He turned to the Frenchman and pointed to the man on the ground. "This man stole a purse and my sister caught him," he said in French.

"Ah, you are civilized. I'm Antoine, the foreman. I see the purse. I will call the police now."

Will caught Bear's eye and, from the slight movement of his head, gathered he might like to interrogate the thief himself. But how to extricate the robber from the situation?

Thinking quickly, Will gave a false name as an introduction. "I'm Stanley. I live on a boat back in America." He looked around and found a similar craft. "It's a V42 like that one over there. Has she been de-teaked yet?"

Most owners of the Vancouver 42's removed their teak decks.

The foreman's shoulders relaxed a bit. "They're nicely built. Rugged and true cutters."

"I can't see from here. Does that one have a center or an aft cockpit?"

The foreman smiled. "Center."

"Those are a little cramped but offer excellent visibility."

"Agreed. Her owner has us doing a complete interior refresh on the Taiwanese joinery, along with removing the worn teak, but we're behind schedule."

A light bulb went off in Will's mind. "You are welcome to call the police. Of course, it might take hours and put you further behind schedule. If you'd like, we could walk the man outside your shop and call from there."

The foreman motioned his men back to work. "That is an excellent idea, my new friend. This has nothing to do with us."

Will signaled Maddy to let the thief stand.

Turning to the foreman, he asked, "Do you offer any private charters, if I have time later?"

"No, but come back after work some night if you want to sail. Bring a warm jacket and I'll show you around."

"Thanks, I appreciate that."

Bear put the thief's arms behind his back and marched him along next to Maddy. When they reached the warehouse entrance, Will waved farewell to the foreman. As they stepped outside, several pedestrians glanced their way.

"Not sure how you did that, Will, but good job," Maddy said. "A narrow street runs along the side of the warehouse. Our guy here snuck under the door over there."

"Sounds a little more private," Bear agreed.

Soon they were around the corner. Maddy put their captive in one of her aikido locks as the men turned their backs to the busy street, creating a shield from prying eyes.

Will looked deep into the thief's one good eye and spoke to him in French. "Why did you steal the purse?"

The man looked down at his shoes.

Will put a hand under the man's chin. "We don't want to hurt you, but need to know some things."

"What things?"

That was a start. "Tell me about the purse."

"It's been a slow week. I needed some francs. She seemed an easy mark."

"That's it?"

"What else would there be?"

"Where's the girl?"

The man squinted. "What girl?"

"The one you and your pals kidnapped yesterday."

The man shook his head. "I work alone. I have no pals."

Maybe the guy was a good liar. "We'll see what the local police have on you."

The man looked at the ground. "I have no friends."

Will continued the questions for several more minutes, but got no further information. Finally, he turned to Bear. "He swears he works alone and knows nothing about the girl."

Bear sighed. "All right. Will, you and Doyle call the cops and wait here with our thief. Maybe he'll be more forthcoming when he hears sirens."

"What are you going to do?" Will asked, wondering how it was he kept being paired with Doyle.

"While we keep our eyes out for Avril's kidnappers, Maddy and I are going to pay a visit to a man at the library famous for his knowledge about Nostradamus."

CHAPTER 22

BEIJING, CHINA

3:00 P.M.

Deep inside People's Liberation Army headquarters, General Wong stalked back and forth across his windowless office. Anger fueled his movements.

Earlier that day, fourteen Chinese Air Force fighter jets had flown into Taiwan's air defense zone to see what type of rise they'd get out of the US president. The latest man to hold the oval office had run as a peace-seeking dove, and Wong's ambitious leadership wanted to see if the American's reputation would hold. So far, the answer from Washington was inconclusive.

Lately, Wong's peers argued endlessly over whether America would defend Taiwan, especially in light of the recent abandonment of Afghanistan to the Taliban.

China's aging leader wanted reunification to crown his legacy. Plus, the old man's father had died in the civil war with the Kuomintang party that had caused many to flee to Taiwan in the first place. It was personal for him. With a military that many argued was the most technologically advanced in the world, he was poised to pluck the rose across the strait. But he'd reiterated in a meeting this morning that he didn't want to go in blind, potentially risking an economic tsunami. He'd worried about the fallout for months, which was why he'd assigned Wong to predict what the new American commander in chief would do when China seized back its rightful territory.

Not one to leave predicting the future to a roll of the dice, Wong had reignited an operation that he'd been nurturing for decades. Long ago, he'd become impressed by Nostradamus's uncanny ability to see the future. If Wong could harness that power, his country's fortunes, and his own place in history, would be assured.

It seemed the young French girl also had her ancestor's gift of prophecy, or a formula.

Regrettably, his men in France had bungled the kidnapping of the young seer. With the world's most elite intelligence service at his disposal, Wong knew she was now in Marseille. His team was also researching who had interrupted the snatch at the market yesterday. Likely the Americans, who were always butting in where they didn't belong.

Wong clenched and unclenched his fists. He'd worked with Seymore a long time, but lately the man was not getting results. What's more, Wong was beginning to wonder if he could trust the greedy expert.

He adjusted his next-generation soft body armor before striding to his desk and picking up the black phone. Dialing Seymore's number, which Wong had memorized from a list of disposable devices, he counted the rings until the phone was answered. One, two, three—

There was a short delay as voice recognition software kicked in.

Seymore's tone was terse. "Hello."

In French, Wong barked, "You lost the girl."

Seymore replied, "I'm not happy about it either."

"I'm past unhappy; this was unacceptable! It's time to add some help. Go hire your friends from the island."

Over the years, they'd used the Corsican mob when Seymore needed additional manpower. Wong thought it was more effective than bringing in resources from mainland China. They knew the turf and blended in better.

Seymore was silent for a long moment. "I'll make the call now."

"Grab the girl. She's in Marseille, headed for your library. Kill anyone who might be helping her."

Wong slammed the phone onto the cradle.

The Americans had gotten close to finding Nostradamus's secret decades earlier; he wouldn't let them near it again.

CHAPTER 23

A s they started off for the library, Maddy shivered, thanks to the cold wind that was rocking the boats.

"Think Will and Doyle can hold the thief until the police show up?"

"He seemed fairly docile, so I expect they'll be fine."

Maddy frowned. "That chase was disappointing. Got my heart rate up for nothing."

"Hey, at least you got some exercise today."

"That's true I suppose, but I was hoping for a clue to find Avril."

His tone turned serious. "I know. I was too."

They walked on in silence for a time, past two different American fast-food joints, and a polished piece of overhead steel art designed to reflect the images of those walking underneath it.

She whispered in his ear. "See anyone of interest in the crowd?"

"No, but I'm still looking."

"Me too."

It didn't take long to traverse the short end of the harbor.

"I have an idea," Bear said.

"Oh?"

"Let's walk by the Port Antique."

"What's that?"

"It's a park. *Mostly* on the way." He looked like a kid hiding the empty cookie jar and swearing he hadn't eaten the missing cookies.

She gave him one of her best I'm-on-to-you looks. "What's in this out-of-the-way park?"

"You know. History stuff."

"What specifically?"

He shrugged. "Archeological remains of a local Roman road, and, even cooler, the Greek walls of Marseille's ancient port."

She knew it would make his day. "Fine. Why not? As long as it doesn't rain on us."

When they arrived at the grassy expanse littered with a few old limestone blocks, they stopped so Bear could ogle the unimpressive ruins. Meanwhile, Maddy kept an eye out for dark-haired teenagers with swaying hips and men with glass eyes.

After a time, they left the park, walked a few blocks down cobblestoned streets lined with ornate sandstone buildings, and neared the library. The building was situated on a street with a trolley track, which reminded her of downtown San Francisco.

"That's it over there," Bear said, pointing.

"Wait, that gorgeous ochre-colored door with the delicious wrought-iron portico?"

"Yeah."

She shook her head. "Puts American buildings to shame."

"Focus, darling."

"Okay, I'm focused. Do you want to scout before we go in?"

"Yes, I've been keeping an eye out, but would like to circle the block. Why don't you do some of your own reconnaissance from . . ." He trailed off, looking around. He tilted his head toward a narrow acupuncture shop across the street with a yin-yang symbol on the overhead sign. "How about the inside of that store over there, in case the rain starts?"

That sparked her interest. "Sure."

Maddy arrived just as a wizened Asian woman wearing sunglasses unlocked the door. She motioned Maddy inside with a white cane. Bells tinkled as Maddy walked in, pushed by a gust of wind.

"Thank you," Maddy said.

The woman replied in French—probably "You're welcome."

With the door closed, Maddy felt transported to another world. The traffic sounds from the busy street were muted, and an earthy scent permeated the space, seeming to seep up from the scarred old floorboards. The light that came through the front windows was swallowed up by the dim interior.

Her tendency was to relax in a place like this, but was it safe? The store was slim, but deep, and shelves on both sides of the center aisle were filled with glass jars holding a variety of herbs. She recognized red clover, but not much else. Mom had never had a garden. Or had she? Maddy would have to ask Will.

Speaking of Will, she was certain Nostradamus had foretold the future using a meditative technique with instructions similar to how she moved energy out her hands, but while she was here . . .

Maddy walked over to the stooped shopkeeper. The woman had white, sightless eyes behind her dark sunglasses. Ah, thus the need for the cane.

"Do you speak English?" Maddy asked.

The shopkeeper shook her head and said something Maddy didn't understand.

Shoot.

As she walked back to the front of the shop to perform Bear's requested surveillance, a tall man in a tailored suit walked by, phone plastered to his ear.

Aha! Maddy had an idea.

She dug her phone from her pocket and pulled up a translate program. She spoke to it, "What is your name?" and the device spat out garbled words in French.

The old woman's eyebrows shot up in understanding. She replied and the program translated, "Lan Fang."

Maddy nodded, getting excited. "How long have you run this shop, Lan?"

"Thirty-five years."

"Where are you from?"

"From Dongguan, China."

"I study martial arts," Maddy said, wanting to build rapport.

"Which ones?"

Communicating through an app was awkward, but it was working. "Aikido."

The woman's upper lip curled momentarily in what Maddy took as distaste. She realized aikido was a Japanese martial art. Too bad she hadn't studied a Chinese fighting art like Kung Fu or Thong fu. She ground her teeth at the faux pas.

"I am an acupuncturist," Fang said.

Maddy had been to a practitioner in the city for a lower back issue once, but had forgotten they also studied herbs. "No needles today?"

"Needles in the afternoon. Herbs in the morning. Qigong in the evening."

Maddy had tried qigong, the ancient practice of moving meditation to circulate energy, but had found it too slow for her taste. "I see. Do you know if there are herbs to induce visions?"

Lan's clouded eyes narrowed. "Visions?"

How could Maddy explain this? "To see the future or the past."

Lan nodded, as if thinking. The clock ticked fourteen times before she answered. "Let me see your chi."

That sounded strange. Especially for a blind woman. But maybe it was a test. Maddy was familiar with those. "You mean with my hands?"

"Yes. But first let me feel the pulses in your wrist."

Maddy glanced over her shoulder, feeling a little guilty for taking so long. But if she was actually wrong about an herbal formula, the delay would be worth it, even if Will would taunt her forever. The shopkeeper took her hand with a firm grip before holding two fingers to Maddy's inner wrist. She felt her heart rate kick up a notch and willed it to slow.

The old woman dropped Maddy's wrist. "You need to work on balancing your liver chi. Staying in the present moment will help. Please send me a ball of chi now."

Maddy committed the advice to memory for later review. Grounding herself through her feet, she took a common aikido stance and a few deep breaths. She lowered her eyes to better focus, and allowed herself to drop into the zone by focusing on the sounds around her. She *listened*. Nearby, the clock ticked. A bus honked. She imagined energy pouring into her center, below her navel, and then pulled that energy through her heart and into her cupped hands. It was what she did to engage the lorandite rings.

When she was ready, she tossed the chi ball to the shopkeeper.

Lan caught it, and with two hands threw it gently toward the front door with a basketball pass motion. Bells jingled softly and the acupuncturist smiled.

Maddy grinned back. "Nice."

"Plants are powerful medicine," Lan said. "They can put us in a state of mind where we can see many things."

"The future?" Maddy asked.

"Perhaps. My teacher once told me it is possible."

Maddy's eyes grew wide. Could she admit this to Will?

The old woman went on, saying, "But you need a formula, with specific herbs and exact amounts."

"Do you have such a formula?"

Lan smiled and bowed slightly, hands to her chest. "I am sorry. I do not."

Maddy hardly had time for a few curse words to bounce around inside her head before Bear's voice summoned her. "You're clear to approach the library."

Maddy turned to leave.

"Before you go," Lan said. "I have a message from your mother."

"What do you mean?"

"She says she loves you, the necklace is a lion, and it was not your fault."

Maddy clutched the dime-sized pendant on the delicate silver chain she always wore under her shirt, the necklace her father had saved for her from her mom with the lion silhouette. It had been Mom's favorite. How on earth had the woman known about that? Maybe the blind-old-woman thing was a sham. None of it made sense.

Maddy rushed out of the shop as if she were running for her life.

CHAPTER 24

Will stared down at the purple purse in his hands. "Exactly what am I supposed to do with this?"

In a deadpan tone, Doyle replied, "It's not a good color for you, so I suggest we give it to the police when they arrive."

Will strained not to roll his eyes. "I've been thinking about that."

"Thinking? Sounds like trouble already."

"Stop. Just stop. I'm still operating on a different time zone. I don't have enough sleep for your witty repartee."

"What's repartee mean?" the kneeling thief asked, in French.

Will ignored the question, but figured they'd better be extra careful about what they said since their prisoner spoke English. He also realized the pickpocket wasn't very bright, as the words sounded similar in both languages.

Sirens blared in a distant part of the city.

"Anyway," Will continued. "I think *you* should turn him in."

Doyle raised a bushy eyebrow, pushing the point of it toward his hairline. "Why's that?"

Will did not want a police report with his name on it in this town too. Bad enough the cops in Saint-Rémy knew him. Best to fly under the radar. Be a ghost.

He glanced down at the thief, then back to Doyle, trying to communicate the need for discretion. "Tell you later."

Doyle's eyes finally lit with understanding. "Okay. Right then. Well, the authorities should be here at any moment."

Will looked at the thief, returning to French. "Last chance to tell us what you know."

The scallywag's thin mustache set in a firm line. "I know nothing about a girl, but now I know a few things about you."

Will flicked his blade from its scabbard and held it to the man's jugular. "You don't know anything about me. Understand?"

The man's Adam's apple made a slow roundtrip down and up his neck. "Um. Yes. I understand now."

He hated to have to threaten the lowlife, but sometimes you needed to speak the tongue of the locals to get your point across.

With his knife, Will flipped the man's black eye patch up, revealing a missing orb. Not a glass eye. They should have thought to check that sooner.

Frustrated, Will sheathed his knife, dumped the purse on the ground, and stalked off to the sound of distant sirens.

In the harbor, Will sat down on a bench to gather his wits and pretended to watch gulls with his thermal-imaging binoculars. Should he have left Doyle alone with the purse snatcher? The sirens had sounded like they were approaching when he'd left. It was probably fine. Nevertheless, he turned so he could see the exit to the alley, as the police had yet to arrive.

His phone rang and he answered, "Hello."

"Will, it's Jags."

"We caught a thief but it was a dead end."

"Okay. But get this. I still see the phone there in Marseille. It's near the library now, but here's the weird thing . . ."

Will interrupted, saying, "Tell me."

"That van is unfortunately registered through shell companies, but a tracking camera picked it up at the other end of town last night."

"And no nearby cameras have picked it up today?"

"That's right."

Before Will had time to consider the implications, a white Mercedes blew around the corner on two wheels and headed up the street to where Will had left Doyle and the thief.

CHAPTER 25

The glass door on the other side of the library swung closed as Maddy walked in and caught the scent of old paper. Instead of going in together, Bear had wanted her to feel out the local Nostradamus expert, Henri Seymore, alone, citing her "charming smile."

Bear had provided no description of Seymore. As soon as she walked through the door, Maddy spotted the librarian behind the center crescent-shaped desk that held his name plate. Bald. Clean shaven. Dark eyebrows and thick lips. He was processing returned books by taking them out of a cart and organizing them into piles.

It was still early, and the library held only a handful of patrons. An elderly woman sat hunched at a computer in the corner and a young man held a book while reading, slouched against a stack of fiction.

Maddy walked toward the desk. After the awkwardly translated conversation with Lan Fang, Maddy hoped Seymore spoke enough English to communicate.

She waited a few moments for Seymore to notice her, but he continued with his work. Not wanting to get off on the wrong foot, she waited, and studied the man and his domain.

He smelled of cigarette smoke, but his dress slacks and tailored shirt were tidy, as was his workspace. Near the desk telephone, a stack of books whose titles contained the word "Nostradamus" sat like a latent time bomb.

When Seymore finally turned to look at Maddy, she startled, struggling not to let shock show on her features.

Her left index finger twitched.

One of his deep brown eyes looked at her intently. The other, a glass eye, swiveled like an unmoored sailboat in a storm.

He spoke first. French words.

She gathered her wits. "Do you speak English?"

He cocked his head. "I do, a little. But I'm sorry, we don't have any titles in English." Seymore turned his back on her again.

She tempered her tone and continued. "Please. I understand you're the local expert on Nostradamus. Is that right?"

Slowly, he returned his gaze to her. "Yes. I've enjoyed researching him."

A tingle went up her spine.

"Great!" She stepped into her false background legend, adding a Valley Girl accent to her voice by drawing out her vowels. "I'm a grad student from Berkeley. You know, in California. I'm studying history and writing a thesis on Nostradamus."

Seymore reached out to shake her hand. "It's a pleasure to meet a fellow fan. How can I help?"

She pumped his hand vigorously, warming to her part. "That's soooo exciting. You've been studying him for years?"

"Yes. I've been watching the world wake up to his brilliance for two generations. How about you?"

"Not nearly so long as you, but I agree. The man was amazing."

"He was. What do you like most about him?"

The question took her off guard. She was supposed to be the one doing the asking and hadn't had nearly enough time to prep. Her brain whirred through all the info Bear and Doyle had discussed. "I love that he devised a method of obscuring his meanings from the Inquisition by using word games. What about you?"

Seymore ran a hand over his bald head. "That's tough. I love his passion. He traveled the entire known world in search of the future."

She put a hand on his arm, attempting to flirt. "Any place interesting?"

"Verejeni, Moldova. Nostradamus went to study with a famous healer there."

Maddy made another mental note. "I hadn't read that. Thank you. Maybe I'll do a research trip."

"Highly recommended."

He seemed too eager. Maybe he was trying to throw her off the trail. "What else can you tell me about the famous prophet?" She leaned close as if they were coconspirators. "Something you've found but isn't common knowledge?"

Seymore gazed deeply into her eyes, as if considering her request. Finally, he relented. "Did you know he intended to write three installments of his quatrains?"

She could honestly answer no.

"It's true. The 1555 edition had the first 353 quatrains, organized by the hundreds. And what's most interesting is the last fifty-eight quatrains of the seventh 'century' have not survived in any edition."

That caught her attention. In addition to some sort of fabled formula, maybe Avril had come across those missing quatrains, or they'd been bequeathed to her. She wondered how far someone would go to acquire them.

Maddy glanced at the glass door. A girl in a yellow rain jacket stood with her palm on the handle, looking through the glass. The dark features and full lips looked familiar. The girl tilted her head slightly and scars became visible on the side of her face and neck. Avril!

For a second, their eyes locked. Avril must've noticed Maddy's eyes, wide with shock and recognition, because when she moved toward the door, Avril bolted.

Maddy took a last look at Seymore while sprinting toward the room's exit. He was bent over, his bony hands reaching toward the black desk phone.

The man cocked his head in her direction. His one good eye seemed fixed on the drama between Avril and Maddy. But his glass eye stared vacantly into the abyss.

CHAPTER 26

OLD PORT OF MARSEILLE
9:50 A.M.

Will tracked the white Mercedes with his eyes.

"Sorry, Jags. Gotta run."

He jumped off the bench and sprinted up the street, following the four-door sedan as it barreled toward where he'd left Doyle and the mustached purse snatcher. He had a bad feeling about that car. With its tinted windows and the way it had taken the corner on two wheels, it sure didn't appear to be a police cruiser.

As he ran, he listened for sirens. The only ones he heard seemed to be in the distance.

His breath came in ragged bursts and he swore that once the mission was over, he'd hit the gym.

Turning the corner, he saw the long muzzle of a silenced gun appear out of the passenger-side window. Doyle dove for cover behind a red Peugeot, leaving the French thief alone, kneeling on the pavement.

Pop. Pop. Light flashed from the barrel.

The pickpocket crumpled sideways as a light rain began to fall.

The assassin's Mercedes sped away, turning the next corner without slowing down.

Will swore and ran to the thief.

Fingers to the carotid. Nothing. No pulse.

Two holes were burned through the man's chest.

Will turned to Doyle. "Are you okay?" he panted.

Doyle's eyes were wide as he looked from the dead man to Will. His dark hair had come out of its top knot and hung over his shoulders. "Better than him."

"I'll say. Let's get out of here."

Doyle checked the pockets of the deceased, but found nothing. "Agreed."

Leaving the stolen purse on the ground, the two men headed briskly back down the hill.

After Will caught his breath, he said, "What the holy hell just happened?"

Doyle rewound his hair into a neat knot on top of his head. "I'd say someone took out our snatcher."

"Don't be daft. Why? Why'd they take him out?"

Doyle shoved his hands in his pockets. "Do I look like I have Nostradamus's crystal ball?"

Will hunched over against the rain. "Oh my god. You're no help."

"Well, let's narrow it down. Either pals he liked to down a Guinness with wanted to spare him some torture, or someone not so friendly thought he might sing once he was in custody."

Will tried to calm down and think. It was hard with adrenaline flooding through his body. "Someone at the shipyard may have made a phone call. I guess we'll never know now."

"Perhaps not. I did manage to get a look at the plate."

"The license on the white car?"

"What other plate? There are no dinner plates here."

"You're insufferable. That's great, though. And it reminds me. Jags got a hit on the van. But it was in the north end of town."

They stepped onto the boulevard that ran around the harbor. Umbrellas had sprouted over the remaining tourists still braving the weather.

"Let's hope we live to see it."

"Why?"

Doyle pointed. "Because that Mercedes with plate AN-126-FD must have decided we're a loose end. It's heading our way."

CHAPTER 27

Maddy rushed after Avril through the glass double doors of the inner sanctum, worried she was leaving Henri Seymore behind. Her gut told her that loose end would come back to bite her at some point soon. Was Seymore the one who had kidnaped Avril? Had Avril escaped from her kidnappers? If so, why was she running? Or was this a trap?

She shoved the questions to the back of her mind for now, certain she needed to get to Avril before anyone else.

The fleet-footed young woman raced through stacks of books, Maddy a good twenty feet behind her. Avril was fast, whipping around corners, her long black hair streaming over her yellow jacket.

Maddy radioed Bear. "Razor one. In pursuit of target on the second floor." She caught her breath. "Librarian has one glass eye. Repeat. One glass eye."

"On my way."

Avril ran into an atrium that reminded Maddy of a suburban American mall in Sacramento. There was glass everywhere, a monstrous arched skylight above, and safety barriers on the runways.

Avril dashed up a flight of glass-lined stairs. She wore bright-blue running shoes, which flashed as she ran.

Maddy lost sight of Avril. Pounding up the stairs behind the girl, Maddy paused at the top, trying to catch her breath. There. To the right. A splash of yellow. The door swung shut.

Maddy sprinted toward the opening and sailed through it. The study area was filled with long tables lit by low-hanging lights. Pale faces looked up from their work as the two women rushed by.

"Avril, wait!" Maddy shouted, earning more looks.

Avril turned for a second, and then ducked down another row of books, tripping over the outstretched feet of a patron sitting in a low-slung arm chair. She recovered and ran on.

Maddy made progress, but not enough.

Avril rushed back into the atrium and around a tall white column before dashing down a long straightaway.

Maddy gave the race everything she had and began to gain. When Avril turned to cross a connection to the other side, Maddy reached out and caught Avril's hand.

"Wait!" Maddy exclaimed. "I'm trying to help."

Avril yanked her hand away.

Maddy was forced to grab the other hand, and moved in close enough to twist that arm around Avril's back into her yellow jacket. "Stop squirming and listen to me."

Avril tried to push Maddy backward. "You're with the men who kidnapped Monique!"

"I am not." *Thank god you speak English*, Maddy thought. "We stopped them from getting her. And I have information about your grandfather."

"What?"

"Stop fighting and I'll tell you."

Avril quit resisting so fast that Maddy felt whiplashed. Not sure she should trust the girl yet, Maddy relaxed the hold on Avril's arm enough to stop it from causing pain.

"Your grandfather is in the hospital, and we believe foreign actors want to kidnap you."

"No kidding!"

"We're trying to get you away from them. That guy up in the central desk, he has a glass eye. Monique saw a similar eye on one of the kidnappers. We need to get you out of here. Now!"

Avril fully relaxed. "I saw them try to get Monique. That's why I ran away."

"They never kidnapped you then?"

"No."

Sensing the fight had gone from the girl, Maddy dropped her arm and turned so they faced each other. Against a colorful blouse, Avril wore a pendant with a tiger's-eye claw and a feline animal face that Maddy assumed was a tiger. A black satchel was slung over the girl's shoulders.

"I'm glad they didn't get you," Maddy said. "We think they blew up your house. Monique is dead and your grandfather is in the hospital."

Avril's lower lip trembled. "I saw that on the news."

Maddy put a hand on the French girl's thin shoulder. "I'm sorry. The upper story collapsed before we could get to her. But I have others here to help now. Will you come with me?"

Avril glanced down the atrium. Henri Seymore was running toward them from about a hundred feet away.

She turned back to Maddy. "It looks like you're the better choice."

"Come on then," Maddy said.

She turned and ran, Avril close behind.

CHAPTER 28

OLD PORT OF MARSEILLE
9:57 A.M.

Will stared at the white Mercedes with the tinted windows. Doyle had to be right. They were loose ends. Panic gripped him and his breath caught in his throat. Where could they hide?

They were out in the open, walking through a sea of tourists next to the harbor. There was nothing but boats and people avoiding the rain.

His heart hammered in his chest. *We're going to be picked off.*

Then he had an idea.

He looked at Doyle. "Quick. Make friends with an umbrella."

Doyle seemed to understand at once, as he found a woman walking alone and stepped close to her, grabbing her umbrella. "Can I carry this for you?"

Unfortunately, there were no other single women walking their way. Will spied a young man, casually dressed. "Excuse me," he said in French. "Can you tell me how to get to the library?"

The young man stopped and Will moved a few inches so that the umbrella was between his face and the Mercedes. Politely, the man moved the umbrella a little further to cover Will's head while he provided directions using his phone. Will pretended to be utterly lost.

Sweat rolled down his back as he visualized the car's location. He expected to hear another *pop* at any second. Would they recognize his pants? Would they kill Doyle? Or the innocent people they'd put in harm's way?

The car purred past. Will buried his face in the helpful young man's phone and then turned. "That way then?"

"No!" The man's patience was wearing thin. He pointed in the other direction. "It is this way."

The deadly white car had slinked off like an alley cat on the prowl.

"Thank you," Will said, his back still to the car. "May I buy you a drink for helping me?"

The man narrowed his eyes. "Not necessary. But you may wish to buy an umbrella. The rain is starting to fall heavily now."

"Where can I get one?"

The man motioned with his head. "That market should have one."

"Great, thanks again."

Will pulled his jacket over his head and ran across the street. Doyle had disappeared into the crowd. Will missed Doyle's brother, Quinn, who'd been more a man of action. Doyle was just a smartass. Now missing.

Will peered down the street from the cover of the doorway. For now, the Mercedes was gone. He needed to gather the team and let them know about the news from Jags regarding the van, and fill them in on the execution of the thief.

He spoke into his molar mic, trying to get Bear and Maddy. "Razor one and two, can you hear me?"

There was no response. He repeated the message, attempting to reach Doyle.

Silence was the only reply.

CHAPTER 29

BIBLIOTHÈQUE L'ALCAZAR

10:04 A.M.

M addy and Avril sprinted into the library lobby just as Bear burst through the doors, gun in hand. His short blond hair and broad shoulders were wet.

With his empty hand, he waved them over. "Here!"

Maddy didn't waste breath with a reply. She ran toward him and he opened the exterior door for them. She hoped he wouldn't get killed bringing up the rear.

Outside, she dashed under the portico and instinctively headed back the way they'd come. She wanted their get-away car and wanted it now. Where was Will?

A cold, steady rain poured from dark skies. No wonder Bear looked wet. Avril put up the canary-yellow hood on her jacket.

Maddy radioed Will. "Razor three."

"There you are!"

She ducked through traffic to cross a busy street. "Running toward you. Found girl. Bad guys on our heels."

"I just found Doyle, but there's trouble here too."

Great. Just great.

She turned a corner, panting. "Can you get the car?"

"I'll try."

"Meet us at the narrow end of the harbor ASAP."

"Roger that."

Avril ran alongside Maddy, Bear just steps behind. Knowing she couldn't maintain a sprint all the way to the harbor, Maddy relaxed into a jog as they cut across the historical park that had so enamored Bear earlier, and moved at a steady pace toward the wharf.

Ahead, the rendezvous point glistened in the rain like a mirage.

Maddy focused and sucked air. *Just need to make it there.*

Avril and Bear were both breathing hard, too. Their collective feet slapped the wet pavement.

Finally, they made it to the short end of the harbor. Most of the tourists had cleared out, leaving only a few stalwart pedestrians who walked with umbrellas held high or sheltered under hooded rain jackets.

Frantically, Maddy looked around the waterfront, seeking Will and their SUV.

"See Will?" she asked Bear.

"No." Then he threw an arm over her and Avril, pushing them to the ground. "Look out!"

The muted sound of a silenced weapon reverberated across the water, and Maddy's left forearm suddenly screamed for attention. Immediately, she covered the wound with her other palm.

Bear grabbed her under her right arm and dragged her up. Avril's eyes were wide, but Maddy saw no blood on the girl.

"Grab a jet ski!" Bear yelled.

Two skis bobbed in the water, tied to a dock beyond a rental kiosk. Seeing the wisdom, Maddy immediately ran for the booth, her left forearm aching with every step. Small chunks of asphalt bit her ankles as she did, thrown up from bullets.

A short, middle-aged man with classic Italian features was bringing his clapboard sign back to the stall. He must have heard the shots because he dropped to the ground and crawled behind a concrete waste receptacle.

Maddy grabbed two sets of keys from atop a table in the kiosk. "Pay you later!" she yelled in his direction.

The rope attaching the jet ski to the dock was merely looped over a post. She pulled the rope off, earning a jolt of sharp pain from her arm, and jumped on, shoving the key into the ignition. She swore when the key didn't fit. Bear was on the other ski, Avril behind him. Maddy tossed him the key and he caught it with one hand.

Using the other key, she fired up the ski, figured out its rudimentary forward/backward transmission lever, and tore away from the dock. Bullets hit the water around her, looking like larger-than-normal raindrops. She veered between small dinghies and world-class yachts, all the while heading for the bridge that spanned the harbor and the promise of the open sea.

The pouring rain made visibility difficult.

She needed to use both arms to steer, which meant every twist of the steering column hurt like hell.

Ahead, a bridge loomed in the semidarkness.

In her earpiece she heard Will's voice. "Look out! They have a car on the bridge!"

She swung her head around, but didn't see the companion jet ski.

Where are Bear and Avril?

CHAPTER 30

OLD PORT OF MARSEILLE
10:20 A.M.

Even a quarter mile away and through pounding rain, Will could tell the white German car with the tinted windows held the high ground in the center of the bridge. From there, it would be too easy for whoever was in the car to use the jet skis as target practice. Heart racing, he gunned his X5 down the slippery road that paralleled the port. He had no plan.

He shouted over the wind from Doyle's lowered window. "Any ideas?"

"Not yet!"

The jet skis were trapped. They might only have minutes until enemy reinforcements arrived. Operating without their own set of backup resources, he had to think of something. Fast.

Will passed a slow-moving tourist bus, empty now, and played chicken with a small Renault. Wanting to avoid the head-on collision, the Renault veered off on a side street and the X5 powered forward.

With a bump that caused Will's head to hit the sunroof, the SUV finally bounced onto the bridge.

"What's the plan?" Doyle yelled.

"Hang on!"

With no better option, Will kamikazed the big SUV directly toward the white sedan. A rifle appeared from a side window, and flashes of light announced incoming fire.

Will swerved, bullets pinging off the hood and the car's side mirror. He floored it.

"What are you—" Doyle was interrupted when a shot pierced the windshield.

A hot poker of agony parted Will's hair, but he held his focus through the pain and kept his foot on the accelerator. Nearing the Mercedes, he swung the steering wheel hard to the right and slammed on the brakes. The back end of the X5 skidded on the wet pavement and hit the trunk of the sedan with a resounding crunch, forcing it forward through the guardrail.

For an instant, the menacing white car teetered like a drop of water suspended from an icicle. Then it crashed headlong into the water.

"Good thinking there, William," Doyle remarked.

"Tried to work it so our air bags didn't deploy."

Will exited the BMW and ran to the railing. The car was submerged in the deep harbor, taillights barely visible and disappearing fast. Bear and Maddy gave the roiling water a wide berth as they passed under the bridge and motored out to the white-capped sea, heading east. Avril gave a quick wave of thanks. Will exhaled in relief, glad the girl was safe.

Back at the site of the wreck, three men swam to the top of the dark water. The first one to surface, a blond, shook his empty fist at them.

Will and Doyle exchanged a glance. Doyle raised an eyebrow.

Will thought about Doyle's implied suggestion to eliminate the threat while the men were helpless. "Nope."

"Your call, but it'll come back to haunt us."

Will jumped back in the car, nodding for Doyle to join him. "Didn't the master remind us to stay in the present?"

Doyle just grunted.

Will put the slightly damaged X5 in gear and sped off to rendezvous with Maddy and Bear. He was looking forward to getting more information from Avril.

As he cleared the bridge, Doyle said, "Uh-oh."

Exasperation colored Will's tone. "Now what?"

"A fast-moving cigar-style boat just picked up our wet rats under the bridge." Doyle paused. "Now it's cleared the harbor and is chasing after the jet skis."

CHAPTER 31

OFF THE COAST OF MARSEILLE
10:32 A.M.

Maddy turned and swore. *That crimson-colored cigar boat is headed our way.*

She bit down on her lower lip. Was it a pleasure boat? In the pouring rain? Nope, the conclusion was inescapable: *There's a speedboat on our tail.*

Holding the throttle open on the jet ski, she willed it to move faster through the rough sea. Rain stung her face and jolts of pain shot up her injured arm with every wave.

Bear and Avril hammered through the water next to her. The girl's yellow hood had come off and long dark hair streamed out from her head.

Maddy yelled, "We have a tail!"

They both remained focused ahead. She ground her teeth together. Would it even make a difference if they knew? They needed to get to the beach. And to Will.

"Razor three. Three, can you read?"

Silence. No reply from her twin.

Oh my god. She thought these molar mics were supposed to have better range since they used tactical radios. The beach, with its tall hotels and gazillion-dollar mansions, wasn't that far. But they needed a rendezvous point. It would do them no good to beach the skis, only to stand there or have to run for it. She'd rather . . .

Her thoughts trailed off as she saw their BMW X5 on the road that ran parallel to the shore.

"Three, can you read me now?"

"Yes. You have a tail."

Bear whipped his head around. When he turned back, his face wore a deep scowl.

She replied, "Need a pickup spot."

"There's an outcropping coming up. Juts into the sea. On the other side is a small arched overpass. Take the jet skis under the bridge. Boat can't follow. We'll wait on the far side."

"Roger."

"Road cuts across so we may lose connection. Hurry!"

The SUV rolled out of sight.

To avoid rain in her face, and to make a smaller target for any trigger-happy pursuers, Maddy hunkered down behind the low windshield. The cigar boat had gained on them, but was still out of gun, and lorandite, range. The pursuers probably had no cannon, but she was acutely aware that Avril's back was to the gunmen.

Poor kid. What a day.

Finally, the ski made it around the spit of land. Ahead, the arches of the ancient-looking bridge beckoned through curtains of rain. The SUV was parked on the other side of the road. The sea calmed as she approached, allowing more speed.

Just in time too, as bullets began to pepper the water around her.

She skipped the jet ski around shallow rocks and under the cover of the overpass. On the far side, she ran it aground. Bear did the same.

They vaulted off the jet skis and ran along the embankment. A final bullet nipped at her heels, and then she was in the shade of the road. There were no steps, so she ran along the old brick wall until a jumble of large rocks provided a natural stairway. Acting like a billy goat, she scrambled up the slippery rocks to the BMW's open back door. Then she tumbled inside and pushed her way to the far window so Avril and Bear could slide in behind her.

The instant the door closed, Will rocketed the car away.

Maddy fell back against the seat, exhausted, hand clutching her wounded arm. She closed her eyes and savored the moment. *I'm alive.*

Bear interrupted her reverie. "Maddy, you're bleeding."

She tried to open her eyes, but they wouldn't budge. "Yeah."

"Avril, switch seats with me."

Maddy recognized the sound of shuffling bodies against a backdrop of squeaky windshield wipers.

Bear gently removed her hand and applied firm pressure to her arm, which hurt again. "Will, we've got to get to a safe spot and have her bullet wound looked after."

"Working on it. I got a new part in my hair, too."

"Hmm, you sure do," Bear said. "Both y'all are lucky."

"I suppose. Don't feel out of danger just yet. I'm trying to drive a diversion route so they can't follow us."

Maddy gave a weak smile. There was a reason they'd called her brother Sir Skeptalot in high school.

"Might be tricky here," Bear said. "If they have a bird in the air, not much opportunity to lose them."

"I know. We need some extra cars to run a proper antisurveillance route."

Avril spoke, her French accent thicker than it had been in the library. "I appreciate the ride, but why not let me out here?"

Maddy couldn't believe her ears.

Bear let loose a deep, throaty chuckle. "You want to tackle those guys alone?"

"You hero types do not seem very prepared."

"Have a better suggestion?"

"Yes, actually. I suggest we head back downtown, lose the car in a hotel with underground parking, and hail a ride to somewhere else."

Bear responded. "Good thinking, but they could track a ride hail. Will, head back downtown and—"

Doyle interrupted. "There is a small city just up the road. Aubagne. Multiple ways in and out of town. Why don't we at least get out of the serpent's nest? Regroup there?"

Maddy opened her eyes. *Too many suggestions.*

Avril pointed. "Look, there is an apartment building up ahead. Why don't we switch cars in the parking garage before we head to Aubagne? I'm sure one of you can hotwire a car, yes?"

Maddy said, "I like that idea."

Will said, "If they're good, they'll eventually figure it out."

"We don't have much choice, Argones," Bear said. "No safe houses in the area. Make it happen."

CHAPTER 32

Wong studied the wall of computer monitors that displayed satellite feeds from around the globe. He zeroed in on the one showing the south of France. "Here they are!" He pointed. "Where is that BMW going?"

The large room held hundreds of seated technicians who worked their keyboards and mouses with a fervor usually reserved for a favorite sports team.

A bespeckled middle-aged man replied to Wong. "Sir, the SUV just entered an underground parking facility."

Understanding that the enemy was attempting to avoid surveillance, he slammed a fist into his open palm.

A minute ticked by, then two. Wong stared at the bank of feeds and threw back half a cup of coffee. "Has the facial recognition software returned any values?"

"Yes, just now. They are Americans, sir. The man who was driving the jet ski is a former marine, now a known VanOps operative."

After several more agonizing minutes, four cars exited the parking structure in short succession. None were the BMW.

"Track them all," he growled, and stalked out of the room.

It would take hours, but they'd find them.

At least his team had confirmed that they were up against American operatives. That was good news because he knew how to compromise a certain diplomat who would soon be meeting with Director Bowman.

CHAPTER 33

A t least the hotel had a pool. That was about the only nice thing Will could say about it. After ditching the BMW, Doyle had hotwired a Jeep Cherokee and waited to exit the parking garage until several other cars were also departing. After, he'd driven them to Aubagne, where they found a drugstore for their bullet wounds and a place to stay.

The Hôtel La Bastide fit the covert ops bill. Underground parking. Rough around the edges. Near the train station and the intersection of several major roads bisecting the town. Will, however, preferred five-star accommodations when he was on a mission. This place was a one-star stretch.

Upon arrival, Bear had called the director to provide an update, and their instructions were to keep Avril safe and find out how she'd managed to predict the Chinese invasion of the Pratas Islands. Then he'd tackled mending their wounds, although he was only a medic by necessity, not training. Will ended up with a sticky antibiotic cream in his hair, while Maddy earned butterfly bandages on her forearm. After, they'd taken a meal, followed by a short rest. He and Doyle were told they'd be sharing a room. Or was it a cell? Will couldn't decide.

Now they sat in the room belonging to the other three, which overlooked the neglected pool. They'd just finished telling Avril about the night her house was bombed.

"I want to speak with my grandfather," Avril said.

Her English was good, the accent plain but not thick.

Now that he had an opportunity to get a good look at her, Will noted she was just a few inches shorter than Bear, had wavy, raven-colored hair down to the middle of her back, rich dark skin, full lips, an aristocratic nose, and hooded eyes under heavy brows. Her sweater was a bright mélange of color. The lower left-hand side of her face held a burn scar that bled into her neck. The mutilation made Will cringe, although he kept the emotion from showing on his features.

"We'll try to patch you through," Bear replied to Avril. "First, why don't you fill us in on how you managed to avoid getting kidnapped?"

Avril had been pacing. Shock from hearing about the explosion lent her a haunted air. "I need a latte." She stopped and crossed her arms. "And I'm not sure I want to tell you that."

"Fair enough," Bear said. "Should we have left you at the library?"

She bit her lower lip. "I would rather be on my own."

"I understand that," Bear said.

Avril stared Bear down. "May I leave then?"

Bear shook his head. "Our orders are to keep you safe."

"Orders? Who do you work for?"

Will was intrigued by her feisty resistance.

Bear popped an ice cube from lunch's leftover beverage into his mouth. "The American government."

She straightened her tiger-eye necklace. "I am a prisoner of who exactly?"

"I can't tell you."

Avril's shoulders tensed. "Well, that inspires trust, now doesn't it?"

Will agreed with Avril. If he were in her shoes, he'd shut his mouth too.

Bear crossed his arms and leaned his cheap wooden chair back against the wall. Doyle sat by the window, looking outside at the pathetic pool. Or watching for unwanted company.

Maddy tucked a stray lock of dark hair behind one of her ears. "Let's phone her grandfather. Maybe he'll give us a vote of confidence."

Bear and Maddy exchanged a glance that Will wished he understood.

Bear nodded. "Argones. Will you see if Jags can get the hospital on the encrypted line?"

Will hated having to deal with grunt duties, like making phone calls. He did it anyway, calling Jags and asking to be connected to Avril's grandfather.

Finally, a weak voice came on the line and whispered in French. "Avril? Is that you?"

"Grandpère!" Avril squeaked.

The conversation continued in French over the speaker phone.

"My little gumdrop. Are you safe?"

Avril glanced around the room. "I'm not sure."

Will realized she didn't know he spoke French. He wasn't going to share that tidbit. Yet.

Sébastien replied, "Are you with the Americans?"

"They say that's who they are."

"One tall, dark-haired woman with long legs, a short and stocky blond man, and the woman's twin brother, who has curly hair and eyelashes like a girl?"

"That's them. There's an Asian-looking man too, with an Irish accent."

Sébastien wheezed. "I don't know the Asian, but the Americans I trust. She and the tall one pulled me out of the house after the explosion."

The tension in Avril's shoulders relaxed. "Their story is true then."

"If that's what they told you, yes." There was a moment's pause, and then the old man said, "I am sorry we lost Monique."

"Me too." She sniffled. "What about you? Are you safe in the hospital?"

"I hope so. My skin was badly damaged in the fire, so I have no choice. The police have a guard at my door."

That worried Will. One local cop wouldn't stand a chance against their determined foes.

A tear crept down the scarred side of Avril's face. She turned away so none of them would see. "Be safe. I miss you."

"I miss you too, gumdrop." The old man's voice became faint. "Stay with the Americans for now, until I can get out of here."

"All right, Grandpère, I will."

The connection dropped and Avril handed the phone back to Will. She switched to English. "He says you saved him from the fire."

Will pointed. "That was mostly Maddy. I'm sorry we couldn't save Monique."

Eyes glistening, Avril turned to his sister. "Thank you."

Maddy replied, "You're welcome. Now that you know we are who we said, can we talk?"

Avril sat down next to Maddy. "Sure."

"Great." Maddy leaned forward and made small talk for a few minutes. After the light came back on in Avril's eyes, Maddy switched gears. "How did you get away when those men came to kidnap you at the market?"

"Monique was flirting with my English teacher, which I found gross. Plus, someone had been following me for weeks and I saw a sedan that looked familiar. I went across the street to get a latte and watch it."

"What happened next?" Maddy asked.

"A dark-green van screeched to the curb. They grabbed Monique and after the shot . . . a man headed my way. I . . ." Her voice faltered for a beat. "I ran out the back door and kept running until I found my way to a friend's empty house. I had been lizard-sitting there and used the key to get in."

Will's respect for Avril ticked up a notch.

"Why did you head to Marseille?" Maddy asked.

"I'd been researching Nostradamus since I got the . . ."

"Got the what?" Will asked.

"Um. Never mind. Anyway, I found out that Henri Seymore worked at the library there in Marseille. He's the most well-known Nostradamus researcher in all of France."

"I see," Maddy said. "Monique saw a glass eye on one of the kidnappers. Did you?"

"No."

"Not even in the car?"

Avril shook her head. "It was too far down the street. But . . . I did see a hunchbacked old man with a glass eye near the Nostradamus Museum a few weeks ago. Ever since, I thought I was being followed by men in a dark car."

Maddy nodded. "And you hadn't talked with Seymore before we arrived?"

"No, you beat me there. When you recognized me, I ran."

Based on what Maddy had told them of the incident in the library, it sure sounded like Seymore had called in the hounds. They had Jags digging up whatever dirt she could find on the librarian. Will hated to assume anything, though. Maybe Seymore was guilty, maybe not. If Will had seen Maddy take off after Avril, he might have called the authorities and gone to investigate. He had to admit the glass eye was damning, though. And why had they taken out the purse thief?

Maddy nodded. "You're a smart girl. Do you remember your mom?"

Will wondered at the change in subject.

Avril titled her head. "I remember her hair. And her smell."

"I lost my mother when I was six. Will and I both did."

Oh, Maddy's trying to bond, Will thought.

Avril seemed to reappraise them both. "What happened?"

"Car accident. We grew up in Lake Tahoe and the roads were icy that day."

Will's jaw grew tight. At least Maddy hadn't brought up that it was his fault.

"I'm sorry," Avril said politely. Then her tone turned bitter. "My mom got drunk and set fire to our apartment. My face burned. She disappeared. I think she is dead."

Maddy put a hand on Avril's arm. "That's hard."

Avril took a deep breath.

"Then your dad died," Maddy said softly. "When was that?"

"Last year. We'd been living in Paris near my grandmother. She died a few years ago. That was Dad's mom. I never knew Mom's mom. When Dad died, I went to live in Provence with Grandpère."

"I'll bet that's all been hard to deal with."

Reminded of his mother's death, Will's face began to burn and his chest felt tight. He tapped his toes on the floor to distract himself.

Avril started to reply, then broke down and began to cry.

As Maddy held her, Will and the men stared at each other, then all moved to the hallway outside and shut the door. Will inhaled. Bear applied balm to his lips. Doyle scratched his beard stubble.

Will was trying to get more comfortable with emotions. He honestly was.

When the sobbing stopped, they gave it a few more minutes, and then knocked.

"Come on in," Maddy said.

Avril's eyeliner had run, making her hooded eyes appear even darker and more mysterious.

"Will you tell them what you told me about your inheritance?" Maddy asked the girl as the men settled back onto the plain sofa and chairs.

Avril nodded, and made eye contact with each of the men in turn. "When my father died, I was given a box."

Bear's eyes lit up. "Can you tell us more about it?"

"It is a small walnut coffer that once belonged to Nostradamus."

CHAPTER 34

3:30 P.M.

Bear's heart fluttered so wildly in his chest that words became trapped in his throat. *A box that once belonged to Nostradamus? Oh dear and precious god.*

Maddy, who had cleverly gotten the girl to open up, had the presence of mind to ask, "May we see it?"

Bear reached over and grabbed Maddy's hand. His palm was covered with sweat.

Avril reached into a black leather satchel, dug around for a minute to extend his agony, and produced a package wrapped in a woolen cap. Not the most high-tech protection, but she'd probably not planned to carry it about the country. She pulled the cap aside, revealing a six-by-four-inch polished walnut box. The dark chest was reinforced with decorative iron bands, and it held a rudimentary three-disk combination lock.

All leaned forward in their seats to study the box.

Maddy said, "This can't be from Nostradamus. It has a combination lock."

Bear touched the disks. "Actually, I've read that the Romans had them, and there are a couple locks an Arab engineer made around 1200 AD in museums in Copenhagen and Boston."

She frowned. "How do we know they were in Europe in the sixteenth century?"

He loved this kind of history. "A mathematician named something like Cardamon or Cardano described one during the time period Nostradamus lived."

"I've heard of him," Will said. "Gerolamo Cardano. He was an Italian. A true Renaissance man. Wrote on science, mathematics, and was an astronomer and physician. He'd have been a peer of Nostradamus."

Avril grabbed the box back from Bear. "Whatever. I got the combination when I was given the box."

She proceeded to dial the numbers 9-6-3.

The box creaked open.

Avril showed it off like she was a game show host. "I like the compartmentalized velvet interior. And the mirror."

Bear took a drink of weak ice tea and wondered why there would be a mirror on a strongbox. Maybe it held jewelry at one point.

"What did you find in there when you opened it up?" Doyle asked.

Avril started at the question. "What makes you think there was something inside?"

Doyle pointed. "I don't see anything in there now, lass."

Bear was itching to get his fingers on the box again, but Will put his hands out first. "Smells like . . ." He put the box to his nose. "Maybe roses?"

Bear could stand it no longer. He grabbed the box from Will and took a sniff. Smelled faintly of roses all right. "His recipe to cure plague included rose hips."

"I read that too," Avril said.

Bear turned to her. "You've been studying up on him?"

"Sure. With a box like this, who wouldn't?"

How'd she predict that invasion? Bear thought as he tried to read her eyes. "Were there herbs in there? Maybe some tablets?"

Avril looked away.

He'd get Maddy to press that point again later, since she'd done a better job than he had getting this far with the kid. "Have you found any hidden compartments?"

Her deep-set eyes grew wide. "No. You think there could be some?"

Bear turned the box over in his hands. "Could be. They made 'em like that all the time."

"Ooh, I didn't know that."

"Hidden screws, little places for a fingernail, that sort of thing. Quite common. Banks and safes are of a more modern time."

While he talked, he shifted his GPS-enabled watch out of the way so his fingers could explore the box. That reminded him . . .

He looked at Maddy. "Do you have any extra trackers?"

"I think so. Are you thinking . . ." She trailed off and met his eyes. "Ah, of course. Good idea."

She pulled a piece of metal that looked like a dime from her backpack and handed it to Avril. "Keep this in your pocket. If we get separated, we'll be able to find you."

"Fine. Whatever." She shoved it into the coin pocket of her jeans. "Let's see what's in the box."

Satisfied that Avril was as safe as he could get her for the moment, Bear turned his attention to the treasure. It felt about the weight he'd expect from a walnut chest bound with iron. He tapped at the sides, top and bottom, but heard nothing that might indicate a hollow space. The rest of the team and Avril watched as he pressed the iron rivets one by one. Nothing happened. But one had felt a little sticky so he went back and pressed that one again. Twice.

A spring-loaded false bottom dropped away. Everyone gasped.

Gently, Bear pulled the bottom away. A collective groan escaped the lips of all present when the velvet-lined compartment proved to be empty.

Bear exhaled, irritated. He poked and prodded the formerly concealed tray. "Whatever was in here is gone now."

When Maddy held out her hand, he gave the box to her. Then he sat back in his chair, crossed his arms, and stared at the offending item. The energy in the room felt like a deflated balloon.

Maddy looked at Avril. "Did you get any instructions, other than the combination?"

"No. The combination was written in marker on tape stuck to the bottom of the box."

As Maddy turned over the false compartment, Bear could make out the remnant of yellow masking tape. Maddy put the compartment on the table.

Will said, "Looks like we'll never know what he left for you. Maybe it was jewelry and one of your other family members has it."

Doyle picked up the chest and examined it. "Don't be jumping the gun, now. Why's there a mirror in it?"

"I wondered the same thing," Bear said.

Doyle began to push around the lid and edges of the mirror. "What were you saying about fingernails?"

Bear leaned forward. "Do you feel something?"

"Maybe."

Doyle made a twisting movement with his finger and the mirror popped away from the lid, revealing another compartment.

Bear's heart thundered in his chest. *Paper. There's paper in there!*

Doyle pulled the thin sheet of folded paper from the cubby hole. A shiver ran down Bear's spine, and he reached for it, but Doyle handed it to Avril.

"I believe this is your birthright."

Avril nodded graciously, like a queen to her subject. "Thank you."

With utmost care, she unfolded the yellowed page. Bear was worried the paper would crack or tear, but it didn't. He moved to stand over her shoulder, and made out five groups of four lines, all written in flowing handwriting.

"What's it say?" he asked.

She put a hand out, as if to say, *All in good time.*

He wiggled his toes. This was too much. A message from Nostradamus. Wow. Like *oh my god times a trillion* wow.

Avril studied the paper. "There are five quatrains," she said. "In French of course. Where's my satchel? I'll translate."

Will produced it. "Here you go."

Avril dug deep and pulled out a paperback-sized leather journal. She put the tip of a pen in her mouth, and then started scribbling and doodling. She crossed out a line, wrote another. Kept writing. Drew some more. Bear tried to look over her shoulder, but she shooed him away so he went to sit back down.

Finally, she looked up. "Ready?"

They all nodded. Bear felt dizzy with anticipation.

"I'll read the French version first:

La formule sera trouvée par ceux qui cherchent
Le fils du soldat guide un vers les cavernes
Commencez par un écrivain de cosmographie de la cour de Marguerite
Pour trouver l'enfant mâle de la créature aux défenses courbes."

Bear was completely lost, but he noted from the expression in Will's eyes that he had followed along.

Maddy asked, "What about the translation?"

"It's crazy. He's saying there is some sort of formula:
The formula will be found by those who seek
The son of the soldier guides one to the caverns
Start with a writer of cosmography from Marguerite's court
To find the male child of the creature with curved tusks."

CHAPTER 35

3:52 P.M.

Avril repeated the first line of the quatrain. "The formula will be found by those who seek." She paused, and glanced at Will, as she found him the least intimidating of the operatives. And it was now obvious he spoke French. She already regretted letting the intense woman under her skin once, Bear's military eyes were icy, and Doyle seemed reserved. She figured them all for spies, probably assassins, and didn't fully trust any of them. "He must be talking about the formula to see his visions."

"Maybe. Although he could be referring to some other formula," Will said. "Say, to cure the plague."

Avril frowned. "No, that would not make sense. He published that recipe in *The Treatise of Cosmetics and Jams*."

"Okay. He was a doctor. Maybe he had a secret formula for, oh, I don't know, treating cancer."

Maddy, Bear, and Doyle screwed up their faces in disbelief.

Avril also gave him a skeptical look. "Seriously? The man was a world-renowned prophet, sought after by kings and queens because of his talent for *telling the future*."

Will's lips tightened. "It's my job to be cynical."

Avril tried to lighten her tone so he wouldn't feel bad. "All right. Good to know. But right now, I am a little excited! This has to be his recipe for seeing the future. Who is with me?"

She scanned the room. Maddy gave a thumbs up. Bear nodded his blond head quickly. Doyle smiled a toothy grin under his thick bushy eyebrows.

Will drummed his fingers on the table. "Looks like I'm outvoted, as usual."

Thinking about the mention of caverns in the second line of the first quatrain, Avril said, "Do not feel bad, Will. It will be fun to travel to some old caves."

"What do the remaining quatrains say?" Bear asked. "Maybe they shed more light on his intentions."

"Oh, right. I haven't read them to you yet. Okay, here is the second one:

Six degrees from Charlemagne
Lies a liege who made a city from the marsh island
Buried to rest in the church of a servant
Above his sarcophagus mark the second line eleven fifteen and seven times

Does that make sense to anyone?"

Everyone shook their heads, but she could see Bear's wheels spinning. All she got was they needed to find a church on a place that used to be a marshy island, so she'd drawn a spire with long blades of grass next to the words.

"Here's the third one then:
The duomo's architect
Pays homage to a night in July
With sacred signs of the zodiac
Of the first the penultimate strikes the mark but of the second take the last and the first of the twins

Anyone know of a duomo?"

For this one, she'd drawn a dome and a ram's profile that reminded her of the Aries zodiac sign.

Doyle replied, "Probably talking about the one in Florence."

"My thought too," Bear said. "Would've been the landmark at the time."

"Keep reading," Maddy suggested.

Avril glanced at the old paper and then read from her notebook.

"South, to the first sanctuary of new citizens

Temple of Jupiter and Juno

The famed sculptor and architect makes his marks in mud

The last letter of the founder is placed behind the mountainous middle

He mentioned a letter, so maybe it's some kind of clue."

The only symbol she'd drawn for the fourth quatrain was a cartoon of Jupiter and its moons.

"Good point. And there's a number of temples for Jupiter and Juno," Bear said. "We'll have to research those."

"And find a sculptor and architect who likes mud," Maddy added with a smile.

"What's the last quatrain?" Will asked.

Avril read from her paper.

"Having collected the parts of the enigma

Take the four in reverse order then twelve steps back in time

Once you know the answer

Look for the medallion deep inside the Oracle's icy crown."

Her voice rose with excitement. "It all leads to a medallion!" She glanced at the bronze circle she'd sketched next to the words, curious about what it looked like.

Maddy nodded. "I note he mentioned an oracle, too, which lends more credence to the theory that the formula is related to his prophetic prowess."

Excitement danced in Bear's eyes. "Sounds like each quatrain leads to a different location where we find a sign. Then put the clues together for a final location. What an incredible find."

Will said, "Well, we need to find the find. Right now, these are just words on paper."

"I'll call the director," Bear replied.

Bear's phone rang and he stood to answer it, walking down the short hallway with a bit of a limp as the rest of them discussed the English versions of the clues.

Buzzing with excitement, Avril reread the French quatrains again to make sure she hadn't missed anything. She still didn't trust the crew, but perhaps they could help her figure out what her ancestor had hidden. And with that prize, she could finally get the plastic surgery on her face and shoulder that her father and grandfather had forbidden.

She wished for her computer, so she could check the news about her grandfather and start researching. Her beloved smartphone was almost as fast. She pulled it out and turned it on, snapping a pic of the page containing the quatrains, sending it to a secure backup location, and then pulling up a search engine.

Maddy snatched the phone from her fingers. "What are you—"

She cut off abruptly when Bear returned to the small space. All traces of excitement had left his face, which now appeared long. He turned his arctic blue eyes on Avril.

"I'm sorry, Avril. Your grandfather is dead."

CHAPTER 36

Sébastien's death hung in the air like a stench, heavy with implied sorrow and the impact the old man's demise would have on Avril's young life.

Will saw the words reach Avril, but it was almost like the sounds didn't make it inside her brain. She tilted her head, as if Bear had spoken in an unfamiliar tongue. Her impish smile disappeared. "What did you say?"

Bear repeated, "Your grandfather. He's gone."

Will felt like he was watching a disaster movie in slow motion. It made his heart ache.

Avril blinked hard twice, and put a hand to her chest. Her mouth moved, but no words came out. Her breath became jagged, like she had the hiccups.

Oh boy. This wasn't good.

Maddy moved to put an arm around Avril's shoulders, but the girl shrugged his sister off, turning instead to stare out the window at the wretched pool. She rotated so fast her long, dark hair almost caught Maddy in the face.

Will wondered about Avril's reaction to Maddy. Maybe his sister had ticked the girl off by taking her phone. Teenagers loved their electronic leashes. Or maybe she was just too raw. He could understand that.

Thoughts flooded Will's mind. *Another setback for Avril. Was it natural causes from the burns? The old man had sounded weak. Or did their enemies track Sébastien down? If so, what was the purpose of killing him? Had he known something? Was it a message?*

Time stretched.

Will twirled his flashlight, listening to the sound of renewed rain outside, as Doyle stared at his feet. Then Bear's phone rang again.

Out of respect for Avril, Bear moved into the bathroom to take the call.

He wasn't gone long. When he came back, Avril turned to him, her hooded eyes red. "Well? What else do you know about his death?"

Bear sighed. "From what we can tell, two armed men overran the single policeman who'd been stationed outside his hospital room. They executed the officer, entered the room, and killed your grandfather before escaping."

That answers that, thought Will grimly.

Her voice rose. "What am I supposed to do now?"

Bear answered, "Our director wants us to continue as your security detail. That was him calling. He expressed his sorrow for your loss and says there's a place we can take you in Lyon where you'll be safe until we can find out who's behind this."

She pointed to the paper and tilted her chin, fire flashing in her dark eyes. "Are you also going to track down these clues?"

Bear nodded.

"Then I am coming with you."

Bear shook his head. "I'm sorry, but those are my orders."

Avril's nostrils flared. "You can tell your director that I have sent the quatrains to a secure, impossible-to-find location, and have scheduled to release them to the public in four days if I am not allowed to travel with you."

Bear raised an eyebrow and turned to Maddy.

Maddy held up the phone. "Avril was doing something before I took it from her and turned it off, so I suppose it's possible."

Bear glowered, clearly displeased by the security breach, which could get them all killed.

"It is *my* phone." Avril stood and crossed her arms over her colorful sweater. "Besides, you want to know how I predicted the invasion, correct?"

Bear's tone was all business. "Yes."

"Is torturing an innocent sixteen-year-old in your playbook?"

"No."

"Then your director has no choice." Her tone was flat. "Once we find the medallion that contains the formula my ancestor hid for me, I will tell you everything."

CHAPTER 37

With the juvenile ultimatum that might endanger them all, on top of the earlier phone antics, Maddy's patience toward Avril was wearing thin.

Two hours and multiple phone calls later, Bear finally announced, "All right. The director has agreed Avril can join us on the mission to find out where the medallion is hidden. He really wants to get his hands on that formula."

Avril's full-lipped smile turned smug.

Maddy picked at the bandage on her forearm. "What's the director's thinking on keeping Avril safe?"

"He thinks she'll be more secure with us than she'd be in that safe house in Lyon," Bear replied. "She knows more about Nostradamus than the rest of us, and in the interest of time and learning whatever we can to stop the invasion of Taiwan, he's willing to have her help."

That's a bunch of bullshit, Maddy thought. *Bowman caved because he needs Avril. But the girl is going to be far more trouble than she's worth.*

"Speaking of Taiwan," Doyle said. "I received another video from my grandparents."

Bear rolled up his sleeves, showing off the cool but rather ghostly lightning scars on his forearms. "Let's see it."

Doyle pulled out his phone to run the video. Worrywart Will took a last look outside before joining. Even Avril huddled around the device to see the latest.

"Wait," Will said. "Can someone give me the background on Taiwan and China? Just a snippet for context?"

Doyle and Bear looked at each other.

"Go ahead," Bear said.

Doyle nodded. "The animosity began in 1927 with war between the Communist Party and the Kuomintang, or KMT. The KMT had been running China since 1919, but the Soviet Union began sending spies and money in an attempt to bolster the Communist Party. The two sides came to blows and fought a brutal civil war off and on for over twenty years. Eventually the KMT retreated to Taiwan in 1949."

Will tapped his foot. "The communists won?"

"Both sides claimed victory. No peace treaty has ever been signed. But the Communist Party has run mainland China since."

"Thanks," Will said. "Quite helpful."

"No problem," Doyle replied. "And here we are, decades later, on the cusp of another major conflict between the parties. Just in the last four years of that war, the commies lost about 1.3 million people and the KMT nationalists over 7.5 million. This new war could kill even more."

They all nodded.

Doyle said, "I'll roll the vid, then translate."

In the video, an older couple sat next to each other on a red sofa. He had his arm around her shoulder and she held the phone out to film themselves. The room they sat in had long windows and was lush with plants and high-end modern furniture. The man, who Maddy supposed was Doyle's grandfather, had a face lined with worry. The woman, who they'd seen in a prior video wielding a long-bladed kitchen knife, spoke in a high, anxious tone, gesticulating often while the man nodded or occasionally added words of emphasis. The video ran for about two minutes before it ended with solemn waves of farewell.

"What did they say?" Avril asked, turning her face in a way that wouldn't let them see her scars.

Doyle's face grew grim. "Talks are ongoing with China about the Taiwan Strait and their invasion of Pratas Island, which everyone fears will mean a full-on attempted takeover of Taiwan. Stores are empty, as the people have stocked up. The entire island is ready to fight and die. It's very tense."

"The director provided some additional details," Bear offered.

Doyle turned to him. "Oh?"

"We, the US that is, are trying to intervene without intervening. China is mad about our aircraft carriers sailing in disputed waters, so they're going to conduct military exercises in the South China Sea tomorrow. Basically, there's a lot of chest thumping going on."

"Sounds to me like fools dumping gasoline on dry fields during a nasty California fire season," Maddy noted.

Will looked at Avril. "Do you have any other insight about what China will do next?"

She shook her head. "Sorry, none at this time."

Wondering again how an untrained teenager had made that original prediction, Maddy picked up the sheet of paper containing the quatrains and doodles. "Seems tracking down the medallion is our best bet." She turned to Bear. "What's the plan?"

"The director wants us to split up. If they're onto us, they're looking for a group. We'll blend better and be able to cover twice as much ground if we divide into two teams."

Maddy thought through the various scenarios for the French girl. Even though she was annoyed at Avril, Maddy knew the right thing to do. Looking at Will she said, "It makes sense for Avril to join Bear and me."

Avril glanced around the room. "I would like to travel with—"

Will put a hand out, cutting her off. He looked angrily at Maddy. "Don't think so. Doyle and I will travel with her."

Did Will really mean that or was he just being difficult and trying to control things again?

"No," Maddy replied sharply. "Neither of us speaks French."

Will drummed his fingers on his thigh. "Bear is a history geek and that puts Doyle and me at a disadvantage."

"A disadvantage? This isn't a race. How are you going to blend in? Two middle-aged men and a sixteen-year-old?"

"Middle-aged? You're a decade off." He pointed at her. "Plus, we were born on the same day."

Doyle, Bear, and Avril exchanged a glance, which made Maddy realize she and Will were bickering again. Well, he wanted to control everything, even her dreams. Maddy took a deep breath to center herself.

Bear interrupted. "Knock it off, you two. Here's the plan: Will and Doyle take quatrains one and three. Maddy and I get two and four. We'll regroup and tackle the fifth together." Bear's phone vibrated. He glanced down at it, and then looked back up at the group. "Jags has ID'd the enemy's green van heading our way. Grab your stuff!"

Maddy stood. "Avril?"

"She goes with them in the car. It'll be safer. They can disguise themselves as gay men with a daughter, or whatever. We're heading for the train station. Let's move out!"

CHAPTER 38

With the brusque announcement that they needed to leave, Avril broke out into a cold sweat. She grabbed the walnut box from the lame hotel table, stuffed it inside her pink woolen cap, and packed it inside her leather satchel. Then she grabbed her bright rain jacket and threw it on, wishing for a black one to better keep to the shadows.

If only I'd been able to foresee the enemy's arrival, we wouldn't be dealing with this urgent fire drill.

"Want me to carry that satchel?" Will asked, concern in his eyes.

She stood. "No, I'm good."

Maddy threw her backpack on her shoulders, and tucked Avril's phone into her own jacket pocket.

"Can I have my phone back?" Avril asked.

"Sorry, no." Maddy's tone was curt. "It could get you killed."

Avril was suddenly glad Will and Doyle were to be her companions.

"What if I get kidnapped?" she snapped.

"Just keep that tracker in your pocket."

She touched the false coin, not thrilled.

Doyle returned from the next room with two small duffels. Probably one was his and one belonged to Will.

Bear moved to the door, a black pistol in his raised hand. "Ready?"

Nods all around. Doyle also had a gun. Maddy and Will did not, which Avril found odd until she remembered that the lone female operative had captured her at the library with a martial arts move. Still, that didn't explain Will's lack of weapon. Maybe they were both concealing their guns. Even the two visible pistols unnerved her.

Avril had seen this kind of action on the television, but never imagined she'd be forced to make a stealthy exit from a sleezy hotel room with a team of covert operatives. For a moment, she was paralyzed with fear. Her legs simply would not move.

As most of the team followed Bear out of the room, Will hung back. "You okay?" he asked.

"Not really," she managed to say. "I am terrified."

He put a hand on the small of her back and gave her a gentle shove. "This is a scary situation. That's an appropriate emotional reaction. But right now, the only way to save your life is to get moving."

With his urging, her feet began to perform their job, knees and hips getting the idea too. She walked out of the hotel room and turned left. Then she ran to catch up, following Doyle's bobbing topknot. She heard Will's harsh breathing behind her. Geez, he was out of shape for a secret agent.

Night had fallen. Rain continued to drench the inn, making rapid, plopping sounds as it pummeled the tile roof. Bear held the lead, and took them to the underground parking garage. They jogged to the Jeep they'd acquired earlier, and Will jumped in the driver's seat. Doyle sat next to him.

Bear held the back door open for Avril. "Get down on the floor."

Avril dove in head first, using her satchel as a makeshift pillow, and the Cherokee roared to life. Bear slammed the door shut, making her toes tremble.

"Ready, Doyle?" Will asked.

"Yes."

Avril felt the car back up and then tear off. Her breath still heaved and she unsuccessfully tried to slow it down. Too much was happening. Who were the bad guys who had killed Monique and her grandfather? Was that librarian, Seymore, behind all this? Were he and his henchmen as close as the team's coworker had warned? Would they shoot at her at any moment? Would her mission to find her ancestor's medallion be aborted before it truly began?

The Jeep took a corner and she swayed with the motion. She recalled Will's words, "This is a scary situation. That's an appropriate emotional reaction." She appreciated the truth, but it frightened her all the more. Her blood pounded in her ears. She clenched her fists and closed her eyes tight against whatever was coming next.

Will shouted, "There's the van!"

Shots rang out and a bullet *thunked* into the door six inches from her head.

CHAPTER 39

As Maddy was about to breathe a sigh of relief that they'd managed to evade the incoming attackers, the Jeep turned a corner and the sound of gunshots echoed through the rain.

All thoughts of making it to the train station left her mind as she and Bear sprinted down a commercial street lined with parked cars. The Jeep's taillights had disappeared in the gloom, but the green van was headed right for her and Bear. The gunmen must have taken a potshot as the vehicles passed one another. But how'd the enemy know it was their car? She'd puzzle that out later.

Cursing Will's "middle-aged" retort, she dove behind a vehicle for cover, and Bear did the same. The van peppered them with bullets as it sped by. Bear got off two shots as the vehicle careened around the corner and slammed on the brakes. She didn't have enough time to use her lorandite rings or her gun; she'd have to get faster with her reflexes.

Maddy pointed. "Quick, this way!"

They'd chosen this hotel partly for its easy access to the station, and had studied the map for escape routes. A narrow street beckoned across the road. It was perfect.

Bear ran with her down the alley. Within fifty feet, the road met up with a cross street, and they ran to the left, onto a residential street lined with thick stucco walls occasionally broken by iron gates.

The sound of screeching tires reached them.

"Maddy, wait. We need to hide."

She tried the nearest gate. Locked. "Where?"

"Can you get over the wall?"

Without answering, she found a toehold, reached up, and pulled herself to the top of the stucco wall. She let herself down the other side as Bear followed suit.

As his boots hit the ground, headlights cut through the curtain of rain. Maddy leaned against the wall for support, her legs trembling, breath held.

Bear peeked through the iron gate as their pursuers rumbled by. When they were gone, he said softly, "That was the van all right. Let's wait here for a sec."

"Okay." Maddy put her hands on her knees as she exhaled. "At least they've lost the Jeep."

"Hope so. These guys are good, whoever they are. They're probably going to patrol the area. How'd they know to shoot up the Jeep?"

"My guess is they used cloud-penetrating satellite feeds to figure out what came out of that parking garage by the beach, after our BMW went in."

"Makes sense," Bear panted.

"Or they may have tracked us through Avril's phone," Maddy whispered. "She turned it on before I realized what she was doing."

"I know. We should have taken it from her earlier."

Maddy adjusted the backpack, trying to get more comfortable. "Think Jags can get any better images of the van from street cams?"

"I'm sure she's trying."

A large dog howled inside the house. Seconds later, a second-floor light switched on.

No choice. They had to hit the street.

CHAPTER 40

Will took a deep breath and looked in the Jeep's rearview mirror again. It had been at least five minutes since the shootout at the crappy Aubagne hotel. "I don't see anyone on our tail."

"Good. I like to hear that," Doyle replied.

A female voice came from the backseat floorboards. "Can I sit up yet?"

"No one is shooting at us," Will said. "Just be ready to drop at my signal."

Avril's head popped up between the driver and passenger seat. "I see you are an optimist."

Will gripped the steering wheel with both hands to hide the adrenaline shakes. "Skeptic. And proud of it."

Avril tossed her hair. "Whatever."

Doyle pulled out his phone. "Where are we headed?"

"How do you say this in America?" Avril asked. "That is the million-dollar question?"

"Yup," Will responded. "First we'll need to get a new car, though, since this one has obviously been tracked. Why don't you both do some research on that first quatrain while I drive?"

"I don't have a device," Avril said.

He thought about giving her his phone before he realized one of the forms he'd signed as a new VanOps operative had expressly forbidden that type of thing. "Doyle has one. Let's help him search."

"That is ridiculous," she snapped.

"Perhaps. No choice, though. Why don't you reread us that first quatrain and help Sherlock Holmes here figure out our destination?"

She grabbed her journal out of the satchel. "*La formule sera trouvée par ceux qui cherchent—*"

Will interrupted. "English!"

"You're impossible.

The formula will be found by those who seek
The son of the soldier guides one to the caverns
Start with a writer of cosmography from Marguerite's court
To find the male child of the creature with curved tusks."

Doyle said, "We need caverns then. Or a cave."

"That is obvious," Avril said in an ultimate bored-teenager tone. "But which one? Perhaps we should start with a writer of cosmography from Marguerite's court as instructed?"

"Sure, I'm easy," Doyle said. "Let's see what the interweb says."

The glow of Doyle's smartphone lit up the interior of the cabin.

"The *interweb*? Are you that old?"

"I remember my mom carrying a wee flip phone."

"Wow. You are that old."

Will cringed. He had a memory of his mom on a land line, making arrangements to go to the birthday party that got her killed.

Doyle gave them a play-by-play of his search results. "Cosmographies speculate about the universe being repeatedly created and destroyed over millennia . . . no, that's not it. Cosmography is a science that attempts to describe heaven and earth . . . nope. The Marguerite Isles . . . no. Rape and Writing in the Heptameron of Marguerite de Navarre. Hmm, not finding anything."

"Who is Marguerite of Navarre? Did she have a court?" Avril asked.

Doyle's fingers moved. "Looks like she was the sixteenth-century queen of Navarre."

"Queens have courts. And the timeframe aligns with when Nostradamus was alive. Tell us more," Will said.

"Says here she was also known as Marguerite of Angoulême and Margaret of Navarre. Her titles were Princess of France, Queen of Navarre, and Duchess of Alençon and Berry."

"Where is Navarre?" Will wanted to know.

"You need to learn European geography," Avril replied. "It's in northern Spain and is famous for Pamplona and the annual running of the bulls."

"Thanks. I think," Will said dryly. "Who was her husband?"

Doyle flashed the screen toward Will, a starburst of light momentarily blinding him. "Henry II of Navarre. Her brother was Francis I, King of France. She and her brother supported cultural salons and the intellectuals of the day."

"Nice. An influencer during the French Renaissance," Avril said. "Then who wrote the cosmology during her reign that Nostradamus mentions?"

"Hold on. Searching." Doyle paused. "This is interesting."

"What?" Avril tried to grab the phone from Doyle's hands, but he pulled it away.

"This guy, François de Belleforest, who died in 1583, translated the Cosmographia of Sebastian Münster, and added quite a bit of new material."

Will checked his mirrors again. Still clear. But for how long? "Sounds like we're getting warm."

"Maybe," Avril said. "What does Belleforest and his cosmography have to do with caverns? We need to find the son of a soldier to guide us to them."

"Let me check his bio," Doyle said. "Trying to read without getting carsick."

"I can read. Give me the phone."

"Hold on, lass," Doyle said, with more patience than Will would have mustered. "All righty. Says on his Wikipedia page he was born into a poor family. Wrote a pastoral novel. Traveled to Paris. Wrote on morality, cosmography, literature, and history."

Avril leaned over the passenger seat. "But who was his father?"

"Looking."

"Look faster. We are driving aimlessly through the French countryside."

"Aha! Here it is. Yes, he was the son of a soldier."

Will tapped his fingers on his jeans. "We're definitely onto something."

Doyle nodded. "Belleforest is our man."

In the rearview mirror, Will saw Avril puff out a breath.

"Does his grave have some sort of signpost to a dark and lonely cavern?" she asked. "How many cave systems are there in Europe anyway?"

Doyle typed. "Here's a list of the ten best European cave systems. They range from Croatia to the Canary Islands. How far afield do you think we need to search?"

Will rubbed his chin, dimly thinking it was time for a shave. "Avril, what do you know about how far Nostradamus may have traveled during his time?"

"I read it took him almost a month to take a coach to Paris. One of his biographers said he wandered all over Europe, though. I think all we can really eliminate is the Americas, Australia, and probably the Far East."

"We are in trouble then," Doyle said.

"Why's that?" Will asked.

"I found a page listing all the caves in Europe. There are hundreds."

CHAPTER 41

7:00 P.M.

Avril exhaled heavily, threw her weight back against the Jeep's seat and pulled out her journal. "If you would give me the phone, I am sure I could figure out which cave we need to visit."

Will tapped his fingers on the steering wheel, impatiently. "You know that using your phone stunt back there at the hotel might have given our location away, right?"

Idly, she doodled in the margins. "I used a privacy-preserving VPN."

"A what?"

"Virtual private network. 'Private' being the key word there. It should have rendered my phone's browsing invisible."

"That *only* works for browsing," Doyle said.

"Of course. I also turned off location settings and Wi-Fi."

"You used your carrier then, to upload that file copy of the quatrains?"

"Yes."

"You're a civilian." Doyle turned to look her in the eye. "The phone carrier has your GPS data. You'd have to have taken your battery out to be truly invisible. We should have done that when you started traveling with us."

Like a balloon, the air deflated from Avril's lungs. *I'm an idiot!* She should have done a search on that, but hadn't anticipated being followed. "How is your phone safe then?"

"Secret military cloaking technology."

She ripped the page out of her notebook and balled it up. "Whatever. We need to find that cavern."

Will shifted in the driver's seat. "Guess we should go through that Wikipedia list then."

"That seems crazy and inefficient. Let's focus. How many of those gazillion EU caves would have been known in the time of Nostradamus?"

Doyle rubbed his scruffy cheek. "Good question, but hard to say. We need reference material from his time."

Avril recalled the quatrain and mentally connected the dots. "Something like, say, a book of cosmology?"

Doyle hit his forehead with his palm. "Brilliant!"

Avril smiled. "Thanks. Let's see if my hunch plays out."

Doyle's fingers were already flying across his phone. "Searching, searching. Bingo!"

Avril couldn't contain her excitement. "What?"

"In François de Belleforest's *Cosmographie Universelle*, which was published in 1557, he wrote that the Rouffignac caverns in the Dordogne region have monochromatic paintings and engravings, also known as petroglyphs. Of it, he says, and I quote, 'paintings in several places as well as the trace or footprints of various kinds of large and small beasts.'"

"Excellent detective work," Will said. "Perhaps we'll even find paintings of creatures with curved tusks. But where's Dordogne?"

"Southwest France," Avril answered in a sunny tone.

"With a pit stop to sleep and change cars, we should be there by morning—if our opponents don't find us."

CHAPTER 42

From the top bunk of the sleeper car, Maddy glanced out the train window, wishing for morning so she could see the French countryside. At the moment, the world rushing past their cocoon was pitch-black. No moon illuminated the hills and vineyards. The wheels clicked, clanked, and clanged on the iron tracks.

Bear was stretched out on the lower bunk, his muscled forearm under his blond head.

"I'm glad we made it out of Aubagne without a further run-in with the men in the van." She spoke just loud enough to be heard over the sounds of the train. "Think they were able to follow us?"

"We were the last passengers on board at Marseille, so I think we've outsmarted them. For now."

She wondered how the others were faring. "Hope so, I could use a good night's sleep."

"Me too. Although this mattress isn't as nice as the one at the vineyard."

"The price we pay for an adrenaline rush."

"I guess."

"I'm still a little wired." Maddy stretched her long legs until her toes hit the cabin wall. "Why don't you tell me a bedtime story about where we're headed? Why'd we take the train to Paris?"

"If you're wide awake, why don't you come join me on this bunk?"

The twinkle in his eyes made it clear he wasn't sleepy either.

She decided to play hard to get. "Maybe, sailor. That's a narrow bunk. Tell me that story first."

He grinned. "Okay. I've been thinking about the second quatrain, but I don't remember all of it, and actually, we all split up so fast we never got a copy." He pulled his phone out and typed while he talked. "But I do remember a key part: a king who made a city from a marsh island."

"You texting Will?"

"Yeah. He can send it."

"Which king drained the swamp, Mr. Living History Channel?"

"That would be Charles, the Duke of Lower Lorraine. He was a distant relative of Charlemagne."

"Aha. The quatrain mentioned Charlemagne."

"Yes. That was the other big clue."

She shook her head. Bear didn't remember what she asked him to get from the grocery, but the pedigree of royals from a thousand years ago stuck in his mind like glue. "What was the marsh island?"

"Saint-Géry Island. The duke constructed a fort on it to protect the western frontier of the Holy Roman Empire from the French kings."

"Those French kings are pesky."

"You have no idea."

"I probably don't."

"That's okay, you're sexy anyway."

She raised an eyebrow. "Let's focus on the story. When did all this happen?"

"Around 979. Charles transferred the relics of Saint Gudula from Moorsel to the Saint Gaugericus chapel on the island."

"Ah. That's a mouthful. Might that be the church the quatrain mentioned?"

Bear nodded. "I'm hoping so."

His phone vibrated. He pulled it out of his pocket and unlocked the device.

"Is that Will getting back to you?"

"No. It's Jags."

"She get any images of the people in the van from traffic cams?"

"Yes, but"—he scrolled—"they were wearing masks. All of them."

"Of course they were." Maddy threw herself back on the bunk and faced the ceiling. "Any info about glass-eyed Seymore?"

"Not yet. Sounds like a DoD network got hacked and her research is on hold."

She tapped her toes on the wall in frustration. "I was thinking . . ." She trailed off.

"About?"

She hesitated, still pulling her thoughts together. "About those reports we got from the director."

"And?"

She rolled over and looked at him. His blue eyes were lit with curiosity. "Seems people, and/or governments, have been looking a long time for the formula Nostradamus hid."

"Agreed. At least thirty-five years."

"What if . . ." The idea sounded a bit far-fetched to her, but she had to voice it. "What if the same operative who uncovered our American agent Leo is still in the field today? What if it's him or her who's on our tail?"

Bear cocked his head to the side, thinking. "I suppose the math could work. If that operative was twenty-five then, they'd be sixty now, and could still be involved. If they're that old, might be as slow as a gator taking a sunbath."

"Not all sixty-year-olds are out to pasture. Seymore looked fairly spry." She considered alternatives. "Or they could have turned all their information over to someone younger."

"True."

"Could even be the wise old alligator pulling the strings."

He smiled. "Guess we'll need to find out."

"We will. Anyway, where are we going? What's that island called today?"

"Brussels."

"Belgium. You know I love chocolate."

"Valentine's Day is coming up fast. Maybe I need to get you some of the good stuff so you'll make babies with me."

Ugh. Not this again. "How'd we get on the baby topic?"

"C'mon. Let's have three."

"Three?" The man hadn't even popped The Question. "I thought you wanted me to join VanOps and have an exciting career."

His blue eyes darted away from hers. "I did."

"And now . . ." She trailed off.

"Well." He made eye contact. "All this getting shot at makes me worry about you."

Her cheeks flushed. "Me? You don't think I can take care of myself?"

He shook his head violently. "No, that's not what I meant."

"You don't actually want to have children with me, you just want me to be on the sidelines?" Her voice rose. "Barefoot and pregnant?"

"No! That's not it at all."

"Bear Thorenson, you can forget all about babies. And practicing in your bunk. I'm going to sleep."

She slashed the light in the room and rolled over to face the wall. Before she had time to mutter more than "Men!" slumber claimed her.

CHAPTER 43

Seymore piloted the loud cigar-style boat out to the deep sea as the bloodred sun crested the horizon.

Yesterday, several of his men who worked freelance for the Corsican Mafia had just finished a hit on a petty thief when he'd ordered them to find the girl. They'd failed miserably.

He still burned with anger and annoyance at the fiasco. They didn't understand the stakes, so he'd brought them out here at dawn. The sea was rough, but he had the throttle down, uncaring that it tossed the men in their seats near the long bow.

After a half hour of the screaming motor, he pulled back and turned off the ignition. The boat rocked in the swells.

As they'd discussed, Raphael drew his Ruger semiautomatic and pointed it at the hired guns up front. "Stand up. All of you. Hands behind your head."

The four men exchanged confused glances, but rose.

Seymore said, "You screwed up yesterday. One simple task. That's all you had."

One began to object and Raphael released the pistol's safety. They shut up.

Seymore put heat into his tone as he slowly spoke each word. "This—will—not—happen—again."

They nodded.

But it wasn't enough. He needed to make an impression so that word would get back to their brethren. "Who screwed up yesterday?"

It took a moment for them to realize what was afoot. Fingers pointed wildly.

The unlucky sod who had more digits pointing at him than the rest began to yell. "No! It wasn't my fault."

Seymore moved to the back of the boat and grabbed an anchor. He handed it, and the heavy chain, to the nearest man without a word.

They knew what to do next.

CHAPTER 44

CAVES OF ROUFFIGNAC, FRANCE
8:45 A.M.

After a short night's rest at a small country inn, Avril walked behind Will and Doyle through the parking lot to their new white Toyota sedan. The day had dawned bright and clear and the air smelled fresh after the prior night's rain. It struck her that Monique and her grandfather would never see the blue sky again. A pressure built behind her eyes.

Doyle put the vehicle in drive and headed down a narrow and unmarked lane. "How old are these petroglyphs we're going to look at?"

Avril welcomed the distraction, wishing she had a computer or phone to do her own research. The men's bickering and high-handed natures were already starting to wear on her. Since she couldn't reply, she pulled out her notebook and began to sketch an image of an elephant inside a cave with zodiac signs on its hide.

Will pulled up an article on his phone. "They date to around twenty-four to twenty-two thousand years ago."

"Anything else interesting?"

"They were tourist attractions during the nineteenth century and recognized as 'genuinely prehistoric' in 1956." He paused, and then added, "They're the largest limestone karst system in this part of France, and have roughly ten kilometers of cavities spread over three levels."

Avril gathered from context that a karst system was some type of topography. She didn't want to ask.

Doyle slowed the car. "Do we walk around inside the cave? Crawl?"

"Looks like an electric train."

Avril frowned. "That is too bad. Would have been neat to see the petroglyphs close up. My dad always wanted to be a painter."

The men didn't seem to know how to respond to her comment about her dead father, and silence descended inside the car. She was glad they didn't ask probing questions.

They turned left at a brown signpost that pointed to the prehistoric caves of Rouffignac. Here the countryside was rolling and studded with oaks. Cows grazed in the fields. Soon they came across a stone-walled restaurant with small tables out front and a gaggle of geese guarding the front door. Starving, they parked and shooed the birds away, ran inside, and obtained some prepacked food, although Avril refused the foie gras, never having developed a taste for liver.

Once they were back in the car, Will said, around a bite of cheese and cracker, "Remember. Once we get to the caverns, we're tourists. No discussing the quatrains outside of the car."

"I remember," Avril said. "No need to be condescending."

"Reminding myself too. Please repeat that last line of the quatrain."

She reined in her irritation. "To find the male child of the creature with curved tusks."

"Okay, got it."

Five minutes later they stopped under trees on the side of the road in an area big enough for only a handful of vehicles. There was only one other parked car. Avril got out and stretched. This time of year, the leafless trees looked like gnarled, arthritic hands trying in vain to clutch the sky. They walked across the street and approached the low-slung cave entrance, which was guarded by an aged man with a ring of hair around the back of his head. At least the cave mouth looked tall enough to stand inside.

As they paid their tickets for the train, a young family departed, all smiles and laughs. Their toddler was gibbering about how much fun he'd had. The attendant motioned Avril and the men inside, where the air immediately felt ten degrees cooler and smelled of damp earth. A guide helped them board the "train."

Avril grimaced. It wasn't much of a train. The cars lacked walls and a ceiling, and there wasn't even a bench on which to sit. They grabbed the railing and the ride began. With its electric engine, the so-called train was silent, and there was no jarring movement. Avril held her breath in anticipation and hoped whoever was chasing them wouldn't find them down here. There was nowhere to hide.

The cave held none of the stalactites or stalagmites Avril had expected. Instead, the interior walls looked like rock, and the floor was made of clay. The conductor showed them the depressions where cave bears had once hibernated, and the vertical claw marks on the walls made her shiver. According to their guide, the rock art was thirteen thousand years old, and came from the Magdalenian culture.

Avril elbowed Will in the ribs. "Thirteen thousand years. Not twenty-three."

He looked down at her through his long lashes. In the ghostly ambient light, his green eyes nearly glowed. "The past is an illusion and the future a mirage."

She whispered, "Smartass."

The docent noted that pieces of manganese dioxide were used to make the black-figure drawings. The engravings, on the other hand, were made with flint chisels, bone, or wooden tools. The black drawings were fascinating: mammoths facing each other, a rhino with two curved horns, the front half of a friendly-looking bison. The engravings didn't move her, though, as many were geometric in nature rather than illustrating the ancient animal kingdom.

When they reached the final cave, she grew almost dizzy looking at early man's version of the Sistine Chapel. The ceiling was adorned with an amazing variety of horses, wooly rhinos, mammoths, bison, snakes, and ibex. The curved tusks of the mammoths reminded her of elephants, and the graceful curves of the ibex horns took her breath away.

As the train wound back up through the chambers, Avril reflected on the last verse of the quatrain: "To find the male child of the creature with curved tusks." Their guide had said 158 of the 255 black line drawings were mammoths. Clearly, those were the curved tusked creatures Nostradamus had intended for them to find.

But she'd seen no evidence of a specific male child. Even if they hadn't seen all the drawings because some of the caverns were off-limits, what the hell was Nostradamus talking about?

CHAPTER 45

BRUSSELS, BELGIUM
8:57 A.M.

Although she'd had strange dreams of a cackling Nostradamus sculpting ram's horns from pliable neon tubes, dreams she was sure were not predicting anything, Maddy had slept well until they'd had to change trains at seven a.m. in Paris. Before leaving the coach, Bear had tried to kiss and make up, but she was still miffed. A half-hour layover in the busy station had fortified them with croissants and espresso before she and her annoying boyfriend hopped the next train to Brussels.

On the morning route, she'd checked in with AJ, who seemed to be enjoying his time with Jags and Deanna. Jags had no news on Seymore except they expected the hack, which was impeding progress on that front, to be resolved soon. Maddy also sent an email to Aunt Carole, hoping Bella the gatekeeper would share it, and wondered briefly about that postcard. When had her mom been in Italy?

In Brussels, after the train pulled into Gare Centrale, they pushed through the Belgian crowd and trotted up the stairs, emerging into the partly sunny day like blinking moles yanked out of their hole.

"Which way?" she asked.

"Just a few blocks north."

A teenaged girl with sapphire-blue hair flew by on a bicycle. Maddy thought of Avril, whose life had been completely uprooted, like a budding flower accidentally pulled with a handful of weeds. Maddy's heart went out to the girl they were attempting to keep safe by finding the medallion of Nostradamus. She had been stressed yesterday, and regretted snapping at Avril over the phone incident.

Late last night, Will had sent them a copy of the quatrains. She and Bear read and reread the second one during the short ride from Paris to Brussels.

Six degrees from Charlemagne
Lies a liege who made a city from the marsh island
Buried to rest in the church of a servant
Above his sarcophagus mark the second line eleven fifteen and seven times

Bear was convinced that the Cathedral of St. Michael and St. Gudula was the burial site of Charles, Duke of Lower Lorraine. It seemed clear to Maddy that the duke was the liege in question, but they'd been unable to find his resting place in their online research.

They set off down an urban street bisected by a boulevard of trees. Bear still limped more than usual from the motorcycle crash in Saint-Rémy. The wind whistled through buildings, reminding her of San Francisco. They passed a brewpub and modern-looking apartments. She and Bear both kept an eye on their surroundings in case they'd somehow been followed.

As they neared a small park, church spires reared up ahead, outlined against a patch of blue sky.

"Is that it?" she asked.

Bear still seemed peeved that they hadn't made love before bed last night. He chewed his gum with an unusual fierceness and didn't make eye contact. "Yeah."

Ah well. They had a job to do and would have to make up later.

Only a handful of people sat on the park benches. She studied them. One had a pile of plastic bags and looked homeless, while another had the dressed-to-the-nines air of a retired man enjoying his coffee in the park no matter the weather. She emptied her mind of thoughts and put herself in an alert mindset, to better keep an eye on them both.

At the end of the park, they turned up a one-way street and got a full look at the cathedral. Four-story white towers flanked both sides of the building, which was accessed by a broad stairway. A flag flew from each of the square towers. Slim arched windows, probably stained glass, made the Gothic stone building appear graceful. Narrow vertical openings in both towers looked like arrow slits, designed for defense.

She and Bear approached with caution, as if they were medieval invaders armed with lances and shields.

He zipped his black leather jacket higher against the cold wind. "Let's walk around the block and scout."

She put her hand on his arm, and he melted a little.

"Sure," she replied.

Up close, she saw the church had been built with large white bricks.

"Took about three hundred years to build," Bear remarked.

"Impressive."

It took nearly fifteen minutes to walk the structure's perimeter. Afterwards, they stood in the paved front plaza and Bear took a last look around.

"Okay," he said. "Let's go in. Stay alert."

They walked up the broad front steps to the church and opened a heavy wooden door.

The plain exterior hadn't prepared her for the interior, and her eyes grew wide. Life-sized sculptures adorned the massive support columns and light streamed in through the stained-glass windows, adding rainbows of light. The heavy scent of frankincense filled the air. No one was in sight and the expansive space was deathly quiet.

It would be a good place for an ambush. She shivered, in spite of the gorgeous architecture, and reminded herself to stay present.

Bear pointed to a sign for the gift shop, and they walked down the rows of wooden chairs to the north transept. The shop was empty, save for an elderly nun in a black veil and tunic. A mahogany-colored rosary adorned her neck. She stopped dusting a glass candle holder, looked over her half-glasses, and said hello in French.

Bear bowed his head in respect. "Good morning, Sister. Do you speak English?"

Tuffs of gray hair framed her round face. She smiled. "I do. Good morning. How may I help you?" she said with a slight French accent.

"I understand you offer tours of the crypts."

"Yes, it's by appointment only. Our next tour is two days from now."

Bear's mouth sagged in disappointment. "We were hoping to see the tomb of Charles, Duke of Lower Lorraine, today. Is there any way to arrange that?"

The nun frowned and put her hand to her chest. "I'm afraid not."

"It's rather important," Maddy said.

"That may be," the nun said. "But I don't believe he's buried here. Father Damon runs the tours of the crypts and the archeological features. I'll ring him."

As she picked up an archaic black desk phone and dialed, Maddy and Bear stepped away to give her some privacy. The conversation was hushed, and in another language, although Maddy wasn't sure it was French.

The nun hung up the phone. "Father Damon says he'll speak with you, but he's on top of the north tower attending to our resident peregrine falcons. You're welcome to go on up."

Five minutes later, as Maddy and Bear exited a steep staircase, a short, white-bearded man turned to greet them. He wore the black garb of a priest, including a white throat collar that matched his long, curly hair and neatly trimmed beard and mustache. His thin frame looked almost skeletal, but he had pink cheeks and friendly dark-brown eyes.

"I'm Father Damon," he said loudly over the rooftop wind.

She and Bear gave aliases.

Maddy wanted to break the conversational ice. "What's the story with the falcons?"

The priest's accent was strong, but she couldn't place it. "They are such mighty hunters. Did you know they're the fastest birds in the world?"

She and Bear both shook their heads.

"Pesticides like DDT wiped them out in the seventies." He frowned and a gust of wind tousled his white hair. "Back in 2004, an ornithologist found a couple nesting up here. Now we have mated pairs all over town."

"That's neat." She meant it.

"It is." Father Damon pointed to an area with a scale. "We bring them here, weigh them, that sort of thing. Most of it is done by wildlife biologists, but I keep the webcam working."

"Where are the birds?" Bear asked.

Father Damon walked over to the edge of the tower, which was delineated by a short stone railing. When they joined him, Maddy gave a little gasp at the view of the city spread out below them.

The priest pointed. "Their nest is inside that cavity, over there."

The wind whistled and seemed to sweep under his cassock. He lost his balance, tripped, and fell toward the edge.

Before she could react, Bear's strong hand grabbed the old man by the back of his frock. Father Damon stumbled, and then got his footing.

He faced them with wide eyes. "You saved my life. Thank you!"

Bear's eyes turned down. "Just happy to help."

Maddy found Bear's modesty endearing, which melted the remaining frost from last night's argument. The old priest could very well have tripped over the edge. She reached over and squeezed Bear's hand.

Father Damon shook his head. "That's never happened. I come up here all the time."

"Good timing, I guess," Bear said.

Father Damon led them back to the stairwell. "Let's step out of the wind, then, for a moment, yes?"

Maddy finally had caught her breath from the trek up and was glad the way back was down.

Father Damon turned to them, looking them in the eye. "You didn't climb all the way up here to hear me ramble on about birds. How can I be of assistance?"

Bear said, "We hope you can help us. We're searching for the tomb of Charles, Duke of Lower Lorraine."

The priest tugged his ear. "The false French king?"

Bear faltered. "I suppose you could call him that. We understand that he established Brussels and brought relics of St. Gudula here."

"That may be true, but I've been in charge of the crypt and the archeology tours here for twenty-two years. The cathedral does contain the unmarked burial place of Dermot O'Mallun, the last Irish-born head of the O'Moloney clan, but no, Charles isn't buried here."

Bear hung his head. Maddy felt sorry for him and put a hand on his back. He'd been so sure Charles was laid to rest here.

She eyed the priest. "Would you happen to know where he *is* buried?"

A twinkle entered the man's brown eyes. "I do, actually. Before I came here, I was a priest in the Netherlands. The false king is buried in the Basilica of Saint Servatius."

They should have known. *Buried to rest in the church of a servant.* "Where's that?"

"In Maastricht, just over the border."

CHAPTER 46

After leaving the cave system, Will slid back into the driver's seat of the Toyota with a sigh.

"I can check petroglyphs off my bucket list, but I'm not seeing the solution to the quatrain about the male child of a creature with curved tusks—are you guys?"

Next to him, Doyle fastened his seat belt. "I think it's pretty clear the curved tusks belong to the mammoth species."

"Given all the mammoth drawings, that conclusion is easy to draw," Avril said. "It is the male child part of the riddle that is trickier."

Will jingled the keys in his hand. "What are baby mammoths called?"

Doyle whipped his phone out. "Since they're related to elephants, I think they're called calves, but let me see." He began to swipe. "Scientists think they ran in mostly female herds, like elephants, while the young males gallivanted around and got themselves killed by falling into pits."

Avril snorted. "Sounds like teenage males all right."

Will gave her the evil eye.

Doyle looked up. "Yes, today anyway, they call them calves."

Will glanced around the parking lot. No other cars had shown up, but he wanted to get moving again. "Do experts differentiate between male and female calves?"

"You mean like a colt versus a filly?" Doyle asked.

"Yeah."

Doyle buried his head again in his phone. "Not that I see so far. Still looking."

Avril piped up. "Since he mentioned the 'son of the soldier' earlier in the quatrain, maybe Nostradamus means 'son' for the 'male child of the creature with curved tusks.'"

"Or maybe he means calf?" Will suggested.

Doyle pulled his seatbelt on. "Maybe it's 'mammoth.' The son of a mammoth is still a mammoth."

"I am sure now," Avril said. "It's son."

Will turned the key, firing up the engine. "Maybe tracking down the other clues will make this one more obvious. Are you guys sure we should head to Florence?"

"I am," Avril said. "That duomo reference seems pretty obvious."

Doyle gave Avril a false glare. "This old man is going to ask the *interweb*."

She rolled her eyes. Will found her both innocent and infuriating, but he also noted a protective streak growing in his heart, rather like how he felt about AJ.

Doyle typed and scrolled. "It appears that the definition of duomo is an Italian cathedral. That means we may be premature in our assessment of Florence. Could be Milan, Siena, Pisa . . . Avril, please repeat the third quatrain."

"The duomo's architect
Pays homage to a night in July
With sacred signs of the zodiac
Of the first the penultimate strikes the mark but of the second take the last and the first of the twins."

Doyle nodded. "We don't just need any old Italian cathedral. We need one with signs of the zodiac."

"Sounds right to me," Will agreed.

"Try searching for duomo zodiac," Avril suggested.

"Hold on, lass." Doyle paused. "Okay, when I search for that, the church in Milan comes up. Largest cathedral in Italy. Took six hundred years to build." Doyle's fingers danced across the phone screen. "Construction started in 1386, so it would have been around during Nostradamus's time."

Avril leaned forward. "Anything related to the zodiac?"

"Not yet," Doyle replied.

Will checked his mirrors. "Since we know we're at least headed to Italy, let's get out of here before trouble finds us. Again."

CHAPTER 47

MAASTRICHT, THE NETHERLANDS
2:50 P.M.

Thanks to the swift magic of rail travel in the EU, less than two hours after saving the life of the old priest atop the cathedral, Maddy and Bear arrived in Maastricht. They immediately left the station, wanting to get to the church as soon as possible. Maddy donned a dark cap against the cold air, glad for thick jeans and her black down jacket.

They were nearly across a pedestrian-and-bikes-only bridge that spanned a wide stretch of emerald water when Bear's phone rang.

He glanced at the device. "It's Will."

"Let's get across the bridge."

Bear answered. "Will, hold on a second."

They made it across the remaining span and glanced around the busy intersection. To their right was an outdoor café, surprisingly busy for a cold winter's day. Maddy touched Bear's arm and pointed. Below the restaurant, a paved walkway ran along the river.

They went down the stairs, both surreptitiously watching for not-so-innocent bystanders.

Once they were walking in relative privacy, Bear spoke again. "Hey, Will, what's up?"

"We're almost to Lyon, then headed to Milan."

He quickly brought them up to speed on what they had, and hadn't, discovered in the caverns. Likewise, Bear summarized their own roadblocks.

"We've been listening to the news," Will added. "All holy hell is breaking out between Taiwan and China."

"The invasion of the outlying islands wasn't enough?" Maddy asked.

"Apparently not. In the last thirty-six hours, Chinese warplanes crossed the median line across the narrow strait that separates the mainland and Taiwan almost forty times."

"Forty!" Doyle yelled in the background.

"Sounds like chest thumping to me," Bear said.

Will responded, "Sure, but after invading Pratas Island? Plus, it involved a combo of fighter jets and bombers. Unlike anything seen in years."

They were silent for a moment, taking in the implications. Maddy figured Doyle was probably about ready to yank his topknot out with worry.

"Have you had any sort of update from the director?" she asked.

"No. But we've been keeping Jags in the loop. You?"

"Not yet," Bear replied. "We'll give them a ring after our upcoming visit."

"Okay. Keep us posted."

"We will."

They rang off, and turned back toward the Basilica of Saint Servatius, but Maddy was still stuck on the situation with Taiwan.

"That doesn't sound good."

Bear pursed his lips. "No. Not at all." He pulled some balm from his pocket and applied it. "But they haven't invaded the main island yet."

He was right. She reminded herself to try for once to live in the moment.

They walked the rest of the way quickly, Maddy noting the distinct differences in architectural styles from Brussels as she continued to scan for company. Where Brussels was all midcentury modern, Maastricht looked like a fairy-tale town. Dark brick buildings clustered together on narrow streets and, as the central business district was a no-cars zone, bicycles were everywhere. Unlocked, too. Maddy compared that to San Francisco, where any unsecured bike would have been stolen in a heartbeat.

They moved around a corner. She pointed at a small stone building with a dark-red tower. "Is that part of the church?"

"I don't think so. When I was looking at the map on the train, it said the distinctive red tower was Saint Jan's. Our destination is beside it."

The church next door was a mixture of dark and light stones, reminding her of a wizened war veteran whose body bore scars but whose mind knew wisdom. "How old is it?"

"It's from the eleventh century."

"Yikes! A thousand years old?"

"Pretty much. Let's go in."

When they entered, Maddy was struck by how different it was from the cathedral they'd seen earlier that morning. This church had carved wooden pews, black-and-white floor tiles, dark granite columns, and a massive blue and gold organ at the back. It gave off a more serious vibe, enough that Bear crossed himself using a fount of holy water.

The church was also busier. Worshipers knelt in pews or stood in naves, studying the stained glass, or sculpture. There was a subtle hint of incense, but the scent was unrecognizable.

Maddy took her cap off and stuck it in her jacket pocket. "Any ideas on how to get into the crypt?"

"Let's head down that hallway."

They left the central part of the nave and walked until they found a series of posters announcing the current exhibition, which was a set of drawings of the basilica. They entered a hall of tall glass cases.

The pockmarked attendant was stout, with broad shoulders, thick legs, and long hair braided into dreadlocks. His wide stance showed a military bearing. He reminded Maddy of a modern-day Viking.

Tired from their travels, Maddy got right to the point. "Is it possible to see the tomb of Charles, Duke of Lower Lorraine? Perhaps on a tour?"

The Viking-esque attendant put his hands on his hips, and looked them up and down with cold sapphire eyes. "Absolutely not. That area is permanently closed."

CHAPTER 48

Four hours after leaving the caves of Rouffignac, Avril woke from a nap feeling sore and hungry. Will was still driving. Doyle yawned and shoved a jacket under his neck. Within a minute, he was making soft snoring sounds.

Will made eye contact with her in his rearview mirror, and then pulled his fancy harmonica from the leather pouch on his belt. The guy was handsome enough in a young-dad way, with his long eyelashes and chiseled cheeks, but his constant negative outlook gave her a headache. He tooted on the instrument a few times, holding it in one hand, and then began to play a soft, sad tune. It put her in a reflective mood.

She pulled out her brown leather-bound journal and began to sketch, wondering how Bear and Maddy were making out with their two quatrains. Contemplating where their clues might lead, she drew the outlines of a church spire and the columns of a ruined temple with little effort. Avril had always wanted a brother, but the way the twins bickered made her glad to be an only child. Maybe it was Will's fault, though, as she was already getting tired of arguing with him.

They passed an Asian restaurant, reminding her of times when Monique would bring in Chinese food. She stared out the window and bit her lip to choke back tears. The reality of having no one else to turn to made her stomach churn. She missed her family. Should she have come with the team? Did she have a choice? Foster care sounded like a prison sentence. She drew the bars of a jail cell on the white paper.

Perhaps it would be safer, though, than this mission. Whoever was after them had taken the lives of those she loved with as little effort as she might use to fry an egg for breakfast. What chance did she stand to live through this? Could Will and Doyle protect her life?

When she noticed where they were, she snapped out of her depressing reverie, and tapped Will on the shoulder. He jerked in his seat, dropping the harmonica into his lap.

"Why so jumpy?" she whispered.

He whispered back, "Habit."

"My gecko can be a little jumpy, too."

"Is he . . . did he . . ."

"I left him at the friend's house where I spent the night."

Will exhaled. "Good. That's good." He paused. "What's his name?"

"Fleck."

"Does he have spots?"

"Yes, he is a leopard gecko."

"Nice."

She picked at her fingernails, and then bit one for good measure. "We are nearing Lyon."

"Why does that matter?"

"I'm hungry and need to stretch my legs. Besides, there is a library here with an old manuscript Nostradamus wrote."

"Think it will help us?"

"No idea, but I have been wanting to take a look."

"Where is it?"

"The Part-Deux business district."

"Okay."

While Will piloted the car the last few miles, Avril wondered about the third quatrain. With a pit stop at the library, this could be a good investigative opportunity. She had some ideas about the endgame. Her fingers itched to do some research of her own.

Doyle woke up when Will shut the car off and they all groaned as they stepped out and stretched. After, they walked toward the building that housed the Nostradamus collection, which, in contrast to the older part of town, had a definite postmodern vibe.

Inside, they made their way to the heritage collections area and found a youngish librarian who ushered them into a back room and showed them the bound manuscript Nostradamus had written about hieroglyphs.

"Here you go," the brown-haired librarian said, pointing. "French manuscript No. 2594. It's called 'The Orus Apollo' and is a rather rough translation of Horapollon of Manuthis's Hieroglyphica, with about ten sections added by Nostradamus. It contains two books of 182-verse epigrams. The paper has been tested, and shown to be from the correct period. It's definitely original, which is why we have it in a locked glass case."

The men murmured their thanks.

As Avril's research had indicated, the epigrams had no punctuation or accents. Neither did the quatrains they were working with, which lent them a new aura of legitimacy. The handwriting looked like a good match, too.

She quickly grew bored and turned to the librarian. "Where is the restroom?"

The librarian pointed. "Down the hall and to the left."

On the way, Avril bumped into a middle-aged woman with curly black hair who wore a nice-smelling perfume.

After taking care of business, Avril ducked out of the bathroom and spied a bank of computers. *Yes!*

She skipped over to the machines and fired up a private browser. With practiced ease, her fingers flew over the keyboard, researching tidbits from the remaining quatrains, starting with Greek maps.

Feeling she'd hit a jackpot, she sucked in a breath. Sometimes she got ahead of herself, though. Wanting to make sure she was correct in reading the breadcrumbs left by her ancestor, she used keywords for 'zodiac' and 'duomo' and discovered that the cathedral in Milan had a series of astrological symbols inlaid on the marble floor next to a brass strip that signified a meridian line. The location didn't fit her theory, but it did make her raise her eyebrows. At solar noon every sunny day, sunshine poured through a ceiling window and lit up the zodiac sign related to the earth's current orbital position. How could Doyle have not seen this?

Before she could celebrate getting one up on Will and Doyle, a heavy hand fell on her back, causing her to jump in her seat.

She whipped around, and realizing it was Will who had interrupted her research, swore silently.

Any additional investigation was going to have to wait.

CHAPTER 49

Maddy wrapped her ponytail around her occasionally traitorous index finger, then unwrapped it, and twisted again. Several hours had passed since she and Bear had been turned away from the Tomb of Charles at the Basilica of Saint Servatius. Starving, they'd regrouped at a local café and called Jags, who told them of a VanOps safe house nearby.

It wasn't exactly a safe *house*, however. It was a safe boat.

Maastricht was a river town, bisected by the Meuse, which, according to Bear, had once been the Holy Roman Empire's western border with the Kingdom of France. At some point, an enterprising VanOps supply steward had acquired an old, floating two-star hotel and converted it into a safe house for operatives working in Belgium, Germany, and the Netherlands. She had to admit it was a private location, and, while not even close to luxurious, was certainly novel. Too bad the rooms were so cramped.

Night had fallen. After a brief meditation on a below-decks bunk to calm her nerves, she stared out over the river from the stern. Lights from the distant town sparkled like gold dust on the water. Bear was downstairs taking a shower in one of the tiny cabins. They were both awaiting the arrival of Director Bowman, who was in the area and wanted to speak with them personally.

Since it was her first official mission, his imminent arrival made her nervous. Had they screwed up? Bear insisted the visit was probably routine, but he'd never heard of a field visit either. Shivering, she tugged her jacket closer.

She felt a hand on her lower back, and then warm lips kissed her neck underneath her ears. Bear smelled fresh and clean.

"Hey, honeypot. I'll keep you warm if you want to come downstairs."

"Tempting, Mr. Thorenson, but isn't the director due any minute?"

The boat swayed lightly underfoot. As if on cue, three dark forms were gliding swiftly up the broad gangplank that connected the floating ship to the riverbank. The center shadow moved like the director, who was probably flanked by bodyguards.

"Let's go greet him," Bear said.

They made it to the side of the boat just as Bowman and his entourage stepped aboard. Handsome as ever, tonight the director wore an unbuttoned camel-colored trench coat, which covered a dark suit with a purple tie. His bodyguards moved fore and aft.

Bowman extended a hand to each of them. "Thorenson. Marshall. Good to see you both. Where can we sit and talk in private?"

Bear nodded to the main cabin. "In there, sir. Other than the manager, we're the only ones here."

"All right. Lead the way."

Bear moved through the door and into the sparsely furnished dining room, which held only a handful of wooden tables and chairs. They sat across from the director at a table with a view of the black, fast-moving river.

Maddy noted that her breathing was shallow and made an effort to deepen it. "To what do we owe the pleasure, Director Bowman?"

The director's baritone was smooth but, as always, his words were rapid-fire. "I was in Paris for a meeting."

"Thanks for making time for us."

Bowman took off his trench coat and hung it over a nearby chair. "Jags brought me up to speed on your progress. Good work so far."

Maddy's shoulders relaxed a notch.

The director pierced them with his eyes. "But we have two serious problems."

Maddy's stomach clenched into a tight ball.

Bowman continued. "Our big-picture problem is that millions of innocent people will die in Taiwan if China invades."

"Wouldn't it also change the balance of power in the Pacific?" Bear asked.

"Yes." Bowman nodded. "Permanently. All the superpowers know the strategic importance of Taiwan. Our allies are behind us should this blow up, but Russia is signaling that they're on China's side."

Maddy saw the problem immediately. "A world war would lead to even more people dying."

"Exactly. This is the type of doomsday scenario we work to avoid."

Imagining the mushroom clouds, she recalled that black human shadows were found etched across the sidewalks of Hiroshima and Nagasaki from the countless bodies blasted to bits. Maddy leaned in. "That's worse than we thought. How can we help?"

"Knowing the future would change everything for China. They want to predict how our government, especially our one-week-old president, would react to an invasion, so they can plan a counter move. We suspect it's the only reason they're holding off. If they get their hands on the medallion Nostradamus hid, we're in for a world of hurt."

"Is China behind the attempted kidnapping of Avril, sir?"

"Given the timing, it's a good theory, but that's for you to find out, son."

Bear nodded.

Bowman glanced at Maddy. "However, we have another problem."

"Oh?" Maddy asked. The tight ball in her stomach did a roller-coaster-worthy loop.

Bowman leaned back in his chair and rubbed his hand across the growth of his new beard, which was black, flecked with silver. "Given the importance of this mission, I've had Jags digging into old CIA files. How much do you know about the operative named Leo?"

Maddy glanced at Bear. "Only what was in the reports. His mission was to find out how Nostradamus saw visions. At some point, the operative had a child while undercover, and had to abort the mission because it was suspected he'd been made. He had to leave the child behind."

Bowman nodded. "What if I told you that Leo was female?"

Maddy raised an eyebrow and shrugged.

The director pulled a letter-sized envelope from his trench coat and put it on the table, unopened. "What if she retired, and moved to California?"

Maddy shook her head. "It's a great place to live. I'm still not seeing your point."

"For security purposes, they didn't record her first or last name." He pulled an old photograph from the envelope and handed it to Maddy. "But we have a black-and-white picture."

The woman in the faded photograph was tall, with full lips and familiar features. She stood unsmiling, with a hand on her hip.

The director added, "Her middle name was Louise."

In her mind's eye, Maddy saw the postcard Will had shown them back at the vineyard. It was signed in her mother's hand: Mary Louise Marshall.

Maddy gasped. Those lips. The resemblance to Aunt Carole. Maddy's heart rate spiked. She shut her eyes hard and swallowed. After a breath, she blinked numerous times in succession. "Are you saying . . ." She trailed off and studied his face.

He nodded, concern welling in his eyes. "I am."

She put a hand to her mouth. "Oh my god. Leo was my mother."

Maddy turned her head away, feeling nauseous. For a long moment, time stood still. The golden lights of the river blurred.

My mother.

Bear put a hand on her thigh, under the table, to steady her.

A whirlpool of emotions tugged at her. Leo, whom she'd assumed to be male, was her mother.

Blinking back tears, she faced the director.

"Did you know?"

"Jags just found out and brought it to my attention."

She studied his face, recalling his earlier words. *Spying is in your blood.* Was he lying? "It never came up during our background checks?"

"No. Their protocol at the time was to obscure first and last names. Hourglass was the last big parapsychology-related mission run by the CIA, before remote viewing made headlines and heads rolled. VanOps was born from those ashes, but they learned their lesson and pushed the new department all the way into the abyss, where we remain, blacker than black."

Maddy touched the envelope on the desk. "Is this her file?"

He pushed the thin white packet toward her. "Yes. You need to burn it after Argones sees it. I don't have time to visit your brother in person, as I need to meet again with the director of national intelligence, but I'll call him when we're done."

Her mom died when she was six, likely seven to ten years after retiring from the CIA. Still. Maddy's eyes narrowed and she yanked on her ponytail.

"Was her death an accident?"

CHAPTER 50

BEIJING, CHINA
MIDNIGHT

General Wong woke to the sound of his encrypted phone ringing. He groaned and sat up to answer the device, grateful his wife of thirty years slept in another room.

The man on the other end of the line spoke rapid Mandarin and brought Wong the news he'd been waiting to hear. The VanOps team had been located.

A French intelligence minister had met with Director Bowman in Paris that evening and had managed to slip a micro audio-activated recording device onto a button of Bowman's tan knee-length trench coat when he used the restroom. Knowing Bowman and the minister met on a regular basis to share notes on China's activities, Wong had the minister's daughter photographed throughout an entire day at her university, and the threat of harm to her had convinced the Frenchman this one small act would be much "appreciated."

The human element. It had been his secret weapon throughout his successful career.

He turned on a bedside lamp, stood, and put on a silk robe. They'd had trouble following the girl after the fiasco at the Marseille harbor. Satellites had tracked her protectors, leading to a tantalizing near-miss in Aubagne, and then they'd disappeared after swapping cars multiple times in busy metro airports.

The news that Bowman had revealed the team's current locations when speaking with an underling after the meeting was especially positive in light of the past failures, but Wong remained angry.

Using the irritation in his voice to motivate the team, he called Seymore on a single-use phone and ordered cleanup crews dispatched to Maastricht and Milan. Then he put the phone aside to be pulverized in the morning.

If tonight's good news didn't turn the tide, he might have to intervene in this mission. Personally.

Wong moved over to the dresser and picked up a knife concealed in a turquoise- and amber-encrusted silver scabbard that had been in his family for generations. He traced his finger over the engraved dragon and its outstretched claws. As a child, he'd been allowed to touch the knife only as a special reward for good schoolwork. His father had given him the weapon on his deathbed.

With a *whoosh*, Wong unsheathed the gray seven-inch blade, and checked the sharpness with his thumb. He could have shaved with it. The handle was made of carved bone and felt good in his hand. For the last several hundred years, his male ancestors had been warriors. Men of war. He was no exception.

Martial arts training had begun when he was old enough to walk, and he still practiced Tai Chi daily in the walled garden behind his home. It kept him strong.

He grabbed a poorly written mystery from his bedside table, threw it into the air, and slashed it with the blade. It parted clean in half, falling to the floor in a flurry of pages.

Satisfied for the moment, he removed his robe and went back to bed.

CHAPTER 51

MAASTRICHT, THE NETHERLANDS
6:05 P.M.

Maddy held onto her rearing temper by a thread as Director Bowman stared out the window at the dark night without answering her question.

"Was my mom's death an accident?" she repeated.

Finally, he turned and faced her. "Her former life as an operative was buried deep. She fell in love with your father and wanted to get off the radar."

"Meaning?"

"The only examination at the scene was done by local Tahoe City sheriffs. There was never a federal investigation."

Maddy's mind reeled.

Bear said what she was thinking. "With no cause, and in the middle of winter, they wouldn't have looked for anything suspicious."

Bowman nodded. "Agreed. She'd been out of the game for eight years at that point."

Maddy shook her head. "But she'd been made in France. Even left a child there. Do you know anything about that?"

"No, there was no information about the love child in the file."

"Anyway, that's why she returned to the States. Someone was onto her. It doesn't look like an accident to me."

Bowman looked her deep in the eyes. "That's why I'm here. To see if you need to leave this mission."

She jerked back, as startled as if she'd stepped on a rattlesnake. "Why? What do you mean?"

"Dynamite-laden information like this is tough to keep quiet. You'd have found out and I wanted to see your reaction for myself. Your brother is a skeptic. He won't believe she was murdered without proof. You, on the other hand . . ." He raised his palms and tilted his head, as if to say her belief was already apparent.

Her voice rose. "What if I do? Assassination is certainly a possibility."

His tone dropped an octave. "If you believe it with your heart, you'll get angry. When you get good and mad, you have a hard time limiting your behavior to that which is appropriate."

She growled, "How do you know that?"

"It's my job to know my operatives."

She wanted to slap him, but that would only prove his point. Instead, she shoved her hands under the table. She wanted this mission. Now, more than ever. If her mother's killer was out there, she'd find him and justice would be served. So angry she could hardly think, she dug her nails into her palms until the skin broke and blood made her fingertips wet.

Bear gently squeezed her thigh, breaking the spell. She released her fists, knowing she had to get her emotions under control.

She took a deep breath and mentally reached deep, grabbing her bucking temper by the reins and forcing it down into her belly where she corralled it. When the time came, she'd let it, and her power, loose.

Putting her fists on the table, she said. "There's no proof she was killed. My behavior will remain appropriate. I give you my word."

Bowman rocked back in his chair, studying her face for any crack in her façade. She held steady under his scrutiny, hoping blood wouldn't drip out of her fists, and eventually, he broke eye contact. "If you find she was killed, do not, I repeat *not*, create an international incident."

"I won't."

He sighed. "All right then. To deal with the roadblock at the basilica, we tried pushing our weight around, but the church wouldn't budge. Instead, Jags has been digging into city records. A subway extension project was recently completed in the area and the church provided a map of the crypt to the contractor. Jags will email you schematics."

"Thank you."

Bowman stood to leave. "I'll leave you a car, too. I want you to find that formula of Nostradamus and keep it out of the hands of the Chinese and anyone else who wants it. And find it as fast as humanly possible."

Maddy wanted to find that medallion too. But now she also had some sharply pointed questions for whoever was on their trail.

CHAPTER 52

MILAN, ITALY
6:30 P.M.

They were almost to Milan.

As far as Will could discern, they hadn't been followed, which made him all the more suspicious. His fingers drummed a relentless beat on his thigh.

It was after dark, and the lights of the city spread butterscotch pools of light along the street. After traveling over the Alps and through Turin, they were coming at the Duomo di Milano from the northwest. The landmark was nestled in the very heart of the old city, not far from Castello Sforzesco.

He glanced in the back seat. Avril's head was thrown back and soft wheezes escaped her lips. After she'd encouraged him to play his harmonica again, he'd riffed some easy blues tunes for her until she nodded off. Her yellow rain jacket was tucked up under her chin, keeping her warm. He'd almost felt bad, back in the library in Lyon, when he'd scared the bejesus out of her while she sat at the computer, but his heart rate was up at the thought she'd disappeared. The little varmint was proud of the information she'd dug up about the church in Milan, though, and he had to admit he was a little satisfied with her discovery as well. He couldn't believe she was getting under his skin like that.

For a short time, a few years ago, his wife was pregnant, a situation that had terrified him and pleased him all at the same time. He hadn't thought much about that unborn child since his wife's death. Probably repressed it. Sixteen-year-old Avril was making him wonder what it would have been like to be a dad.

His phone rang and the screen lit up with Director Bowman's name. Five minutes later, after hearing the shocking news, Will rang off with a trembling hand.

"You okay there, William? You look pasty white, like the inside of a good Irish potato."

Will gripped the steering wheel with both hands. "Just give me a second."

"Sure, buddy."

Thoughts buzzed around inside Will's head like bees at a barbeque. His mother had been an operative? She was Leo, of the Hourglass files? He blinked hard a few times, trying to make sense of it all. He'd always been told that his mother was born and raised in a small house in East Sacramento not far from the university campus. She and her sister, Carole, had grown up eating apples from their backyard and playing on the banks of the American River. For college, she'd gone somewhere back east—was it Brown?—and after working in the nation's capital as a secretary for a few years, had met his father and they'd moved to the Lake Tahoe basin to raise a family. He and Maddy had come along a few years later.

Could Bowman be playing tricks to motivate them? It didn't seem likely, but Will would keep the option open as he gathered more data. The only overlap he could see was the Washington DC connection. Maybe she'd been working undercover while she was supposed to be an administrative assistant. It seemed a plausible cover story. But really? His *mother*?

And what had happened to the operative's unplanned love child? Did that mean he had a half brother or sister out there somewhere? Perhaps Rome? Was that why Mom had visited the museum and sent that morbid postcard?

Doyle pointed. "Hey, that's the duomo over there."

Will decided to put his questions and outraged skepticism on hold for now. He piloted the car around the Piazza del Duomo to scout the area and gestured to the back seat. "Could you wake her up?"

Doyle reached over the seat and touched Avril's leg. "Hey, Sleeping Beauty. We're almost there."

Avril groaned, sat up, and then plopped back into the seat with an exaggerated sigh. "I thought we would never get here. Hey, it's dark out. I must have slept for hours."

"Yep. Old Doyle and I have been keeping the world safe while you slept."

"Thanks. I guess."

He knew she was joking. He liked the teasing and sensed she did too.

She craned her neck. "Wow. Is that the duomo?"

Doyle turned around in his seat. "It is. An impressive bit of architecture, wouldn't you say?"

"It's all lacy and fairy-tale like."

"I believe they call the style Gothic."

The buildings surrounding the church struck Will as classically European. They were generally two to three stories tall with arches on the second stories and red-tiled roofs. After driving a lap around the pedestrian-only area, he decided to park a block over from the grand plaza.

They approached it warily, all banter between them gone, as if the car was a bubble of safety that burst the instant they opened the door. The plaza beneath their feet boasted stones in a gray and white geometric pattern. Will wondered if it was a chessboard, art, or some other random design. In the square, people were still milling about, which might mean that the church hadn't closed yet. Will had discovered that Europeans tended to start and end their days later than most Americans.

Close enough to see the cathedral's filigree, Will could understand why it had taken six centuries to build. A forest of open pinnacles and lofty spires were set upon delicate flying buttresses. The building was beyond ornate. It was intense. Each tall, arched window, for instance, had eight small statues surrounding the pane of glass. It would take him two years to sculpt just one.

"Hey, Doyle, will you stay outside and guard our backs?"

Surprise clouded Doyle's features for a moment. "Sure. No problem."

Doyle peeled off.

Will and Avril climbed the short stone steps and entered the marble church through the intricately carved gray doors. Just inside the vast space they stopped and took it all in. Will was struck by the devotion it had taken to make such a palace of divine splendor. Fifty-two columns held the ceiling aloft, as if each weekly marker held the prayers of thousands set in stone. The stained glass must be magnificent during the day.

Avril tugged at his sleeve and pointed to the floor. "It's what I told you about."

He hoped she'd washed her hands after the fries they'd eaten earlier; this particular Tony Barrister Gray Label indigo linen jacket had set him back a few hundred bucks. "Part of that sundial?"

"Yes, I think so."

She'd told him that the church, the largest in Italy, contained a gigantic sundial built in 1786 by astronomers of the Astronomical Observatory. Holes in the ceiling lit up areas on the floor at different times. At summer solstice, for instance, the ray lit up the gilded brass strip running from left to right. At long intervals, the strip was bordered by the twelve zodiac signs, which would be set alight at the appropriate time of year.

Will wondered about the symbolism of such a pagan artifact in a Catholic church, but that wasn't why they were here. The words of the quatrain rumbled in his head:

The duomo's architect
Pays homage to a night in July
With sacred signs of the zodiac
Of the first the penultimate strikes the mark but of the second take the last and the first of the twins

"I see it," he whispered. "How does it help us?"

"I am not sure yet."

"The problem is that it was built more than two hundred years too late. Any ideas about the night in July?"

"Both Cancer and Leo occur in July."

He walked over to the crab sign, Avril on his heels. The sea creature on the tile had two black claws above its head as if it was trying to clap. The nearby lion, which was inlaid cattycorner to a sketch of twin heads, sported a bushy mane and had one paw raised, and a tail that looked like it might twitch off the floor at any moment. The artistry was exceptional, but he didn't get where this was going.

He pointed between the crab and the lion. "Which one pays homage to a night in July?"

She shrunk in on herself. "I don't know."

He hadn't meant to make her feel bad. He said, "Maybe it's both. The clue mentions a 'first' and 'second.' Perhaps the first is Cancer and the second is Leo."

"Could be. I was thinking it was the architect's first and last name, though."

"Did you research him?"

She put her hands on her hips. "Someone interrupted me."

"Right. Let's sit down in a pew and I'll look it up."

"Fine."

They moved to the end of one of the old walnut pews. Tourists and churchgoers floated around them like butterflies, oblivious to their mission. None looked suspicious.

He grabbed his phone and researched architects for the Milan duomo.

"This can't be right," he said after a few minutes.

"What?"

"Look. Simone da Orsenigo was the first architect in 1387. But there is a page full of others who worked on this church. An entire page!"

She peered down at the screen. "What about before Nostradamus would have died?"

"A page and a half."

Folding her hands over her arms she leaned back and glanced up at the ceiling. "Is any one of them considered the dome's architect?"

"Well, in 1488, both Leonardo da Vinci and someone named Donato Bramante created models to design the central cupola in a competition, but Leonardo withdrew his submission later, so it's not him. Ludovico Sforza, whose name is a mouthful, is given credit for completing the octagonal cupola in 1510. They must have named the nearby castle after him."

"I suppose the timing could work," she said softly.

"Sort of. But the sundial part wasn't built until after Nostradamus was long dead. And it just doesn't feel right. There's no real reference to July here, and the original architect's name is in three parts. I think we're in the wrong spot."

"Sorry, it is my fault."

"Don't worry about it."

"That is easy for you to say. This whole thing is my doing. I feel like I have Monique's and Grandfather's blood on my hands."

He looked at her for a long moment and touched the scar on his chin. "I can understand that. It was my fault my mom died. I got this scar that day."

She put a hand to the scar on her neck and nodded once.

Taking a breath, she tilted her head back and peered up at the dome.

He sat back in the pew, at a loss for where to go next.

They sat that way for a few minutes. Still looking at the dome, Avril said, "I think that duomo reference points to Florence."

"I don't have a better plan, and it's just a few hours south. Let's get moving. I don't like spending too much time in one place."

CHAPTER 53

MAASTRICHT, THE NETHERLANDS
JANUARY 29, 1:37 A.M.

It was well after midnight and Sint Servaasklooster, the cobblestoned street that bordered the basilica, was devoid of traffic, pedestrian and otherwise. Still, nervous sweat made the back of Maddy's shirt damp. To compensate, she *listened*, quieting her mind to be ready for action.

Traffic buzzed a few streets away, and a talkative night bird called to a mate.

She and Bear wore nightclub black, which doubled as effective mission-ware. Tight-fitting leather gloves covered their prints. They'd also donned their custom-fit bone-conducting molar microphones to better communicate should they become separated.

She spoke into the mic now, softly. "You sure this is the best plan?"

"I am."

They'd gone over their options a few times since the director had dropped the schematics—and the bombshell about her mother being a CIA operative—in their laps. Unfortunately, there was no good way to access the crypt from the subway; the spaghetti-like mess of underground rail lines wasn't close enough to the church, and they didn't have any high-tech gear to tunnel through forty feet of bedrock. That left a frontal approach through the basilica.

Bear turned to the church door, which was about three feet wide and made of pine planks, and lay between two sets of rough-hewn stone walls that connected the buildings on either side of the street. Each held a larger arch for vehicles, and a smaller arch for pedestrians. The space in between the walls was secluded, and anyone walking their way would be easily heard.

The door handles were iron and god-only-knew how old. Bear pushed on the door, and then held a penlight to it. "Our usual tools aren't going to work on this."

"Why not?" She bent down. "Ah, I see. There's not even a lock."

"No. It's probably got a two-by-four on the other side, barricading entry."

"Seriously old school." She gently shoved the door; it didn't budge, and she swore. "But none of the other doors looked any easier to breach."

"I know."

They retreated.

"I thought Catholic churches were always unlocked." She pointed to a door four windows down the brick structure, before the next archway. "What about that one?"

"Let's look," he agreed.

The door had a saint or apostle statue above it, and was made of the same pine planks as the first door they'd tried. However, one side of the stone threshold was worn down from centuries of use, an iron plaque boasted the number '14,' and there were small see-through grates above the handles.

"What are those grates for?" she asked.

"No clue." He put his muscled shoulder into the door. "There's no bloody lock here either."

"Effective security. Maybe we'll give these low-tech tips to Will for the vineyard."

His teeth gleamed white for an instant.

"We need a plan C," he said.

"These are single-pane windows," she offered.

"Not a good option. Noise and attention are not our friends."

"Hmm. There's a skinny utility pipe running to the second floor."

"Might work for you. I'm too big." He scanned the area. "There!"

He walked over to where the stone wall met the building and shone the penlight on a wide drain pipe. Maddy joined him and put her hands on it, noting that there were metal straps attaching it to the bricks, and that there was enough room for her fingers to circle it. She tugged. "Seems sturdy."

Looking up, she saw that the pipe terminated next to three windows atop the archway wall.

Bear gestured. "Ladies first."

She shook her head at him and began to climb, making good progress as she pretended to be Spiderman. But it was awkward going, and her fingers and the mostly healed wound on her forearm began to ache. Soon she reached the highest point and moved onto the flat top of the stone wall.

Her location gave her a good vantage point and she looked up and down the street. All the buildings nearby were lightless, as if asleep for the night. "Coast is clear."

Bear hustled up, not even looking winded as he joined her. He was such a brute. At times like these, she was especially glad he was her man.

"You realize we just came up to the roof when we need to be down in the crypt," she said.

"I do, but getting access to the building was the hard part."

"Roof's pretty steep up here."

"It is. But I have an idea."

Using the drain pipe for balance, he reached over to one of the third-floor windows and pushed on it. When it gave a little, he pressed harder, until it opened. Stretching, he got one foot on the sill, and then swung inside. Maddy followed.

They landed inside an industrial-looking bathroom, with a single stall and standard porcelain wall sink. Maddy dusted off her gloved hands on her pants and donned a balaclava to hide her features should they be seen. Bear did the same after blowing a small bubble with his gum and grinning. He loved the cloak-and-dagger part of their job. It was not her favorite, though, and she broke out in a full-body sweat.

They needed to get to ground level, and behind the altar. Bear led the way, into the dark hallway, down a set of creaky stairs, and into the back of the main sanctuary. They expected no resistance, as the schematic had shown them that priests and nuns slept in a building behind the one that housed the relics. Nevertheless, they crept silently and used the penlight only when necessary.

Her mom had taken them to church when they were little. While she and Bear skirted the side wall, Maddy shook her head in disbelief that her mother had been an operative. That revelation spawned a host of unanswered questions. They'd had no opportunity to connect with Will, and she wondered what he was thinking. And should they tell Bella, who still didn't know the full story about what they did? Did Aunt Carole know what her sister had been up to while she lived in France? How deep had her mom's cover been? Was the unplanned love child, Maddy's half sibling, still alive?

There wasn't much to peruse in the sparse file, and Maddy had spent most of her time studying the photograph. She didn't have many pictures of her mom, much less one where she was a fresh-faced young woman, just out of college. The file hadn't said why or how she'd been recruited. The biggest unanswered question was which foreign power had discovered her mom was undercover.

Bear stopped suddenly and she bumped into his back. She needed to stay focused. They were at the door behind the altar. He turned the knob slowly, and then stepped through when it swung open. It creaked.

A nightlight glowed, bathing the new room in ghostly light. She tensed for an encounter.

There was a plain table in the center of the space, and four chairs around it. A countertop ran the length of one wall with a sink. On another wall, an open closet held ceremonial frocks on hangers. The room was empty, and she breathed a little easier.

The stone wall in back held another broad door bound with iron. It looked promising, and was even more so when it opened to a set of descending stairs. They took them silently, until the stairs reversed left at a small landing. The smell of damp earth enveloped them. Finally, the stairway ended in a cavernous room.

They'd both studied the schematic, so Maddy knew there were four crypts down here. Using the penlight, they passed several niches, and continued on until they went through an arched opening straight ahead. A small gate proved no obstacle.

A stone tomb lay to the left, taking up the bulk of the room. It and the rock walls were the color of dried blood. The sarcophagus lay on a rock foundation and had a four-inch-thick lid covering the resting place of the duke.

What they'd come for, however, was above the lid. Mentally, she recalled the relevant part of the quatrain: *Above his sarcophagus mark the second line eleven fifteen and seven times.*

Words were chiseled into the wall with dots as separators. She shivered as she studied them:

SEPVLCRVM
KAROLI * COMITIS * GENEROSE * STIRPIS
FILII * LOTHOVICHI * FRATRIS * LOTHARII
FRANCOVRM * REGVM * ANNO * DOM MI

"What's it mean?" she asked.

Bear put his hand up as if to touch the words. He hesitated, glancing her way. "I have absolutely no idea."

CHAPTER 54

Bear touched the engraved words over the sarcophagus with reverence. The stone was cool to the touch. "I don't know what it means, but it's pretty cool."

"Stop geeking out," Maddy scolded, but without any heat. "We need to figure it out and leave before somebody finds us down here."

Still, he was grinning from ear to ear. Since he'd been young, he'd been in love with history. Everything from dinosaurs, pyramids, and medieval knights in shining armor to real-life kings and queens. He'd loved his subscription to *National Geographic* and still watched the History Channel religiously. Right here, right now, he was standing next to the crypt of a man who had once claimed to be the French king.

What a story, too! Charles, brother of King Lothair, had claimed the king's wife was having an affair with a bishop. The queen was exonerated, but the accusation caused a mega rift between the two brothers. Charles fled to Germany, where his cousin Otto ruled. At one point, Otto and Charles invaded France, and anointed Charles as king, but they were eventually forced back to Germany by the king and Hugh Capet.

Maddy elbowed him. "Seriously. Stop the King Arthur fantasy. What does it mean to mark something? The quatrain said above his sarcophagus mark the second line eleven, fifteen, and seven times."

He stared at the words of the second line. "It's in Latin. Are we supposed to get the English equivalent?"

"I don't know. 'Anno' in the fourth line is the only word I recognize. It means 'year.' And why is the order eleven, fifteen, and seven, and not seven, eleven, and fifteen?"

He popped his knuckles. "Hard to say. Maybe it's an important order. Is that a G or a C? *Cenerose* or *generose*?"

Maddy tugged at her balaclava. "I can't tell. What position is it in?"

His balaclava itched, too. "Fourteen, unless those dots in between mean something."

"Maybe this clue is about the letters, not the words."

He looked around, hesitant to leave. "You could be right. Let's count them." He used his finger. "T is in the eleventh position." He kept going. "E is fifteen." Going back to the beginning he counted out seven spaces. "C."

"TEC?"

"Yeah."

"That doesn't help." She shook her head. "I say we get some pics and get the hell out of here. Study it later from the comfort of our coffin-esque boat cabin."

"Sounds smart," he agreed.

She pulled a phone from her pocket and snapped some images of the entire crypt, focusing on the inscription. He studied the chiseled words. LOTHARII was pretty close to Lothair, the name of Charles's brother. Maybe FRATIS meant brother, like brotherhood, or fraternity. Did all that matter, though, when they were to focus on the second line?

Maddy put the phone away. "Okay, let's leave."

He nodded, moving away using the penlight but wishing he could lead with his weapon, which felt more natural. Except they were in a church and he'd probably burn in hell for even breaking in. The last thing he wanted to do was harm a man of God.

They passed the other crypts and swiftly moved up the stairs. The area behind the altar smelled of beeswax and was still empty.

They hugged the shadows on their way toward the back of the church while Bear continued mulling over the puzzle. KAROLI * COMITIS * GENEROSE * STIRPIS. Eleven, fifteen, and seven.

He tried translating the Latin. "Carole commits generous stripes." No, that couldn't be it. TEC then. He'd need to study the pictures Maddy had taken, but was starting to think TEC was the clue. But what did it mean? They hit the back of the church and his nostrils caught the memory of incense. What was old Nostradamus up to with this setup? Why not just tell his offspring where the medallion was located? Bear chewed his gum thoughtfully as they sped up the stairs toward their window escape.

Maybe Nostradamus didn't think his kids should have the power of knowing the future. Bear was sure his and Maddy's kids would be angels, but he'd also known his fair share of little demons. That might explain this secretive treasure hunt. It wouldn't be the first time an important man or woman had wanted to disinherit their progeny. And if the guy was for real and truly had a recipe for success that could be replicated, maybe he'd seen a vision that had scared him away from passing his secrets to his descendants directly. That would make sense.

Bear poked his head out of the window and glanced up and down the street below. Empty. But his gut told him it wouldn't be long before the enemy caught a whiff of their trail.

CHAPTER 55

Back on the river boat, Maddy stared at the computer screen. Like all the VanOps safe houses she'd seen, this one had a hidden computer room. After a too-short sleep and a shower, she'd slipped into the closet-sized space located near the engine and fired up the machine to look at their only prize from last night's prowl around the basilica.

As she downloaded the pics of the inscriptions, she was distracted by a mental image of the glass-eyed librarian in Marseille glaring at them through the stacks. Jags was still struggling to bring up much data on Seymore's background. However, this computer was unattached to the hacked DoD network, and would hopefully allow Maddy to produce material on the man.

Before joining VanOps, Maddy had been a computer application designer and a part-time aikido instructor. The interconnectedness of data and applications fascinated her. Like shiny silver threads spun from a giant spider, the web part of "world wide web" made for a great visual. She'd never been a hacker, at least not until her VanOps training commenced, but with her degree and background in tech, she had sailed through those modules. She hated to admit it, but that had been easier than learning to shoot her firearm.

Her fingers flew across the keyboard as she used password-hacking programs to break into the human resources database at the Marseille Library. It didn't take long to find him. Henri Seymore had worked there for over thirty years. It seemed the library never updated their employee photographs, because Seymore's hiring picture showed a curly-haired, clean-shaven young man. The glass eye was obvious, even then, but he'd lost his hair in the intervening years. The database was full of performance information. It seemed he was a model employee.

More interesting than his annual reviews, though, was a stored resume from his initial job application. It contained a reference to a former career in the French army.

Maddy sat back in her chair. *Former French military.*

She'd left the door open and heard Bear walking down the hall. Looking over her shoulder, she smiled at him. He wore a short-sleeved white T-shirt, even in the cold weather, and the lightning scars on his forearms stood out because he was carrying two cups of coffee. One steaming, his probably iced.

Grateful, she reached for the hot one.

He pulled back and offered his lips. "It'll cost you a kiss."

His mouth was hard to resist. She gave in.

Before she got lost in their passion, he pulled back. Probably a good thing. Work to do.

Bear handed her the hot coffee with a grin. "How's it going? Any progress on the Latin?"

She grimaced, having forgotten she was supposed to translate. "I'm not sure we need to do that. We have the three letters, TEC. I've been tracking down more information on that librarian from Marseille."

"The one you think called in the posse who attacked us at the marina?"

"Bingo. His behavior was menacing, and that glass eye matched what the au pair told us about the kidnappers."

"You're not obsessing over the possible murder of your mother, are you?"

She gave him a don't-mess-with-me look. "I just want to know the players we're up against. Seymore is one of them."

He put his hands up in mock surrender. "Fine, we can look at the Latin in a minute. What have you found out?"

She sipped her coffee. It was almost too hot, but strong and black. "He's been working at the library for thirty years. Before that he worked for the French military."

Bear's eyebrows shot up. "Maybe he's doing some side work?"

"That was my next stop. To follow the money trail."

"Don't let me stop you."

Maddy turned her attention back to the keyboard. She plugged in some parameters to search French banks for names similar to Henri Seymore or any accounts with his fifteen-digit national identification number. "This might take a minute. Want me to translate that inscription while we're waiting?"

"Sure."

She pulled up a translation application and plugged in the words from the crypt:

SEPVLCRVM
KAROLI * COMITIS * CENEROSE * STIRPIS
FILII * LOTHOVICHI * FRATRIS * LOTHARII
FRANCOVRM * REGVM * ANNO * DOM MI

It spit back:

Grave
Charles Earl CENEROSE Blood
Son Louis IV Brother Lothair
FRANCOVRM King Year Lord

"It doesn't like a couple of those words," she said.

"Try a G instead of a C on that first one."

She did. "Ah, that translates to generous."

"Makes more sense. What about FRANCOVRM? Can you replace the V with a U?"

"That brings back Frankcourt."

He leaned back on the doorframe. "Maybe it's just Frank, like a Frank king."

"Could be. That gives us:
Grave
Charles Earl Generous Blood
Son Louis IV Brother Lothair
Frank King Year Lord."

She pulled her ponytail over her shoulder. "Basically, it's the grave of Charles of the generous blood. Louis and Lothair are his brother and father, right?"

Using his mouth, Bear grabbed an ice cube from his cup. His favorite beverage was iced sweet tea, but it was apparent he'd had to settle for coffee here. "Yes."

"I still think we need to focus on letters in the second line."

"TEC doesn't mean much."

"Then maybe we should start with the end in mind. I think he said . . . wait, hold on . . ." She pulled up a note on her phone. "Right, here it is:

Having collected the parts of the enigma
Take the four in reverse order then twelve steps back in time
Once you know the answer
Look for the medallion deep inside the Oracle's icy crown

That means TEC is just a part of the enigma and we're trying to find the Oracle's icy crown. Have any ideas on an oracle? Or icy crown?"

He shook his head. "None."

"Yeah, me neither."

Bear scowled. "Did those programs return anything on Seymore?"

She switched screens and blew out an annoyed breath. "No."

"Let's have Jags find someone who can dig deeper. My gut says we need to get moving." He peeled away from the doorway and headed off down the narrow hall. "I have some ideas on the fourth quatrain."

"Oh? You've figured out the 'sanctuary of new citizens?'"
He spoke over his shoulder. "I'll fill you in on the road."

CHAPTER 56

Inside the Duomo Café, Will's phone buzzed with the promised text message from Bear containing the Latin inscription they'd found above the sarcophagus. Will would look at it later. The lovebirds were encouraged by their success, and he wished he had something equally exciting to report. So far, *nada*.

He joined Doyle and Avril in the street adjacent to Brunelleschi's Dome, which was the highest part of Cattedrale di Santa Maria del Fiore, known in English as Cathedral of Saint Mary of the Flower or simply the duomo. He liked the sound of the Italian version better. All the nearby buildings had a classic Italian feel. He loved this city.

Had his mother ever been to Florence on one of her operations? How odd that she'd been in Rome at one point. Had her trip there been related to the Hourglass mission?

Will nudged Avril. "You sure you're old enough to drink coffee?"

She tossed her dark mane over her shoulder. "I am French. I was bottle-fed lattes."

Will laughed. "Let's go find homage to a night in July."

They set off down the street. The church that housed the famous dome seemed drab in comparison to the Gothic monument in Milan, or maybe it was just the overcast sky. This house of the Lord had far fewer windows, and other than the dome above, was a study in arches and green rectangles. No filigree or flying buttresses here.

Avril stopped dead in her tracks. "Oh my god, the line to get in is around the block!"

Will shrugged. "Good things come to those who wait."

"But I still don't have my phone," she whined. "I have not been able to check TikTok in days."

"Guess you'll have to entertain yourself people-watching like we did in the stone ages."

"Fine."

She crossed her arms over her jacket and hopped from foot to foot to stay warm. Eventually, she pulled her brown journal from her satchel and started to sketch zodiac signs and medallions of different shapes and sizes.

After they joined the queue, Will and Doyle sipped their coffees and watched the crowd, but not for entertainment. At one point, Will's hackles rose when two men on Vespa motorbikes crept around the block, but they never slowed, and Will's shoulders relaxed when they moved on.

A half an hour later the three of them were finally admitted into the church through the central set of bronze doors.

As he moved through the incongruous metal detector, Will was surprised to see no pews. There were a few chairs set up near the altar, but the vast space looked more like an empty museum than a house of worship. The relatively plain stone columns were huge, and the floor showed off a lovely collection of marble tile designs. People crowded the space. To the far right, a short man in a gray jacket gave spectators a tour. Along the left wall, a woman in a black robe stood motionless in front of a statue, head bowed.

Without any discussion, they all headed for the dome.

Once they were underneath the architectural marvel, Will craned his neck up. Not only was it an impressive feat of engineering for its time, it was also pleasing to the eye. Above the dome's round stained-glass windows were four rows of religious paintings, topped by a fifth row painted as if it were a playhouse balustrade with onlookers gazing down at all the angels, apostles, and saints.

Even the artist considered life to be theater, Will thought.

"It's keen," Doyle said. "But I'm not getting any reference to July."

"Nor am I," Will replied. "Maybe we can find a local, or a historian."

They ambled toward the doors, but Avril tapped Will's arm.

"What about that tour guide?" she asked. "He is done with his group."

It was true. The gaggle was filing out the door, and the guide was collecting tips with an exhausted smile.

"You two wait here."

Without waiting for a reply, Will made a beeline for the guide. Up close, the gray jacket looked worn and had a stain on the right pocket.

"Excuse me," he said in Italian once the last tourist had departed.

The man turned bloodshot eyes the color of mud toward Will. "I'm done for the day. It's time for a drink."

Will was startled, but persevered. "We're looking for buildings designed by this dome's architect. Brunelleschi, right?"

The set of the middle-aged guide's jaw said the last thing he wanted to do was answer more questions. "I hate Americans. Plus, I only do tours for the church here."

Will's blood pressure thundered in his ears. "But there are other buildings?"

"I don't know. Bugger off." The guide turned and stalked out of the church.

Grumbling under his breath, Will rejoined the others. "He didn't know."

"Looked like a friendly chap." Doyle idly moved his watch strap around his wrist. "I suppose we could find a library."

Avril pointed. "Why don't I go ask that old woman? She looks like she's lived in this town since Nostradamus was alive."

"Be nice," Will chided. "Do you speak Italian?"

"Not much."

"I'll go then."

He marched over to the stooped old woman, who was parked in front of a chiseled statue, her head bent, her hands folded in the universal sign of prayer. She was shorter than average, and her aged face was heavily lined. Will tapped his toes as he waited for the supplications to cease. The way his day was going, she'd probably spit on him.

Finally, the woman made the sign of the cross. She jumped back an inch when she saw Will.

"I'm sorry," he said in Italian, giving her his most winsome smile. "I was struck by the statue. Could you tell me about it?"

"Saint Reparta?" The woman's voice was deep, and it cracked with age.

"Is that who it is? What's her story?"

She looked back at the statue, face softening. "She was a young woman, under twenty, when she was tortured and killed for her faith. They tried to burn her alive, but she was saved by rain. She refused to turn from her conviction even after being forced to drink boiling pitch, so they chopped off her head. Until the High Middle Ages, she was the patroness of Florence. I come here and talk to her whenever I've had a bad day. It gives me perspective."

"Have you lived here your whole life?"

She gave him a Mona Lisa smile. "I have. All eighty-four years."

He dropped a bill into the offering box at the base of the saint's statue. "Perhaps you could help me. I'm seeking buildings designed by Brunelleschi. Do you know of any others?"

She cocked her head. "My mother was a sculptor and a huge fan of his work. I believe he designed a home for orphans called Ospedale degli Innocenti, the white-walled Basilica of San Lorenzo, the Basilica of Santo Spirito, and the small Pazzi Chapel. Let's see. What else? There's the octagonal Santa Maria degli Angeli, which I really love, and of course this church. Did you know there's a stairway between the inner and outer domes? I got to see it once when I was a girl."

He nodded his thanks. "That's so very helpful. Would you happen to know if any of them pay homage to a night in July?"

She squinted and tilted her chin. "My mother considered the Pazzi Chapel to be the pinnacle of Brunelleschi's career. It has a dome fresco half painted with signs of the zodiac that many scholars believe honors the consecration of the high altar below it, which happened in July in the early fourteen hundreds."

"How'd you remember that it happened in July?"

"July ninth was my mother's birthday. A special day."

He put another bill in the offering box. "You're quite kind."

"Would you like me to walk you there?"

"Thank you, but no. I can find it from here."

Plus, he didn't want to put such a caring old woman in harm's way if trouble found them any time soon.

CHAPTER 57

Over the years, Bear had found his gut to be a fairly accurate barometer of brewing trouble. This morning, he felt the pressure of needing to move, and fast. Within an hour of deciding to leave the floating safe house, Bear had told Jags where they were headed and asked her to find someone to explore the finances of Henri Seymore.

As soon as they left the boat, they jumped in the midnight-black Porsche Cayenne coupe the director had left. Bear felt mission-sharp and ready to hit the road.

From the passenger seat, Maddy waved her hand in front of her nose. "God, this car smells like stale cigarette smoke. Can you tell me now where we're going?"

"Aachen first."

"That has to be the name of a German town."

"It is."

She played around with the radio buttons and found a nineties rock station. "Okay, why there?"

"I want to pick up the autobahn."

"Aha. We must be heading somewhere fast."

He gunned the engine, accelerating around a beige truck belching diesel smoke in the passenger lane. "The director said to use speed and my gut is telling me we need to get goin'."

She reached for her phone. "If you tell me our destination, I'll check the fastest route."

Feeling ornery, he reached over and grabbed her hand. "It's somewhere romantic."

She put the phone down, clearly wanting to play along. "We've already been to the south of France. Hmm, the fjords of Norway?"

He shook his head.

She touched a contemplative finger to her lips. "Paris?"

"Nope."

"Give me a hint."

Bear chewed on the icy remains of his coffee. "You already have a clue. That entire fourth quatrain."

"You're intolerable!" She chuckled and pulled out her phone. "Fine. I've been so focused on the 'TEC' result from the last one, and researching our enemy, that I've failed to memorize that quatrain. Ah, here it is:

South, to the first sanctuary of new citizens

Temple of Jupiter and Juno

The famed sculptor and architect makes his marks in mud

The last letter of the founder is placed behind the mountainous middle

At least I can say we're probably headed south."

"That's a good guess." He adjusted the rearview mirror to better see the Ferrari acting like a tail behind them. Bear's heart rate ticked up. "What about the rest?"

"No idea. But let's see if keyword 'sanctuary of new citizens' does anything for me." She typed and swiped.

"Any results?"

She pursed her lips. "No. Just a bunch of articles about cities in the US that offer sanctuary for immigrants."

"Hmm. Tricky."

"Nothing about new citizens either."

"How about those temples?"

"Let's see." She paused. "This is more promising."

His head swiveled as he checked the mirrors. "Oh?"

"Looks like there was a temple to Juno Moneta in the center of Rome. Here's a fun tangent—they minted coins next to the temple and Moneta spawned the word 'money.'"

"Look out. You'll become a history buff next."

She whacked him with her left hand. "Stop."

"Do they know where that temple stood?"

She read further. "No. Its location is a bit of an enigma. However, looks like all scholars agree it was on the summit of a hill."

The drab landscape rushing by was cloaked in winter gray. Bear's eyes flicked to the rearview mirror again. "Okay, what about the temple of Jupiter?"

"Sorry to interrupt, but are we being followed? You keep checking the mirrors."

"Maybe. There's a baby-blue Ferrari lurking back there."

"Comforting. Glad the director left us a fast car, but against a Ferrari?"

"Could get interesting."

"Guess you'll tell me when to worry, so let's see." She flipped through some more internet pages. "Here we go! The temple of Jupiter was also in Rome. On Capitoline Hill."

He nodded. "It was the most important temple in ancient Rome. Probably built in the sixth century BCE."

"You knew this all along?"

"Yeah. Jupiter was the special guardian god of Rome, so most victory marches ended on top of Capitoline Hill. Winning generals would make sacrifices at the temple to thank Jupiter for their luck in battle."

"What's the part about new citizens?"

"I'm not exactly sure, but being a citizen in Rome was a big deal. Voting, holding property, making contracts, that type of thing."

She eyed him sideways. "Were women citizens?"

"Um. From what I recall, yes . . ." He trailed off.

"I feel a 'but' coming on."

"But they had no rights."

She slammed her hand on her thigh. "That's a cockamamie bunch of shit."

"It was, yes," he quickly agreed.

"Why do you think my mom visited Italy? Now that we know she was an operative, it puts that visit in a different light."

Bear visualized the card, with its memento mori mosaic of a skeleton and arcane message to remember death. A chill ran up his spine. "Remind me. Was there a date on the postcard?"

"No."

"Doesn't help us much then, does it?"

"I wonder if Aunt Carole knows anything. Could have simply been a holiday."

"Think your aunt is taking phone calls yet?"

"I don't know. She wasn't before we left. And I have to go through my sister, the ten-ton gorilla."

"I hope you and Bella make up at some point."

"Me too. But she's still mad we can't tell her about our work."

"Even though it's for her own good?"

"Yes. I suppose I might be upset too," she admitted. "Think we should fill her in about Mom?"

"That's up to you. It might be a way to thaw your relationship, though."

"I'll think about it." She changed the subject. "Meanwhile, I guess we're going to romantic Rome. Shall I check the directions?"

He downshifted and sped around a corner. "Sure."

She pulled up a map app. "It'll take us about ten hours to get to Italy. Looks like after crossing the German border near Aachen, we head just a little north to stay on the autobahn through Cologne, then we drive almost due south. We hit Frankfurt, Wurzburg, Stuttgart, and that'll take us all the way to Switzerland. We'll cut through the heart of army-knife country, and be in Milan in a few hours after slicing through the Swiss border."

He smiled at all the knife references. "If I remember correctly, Florence is on the way to Rome. Should we hook up with Will?"

"Let me check in with them and see."

"Okay. Just hold on tight for a minute. I'm going to see if I can lose our friends back there."

CHAPTER 58

Flanked by the two operatives, Avril walked through the quiet courtyard and down the crushed stone path toward the portico of the Pazzi Chapel. The soles of their shoes crunched on the gravel and a crow cawed in the distance. The air felt heavy, like it was going to rain.

To their left was a stone church behind an arched walkway, and to the right, the curves of another building. Probably where the priests abused the altar boys, she thought. The silence sent a chill up her spine.

She glanced between Will and Doyle, both stone-faced as they bookended her journey toward the Renaissance chapel. Were they guarding her to keep her safe? Or was she a prisoner? It was rather hard to tell.

They probably just wanted the formula, and then she'd end up in an orphanage in Paris.

It all seemed surreal, this outing with the two men. Like a dream, or a holiday. She'd wake up and go back home, and Monique would be laughing, her blonde head bobbing and green eyes smiling as she made roasted chicken for dinner.

Avril touched the necklace at her neck for comfort. It was from her grandmother, whom she'd never met. Monique had been the mother Avril had never had.

A scraping sound near the stone church caused both men to stop and reach for their weapons. After a moment, they relaxed and kept moving.

Avril would have to worry about the orphanage later. Right now, she needed to stay alive.

At the end of the long courtyard, they walked under the archway and onto the chapel's columned porch. A Greek-looking triangle decorated the top of the door frame.

Will motioned her forward. "Ladies first."

Doyle put a hand on her arm. "Wait, let me clear the space."

All of this watching for bad guys was getting on her nerves.

"Good idea," Will replied, turning to scout the courtyard.

Thirty seconds after Doyle entered the sacred space, he pulled the door back open. "Clear. Place is empty and there's nowhere to hide." As they entered, Doyle stayed rooted. "I'll keep an eye out."

The chapel was small and square, maybe twenty by twenty meters, but well proportioned. Her eyes were drawn up, to the dome above their heads. In contrast to the duomo, this cupola was white, with ribbing and portholes between each rib. At eye level, three of the four walls were mostly arches adorned with simple designs. She walked toward the fourth wall. Three wide stairs led to a stone altar in a niche below a stained-glass window. Above was a cupola. Half was painted a gray-blue color, but the other half held zodiac symbols.

She tugged at Will's sleeve and pointed. "There it is! See?"

He looked up.

Just then, Doyle yelled, "We have company!"

Before she could react, Will grabbed her elbow and pulled her toward the door.

She heard a *whomp*, and Doyle swore.

Her heart began to thump wildly. She felt like a scared rabbit, too terrified to move.

Will put his body in front of hers, a six-inch knife appearing in each of his hands. The sight made her stiffen.

When he reached the door, it jerked open and he was yanked out by his shoulders. A man wearing a knitted cap and sunglasses slipped inside and behind her. Before she could scream, he pressed a cold blade against the scar on the side of her throat.

CHAPTER 59

Will was yanked out of the Pazzi Chapel and thrown forward, onto the gravel walkway. As soon as he stopped rolling, he threw the blade in his right hand toward the man standing in the doorway just as the man's gun popped.

Will logrolled into the grass. Tufts of smoke rose from the pebbles where he'd been an instant before. A rock chip sliced across his temple, burning.

The shooter fell back and hit his head on the side of the chapel, a knife in his chest. On the porch, Doyle and another man traded punches. Will needed to rescue Avril. He'd felt another attacker sweep by him as he'd been tossed out of the church.

Switching his spare knife to his dominant hand, he vaulted the low stone railing, and stabbed Doyle's attacker in the back of his upper thigh. The man yelped and lost his hold on Doyle, who collapsed. After pulling the knife, Will put his hands under the man's arms and thrust the human shield through the door, where Avril was struggling in the arms of a man with a cap and sunglasses. Will stabbed his blade into the man's face, shattering the glasses and nailing an eye. The stricken man dropped his dagger from Avril's neck to clutch at his face before he fell to the floor, dead.

Will released his hold on the man he'd used as armor. As the bastard slunk to the floor, Will hit him in the back of the neck to knock him unconscious, collected his knife from the lifeless fellow, and then checked both men for ID. They had no passports, no wallet, nothing. Not even a phone.

For an instant, he stared at the one who was still breathing, considering how to interrogate him. It was a tremendous opportunity to gather intel. However, although information would be useful, it simply wasn't practical to drag the man around town and this place could be overrun with more of the enemy, or the police, at any moment.

He grabbed Avril by the arm and pulled her out the door. He hoped he wouldn't regret not killing the surviving attacker.

She tugged his hand and pointed at his face. "You're bleeding."

He swiped at it and his fingers came away bloody. "It's not bad. I'll deal with it later."

On the porch, Doyle was staggering to his feet. Stopping only to seize his other blade from the chest of the first man, Will ran for the far end of the courtyard, holding Avril's hand. The crunching sound of feet behind him provided reassurance that his wingman was at his back.

Will realized he'd come to count on Doyle. Yes, he was different than his brother, Quinn, but Doyle had redeemable qualities. For one thing, that big, attentive brain of his had just given them a lifesaving warning, and he was no slacker in a fight.

Once outside, they moderated into a walk, heading left, and then strode against traffic up a one-way alley. No one pursued them. Avril was shaking, so he put his arm around her as they headed away from the scene of the assault.

Blood dripped down the side of his cheek. He grabbed a paper napkin from a street vendor and used it to clean his face and put pressure on the wound.

They passed a pizza joint and several apartment buildings. They needed a place to stop, but he didn't want to head into a restaurant. Avril's breathing came in ragged gasps and he told her to breathe from her abdomen. He continued to watch for signs of pursuit. The end of the alley opened into a wider street and again they took a left. That led them across a bridge and into a warren of narrow streets. They went into several stores, bought different jackets, and left at different times in an attempt to confuse any satellite watchers.

Finally, he spied a small hotel. They booked a room in the pensione and climbed a narrow staircase. It held a queen bed and a patterned navy-blue couch, and had a shared bathroom down the hall.

Doyle dropped onto the couch, Avril sat on the bed, eyes still wide, and Will walked to the window to check the street. They should be safe here, for now, even if they needed to take turns at a watch.

Telling his heart rate to slow, he turned to Avril. "Are you okay?"

She put a hand to her throat. "I have always wanted surgery to remove these scars, but not that way."

Unsure how to respond, he let that comment pass, instead walking over to turn her head to the side. "No blood. I'm sorry you had to experience that. We let you down and I apologize."

"I'm so sorry, lass," Doyle echoed. "They were on me before I could stop them."

"No." Her head swiveled between the men. "You saved my life. It is my fault you were injured!"

"Don't be silly." Will grunted. "It's our job. It shouldn't have come to that." He turned to Doyle. "Where did they come from?"

"The church. They must've been hiding there, behind the rock wall, waiting for us."

Will's eyes narrowed. "Perfect place for an ambush."

"I'll say," Doyle agreed. "Quiet and isolated. But how'd they know we'd be there?"

Will turned his eyes back to the street; things still seemed quiet. "That's what I'm wondering. We've been compromised somehow, which raises all sorts of questions about our adversary."

Avril's chest had finally stopped heaving. "What do you mean?"

"Our communications system is encrypted using the best software in the world. Either they've hacked it, we've been tracked somehow, or there's a mole in our midst."

CHAPTER 60

The gray hues of dusk deepened into the black tones of a rainy winter evening. After leaving the grocery store, Maddy drove the Porsche coupe back onto the wet highway. "I can't believe we outran the Ferrari. Think we lost them for good?"

"Hard to say," Bear replied. "They could have just needed to refuel."

"Even though dinner at that fancy place on the river would have been nice, I'm glad we got a bathroom break and some food." She stuck a carrot in her mouth. "And it's even my turn to drive before we hit some of those switchbacks in the Alps. Maybe I should play the lottery."

"I wouldn't celebrate too early."

"Agreed. That text from Will that they were attacked makes me worry."

Bear took a bite out of a prepackaged turkey sandwich. "Worry that Seymore and his gang are on our tail in a baby-blue civilian race car?"

"Exactly," she agreed. Pushing the accelerator to the floor, she patted the steering wheel. "At least our ride has some juice."

He smiled. "It does. Handles well too."

"Let's just hope the snow holds off."

"True. It's built for speed, not the white stuff."

After a minute of driving, she said, "Swiss countryside is lovely, but we can't see much of it now that it's dark. Plus, it's a decent hour back in California, and Will was okay with telling Bella about Mom. We really need to hear what Aunt Carole knows about that postcard. Shall we give sis a ring?"

"Why not?"

Intellectually, Maddy knew calling was a good idea, but her gut clenched into a fistful of tiny knots anyway. Just over a year ago, she and Bella had a blow-out fight at her loft in San Francisco, and the aftershocks lingered on both sides.

"Let's use your phone on speaker." She smiled grimly. "She'll pick up for you."

Bella answered on the third ring. "Oh my god, Bear, is Maddy okay?"

Maddy's shoulders relaxed. It was a good start. "I'm here, Bella."

"Oh." Bella's tone turned icy. "I thought maybe you were dead."

"Not yet." Maddy checked her mirrors. "Could happen later today, though." Rain began to spatter the windshield and Maddy turned on the wipers.

"What do you want?" Bella asked. "I'm getting these kids fed and it's the usual whirlwind of not wanting to get dressed for school. You'd think the toothbrush was used to clean the toilet the way they avoid it."

Is there a way to break this news gently? Maddy thought not. "Bella, Mom was an operative for the CIA."

The sound of a breaking dish, perhaps a cereal bowl, came through the speaker phone. Maddy and Bear made eye contact and both chuckled softly.

Bella's voice spiked two octaves higher. "Wait! What?"

Maddy winced. "Bella, I know you don't trust me—"

"Damn right!"

"Just listen a moment, okay?" Maddy paused to gather her thoughts. "I can't tell you how we found out, but information has come to our attention—"

Bella interrupted. "Our? Will thinks this, too?"

"He does." Maddy forged ahead. "We've learned that Mom worked for the CIA, undercover, during the seventies. This would have been a good couple of years before Will and I were born."

"You're pulling my leg. It's not even April Fool's Day."

A shadowed alpine lake rushed by on their left. "It's not and I'm not."

"You have to be. Mom wasn't a sneaky liar."

Maddy tried to ignore the gut punch, but the knots drew tighter. "She died when we were six. You were three. We know hardly anything from before she met Dad, and with him gone, we have no one to ask."

"We could ask Aunt Carole."

Maddy pumped her fist, but decided to work her sister into the idea a little more. "I'm not sure that's a good idea."

"Why? She'd know."

"Is she feeling well enough to chat about something like that?"

"I think so. Yesterday was a pretty good day. She should be getting out of the skilled nursing facility in less than a week. We've got a room prepared for her here."

Maddy ground her teeth.

The highway in Switzerland was a divided four-lane affair. In this section, sharp cliffs squeezed either side of the road. Maddy could sense the conversation balanced on a similar precarious edge. "Why don't we discuss that when we get back?"

"When exactly will that be?"

"Fair point," Maddy acknowledged. She took a deep breath. "Bella, *for your own protection*, we can't discuss our work. For that, I am truly and deeply sorry. What I can tell you is that some things run in the family. Do you understand?"

That was as close to admitting they worked for VanOps as Maddy could come.

Bella was silent for a long minute. "Apology under consideration."

"That's all I can ask."

Bella took a breath. "I'm heading over to visit Auntie for lunch in a few hours. Want me to pick her brain about Mom?"

"That would be fantastic. And if she could give us a call, it would be even better."

"I'll mention it."

"Thanks, Bella." Maddy looked in her rearview and saw the blue Ferrari was back and closing in fast. Bear tugged at her elbow, signaling they needed to ring off. "Hey, Bella?"

"Yeah?"

Maddy's eyes began to water. "If I do die today, know that I love you." Before Bella had time to respond, Maddy added, "Gotta go."

Bear hung up and Maddy downshifted into the coming turn.

CHAPTER 61

FLORENCE, ITALY
5:30 P.M.

Three steps. Turn. Three steps. Turn.

Feeling like a caged animal, Will paced in front of the window of the pensione. Dread gnawed at his gut. He hated failing at anything, and this afternoon's debacle at the Pazzi Chapel made him feel like the mission was spinning out of control. There were way too many questions, ranging from his mother's possible covert activities to how the enemy was tracking them. Worse, Avril was getting on his nerves.

She sat with her back to the wall on the bed, knees hunched to her chest. "Based on everything we have researched, I think the answer to this quatrain is the name of the architect."

Doyle sat on the navy-blue couch, stretching his back. "But it talks about twins, and the zodiac. Surely it's got something to do with Gemini."

Will had the quatrain memorized by now and repeated it.

"The duomo's architect
Pays homage to a night in July
With sacred signs of the zodiac
Of the first the penultimate strikes the mark but of the second take the last and the first of the twins."

He looked at Avril. "You have to admit, he has a point."

She pounded her palm on the bed. "No! I disagree. You are not listening."

Will swung his flashlight around his finger. "I think it's either the name of the chapel or there's a clue we missed."

"Oh, come on," she said. "Remember, the chapel was commissioned to Brunelleschi by Andrea de' Pazzi in 1429. It has to be the architect, Filippo Brunelleschi, and the clue is PIE. PIE! The twins are the two E's in his last name." Her face was flushed with anger. "If it's the Pazzi Chapel it would be ZLZ. Few words have that many Z's."

Doyle took his hair down and retied his topknot. "If it's Cancer, which happens in the beginning of July, and Gemini, it would be EIG."

Will threw up his hands. "I need to get back in there."

Avril untucked her legs and dangled them over the side of the bed. "If we can figure this out, you will not be hurt again. I want to come with you."

He pursed his lips. "Absolutely not. You're going to stay here with Mr. Samurai." He looked at Doyle and pointed to the topknot. "Why do you wear that anyway? No offense. Just curious."

"Makes a great disguise, don't you think?"

"Do not change the subject," Avril insisted. "I need to get out of this room. I am feeling cooped up."

He'd noticed her agitation growing as the day wore on. After sketching in her journal, she'd bounced on the bed until the squeaking had made him yell at her to stop. Then, she'd developed this architect theory. She sure had a stubborn, independent streak. He tried to remember being sixteen, but his life had been safe and boring, nothing like the day she'd had.

His eyes bore into hers. "I'm going. Alone. Understood?"

She dramatically threw herself back on the bed, springs squealing in defiance.

Will looked at Doyle. "Order some food. Guard the house. I'll be back."

Doyle shot him a wary look. "Are you sure about going alone?"

Will realized it might be reckless to do the recon solo, but he sure as hell wasn't going to leave Avril in the room by herself. "Positive."

"All right then." Doyle saluted. "Aye aye, sir."

I'm surrounded by jokers, Will thought, as he left and headed downstairs.

As soon as he stepped outside, he took a deep breath of the damp night air. The cold wind was refreshing after the stuffy space, and a fog was settling over the medieval city. Perfect. It would give him some cover.

He retraced their steps from that morning, berating himself again for letting Avril get so close to harm's way. Why had the director even agreed she could come along? It was stupid to send a teenager on a covert mission, and even if she had answers, she should be locked up tight in a national security facility.

Crossing the bridge through a thick band of mist, he worried about what would happen when the mission was over. She had no family. When she was argumentative, it was tempting to want to throw her to the wolves of an orphanage, but he'd had a college friend who grew up in the foster system and bore ugly emotional scars from the experience. No, he wouldn't wish that on even a difficult teenager. But what choice did they have? He couldn't adopt her, and Bear had confided to Will recently that he wanted kids with Maddy. Their inn was full. He'd have to deal with it later, if he was able to get her out of this mess in one piece.

Frustrated and cold, he walked faster.

Once back at the Pazzi Chapel, he circled the area, scouting for anyone who might be watching for his return. While eating a savory ham and cheese panini at the plate glass window of a nearby restaurant, he mulled over how they'd been ambushed and realized that was a big part of why he was out of sorts. He felt vulnerable and hated the feeling. He should report the morning's incident back to HQS, but what if there was a mole? Comms were so connected these days it was difficult to source a leak.

After a time, he decided to enter through the church next door to the chapel. It was a neo-Gothic Franciscan building that held the tombs of Michelangelo and Galileo. In Italian, it was called the Basilica di Santa Croce di Firenze. He rolled the words around in his mouth with pleasure.

Walking up to the carved front doors, he swore under his breath—they had no handle and no lock. He walked around the corner and under an arched wooden walkway. A door at the end looked promising . . . until he got there. It also had no way in. He glanced at the stained-glass windows. Not an option.

Harrumphing, he strode back to the front of the church and ended up back at the glass-fronted door they'd fled through earlier. He didn't like it. Sure, he could pick the lock, but the street was not exactly devoid of people. Peering between the bars of the iron fence, he caught a glimpse of the long, narrow courtyard they'd run along that morning. The chapel would be in the back.

Waiting until the street was deserted, he used the nearby bike rack to scramble up and over the tall fence, dropping lightly to his feet on the other side.

Hugging the wall, he walked around the corner and stopped to catch his breath. Reflexively, he checked his scabbards and released the safety straps. He'd cleaned his knives in the tiny bathroom at the pensione and they were ready for use.

Listening, he tried to detect the echoes of anyone who might be lying in wait. The night was full of city sounds. A car horn beeped, young men yelled jovially at one another, and a canine ankle-biter yipped. Inside the courtyard, nothing moved.

Once his breathing was back to normal and his eyesight had adjusted, he worked his way to the chapel through wisps of gray fog, only hesitating slightly when he saw the crime scene tape ribboned across the balustrade. Hours earlier, he'd killed a man there. He didn't have the same compunction about killing as his sister, but he didn't like the necessity of it either. When he spotted the black pool of blood staining the porch's floor, he reminded himself there'd been no choice, but clenched his jaw as he passed by.

The massive doors were three times his height and solid wood, and, again, there was no lock. He thrust his fingers inside the grill, but his hand didn't go all the way through. Angry, he pushed the door and was surprised when it swung open on silent hinges.

Moving fast, he stepped through, expecting an ambush. When the space proved empty, he closed the door behind him, silently thanking the police or clergy who'd gotten their communication lines crossed and had left it open.

Inside, he glanced around. There'd been no time for a full examination earlier. The walls were simple, there were no pews, and probably no secret staircase to a crypt. Nevertheless, he climbed over the security ropes to the altar and poked around. He found no hidden chamber, or hinged cupboard.

He was starting to believe the quatrains led to words, and not objects.

Still, he explored every corner of the room, and each inch of the crimson-colored marble floor.

Eventually, he gave up, closed the doors on their silent hinges, and cautiously made his way back to the pensione.

CHAPTER 62

With her foot pressing the Porsche's gas pedal and her blood pressure spiking into the red zone, Maddy turned to Bear. "I don't think we can lose the Ferrari on a four-lane highway."

"I think you're right," Bear growled. "Plus, there's a lengthy tunnel coming up."

"A tunnel? That's not good. Civilians could get caught in the crossfire."

"Yep. But see the marker ahead for the side road? Let's take that."

The rain made it hard to see the sign, but she zeroed in on it after two beats. "Okay."

With the blue Ferrari zipping in and out of traffic behind them, Maddy revved the engine as hot as it would go. Then, at the last instant, she swerved onto the exit. Her evasion tactic was unsuccessful, and the lights of the Ferrari followed them.

"Now what?"

The highway on the left began to recede as she drove up a narrow two-lane road.

Bear was swiping like mad on his phone. "From what I can tell, we're on the Emmetterstrasse."

"Not helpful."

"I know, but all I can see is that this is a winding road, up into the mountains. We best be ready for them."

Bear drew his 9 mm Glock from his leather armpit holster and turned around to face their pursuers.

Tensing for bullets, Maddy kept her eyes straight ahead. Her left hand gripped the steering wheel so hard her knuckles turned bright white, and her right hand worked the gears. They spun around a curve, tires struggling for purchase. To the left, the lake was hundreds of feet below, at the bottom of a bluff. A meager three-foot-tall metal guardrail was all that separated car from cliff. There was no room to run on the right either, as a gray stone wall stood where a shoulder should be.

The Ferrari was directly behind her now, its headlights dancing through their vehicle like supernatural strobe lights. It attempted to pass, but a large yellow bus came from the opposite direction, throwing water and thwarting the bid.

They continued to climb through the night. The rain turned icy.

The next right turn was sharp and Maddy took it so fast and wide that the back end of the Porsche nearly clipped the granite wall. The Ferrari was able to stay in its own lane, gaining on her.

The guardrail and lake were now on their right, with a tall rock wall to their left.

The Ferrari revved and bumped her back bumper.

She ground her teeth. "He's playing with us."

Bear's breath was coming fast and hard. "They just crossed a line."

He aimed and fired.

Even though she expected it, the roar of the unsilenced gunshot made her jump. Her ears rang. Their back window spiderwebbed, before exploding into a thousand pebbles of glass. In their rearview mirror she saw the pieces fly into the abyss. With the lights blinding her, she couldn't see much, but imagined the debris flying through the Ferrari's broken windshield and stinging the driver. She wished him no harm, just wanted him to back off. Maybe . . .

Taking advantage of the confusion, she slammed on the brakes.

The Ferrari crashed into the back of the Porsche, whiplashing her neck. She downshifted and accelerated again, trying to pull away. The next curve came up fast, and she pushed the car up the hill, hoping the enemy got the message.

No luck.

The baby-blue Ferrari roared up behind them again. Bear traded shots with the passenger. A bullet ripped past her ear and through the windshield, spidering her vision.

Pop!

Her left rear tire blew out. The Porsche fishtailed violently. She tried to keep it on the icy road and failed. It plowed to the left, cutting through the metal guardrail like a hot knife through butter, and plunged over the cliff.

The coupe headed nose first down the steep embankment. Maddy wrestled the wheel, keeping the front tires aiming down at an angle, while braking. They slammed onto the paved road they'd just come up, broke through a second guardrail, and hurtled down the mountain. The car crushed every small tree in its path. The front left tire hit a large rock and the car flipped on its side, and began to roll. The airbags deployed. Maddy closed her eyes and hung on tightly while the car continued to roll brutally down the hill. It seemed forever before they finally came to a stop against a thick tree.

Dazed, Maddy took stock. The back of her head hurt. Her breath came in jagged bursts. She felt dizzy and disoriented. A concussion or just a hangover from the bad ride? No sharp pain. The side airbag deflated with a hiss. She forced her eyes open.

She turned to Bear. Blood ran down his nose from a gash in his forehead. Worse, his eyes were closed and his face slack.

"Bear." She put her hands to his face and neck, feeling vainly for a pulse. "Bear!"

CHAPTER 63

5:50 P.M.

Maddy pulled her hands away from Bear's carotid. *I can't feel a pulse!*

A rush of energy exploded away from his body, feeling like the very essence of him was disappearing into the void.

Panic spiked through her and memories from every CPR class she'd ever taken fled, like water from a spilled glass.

He was such a good man. In her mind's eye she saw him tossing a football with AJ at the vineyard, the day before they'd all gone skiing. The two of them had played on the lawn near the house, while Bear answered questions about how to hold the ball properly and where to place AJ's small fingers. When they were done, they'd walked toward the house, both wearing toothy smiles. Bear had put his arm on AJ's shoulders and had told him that he had a good arm. Her redheaded boy was so happy he'd nearly bowled her over with the strength of his hug.

The Porsche settled against the tree with a groan, bringing her back to the present. She needed to get Bear out of the car to attempt CPR. Yanking on her door lever, she swore. It didn't open. The engine had died when the car rolled to a stop. With a shaking hand, she turned the key. The engine wouldn't start, so rolling down the window was not an option.

It was a cold night but sweat rolled into her eyes. She couldn't lose him. It seemed like they'd just found each other. She slammed her hand on the steering wheel.

In desperation, she straddled Bear and yanked at the handle of his door.

It creaked open. Clumps of broken glass dropped to the ground like the hard rain that was falling outside the car.

She pushed the door wide and got a leg out, then two. Kicking the glass away first, she unbuckled Bear's seatbelt and pulled his legs out, and then manhandled him to the ground. The car probably wouldn't explode, but to be on the safe side, she dragged him ten feet away to a level spot underneath the gnarled branches of an overhanging evergreen. It provided a bit of protection from the weather.

Again, her fingers dug for a pulse at his carotid artery. Nothing.

She wailed and pounded on his chest, knowing it was a temper tantrum and not proper technique. Closing her eyes hard, she tried to remember details from the class she'd taken six months ago in a bland classroom. There was something about airway obstruction. She tilted his head to the side and swept his mouth. That didn't help.

Okay. She was going to have to try giving him CPR. She bent down and breathed two breaths into his mouth. Muscle memory led her hand to close off his nose, and she remembered to watch his chest. It rose as it should.

Locking her arms out straight and placing one hand atop the other, she found the center of his breastbone and began to compress. Was it fifteen to two? Ten to one? She swore again and decided it was going to be fifteen compressions to two breaths. It was better than nothing.

She pressed his chest fifteen times and then gave him two breaths. Repeated the motion.

Rain dripped off her hair and ran down her cheeks.

"Damn it, Bear! Don't you leave me now!"

He sure had a thick chest. One she loved to curl into before they fell asleep. Tears began to creep out of her eyes. She couldn't brush them away. One fell on his face.

He coughed.

Astonished, she sat back on her heels. "Bear?"

He rolled toward her and reached a hand out to wipe the tears from her face. "Maddy. Why are you crying?"

She grabbed his hand and kissed it, then bent down and kissed him. "I thought you were dead!"

He shook his head, as if to clear it. "I saw the whole thing."

"What do you mean?"

"You pulled me out of the car, right? After you couldn't get out your side?"

She frowned. "Yes. What do you mean, you saw it?"

"I was floating above my body. Felt wonderful, like I was home on the porch having sweet tea on a nice summer evening with my pops."

"And you saw me?"

"I did. Was trying to tell you I was fine, not to worry, but you couldn't hear me, I guess. There was a light in the sky, all around us actually, and it felt all soft and warm and full of love."

She put a hand to her mouth. "You really were dead."

"I guess I was. Even caught a glimpse of my dad. He gave me a salute and a wink. Then, for an instant, I saw the space beyond space. My heart melted. Could have lasted an hour, or an eternity. Then I woke up. Strangest thing."

She lay down on the ground and hugged him. He felt strong and solid and real. "I'm mega-ultra-really glad you came back."

"Me too. But if that's dyin', I think I'll be happy enough to go back someday."

She was a little jealous of his extraordinary experience. He'd even gotten to see his dad. "That's good to know, but don't be heading back any time soon!"

They lay like that for a time. Had she really felt his spirit explode into the void, since he hadn't really died? It was probably the adrenaline or shock from the accident. Her heart began to beat in time with his.

Eventually, Bear stirred. "Is your body okay? That was quite the tumble."

"I might have a little concussion, but otherwise I'm fine."

He stood and limped to the car, where he grabbed his weapon and holstered it under his arm. "We should both get checked out. I've got a ringer of a headache myself."

The icy rain turned to light snow.

She struggled to her feet, aware now of the cold. "Okay. Let's see if we can find our way off this mountain before someone comes to finish killing us off."

CHAPTER 64

MARSEILLE, FRANCE
6:10 P.M.

Seymore's phone rang. He gave a brusque greeting.

"I don't think they'll be walking away from this one," said the man on the phone.

The voice was high-pitched. They'd always called him Squeaky.

Looking through his living room's French doors down at the rain-dimmed lights of the harbor, Seymore lit a cigarette with his favorite gold lighter.

Squeaky was one of his hired men, a fellow from his army days who liked to make extra money now and again.

"We are in the Swiss Alps. The two in the car went tumbling over a cliff after a high-speed chase," Squeaky continued.

At last, something was going right. Seymore took a long, sweet drag and exhaled slowly, forming the smoke into a ring.

The heat of anger began to cool in his gut.

First there was the miss in Marseille. He'd been so furious, he'd had the group turn on one of the others at sea. They'd beat their comrade to a pulp before dumping him into deep water wearing an anchor around his ankles.

Then there were Raphael's failures in Milan and at the Pazzi Chapel. He'd been too late at the former, but had a chance to make up for it at the chapel. Instead, two of Seymore's men were dead. Raphael had attempted to clean the scene but he'd had to run, leaving the bodies behind and opening the door to an unpleasant criminal investigation.

Seymore's benefactor expected results, especially after providing intelligence on the enemies' whereabouts and details about the medallion. When their patron didn't get his preferred outcomes, he was *extremely* displeased. The creepy man was a martial arts master with a knife fetish and had threatened to cut Seymore into pieces with his favorite blade.

Now, however, that unpleasantness was in the rearview mirror. Seymore drew pleasure from the thought of the Americans flipping end over end. "Excellent. Did the car burst into flames?"

"Um, I don't think so. But they went through two guardrails and down a steep cliff."

Seymore's face turned deep red.

"Not good enough," he roared. "I want you to make sure they're dead."

"But it's steep."

God, but it was hard to hire good help. He hissed, "I don't care if it's a slide to Hades itself." He took a quick puff and exhaled smoke through his nose. "Get your asses in gear and go confirm the kill."

"Will do."

The phone went dead. He threw it into the woodstove with a *thunk* and watched the plastic melt.

CHAPTER 65

Maddy glanced around at the frost-covered forest. "At least it seems we lost our pursuers."

"For now," Bear said. "I don't know how they got on our tail. Until we figure that out, we're vulnerable. Plus, they could be coming to confirm we're dead."

With only the light from her cracked phone to guide them, they stumbled further down the steep mountain. Now that night had fallen, the temperature was well below freezing, and light snow continued to fall. Normally, the flakes would have lent an aura of romance and mystery to the forest, but Maddy's head hurt and she was cold, even wearing a light down jacket and her black cabbie cap. Her left index finger twitched violently inside her pocket.

With her other hand, she held Bear's, and the heat from his fingers made a welcome contrast to the air that chilled her nose and ears. However, it wasn't enough to make up for the adrenaline hangover, which sucked the wind out of the gratefulness she'd felt at Bear's revival. Now, she just wanted to rest somewhere warm and take an anti-inflammatory to ease the ache in her head.

"Hold up a sec," Bear said.

He pulled off to the side and vomited behind a tree.

Her stomach churned in commiseration. "You okay?"

He wiped his mouth with the back of his hand. "Yeah. Let's keep going."

"Wait." She checked his eyes using the phone light. Both pupils were the same. "You sure must have rung your bell."

His half grin made it apparent he was still in pain. "'Cause it killed me for a minute?"

"Exactly."

"I'm glad to be alive, but it'd be nice to have a safe place to rest for the night."

"It would." She grabbed his hand and they set off again, half-sliding down the hill because the terrain was so steep. "Think we'll find civilization?"

"If we can get down to that big lake, there's bound to be houses."

She wished for proper snow boots. Her toes felt like they were being bitten by hungry fire ants. Frostbite worried her. "It's still quite a way down."

"I know, but we can't sleep in the snow tonight."

With her head hurting and his probably worse, she decided to shut up. They slid from tree to tree in the darkness. If there was a moon, it was hidden behind the snow clouds. There was no wind. Silence settled on them, like the blanket of snow on their shoulders, and soon all she heard was their breath and the squishing sounds of their shoes. It reminded her of winter days growing up in Lake Tahoe, when she and Will would hike the woods behind their house in a white world devoid of sound. She wondered why she and Bear didn't hear the highway, and then she recalled it was buried in a long tunnel.

After a time, the steep embankment began to level out, and they entered a clearing.

"A meadow, you think?" she asked.

"Maybe an iced-over lake."

A sound to her right caught her attention. "Do you hear that?"

"A helo. Think it's ours or theirs?"

"Why don't we step back into the trees and wait to find out?"

"Good idea."

They shuffled back ten paces and watched the big black bird land in the middle of the clearing, causing a whirlwind of snow. Her phone buzzed. She raised an eyebrow. They must finally have reception.

A text from Jags.

Helo near your location. Friendly. Find it if you can.

Maddy exhaled with relief. "Jags says it's friendly."

Bear drew his weapon anyway. "Let's go see."

They walked out of the forest and waved their arms. The helicopter's rotors slowed to a lazy whirr, and then four men carrying two stretchers ran toward them.

Bear pointed his weapon at them. "Stop right there."

They did, but not before the one closest spoke. "Are you Thorenson and Marshall?"

Bear nodded. "We are. Can you prove who you are?"

"Sir, your GPS-enabled smartwatch indicated you flatlined."

Bear turned to Maddy. "Doubt anyone else would have my watch data."

"Agreed," Maddy said. "And we got the text from Jags on the secure phone."

The medic motioned to the stretcher with his head. "Would you like a ride to the helo?"

Bear waved them off. "Just a hot beverage once we're on board."

The medic looked at Maddy with a question in his eyes. The stretcher looked tempting, but Maddy could tough it out. She shook her head.

Together, the six of them walked back to the helicopter. She noted Bear's limp was much worse than usual. Then again, she wasn't so steady herself. Under the rotors, she saw no markings or flags on their transport.

Once inside the cabin, Maddy began to shiver violently. The medics removed her wet clothes, and helped her towel off. They gave her dry sweatpants, a red wool shirt, and a blanket, and then soaked her toes in cool water that felt like it was boiling. Plying her with warm coffee, they told her she'd narrowly avoided frostnip, which she knew was the precursor to frostbite. As the helicopter took off into the sky, Bear got the same black ops spa treatment.

When they were finally warm, Bear asked to speak with the director or Jags, knowing the two were in near constant communication. The medics gave them headsets and connected them to Jags.

"Thanks for the ride," Bear said.

"Thought we lost you," Jags responded, her deep voice more throaty than usual.

Bear grinned at Maddy. "I'm too ornery."

"Glad to hear it, soldier. But you're going to have to get checked out before you head back to the field."

"Let's make it a hospital near Will."

"Good idea. He thinks comms have been compromised so said he'll meet you at the postcard place that you told me about in Maastricht."

"Okay. Have any news while these boys ferry us there?"

"Yes. Our man in Russia said they are not a player in this game."

"Hmm. What else?"

"I finally found someone who could follow the money trail."

Maddy noted how both Jags and Bear were watching their language, carefully avoiding names and places. She had to ask her question, though. "Where's it lead?"

"Straight back to China."

"I thought so," Maddy said.

"It was a good hunch, but you'd both better be careful, because this mission puts you right in the crosshairs of a red-alert international crisis."

CHAPTER 66

THE NATIONAL MUSEUM'S BATHS OF DIOCLETIAN, ROME, ITALY
JANUARY 30, 11:30 A.M.

Will shivered as he stared at the black-and-white tile mosaic of a skeleton resting on a bed of nails above the Greek words *gnōthi sauton*. It matched the image on his mother's postcard. *She was here!* He was standing in the exact same place that she had stood over thirty years ago, breathing the same recycled museum air.

Will still couldn't get used to the idea that his mother, the woman who had nursed him and put bandages on his skinned knees, had been a covert operative. He also couldn't trust that Bowman hadn't known, not with that *spying is in your blood* comment. Maddy was giving Bowman the benefit of the doubt. Will was giving Bowman the benefit of years of skepticism. The director had probably known when he'd hired them.

Will shook his head to clear it. More importantly, why had she sent *this* image back home?

"What do you think it means?" Avril asked. She was sandwiched between him and Doyle.

He pointed to the white museum card. "The Greek words on the mosaic, which translate to 'Know Thyself,' or *nosce te ipsum* in Latin, combine with the skeleton to convey a famous warning: *Respice post te; hominem te esse memento; memento mori.* 'Look behind; remember that you are mortal; remember death.'"

She gave him the rolling-eyed "adults are so stupid" look. "I can read. But what do you think is the point?"

Doyle put a hand on her shoulder. "Lass, the Greeks were big on this type of philosophy. The idea is to keep in mind how little time we have on earth. Appreciate it."

She put her hands on her hips. "That is *exactly* why I want to explore. I am certain Nostradamus spent time in Rome."

Will ushered the two of them down the museum aisle. He lowered his voice. "If Bear and Maddy don't join us here, we'll go get them at the hospital."

It was Bear who had figured the fourth quatrain led to Rome, but they all still needed to determine why.

Avril hissed. "I want to go now. You two stand out like middle-age tourists. I can buy a hat at the museum store and find some sunglasses."

Will couldn't believe he was hearing this. "Did yesterday's little incident in Florence not convince you that you're unsafe?"

"I think I would be safer alone."

Will and Doyle made eye contact over her head. It was clear from the tilt of Doyle's bushy eyebrows that the Irishman didn't like what she was saying any more than Will did.

Will put his hands on his knees to level with her, eye-to-eye. "Avril. That is absolutely not true. We're both trained in methods to keep you safe. You're a smart girl, but you don't have the skills or experience we do."

She moved around him and kept walking. He exhaled, stood, and followed. She stopped in front of a brown-and-blue-themed mosaic titled "Mosaic with Nilotic Landscape." He studied the birds, alligators, and horned rhinos, wondering what had captured her attention.

Crossing her arms, she said, "S-O-N," enunciating each letter.

"What do you mean?"

"This reminds me of those wooly mammoths from the caves. I think that quatrain's answer is S-O-N."

Doyle studied the picture, hand on his chin.

Will looked again at the mosaic. "Sorry, I'm not seeing it."

She exhaled strongly and threw her hands in the air as she headed down the hallway, speaking over her shoulder. "That is my point."

CHAPTER 67

CAPITOLINE HILL, ROME, ITALY
3:45 P.M.

Maddy stood at the bottom of the long stretch of ramp that led up to the plaza. She turned to Will. "Thanks for waiting for us to bust out of the hospital."

"We considered standing you up at the museum while we solved the riddle and got all the glory, but I was outvoted." He jerked his chin toward Doyle and Avril. "They thought you might still be useful, even if you are gimpy."

"Bah. I'm no gimp."

He gave her a look that told her he knew she was lying. It had been a rough night at the hospital. Between the CT scans and the MRIs, she and Bear hadn't slept much. They'd been held until midafternoon, had met the rest of the team on the steps of the museum, taxied over here, and now light was fading from the overcast sky.

Bear stood off to the side with Avril and Doyle, examining a basalt lion fountain with water spewing out of its mouth. She didn't understand how Doyle could remain so calm when his grandparents' lives were threatened.

"You up for this ramp after all that beauty rest?" Will asked.

Beauty rest. Right. If it wouldn't have taken so much bloody effort, she'd have punched him. "Of course I am." *Thanks to the pain pills.*

Both she and Bear had been diagnosed with mild concussions and released, pending plenty of rest and little activity. She hoped her brain would forgive her for not following the doc's orders. Besides the head injuries, Bear had a black eye, her neck didn't want to turn more than thirty degrees, and the rest of her felt like she'd been beaten by a baseball bat.

"Let's get started then." Will began to walk up the slope. "Bear said Michelangelo designed this as a ramp instead of stairs so horses could use it."

"Works for me." It was definitely wide enough for six to eight horses abreast. Mostly she was grateful to not have to deal with stairs. Even with the painkillers, her head thumped, making her eyes squint and her mood poor. "Jags said you think our comms are compromised."

"They're tracking us somehow."

"Guess we better hurry then."

They picked up the pace.

A minute later she asked, "What did you find inside the museum? Anything interesting?"

"No. It was just a bigger image of that postcard."

She checked behind them, turning her whole body since her neck didn't want to rotate. The rest of their tribe was following, Bear still limping more than he should. There was no sign of Seymore or anyone that looked out of place. "That's so frustrating. Why did Mom visit and send that morbid card?"

"Wish I knew. It's annoying as hell." Will flicked a piece of lint off his silk shirt. "Did Aunt Carole call you yet?"

Maddy clenched her jaw. "No. We did speak with Bella. She's going to ask Aunt Carole."

Before Will could comment further, Bear came up behind her and looped his arm through hers. "How's it going?"

Doyle and Avril moved to flank Will.

Maddy squeezed Bear's arm. "Why don't you tell us about this place to keep my mind off the climb?" *And this same old argument with my brother?*

"Sure. Hey Avril, why don't you remind us of the relevant quatrain?"

Avril combed some of her long hair over the burned side of her face. She blew out an exasperated breath. "Still have not memorized it yet?

South, to the first sanctuary of new citizens

Temple of Jupiter and Juno

The famed sculptor and architect makes his marks in mud

The last letter of the founder is placed behind the mountainous middle

There you go," she finished.

"Thanks," Bear said, ignoring her commentary. "The reason that we're climbing the famous Cordonata Capitolina is that the clues made it clear we needed to come here."

"Please elucidate," Will said.

"According to myth, the top of this hill is where Romulus, the founder of Rome, established the first sanctuary for new Roman citizens after killing his twin brother, Remus. The temple of Jupiter and Juno is behind that big building in the center, and Michelangelo, a rather famous sculptor and architect—perhaps you've heard of him?—redesigned the plaza when it was all a muddy, medieval mess."

"Sounds like we know the founder's name then, right?" Maddy said. "Romulus."

"I'd bet on it," Bear said.

Avril piped up. "What is the mountainous middle then?"

"That's what we're here to find out," Bear replied.

They approached the top of the ramp, which was flanked by statues twice the normal size, each of a sculpted male who stood next to a horse. The men wore capes, but no other clothes. Maddy didn't quite understand the fascination sculptors had with nudes, but maybe she was a prude.

An open square waited at the end of the ramp, surrounded on three sides by Renaissance buildings. Another statue held center stage, this time a bronze man on horseback. The paving stones marked a twelve-pointed star.

"Think that's got anything to do with the mountainous middle?" Maddy said, pointing to the statue.

Before Bear could respond, Avril shot off toward the rear of the building to the right. "I need to use the restroom."

Maddy shook off Bear's arm. "I'll go with her. Safety in numbers and all."

"Good thinking," he said.

"Avril, hold up!"

The girl stopped, tapping her foot, and Maddy joined her. Avril's forehead was beaded with sweat and she wouldn't meet Maddy's eye.

Maddy asked, "Everything okay?"

"Yes."

Maddy put a hand on her hip and raised an eyebrow.

"It is Will. He does not listen to me. And he is going to get hurt!"

Maddy could understand her brother not listening, but wanted clarity on the last comment. "What do you mean?"

"I need to go! See you in the bathroom." Avril sprinted off.

Maddy followed along the white lines of the humongous star, too tired to keep up with Avril's energetic pace. Tourists on single-wheeled scooters rushed by, laughing, slowing Maddy's progress further. She'd catch up with the girl in the bathroom.

Maddy spied the universal restroom sign and followed around the edge of the building. Ahead, the lavatory door swung closed.

Maddy entered. There were three stalls, one open.

She did her business and when she exited, looked to the sinks for Avril. She wasn't there.

Maddy checked under the stalls, and didn't see Avril's bright-blue running shoes.

Heart rate rising, Maddy opened the exterior door. From the corner, she saw the team standing next to the bronze statue. Turning the other way, she saw a group of tourists taking selfies above a garden of ruins.

Avril, though, was nowhere to be seen.

CHAPTER 68

3:55 P.M.

Will knew something was wrong the instant he saw Maddy rushing toward him. A minute ago, she'd looked like she could barely walk and now she was moving at a near jog.

He met her halfway. "What's wrong? Where's Avril?"

Maddy leaned over, hands on her knees. "She's gone. I don't know."

Bear put an arm around Maddy's shoulders as soon as he caught up. His face looked pale in contrast to his black eye. "What happened?"

Maddy panted. "Thought she entered ahead of me. Came out and she was gone."

Bear took charge, leveling a steely gaze at the other two men. "You two. Take north of here." He motioned with his blond head. "Up to Vatican City. We'll go south."

"Okay. But don't call Jags yet. I don't know how they keep finding us." Will turned on his heel, and then turned back. "Did Jags know we'd be here?"

Bear hesitated an instant, and nodded grimly. "More or less. As we left Maastricht, I gave her the quatrains and told her we'd be heading to Rome. That was before they attacked you in Florence and us in the Alps."

Will squeezed his eyes shut and swore. A rock sat heavy in his gut, shocking in its intensity. Could Jags be a mole? He felt sucker-punched.

"What about Avril's tracker?" Bear asked.

In Will's worry, he'd forgotten about that. "Good idea." He pulled out his phone and swiped as fast as his fingers would let him. The app showed a blinking dot a block away, moving north.

"Go! In case that's a decoy, we'll keep to the plan," Bear said.

Will and Doyle sprinted down the broad ramp, crossed several streets filled with honking bumper-to-bumper traffic, and entered Piazza di San Marco.

But after searching the bare stone plaza, all they found was the silver device in a trash can next to a park bench.

He turned to Doyle, tracker held aloft. "Did she run?"

Doyle put his hands on his hips, breathing hard. "Or was she taken?"

Will turned his head, searching the plaza. "The better question is—"

The men made eye contact and spoke at the same time.

"Where is she now?"

CHAPTER 69

5:44 P.M.

The last vestiges of light were draining out of the sky as Maddy and Bear hurried along the back alleys of Rome. They'd made a full circle of the area south of Capitoline Hill and were heading back to the square where they'd begun the search.

"Ugh," Maddy said, slightly out of breath. "I still can't believe a sixteen-year-old gave me the slip."

"We've been over this," Bear replied. "The more likely scenario is that she was snatched."

Maddy yanked on her cap, and grimaced at the ensuing head pain. Bloody concussion. "Why didn't they take me too, then?"

"Hard to say. Maybe they knew you'd give them trouble."

"Do you mean to say I'm more trouble than I'm worth?" she snapped.

He held up his hands. "Whoa, Nellie. I was talking about your aikido skills."

She glanced at him. "Sorry. This is just so frustrating. We've walked around half the old city."

He grabbed her hand. "I hope she's safe."

"Me too." Maddy wrestled her emotions under control. "Think she really tossed her GPS tracker into that trash can?"

Will had radioed them with that update, and they'd decided to keep searching anyway.

Bear stopped to admire a weathered replica of a she-wolf statue atop a column. "Either that, or our opponents did."

She dropped his hand and glanced up at the sculpture despite her sore neck. "That skinny wolf has some mean fangs. And why are there babes at her teats?"

"It's supposed to represent Romulus and Remus, the mythical twins fathered by the war god Mars and sent down the river in a trough. They were found nearby and suckled by a wolf until humans raised them."

"Whatever. I'm not in the mood." Maddy grimaced and pounded her right fist into her left palm. "I feel sorry for Avril. She's just so young."

"She is. At sixteen, I had only recently moved to Lake Tahoe."

"That's right." Maddy took a deep breath to calm down. "You were a sophomore. I remember you were the new kid. Everybody loved your skills as a running back."

"I had fun playing football." He looked her in the eye. "Liked meeting you better."

She kissed him softly. "Glad I finally came to my senses?"

"Over the moon. That decade and a half of unrequited love was hard on my tender heart."

She hugged him and thought about making an innuendo, but decided to save that for later.

Bear seemed to have turned back to the Avril situation. He stretched his massive shoulders. "To find the girl, I suspect we're going to have to figure out where Nostradamus hid his formula. If I'd kidnapped her, she'd be tied up tight somewhere and out of the way by now."

"What if she just ran away?"

"In that case, a smarty-pants like her will try to beat us to the endgame."

"I think you're right. She seemed like she was trying to tell me something before we got to the restroom. Like Will wasn't listening to her. And that it was all her fault. I feel bad I couldn't get more out of her."

"Don't blame yourself. She could have told you more."

"I suppose."

"Well, whether she's nailed the puzzle or been taken, we need to get a step ahead. If we can get there first, we can secure the medallion."

"Wherever 'there' is."

Bear ignored her snide comment. "When she shows up, with or without the enemy, we whisk her away to safety."

Maddy sighed. "I suppose you're right. I just hate giving up the hunt."

"We've been looking for hours. So have Will and Doyle. There's nowhere else to search."

"I know."

"We can have Jags check the local cameras and police databases." He grabbed Maddy's hand again, gently tugging her away. "But I think we need to face facts and head to the safe house in Castel Gandolfo to regroup."

When they reached the end of the square near the cape-wearing nudes, Maddy said, "While we're walking back down the ramp, let's revisit the clues. Will's third quatrain, the one about the duomo . . ."

"What about it?"

"I know the clue led to the Pazzi Chapel, but I've been thinking about Brunelleschi, the architect."

As they crossed the cobbled street, Bear swiped the eyebrow above his bruised eye. "And?"

"Well, if we're working with letters and follow the instructions, which were, '*Of the first the penultimate strikes the mark but of the second take the last and the first of the twins,*' then that sounds like two words. It's either Filippo Brunelleschi, which gives us PIE. Or if we work with the chapel, we get IL and there's no twins. At least with Brunelleschi, there's two double letters, 'E' and 'L.'"

"Sorry to change the subject, but pie sounds good. Apple. Or maybe pumpkin. Want to find some food?"

Her stomach grumbled. "Sure. We could grab something from that restaurant up the street that we passed on our way here a few hours ago."

Keeping an eye out for nefarious company, they hustled down the street a few blocks to a red-and-white awning.

The restaurant's wrought-iron patio tables were loosely stacked atop one another, waiting for a warmer day. A crooked black-chalk placard announced the day's menu. Maddy resisted the urge to straighten the sign.

Soon, she and Bear were seated across from one another at a red-leather booth in the back. Bear, as was his habit, faced the door like a Mafia bodyguard. For an instant, he rubbed his forehead as if warding off a headache.

He's still suffering the aftereffects of our accident as well. "Your head still hurt?"

"A little." He tried to grin. "I'll be fine. Just need some grub."

Once they'd ordered calamari as an appetizer, Maddy took out a pen and wrote on a white napkin. "I like PIE better than using the chapel's info. Plus, we have TEC from the sarcophagus."

"I think it's all going to spell something."

The waitress brought a carafe of water "with gas." A glass of Italian red sounded nice, but Maddy wanted a clear head. And there were the pain pills. She nodded. "Yes, it does seem we're going to spell out a word or phrase."

"Okay, so what about the quatrain from here in Rome then?" Bear said. "What's the mountainous middle?"

She took a sip of the carbonated water. "What was that one again?"

"The last letter of the founder is placed behind the mountainous middle."

"We know the founder's name was Romulus. The last letter gives us S. But what's the middle?"

"Maybe it was that statue in the middle of the square."

The scents in this place are amazing, she thought, distracted. "Could be. Who was the man on horseback with his arm raised in a victory salute?"

"Marcus Aurelius. Michelangelo provided an unassuming pedestal for it. Apparently, he didn't like the old Roman."

"Who was Marcus again?"

Bear chewed an ice cube. "A Roman emperor from around 170 AD."

"Maybe we use his initials for the second part of the clue that goes in front of the S? MA, which becomes MAS?"

Bear leaned forward, a new light in his Scandinavian blue eyes. "That would make sense."

The waitress brought the squid and took their order of grilled local whitefish in tomato sauce with mushrooms, atop a bed of house-made rigatoni.

Maddy chewed a fried calamari bite. "It would make total sense. His statue is in the absolute center of the square."

"Not sure why it would be mountainous, but the statue is larger-than-life size," Bear added around a bite of food. "The impression I got is one of power. A conquering hero."

"Let's go with it for now." Maddy put her fork down and wrote on the napkin. "That gives us MAS, PIE, and TEC."

"We just don't have the first quatrain then."

"Right." Maddy exhaled. "And we need them all to find the medallion. *Having collected the parts of the enigma, take the four in reverse order then twelve steps back in time*. The reverse order part I get—we need to start with this last one. But twelve steps back in time?"

Bear shook his head. "We're getting close."

"Not close enough." Maddy threw down her pen. "Avril is out there somewhere. And if our enemy has her in their clutches, I hate to think about what they'll do to get information out of her."

CHAPTER 70

Will was in front, using his flashlight to light the way.

"It seems so quiet without Avril," he said.

The rest of the team didn't comment, but the concerned silence was palpable.

They were in the tunnel on the way to the safe house at the abandoned vineyard near Lake Albano, on the outskirts of scenic Castel Gandolfo, home to the pope's summer palace. Given the kerfuffle with comms, they'd used their radios to discuss regrouping. Will hoped the leak was with headquarters and not with their field gear.

The tunnel was dry and smelled musty. There were no cobwebs, which gave him hope that there'd be some food stored in the basement of the villa at the other end.

Eventually, Maddy broke the silence. "Bear and I are thinking we're going to have to solve the remaining quatrains to find her."

Doyle dragged his hand along the tunnel wall. "I've been thinking the same thing," he said. "Either the bad guys got her and she's told them all by now, or she's trying to figure it out on her own."

"Yes," Maddy agreed. "Either way, we need to find our way to the oracle's icy crown."

"Wherever that is," Will mumbled.

Maddy smacked him on the shoulder. "Knock it off, Will. You act like she's dead."

He turned his head. "She could be!"

"Or she could be alive, hoping we'll rescue her. Moping isn't going to solve anything."

"I'm not moping." But he was lying. And knew Maddy knew. "Fine. Let's try to figure it out while we walk. It's a long tunnel."

"Good," Maddy said with false cheer. "Bear and I were talking at dinner. It seems we have good working theories for all the quatrains except the first one. Can you tell us what you saw there?"

Will was silent. Not moping.

After a few beats, Doyle cleared his throat. "Um, well, we took this little train down into the caves. There was a lot of art drawn on the walls. Mostly mammoths, which might be the creature with the curved tusks."

"Remind me of the full quatrain," Maddy said.

Doyle recited from memory.

"The formula will be found by those who seek
The son of the soldier guides one to the caverns
Start with a writer of cosmography from Marguerite's court
To find the male child of the creature with curved tusks."

"Okay," Maddy said. "It's clearly about the male child of the mammoth. What three-letter ideas have you both had?"

Will narrowed his eyes in thought. "Why three letters?"

"The other quatrains seem to have just three. TEC, from the sarcophagus, MAS from Romulus, and I'm thinking PIE from Pazzi's Chapel."

"Avril thought that one was PIE, too." Will got a sinking feeling in his gut. "We really didn't have any ideas for the first quatrain."

"Avril thought it was SON," Doyle said.

Will felt bad for not listening to her.

Bear whistled. "That clever son of a bitch. Nostradamus used the word 'son' in the second line of the first quatrain, saying the son of the soldier guides one to the caverns. He was leading us with baby steps. A clue within a clue."

"I see. You're saying for the first quatrain he gave us the answer within the quatrain itself." Maddy's tone of voice shifted into confident. "I think Avril was right about both answers: PIE and SON."

Abruptly, a door appeared out of the darkness. From his waistband, Will pulled his Strider SMF, a framelock folding knife with a tiger pattern on the steel blade used by marines and gifted to him by Bear. Doyle and Bear drew their weapons. Will could almost sense Maddy focus her energy.

Bear pushed in front, gun at the ready. "Follow me."

He slid a cover off a retinal scanner, put his eye to it, and thrust open the door.

The room was quiet and dark. All four of them cleared the space, efficiently checking the nooks and corners for any sign the house had been compromised.

They found nothing.

Will relaxed, and sat down on a cot with a sigh. It had been a long, horrible day. He hated to think about where Avril was now.

He turned to his sister, a note of pleading in his voice. "Maddy, please try to use your dreams to find Avril tonight."

CHAPTER 71

Maddy had given in to Will's ridiculous request that she try to have a dream about Avril.

In the morning, the team joined together and sat around a safe-house table lit only by a battery-operated lantern. Maddy had slept fitfully for four hours on a hard cot, after taking her turn at watch.

Her brother glanced at her, a hopeful question in his eyes.

She shook her head no. He dropped his gaze and sighed.

When not sleeping, she'd been trying to figure out the final quatrain. She had wracked her brain all night.

The team began to brainstorm about the last clue.

"Let's go over it one more time," Bear ordered several hours later. "What are the puzzle pieces we have so far?"

Doyle stared at a page of paper on which he'd scribbled their clues. He enunciated every letter as he rattled them off. "S-O-N, T-E-C, P-I-E, M-A-S."

Will said, "It says to take them in reverse order after collecting all the parts of the enigma. So M-A-S first, then P-I-E, T-E-C, and S-O-N."

"But *maspietecson* doesn't make sense." Maddy pushed her wooden chair back from the rickety table. "What the hell does it mean?"

The only answer she got was blank stares. At least Bear had the decency to shrug.

Will said, "I don't know, but it's what the quatrain told us to do."

She stretched her neck. *These quatrains are ridiculous.* "We'll never find Avril or the formula at this rate. We're probably completely off base. I'm going to stretch my legs."

Bear touched her arm. "Maddy, this old stone farmhouse is supposed to be deserted. We can't just go for a joy walk up there. If a local sees you it will blow security."

"Watch me." Maddy pushed his arm away and stood. "I can't think down here. I need some fresh air. Besides, this house is in the middle of a vineyard. The grapes are tall enough that I won't be seen."

Bear huffed.

"Plus," she added. "It looked like rain last time I poked my head upstairs. Who's going to be lurking about in a storm?"

Doyle said, "I'll come with you. Could use a spot of air myself."

Maddy offered Doyle her arm like a queen to her consort. "Come along then."

The two of them walked to the ladder. Doyle went up first, unlatching the oxidized iron bolt and pushing up the trapdoor. "Definitely rustic accommodations," he said. "Nothing like the papal palace on the other side of the lake."

"At least the stored food wasn't bad."

Doyle climbed the ladder. "For breakfast. Not sure I want to eat it for long."

"Agreed." Maddy followed him up, still sore from the car wreck. "We need to figure out this clue."

"I know. I'm worried sick for my family, and the whole country of Taiwan, actually."

Above, the stone farmhouse was a ruin. There were no windows, doors, or furniture. At least the roof was watertight, and the plank flooring solid, but nature was working hard to reclaim the place.

"I'm concerned, too." Maddy walked to an opening, glancing out. "And about Avril."

Outside the rock walls, a cold rain fell, slamming into the half-buried patio stones like vengeful tears from an angry god. Water puddles dotted the landscape and a wicked wind blew ripples across the small bodies of water. "Even the weather isn't cooperating with us."

"It's been raining for a bloody week." Doyle moved to stand beside her. "Not the best day for a walk in the fields, eh?"

"No." Glad for her down jacket, she walked along the stone walls, tracing the rocks with her fingers. "I guess I can pace. Moving helps me think."

"Okay. Let's consider what old Nostradamus said. '*Take the four in reverse order then twelve steps back in time.*'"

She reached in her jacket pocket and found a piece of wrapped dark chocolate. Pulling it out, she unwrapped it and took a bite. "I think we've got the reverse order part. Putting the three-letter clues in 4-3-2-1 order is what got us to *maspietecson*. But what's the twelve steps back in time?"

Reversing her steps, she walked backward along the stone walls. Maybe the chocolate would help her think.

Doyle tugged at the dark beard that had grown in the last few days. "Could he be referring to a different time period in history?"

"Or does *maspietecson* have some sort of meaning we don't know about?" She finished the chocolate and pulled the phone out of her pocket. It was running low on battery. This godforsaken dump of a safe house didn't even have electricity, just solar power for the retinal scanner. "I haven't run a search. Let me try that."

She typed the word into a private search engine and scrolled through the results.

He looked over her shoulder. "Anything?"

"No. It's like a nonsense word." She tucked a stray hair behind her ear. "With those ancient caves, could he be talking about something from twelve epochs ago? Twelve centuries ago?"

From below, Will poked his head through the trapdoor. "You're so off base you're not even on the same playing field."

Maddy clenched her jaw. "Oh? I suppose you've figured the whole thing out?"

He gave her a cocky, toothy smile. "Actually, yes."

"Make a believer out of me."

"There are twelve letters in *maspietecson*."

Maddy's eyes grew wide. "Oh my god. We flip the whole word?" She frowned. "Wait. And get what?"

"*Nosceteipsam*."

Maddy wanted to kick the trapdoor down on his head. She went down on one knee so she could look him in the eyes. "That's more nonsense."

He raised an eyebrow. "Not if you speak Latin."

She yanked on his ear. "For the love of all things holy. What?"

"We were off a letter, that mountainous middle was MU not MA, but I figured it out."

"Just tell me already!"

"*Nosceteipsum* is *Nosce Te Ipsum* in Latin, or—drumroll please— Know thyself."

"And?"

Bear yelled from below. "Delphi!"

Then she knew. *The Oracle's icy crown.* That 'Know thyself' inscription was on a column at the temple of the Oracle of Delphi, in Greece. It was so famous, even she'd heard of it.

"Gotcha." She smiled broadly at him. "Nice work."

"Thanks. A version of 'Know Thyself' was on Mom's postcard. It was fresh in my mind."

"Really? That's what the garbled mess said?"

"Yes, but it was in Greek."

"Huh. Mom must've been closer to figuring this out than we thought. But what's the icy crown part?"

"Don't know yet. We'll have to see when we get there."

Bear bellowed, "Get your sorry butts back down here. We're heading out."

Maddy took a last look outside. With a storm like that, getting there was going to be tough.

CHAPTER 72

ROME, ITALY
1:45 P.M.

In her worst nightmares, Avril had never imagined herself strapped to a chair in a dark underground torture chamber. It was unreal, like a comic book, or bad movie. She kept hoping to wake up, but every time she raised her head, she saw Seymore sitting at a scarred wooden table playing with a gleaming gold lighter.

Click. Hiss.

The sound made her skin crawl and she sat back in the hard chair as far as she could. That wasn't much—they'd strapped her in tightly using leather bonds smelling of sweat and fear. Her wrists were so thin they'd needed to punch new holes in the leather, but that hadn't stopped them.

She closed her eyes and mentally kicked herself again. When she'd ditched Maddy in the restroom yesterday, Avril's secondary goal had been to prove to the team why they should've been listening to her all along. She was convinced she knew where Nostradamus was leading them, and the visit to the museum had only confirmed her suspicions. Using the little bit of bitcoin she had stored in an online wallet for emergencies, she'd planned to exchange the cryptocurrency for cash to buy a wig and pass as a blonde American.

Her *primary* objective was to keep Will and the rest of the team safe. It was her fault this whole thing had been set in motion. If she could get to the medallion first, she had a chance to set it right.

It had sounded so reasonable. But the plan had gone to pieces within ten minutes of giving Maddy the slip. Avril had run around the back side of the building and down Capitoline Hill. She'd dropped the tracking device in a trash can. As she was leaving Piazza di San Marco, a foul-smelling handkerchief was placed over her mouth and she'd woken up gagged inside a van. Later, she was blindfolded and dumped in a tiny bedroom with a narrow cot and rank blanket. Hours ago, she'd been brought to this chamber. Now she wished she had the silver tracking device back, because she had no way to signal to the team that she was stuck in this living hell.

Click. Hiss.

It concerned her that Seymore made no attempt to hide his face or bald head as he interrogated her. That meant they planned to kill her once she was no longer useful. She didn't dwell on such unpleasantness. Instead, her mind was busy trying to figure out how to buy time.

Twice, she'd zoned out and thought she heard Will playing his harmonica. Each time, a goon behind her had poked her shoulder hard enough to make her pay attention.

Seymore would click the lighter and repeat his question, "Where is the medallion?"

She would shake her head.

He'd continue with the lighter.

Click. Hiss.

Try as she might, she couldn't tear her eyes from the flame. When she did have nightmares, they usually took place in a darkened room with candles everywhere. The curtains would catch on fire first, and even though she'd try to run, the flames would encroach on her, inch by horrible inch, until her hair began to burn with a sickening smell and a crackle that sounded like it was emanating from the depths of Hades.

He moved to a different chair. Closer to her.

Click. "Where is the medallion?"

The flame was blue, surrounded by yellow.

It would hurt if he burned her skin. She knew that was his point. Sweat ran down her forehead into her eyes and she began to tremble uncontrollably.

He'd read her journal from front to back and knew almost as much as she did. Good thing she hadn't written everything down.

She wanted to give the VanOps team as much time as she could. But how long could she hold out once the pain started?

CHAPTER 73

OSTIA, ROME, ITALY
5:44 P.M.

In a harbor due west of Rome, Maddy looked at the modern, steel-bowed yacht they'd been told to expect and groaned. "Are you sure we can't fly to Greece?"

To have any hope of stopping China's aggressive tactics and rescuing Avril, they needed to get there first.

Will wore a baseball cap, warding off the rain. He shook his head. "I've been trying for hours to find flights, military and commercial."

Doyle said, "Look at the wind, Madeline."

She crossed her arms, hating to admit that beyond the harbor, the sea heaved in a violent, white-capped frenzy.

Will continued, "There are really nasty crosswinds today. Due to wind limits, planes and helicopters are grounded. Besides, this is an amazing vessel. She's built for a hurricane."

That didn't make Maddy feel any better. Her stomach churned. She turned to Bear. "You're the helo pilot of the family—what do you think?"

Bear put his hands on his hips and stared out to sea. He wore a black rain jacket with the hood pulled up. The eggplant bruise around his eye was starting to turn yellow as it healed. "Even if I had a platoon of marines I needed to rescue from enemy fire, I wouldn't brave it . . ."

"Are you sure?"

"It would be a suicide mission." He angrily popped a gum bubble. "It's really not a wind I want to fly in."

Inside her down jacket, Maddy clenched her fists. Her index finger was twitching. "Great. Well then, let's get on the vomit comet and out of the rain."

Will said, "I just hope our enemies don't beat us there."

Maddy looked at her brother as he set off down the dock. Will had whispered to her that he thought the mole was Doyle, or Jags, but he was so paranoid, he probably thought it was her and didn't have the balls to say it. She and Bear disagreed, but had no other theory. To try to limit the spread of information, they were paying for the boat with personal funds instead of looping Jags and the director in on their destination.

Still, their only advantage was speed, and taking this boat wasn't going to help.

A tan, middle-aged woman with sunbaked crow's feet spreading from light green eyes met them at the gangplank. She wore a cherry-red raincoat over her slim build and had tousled blonde hair that whipped about in the wind.

The woman gestured. "Come aboard."

"Where's Chris?" Will asked. "I thought he was our captain."

"I'm Christine." She smiled. "But you can call me Chris."

While Will and Doyle recovered from their misogynistic assumption and began to flirt, Maddy said, "I'm cold and tired. Do you have an antinausea pill and a bed?"

"Yes, everything you need for a comfortable journey. Follow me."

Maddy did as suggested, with Bear at her heels. She didn't care if Will and Doyle found a cabin later, or even managed to take turns with their captain—she wanted a bed now. Chris took them below decks, and Maddy was impressed with the leather and steel accoutrements. They ended up in a master suite that was larger than her San Francisco loft. It had a 180-degree view, a workout area, a jacuzzi, a desk, a library, and a bar with an eighteen-foot widescreen television behind it.

Maddy turned a full circle, taking it all in. "I expected something . . ." She trailed off.

Bear completed her sentence. "Less lavish."

"She's a prototype," Chris said. "My father designed it. You're lucky I was in the area showing it off to potential buyers. This will be a good test run." She turned to Bear. "You're the leader of the group, right?"

He nodded.

"Then my orders are to give you the captain's cabin." She spread her arms wide. "It's all yours."

"You're very kind," Bear drawled.

"With all this, is it really built to withstand a hurricane?" Maddy asked.

"Actually, yes. My father was inspired, if you could call it that, by Hurricane Andrew. He designed her to accommodate adventure seekers and, as an alternative market, rescue teams. She's also environmentally friendly."

"I appreciate the saving-the-world gesture," Maddy said, "but right now I'm worried about my stomach. How rough will the crossing to Greece be?"

Chris handed Maddy a pill packet from her front pocket. "We'll find out. This should take the edge off."

Maddy thanked Chris and the captain left, shutting the door softly behind her.

Bear turned to Maddy. "It'll take us all night to get to Greece. Want to take a nap?"

Maddy yawned and nodded. The bed looked inviting and she was exhausted. She undressed, placing her wet clothes across the bathtub.

Bear also undressed, put all of their clothes outside the door, locked it, and got under the sheets.

She snuggled up to him. The flannel sheets felt soft as a cloud. "Think they'll wash our clothes?"

"Hope so."

"What do you think the icy crown is?"

He stroked her hair. "Right now, I'm not sure I care."

Little knots of tension began to unwind like they were being softly batted by kittens. "No?"

"Nope. In this moment, I'm tired and sore, but it feels really good to lie here with you."

She had to agree, grateful he was alive.

He rubbed her neck muscles. "This feel good?"

She murmured, melting. "You know it does."

"Do you want to talk about . . ." He trailed off.

She stiffened for a moment, knowing he meant making babies. Commitment. But for reasons she couldn't fathom, she answered, "No."

"Okay. Topic tabled." His hands began to explore other parts of her body. "Why don't we just rock the boat before we get out to sea?"

His logic made sense, so she kissed him, and forgot all about their mission, Avril, and the medallion, for a time.

When she woke later, the expansive bow view revealed only rain-lashed darkness, and she worried that it was a portent of what they'd find when they finally arrived at the oracle's ancient temple.

CHAPTER 74

Seymore sat back in his chair as Avril sobbed, her face harshly lit by the basement's sole light. It had taken longer than he thought to break the sixteen-year-old, but she'd finally begun to spit out what she knew five minutes ago. He'd learned a long time ago that the threat of pain was often worse than pain itself, and so he'd bided his time and played on her fears with his gold lighter. With scars like that, he knew fire would be her weakness.

Psychological torture was so much more sophisticated than drawing blood. He was no sadist—he just wanted results. Every half hour or so, he'd scooted closer to her. She'd grown tired, but Raphael hadn't let her sleep. Every time her eyes closed, he'd poke her in the arm or ribs. The whole process was like slow-roasting a chicken.

When her eyes held the right combination of exhaustion and panic, he simply brought the lighter up to her jaw, just close enough so she could feel the heat. That's all it took. Words had flowed from her mouth like water from a broken dam.

Raphael was recording the entire confession for General Wong, who was sleeping his jet lag off in a comfortable bed upstairs, above the basement of the rented villa. Their benefactor, who had come from China to personally oversee this last phase of the mission, would finally be pleased. From Wong's covert surveillance of the VanOps team,

Seymore had been able to deduce the team would eventually be at Capitoline Hill.

When the girl had been stupid enough to bolt, his team had picked her up as easy as plucking a book from a bookshelf.

With her tearful revelations, the girl had just filled in the last missing pieces. It seemed the American team didn't know the final destination yet. Seymore needed the warrior's intelligence for just a while longer, and then he would turn on the old wolf.

Seymore lit a cigarette. "Tell me where you think the medallion is hidden."

Her words were slurred. "I told you. Delphi."

He'd read her journal, but wanted to see what else the girl knew. Although she lacked street smarts, she'd been clever at solving Nostradamus's puzzles. "Why do you think that?"

"Know thyself."

"What about it?"

"With the oracle's icy crown. Together. Has to be Delphi."

He took a long, slow drag from his unfiltered cigarette, enjoying the way the smoke felt when it hit his lungs. "If I believe you—if—where exactly in Delphi are we hunting?"

He clicked his lighter. Sapphire flame shot centimeters into the air.

Her body shuddered violently. "Not sure."

"But you suspect . . ." He trailed off.

"Don't know."

"Does the VanOps team know?"

She shook her head, which then drooped onto her chest. Raphael poked her.

Seymore took a drink of water. "What's the icy crown?"

"Need to see it. Need to see Delphi."

He considered her request. At this point, the odds of her lying or withholding information were slim. She'd sketched some temples in her notebook. It was also believable that the team had yet to figure out the last bit of the puzzle. He could always eliminate her once he had the medallion.

On his phone, he pulled up a map of the area, and a weather report. Ice and snow were present at Delphi and in the mountains surrounding the area.

Tapping out his cigarette, he made a decision.

Making eye contact with his short assistant, Seymore said, "Blindfold the girl and take her back to her room. Guard her well. Obtain a helicopter, snowmobiles, and whatever equipment we might need for a mission in freezing weather. As soon as the squall clears, we're going to Greece."

CHAPTER 75

TYRRHENIAN SEA
6:30 A.M.

Maddy woke to a heaving ship and the sounds of Bear's light snores. No dreams had come to her in the night. Slipping out of bed, she shuffled from one piece of bolted furniture to the next on the way to the restroom, before getting back under the sheets next to her man. It was barely light outside and they were nowhere near landfall, so she curled up next to him and dozed, happy that they'd had time to connect in the middle of a mission.

When he woke, he put his arms around her and rocked her world again.

An hour later, she was freshly showered and up in the dining nest at the top of the boat. Her neck had regained mobility and the rest of her felt decent, too. She sat at a heavy glass table that was secured to the floor, surrounded by her brother, her lover, and her friend. All three men had shaved and wore freshly laundered clothing. The ship was still being tossed like a toy across the sea, making the experience seem like a stomach-lurching roller-coaster ride, but the pills were doing their job. She hoped they'd be reimbursed for this expensive trip. "Testing" the boat had set them back twenty thousand dollars.

A waiter in black slacks, a white pressed shirt, and black silk tie served their coffee in lidded mugs made of sterling silver. She held onto her container so that it wouldn't topple to the floor. She wasn't sure she could eat, but her stomach seemed to feel more solid up here where she could see the horizon. All the men ordered bacon with eggs. She went for yogurt and fruit to be on the safe side.

After ordering, her glowing mood began to fade, mostly thanks to Will.

"Before you lovebirds arrived, we checked the weather with Chris," he said. "It's still blizzard conditions around Delphi. Sea level has minimal precipitation, but the higher elevations, like the temple site, may have snow."

"No storm lasts forever," she replied.

"We also got a shore-to-ship news alert. Things are heating up in Taiwan."

She was never sure if she should take him at his word, given he was such a worrywart.

Maddy tilted her head. "Now what?"

"Talks have broken off."

"Was there ever any real hope there anyway?" she snipped.

"Perhaps not, but—"

Doyle interrupted their argument. "China has taken more outlying islands. Kinmen and Matsu. This is bad, Madeline. Millions are on alert and hunkering down." His eyes got glassy and he looked away. "Including my grandparents."

"I see," she said, more softly. "Invasion is looking more real by the second."

"Exactly." Doyle blinked hard and sat back in his chair. "I've been worried. Now I'm ready to panic. We're running out of time."

She put a hand on his. "We'll stop this. Somehow."

Will grimaced. "About that." He turned to Bear. "What can we expect to find when we get to Delphi?"

Bear rubbed at the remains of his black eye. "I'm not sure. But I can fill you in on some history."

Maddy took a sip of her steaming coffee, glad her boyfriend was a history geek and could take over this part of the conversation. The waiter brought their food. Maddy wondered what Avril was eating this morning and pursed her lips before half-heartedly stirring her yogurt.

Bear held his plate down with one hand and consumed half a strip of bacon with the other.

"Where we're headed is the Temple of Apollo," he said. "The high priestess there was called either the Pythia or the Oracle."

"What time period are we talking about?" Will asked around a mouthful of egg.

"Historians don't agree on when the Oracle began prophesying. It was at least as far back as 800 BC, and maybe as far back as 1400 BC."

Will raised an eyebrow.

"The old girls got around the proverbial block," Doyle said.

The muscles of Bear's bare forearms rippled as he ate, causing his lightning scars to wave like trees in a storm. "There were a lot of old girls involved," he said. "Centuries' worth. The Oracles were consulted until 400 AD."

"That's anywhere from twelve hundred to eighteen hundred years. A long time." Maddy popped a grape in her mouth and considered, thinking about her own experiences with premonitory dreams. "How did one become an Oracle?"

"Not sure. What we do know is that they were chosen from every walk of life. There was only one at a time, and when she passed on, the next one was picked. Since it wasn't just the wealthy, there's speculation that ability played into the choosing."

Will scrunched his face. "Let me get this straight. For well over a thousand years, some of the most learned men of the time consulted a fairy godmother for answers to life's most pressing questions?"

Bear nodded. "Absolutely. Cicero, the famous Roman, noted that no expedition was begun, no group sent out, without the approval of the Oracle."

Will frowned. "Was the Oracle accurate then? Or was it some sort of mass hysteria?"

"They believed her to be accurate," Bear replied. "I found it interesting that over six hundred prophetic statements have survived, and over half came true."

"Half?" Maddy exclaimed.

Bear nodded, taking the opportunity to eat more eggs.

"That's incredible," she said.

The ship churned up an immense wave, hovered at the top, and then rushed down the other side. They all held onto their plates and coffee.

Will's eyes narrowed. "What proof do you have?"

"I remember a few stories," Bear replied.

"Such as?"

"You might appreciate this one: Philip II of Macedon had a devilish black colt that no one could ride. In a trance, the Oracle stated that whoever could ride the horse would conquer the world, but neither Philip nor his generals were able to mount that black pony."

"I remain unimpressed."

Bear grinned. "I'm not done with the story. Philip's son, Alexander, realized that the horse was afraid of his own shadow and managed to tame him."

"So what?"

"Alexander rode the horse to great victory."

Will shrugged.

"You might recognize Alexander from his full name: Alexander the Great."

Will sat back in his chair, a tone of defeat on his lips. "Oh."

"There are hundreds of stories like that," Bear said.

Maddy imagined the Oracle wearing flowing robes and seeing one supplicant after another. Her brother was still holding on to his theory that Nostradamus used herbs in his recipe. She didn't want to add fuel to Will's fire, but had to ask. "Have scientists studied the phenomenon? Is there anything local to that part of Greece that may have put the women in a trance?"

A sparkle entered Bear's eye as he looked at her. "Oh yes. It's been studied for over a hundred years."

Will sat forward in his seat. "And?"

"There are two working theories right now." Bear raised a finger. "The first, and this one was noted by the philosopher Plutarch, who was a priest of the temple, is that there were underground vapors that would collect in the Oracle's chamber. Scientists think the vapors, if they existed, were likely ethylene, and traces of that gas have been found in the town's water supply."

Before Will could get an egotistical comment out of his mouth, Maddy asked, "What's the other theory?"

Bear raised two fingers. "Oleander."

"Really?" she asked. "We have a lot of that planted around California highways. But isn't it toxic?"

"Yes, ma'am. Very. But they didn't know that and smoked it. And chewed the leaves."

Maddy grimaced. "Eww."

"I know. They may have burnt it in the underground chamber. The fumes would have come up through a chasm in the floor."

Bad for them, but promising info for us, she thought. "Okay, so maybe Nostradamus knew about this."

"It's possible," Bear agreed. "There's one other option."

Maddy finished her Greek yogurt. "What's that?"

"Nearby barley was tainted with a fungus that caused visions."

"What kind of fungus? Mushrooms?"

"Ergot. It grew on the barley near Eleusis and some think it was once used as part of the Eleusinian Mysteries initiation rite, in a special drink. The fungus contains LSD-like psychedelic chemicals."

She considered this information. "Were those Eleusinian visions considered prophetic?"

Bear took a moment to think. "Not that I recall."

Will nodded. "I knew it. Science. My best guess is Nostradamus's recipe contains either ethylene gas or oleander."

Bear finished his bacon. "Makes sense."

Maddy scowled at them both.

Doyle folded his napkin and set it by his empty plate. "All very curious. Bear, what's the reference to knowing thyself all about?"

Bear nodded. "I'm not sure if that was just part of the quatrain and it's a clue, or if it means anything further. In the forecourt of the temple, inscribed on a column, were an enigmatic letter 'E' and three quotes:

'Surety brings ruin,' 'Nothing to excess,' and 'Know thyself.' It's thought they were part of the ritual."

"I see. Good advice if nothing else."

The waiter came to take their plates.

Maddy thought the first two statements wise. But in terms of knowing herself, there were parts of her psyche she didn't want to probe. Why had the prophet chosen that saying? It niggled at a corner of her mind she'd grown used to respecting.

Perhaps he was referencing the zodiac. She and Will were born in mid-June under the sign of Gemini. She'd never found much wisdom in the aspects and rising signs of astrology, but Nostradamus was an expert in horoscopes. Could knowing your personality tie in with knowing the future? She could see how it might be prognostic on a personal, behavioral level, but not in predicting world events.

And then there were the clues Nostradamus had left behind . . . the son, the architect, the king, the founder. Those were all identities, labels, not the real person inside. Who was underneath the identities and personalities?

Maddy glanced at Bear's chiseled features. He caught her eye and winked, making her smile. She *had* felt his spirit leave his body. It wasn't just her imagination. The only conclusion: souls were real.

Was Nostradamus talking about souls? She had no idea.

Then she recalled the Oracle's words—"Surety brings ruin"—and her overconfident comment to Doyle about stopping this somehow.

Was ruin where they were headed?

CHAPTER 76

After the yacht landed in Patras, the VanOps team rented a pearl-white SUV to drive the two hours through Greece toward Delphi. Will couldn't help but somberly note the similarities between the name of the northern Peloponnese Grecian city and Pratas Island near Taiwan, where hundreds of soldiers had recently met their demise at the hands of the PLA.

As Bear drove, Will also wondered if Avril was still alive. The weather matched his misgivings—most of the trip would have had scenic views of the Gulf of Corinth had it not been for the leaden clouds and violent rain that lashed the vehicle from all sides.

The team was quiet. Will thought about playing his harmonica, but didn't have it in him.

Outside Delphi, the road cut back and forth in a series of switchbacks.

"Are we there yet?" Maddy asked from the back seat. "I'm getting car sick."

Bear looked over his shoulder. "Do you want to drive?"

"Sure, thanks."

Bear stopped at a pullout near where a creek dipped under the road. Normally, the stream was likely a trickle, but with the volume of rain over the last twenty-four hours, it gushed past with such ferocity they had to raise their voices to make small talk as they switched seats.

Twenty-three minutes later, Maddy parked the car near steps that led to a path up to their destination: the temple ruins. With the downpour, theirs was the lone vehicle.

"Who wants to stretch their legs?" she asked.

Thinking of the climb, Will sighed. "It's still raining."

She glared at him. "If you want to get your little French friend back, you better buck up."

He slammed the door.

A square-jawed young man with a missing front tooth accepted money for their right to enter the archeological site. As they started up the paved walkway, the clouds broke and a mountain appeared ahead, swathed in white snow.

The walk up to the ruins was painfully steep, paving stones quickly turning to dirt. As a rule, Will avoided exercise whenever possible, and, in his view, this path was appropriate only for goats. At least everyone was huffing and puffing almost as much as he was. Except Bear, who maintained his hard-won marine physique.

The rain turned to mist.

After walking by a courtyard marked by a series of snub-nosed columns, they passed the only standing building in sight, labeled "The Treasury." The center of the left column had been repaired and the stone building leaned a little. They moved on up the hill to the sounds of the haunting wind whipping among the Greek graveyard. Soon they came across a set of five columns, surrounded by patches of snow.

"This place is amazing!" Bear said, eyes alight with fascination.

Will didn't understand the captivation with dead civilizations, but Bear's interest had come in handy on occasion. "I'm glad your History Channel fetish is getting a tickle, but I sense old Nostradamus wanted us here for some other reason."

Bear pointed. "You're right. This is it."

Will asked, "Is what?"

"The Temple of Apollo, where the oracles sat and delivered the prophecies that changed the course of mankind."

"Doesn't look like much," Will observed. Even the world's greatest civilizations couldn't stop the onslaught of time.

"Check out the outline of the temple. See where the walls stood?"

"Sure," Will admitted. It was larger than he first thought.

Maddy walked up a few stairs and stood next to a column. "Let's search it."

Will stopped. "Anyone know what we're looking for?"

Doyle had refused to utilize his jacket's hood, and his bushy eyebrows dripped. "William, my friend, it's the icy crown we seek."

Will threw up his hands in mock disgust. "Of course. But what does that look like?"

They spread out, each taking about ten feet and walking the length of the building. He kicked through two piles of slush as he walked, nothing catching his eye.

They reconvened at the end of the temple.

"See anything noteworthy?" Bear asked.

They all shook their wet heads with disappointed eyes. *So much for the famous Temple of Apollo*, Will thought.

"Let's explore the rest of the site then," Bear ordered.

Of course, that meant more uphill walking.

Rain fell harder the higher they climbed. To distract himself from the physical discomfort, Will compared the wet archeological site to the many ruins he'd seen over the years. There were the usual quarried blocks that made up the walls of god-knew-what building two thousand years ago. Slightly more interesting was the well-preserved theater cut into the hillside like half a bowl. The seats probably held a couple hundred people and Will could almost hear men in white tunics orating about one philosophical treatise or another while raising a hand and walking back and forth in front of the captive crowd.

The team stopped to catch their breath here. Barely visible between the sheets of rain, a long valley stretched out far below.

Maddy had her hands on her hips. "I think we need to keep going to the top."

Bear, who listened to Maddy far more often than Will would have liked, nodded and started walking again.

They continued to climb. Rain turned to large snowflakes and then stopped altogether. Will thought about all the horrid situations Avril could be experiencing and walking up a hill suddenly didn't seem so bad. He picked up his pace.

After what seemed like forever, the path leveled out near some trees that looked like cedars from the forests back in California. Will wanted to sit down and rest, but all the stone benches were covered in a dusting of snow.

He looked at the group. "Now what?"

No one answered so he slowly turned around. Wind had blown the clouds high enough to get their bearings. Dusk darkened the green valley below, which beckoned to him with thoughts of dinner. Behind them was a large, snow-covered mountain.

Doyle likewise was taking in the scenery and muttering under his breath about the icy crown.

Bear put his arm around Maddy's waist as if they were on a honeymoon.

"Hey!" Doyle shouted. Like a hunting dog, he was pointing at the snow-topped mountain nearby. "This site is home to the oracles, right?"

"Yes, the Temple of Apollo below," Bear said. "Why?"

"That jagged mountain looks like an icy crown to me. The oracle's icy crown."

They all walked over and stood by Doyle, gazing up at the white-covered mass overlooking the temple site as well as the valley.

Will squinted, trying to see the pointed mountain as a crown. Maybe . . .

Maddy tugged her ear. "Doyle, you're brilliant! Bear, is there anything special about that mountain?"

Bear tilted his head. "I believe that's the famed Mount Parnassus, home of the Corycian Cave."

Maddy smiled. "Somehow, I sense you know its history."

Bear pecked her cheek. "I'll spare you the details, but not only did locals use it for refuge during invasions, it also was sacred to the Corycian nymphs and the Muses. Pan was worshiped there, and it was believed to be the home of Dionysus."

"Seems important. Anything else?" Maddy asked.

"I'll do more research when we get cell reception, but it's supposed to be huge. It would be an excellent place to hide something like a medallion."

Maddy's green eyes glowed. "A cavern. Full circle from the caves in France. We have to search it."

Will spoke up. "That's all well and good, but do you see all the snow up there? We'll need supplies. And it's getting dark."

Maddy moved off at a trot. "Guess we best hurry then, eh?"

CHAPTER 77

DELPHI, GREECE

7:10 P.M.

Avril stared out the window of the helicopter as it flew across the dark shadow of the Greek mainland. Her hands were zip-tied together, but at least there was no gag in her mouth. Seymore sat next to her on a jump seat.

They'd been in the air long enough that she supposed they'd be getting close to Delphi, where she'd finally be forced to tell Seymore and his crew about the location of the medallion. Based on her brief research in Lyon, she was over ninety percent certain the medallion was hidden inside the Corycian Cave.

If Will and Doyle had been more welcoming to her ideas, she'd have shared her theory with them, but they hadn't even wanted to entertain her supposition that the first quatrain's answer was SON, even though it was super obvious. Nor had they been interested in hearing about PIE as the Pazzi Chapel answer. She hoped they'd eventually figured out the ultimate destination on their own, as they were her only hope of leaving Greece alive.

Back in that torture chamber, she'd done her best to stall, finally giving up Delphi when it was clear Seymore was done waiting. She was proud of herself for two things. First, she'd managed to keep her secret about how she'd made that Pratas prediction, and second, that she'd negotiated coming along to the oracle's icy crown by concealing her theory about the cave. Her pride had limits, though, because the only thing waiting for her after they found the medallion was a bullet.

She chewed the inside of her lip. Was there anything else she could do to save her skin?

The odds of eking out any mercy from Seymore or his boss were low. The headman apparently wanted to remain mysterious, as he hadn't spoken a word and wore a mask with crimson, white, and midnight markings to hide his features. The guise reminded her of a theater mask, like one she'd seen in Paris on a poster announcing a show. She guessed he wore it for anonymity, or perhaps to spook his team. He also wore a business suit and gloves, so even his skin tone was hidden. Who was he?

Someone creepy, that was certain, although the mask would make an awesome painting. She longed for her sketchbook, as a pen, or charcoal, in her hand always relaxed her.

Besides the boss man and Seymore, there were nine other men wearing tactical gear crammed inside the helicopter. Behind them, five sleek snowmobiles had been loaded up in the back bay. All she could see of the single pilot was a metal clipboard on his knee that she guessed held some sort of instructions.

The helicopter shook in the wind. She'd overheard a conversation about the storm dying out about the time they were due to arrive, but at the moment it still raged.

Seymore pointed out the window. "We're almost to Delphi. Now what?"

She ground her teeth. There was really no way to avoid telling, but maybe she could stall a little longer. "Once we get there, have him circle the area."

Seymore gave instructions to the pilot.

Minutes later, the helicopter banked, and Delphi appeared below. In ever widening circles, the pilot flew rings around the ruins.

The boss man began to tap his foot. Time was up.

Avril pointed and spoke with false enthusiasm. "There it is! Nostradamus instructed us to find 'the oracle's icy crown.' Delphi is where the famous Greek oracles occupied the Temple of Apollo and the jagged mountain rears up over the valley and is covered in snow."

Seymore's teeth were bright in the dim light. "Where exactly?"

Might as well tell him the truth. "See that hollow part way up Mount Parnassus? It's called the Corycian Cave. With the first quatrain leading us to the Caverns of Rouffignac, it has to be the place."

"I see." He glanced out the window.

"I think I know where inside to search for the medallion," she lied.

Seymore loosened his seatbelt and whispered in the ear of the masked leader. The man's eyes bore into hers, as if trying to read her face. Then he nodded, and Seymore moved to the front of the aircraft to give instructions to the pilot.

She sucked in a breath. *Will they throw me out of the helicopter now?*

CHAPTER 78

MOUNT PARNASSUS, GREECE
7:15 P.M.

The swirling snow limited Maddy's visibility as they telemarked up the mountain into the icy wind. They'd been able to get a quick bite and cross-country ski supplies in the postcard-perfect town of Arachova. After, they'd barely been able to traverse the slippery slope to a chalet roughly across and below the cave, before the snow-plowed section of road ended. She wished they'd been able to get an all-terrain vehicle or snowmobile, but the town was fresh out of both.

Chunks of snow bit into her cheeks and she wondered if they were slicing the skin, leaving trails of blood that might end up looking like war paint. The ski boots weren't even close to a perfect fit, scrunching her toes painfully with every stroke, and the headlamp on her forehead provided only a ghostly circle of light. No goggles had been available to keep the snow from her eyes in the whiteout conditions.

The wind howled louder, as if the cave was haunted with banshees who didn't want them to approach. She supposed she should be grateful the team hadn't been relegated to snowshoes, but she wasn't.

Her stomach churned with anxiety. The Corycian Cave was close, but still far enough away that her imagination played tricks on her. What if they found nothing in the dark grotto? How would they get Avril back and stop the Chinese from invading Taiwan?

Bear skied next to her. Meanwhile, her loyal brother was showing Doyle a few ski tricks; Doyle hadn't grown up on a mountain like the three of them.

Her breath huffed in and out, causing trails of condensation to escape. She remembered one time when she and Will had been playing in a similar snowstorm. Mom had told them to stay in the front yard where they could see the house, and, happy to be out in it, they'd complied, laughing and making snow angels. Was that the time they'd attempted an igloo? Maybe. She remembered Mom calling them inside for a cup of hot chocolate in front of the cheery woodstove. And that was all. It was one of the few memories she had of her mom, and she held it close.

Bear glanced over at her. "You doin' all right?"

"When's the downhill part start?"

"We're getting close, I think. We should hit the track that heads down to the cave any minute."

"Hey, the wind stopped."

His head swiveled. "It sure did. Maybe it'll be easier going."

"I hope so. I'm tired of fighting it."

He pointed with a pole. "That might be the road ahead."

The mountain flattened out and they skied through the blanketed trees toward an opening. At the edge of the forest, they stopped. The woodland was quiet, except for their breath.

Sweat from the exertion soaked the small of her back.

"Looks like a road," she said.

A thin ribbon of white stretched in both directions. With the cessation of the wind, the snow now fell straight down, like ethereal white arrows.

Bear gestured. "We go left."

"I know." She remembered the map. "Shall we wait for Will and Doyle?"

He shook his head, making the headlamp's light dance madly. "No. I want to get to the cave."

"Good. Me too. Think this is why Nostradamus had a cave clue?"

"Could be."

They pushed onto the road. Although no downhill ski run, there was enough of a slope that they both got a little speed by bending over and tucking their poles like they were slalom racers. She narrowed her eyes to minimize the snow's intrusion.

Bear abruptly turned his skis and stopped, causing a cloud of snow to spray her back. She stopped too, and turned to face him. His eyes were darting around the sky, searching for something.

She heard it too. "A helo?"

He swiped at his forehead. "Your headlamp!"

With her thick mittens, it took her three tries before she got it turned off. An instant later, a helicopter flew overhead, heading in the direction of the cave.

"Looks like a Russian Mi-14, but with a lot of cargo space and a Chinese flag." Bear's eyes were wide disks of white in the darkness. "Did they see us?"

"I don't know." Her heart beat in her throat. "Are they who I think they are?"

CHAPTER 79

Avril squeezed her zip-tied hands until they hurt in an attempt to relieve her anxiety. Being thrown from a moving helicopter would be beyond awful. She'd read once about a seventeen-year-old German girl who'd fallen from a lightning-struck plane in South America and survived, but highly doubted she'd have the luck to gently crash into a stand of trees. More likely, she'd be flattened, like one of the pancakes Monique used to make for breakfast.

After giving instructions to the pilot, Seymore sat down next to Avril and looked at her, his glass eye slowly rotating away in a way that caused her stomach to flutter.

He swiped his palm over his bald pate. "I've been searching for this formula for more than forty years, well before you were born. You know where it is in the cave?"

She put on a blank face, trying not to show her cards. "I believe I do."

"Where? What part of the cave?"

"It's too hard to describe with only rocks as landmarks. I'll show you."

His heavy lips pursed with anger and he put his hand on her arm, grabbing the flesh painfully. "Tell me."

Her courage came from desperation. "No."

The masked man kicked Seymore in the foot. Releasing her arm, he made a noncommittal grunt and sat back in his seat.

She nodded her thanks to the boss, but his flinty eyes stared back vacantly. He was like a cruel master keeping his doberman on a tight leash. At some point, though, she'd no longer be useful, and then she'd be fed to the dogs.

The helicopter banked, circling.

Probably trying to find a place to set down, she thought.

The wind buffeted the machine as the pilot brought it straight down for a landing. Outside, there was a small clearing beneath a handful of houses covered by snow. The icy mountain reared up beyond the homes.

The cave mouth must be at least a thousand meters up the slope.

The instant the metal bird touched ground, the men around her sprang into action. The back hatch was raised and the snowmobiles were fired up with a chorus of roars. Exhaust fumes filled the small cabin as each of the machines rumbled down the ramp.

Seymore took her by the elbow and led her toward the front ski. When she hesitated, he smacked her face and she took the hint, awkwardly raising her leg to sit down on the black bench next to the controls. He got on behind her, and another man joined in the back. Seymore gave it some gas, and it shot up the mountain like a rocket. She wished for a heavier jacket and proper boots.

The masked man and the pilot had stayed in the helicopter. Five snowmobiles carrying ten men raced toward the cave through lightly falling snow.

While the icy wind whipped her face, Avril urged her brain to do its job. *Think!* Where would Nostradamus have hidden his precious formula? She tried to reason like the old seer. He had them visit a cave, a crypt, a chapel, and Capitoline Hill. Were there more clues in the quatrains that she'd missed? Where would he hide a medallion?

Avril searched the surrounding forest for any sign that the VanOps team was in the area. Nothing stirred.

The snowmobiles pulled up on a narrow ledge in front of the cave, stopping in two rows—two skis in front, three behind.

She shivered. Although she was glad the freezing ride was done, she now had to find an object hidden hundreds of years in the past. And as soon as she did, she'd be killed and left here to rot.

However, she had no choice. Will's favorite harmonica tune played in her head and she prayed he was nearby, watching. All she could do was find the medallion and hope.

CHAPTER 80

7:42 P.M.

From the relative safety of the snow-covered firs above the cave, Maddy peered at the crowd of snowmobiles, huddled before the entrance like a noisy motorcycle gang in front of a bar.

Avril sat on the front of one of the snowmobiles, looking scared, but alive. A knot of tension in Maddy's gut relaxed . . . until the goons stood and she got a glimpse of their submachine guns.

Maddy pulled back, huddling next to Bear as she tried to follow the activity below. Will and Doyle were about ten paces back, awaiting Bear's orders.

Maddy subvocalized into her molar mic, "Now what? They're about to head inside."

"I'm thinking," Bear replied.

"How deep is the cave? Is there a back exit?"

"Not quite the size of a football field. I don't think so."

The men below turned off the snowmobiles, stood and began to talk among themselves. They were just far enough away that she couldn't hear what they were saying. Avril stood nearby, her thin shoulders hunched.

The adrenaline rushing through Maddy made her irritable. She clenched her fists, wanting action and wanting it now. "Are you sure this is even the right cave?"

"It's pretty much the only cave up here, and our enemies are standing outside it. Yes, I'm sure."

That was a stupid question, she thought.

On the way here, Bear had mentioned French archeologists had excavated the cavern in the late sixties, discovering all kinds of artifacts, like a Neolithic male figurine, bone flutes, iron and bronze rings, and fifty thousand terracotta figurines. They had also found almost twenty-five thousand knucklebones used for prophecy. The numbers made her head dizzy. After all that excavation, what treasures could possibly be left inside? Was the medallion actually in there, or did Nostradamus leave a clue to point to another location?

More importantly, what kind of plan was Bear concocting?

"Think we could get reinforcements here?" she asked.

He shook his head. "Not in time."

"They could use Avril as a human shield."

"I'm trying to avoid that scenario."

"We're outnumbered more than two to one. There must be ten of them."

He glared at her, frowning. "I know."

She should shut up so he could think. He was the military strategist who studied battle plans, not her. Aikido was her thing. Which meant she should be focusing on how they could use the enemies' strength and energy against themselves.

The noisy machines might be useful.

"As soon as they head inside, what do you think about riding the snowmobiles into the cave in a blaze of glory?"

He shook his head slightly. "There's no snow in the cave."

"They work on roads, just not as well. And they would provide some cover."

"There's no stealth involved." His blue eyes met hers.

She put a finger up. "What about—"

"Wait. I have an idea. Here's what we're going to do."

The two of them brainstormed. He actually liked part of her idea.

As they firmed up the plan, her eyes narrowed with the grim hope that some of the questions about her mother might finally find answers.

The men below moved away from the snowmobiles. Two stout, broad-shouldered goons stopped to guard the wide entrance. The rest headed toward the cave, pushing a slight, yellow-jacketed figure in front of them.

CHAPTER 81

7:44 P.M.

T he opening of the cavern, with its oval shape and tongue-like boulder, reminded Avril of an evil, gaping mouth.

As they walked through the entrance, Seymore held her upper arm in an iron grip while two goons led the way with flashlights. The beams revealed an enormous cavern whose ceiling and walls were made of rough gray stone. Light flickered across the space, quickly swallowed up by the darkness of the earth's bowels, but she estimated it to be at least the size of the gymnasium at school.

Where did Nostradamus hide his secrets? she wondered.

Seymore shook her arm as soon as they reached the center of the cave, where a wide circle of stones was the only obvious sign of human inhabitants.

"Okay. Where is the medallion?"

"I need to examine the cave. Let's walk to the back."

"Fine," Seymore growled. "But if you're messing with me, I'll put a bullet between your eyes."

"I'm not." She swallowed the bile in her throat. "It's just that everything looks alike. I have to find it."

Light glinted off his bald head. "You'd better hurry."

She stumbled over a rock as they moved toward the back. It was awkward walking among the stalagmites with her hands bound. She considered asking him to cut the ties, but her cheek still burned from where he'd hit her earlier.

With her stomach clenching so hard she might vomit, her eyes scanned the walls, ceiling, and floor, looking for any sort of clue. Nothing grabbed her attention.

All hopes of rescue faded in the gloom of the cave. She was on her own.

CHAPTER 82

Will subvocalized, "Bear, what's the plan?"

Will had gotten a quick glimpse of Avril near the cave before he was shunted to the rear of the group. Earlier, using his binoculars, he'd seen one of the men smack Avril's face. It had taken all of Will's self-possession, and Doyle's strong hand on his shoulder, to not rush the enemy in a kamikaze surprise. The sense of relief he felt at seeing her sent a glow throughout his body, even warming his cold toes.

She's alive!

Realizing that he'd risk his life for her surprised him. He thought his heart too jaded, too scarred, to care about someone again, but he did, in a parental way. Now she was inside a cave with eight thugs who would probably kill her once she was no longer useful.

Time was running out on the hourglass that was her life. And perhaps his. If he needed to die to rescue her, so be it.

They needed a plan.

"Bear," he whispered again.

Bear's voice came into Will's ear. "Yeah. Here's what we're going to do."

Will's heart hammered in his chest while he listened. Direct enemy confrontation was *not* his favorite part of the job. But they had no choice.

He and Doyle moved into position on either side of the cave mouth. Guards patrolled ten feet below, rifles at the ready.

On Doyle's count of five, Will launched himself into the air, aiming for the back of the sentry on his side.

He caught the man as he was turning, so his chest hit the guard's right shoulder and they tumbled together into the snow. Will tried to clasp his arms around the man as they fell, but the guy was too broad. At least the rifle dropped to the ground.

The impact almost knocked the air out of Will, but he recovered first. Not wanting to kill, he punched the man in the upper stomach. Air burst from the soldier's lungs but the guard already had a roundhouse punch in motion. The swing collided with Will's jaw and caused him to see stars.

Will shook his head, attempting to clear it as the lookout rolled over, trying to pin Will, but he kept rolling and managed a cuff below the chin. The man's head snapped back. Will whacked Avril's captor in the carotid, aiming to cut off the man's blood supply. The enemy's eyes fluttered for an instant.

It was the opening he needed. Will hit the foe in the gut. Then, when the man bent over, Will followed up with a hard smack to the back of the neck using the butt of his hand. The sentinel crumpled.

Will stood and took a deep breath, inventorying his body for damage. He moved his mouth, noting a sore jaw. Not broken, though. Bending over, he picked up the semiautomatic rifle and stuffed a glove in the gaping mouth before quickly zip tying the man's hands and feet.

That hadn't exactly gone to plan, but it had gotten the job done. The next part, however, would be twice as dangerous.

CHAPTER 83

Avril knew she was playing a dangerous game. If she couldn't find the medallion, she was doomed. Even if she found it, her existence would be snuffed out like a candle.

While they walked toward the rear of the cave, she thought back over her brief life. She didn't remember her mother. Her father had raised her, and on weekends, took her to the museums of Paris. It was the only activity they did together. He'd wanted to be a painter, he'd told her once at a café after a trip to the Louvre. When she was young, he'd hold her hand as they looked at the work of Dutch masters, Spanish impressionists, and American cubists. As she grew old enough to comment on the art, they'd laugh at some pieces and cry at others, but he always seemed distant. She never felt she knew him.

He died young. Maybe she would too.

No. I can't think like that! She reminded herself to focus.

Nostradamus had given them the quatrains for a reason. He was methodical and thorough. The clues he'd provided had led here.

Mentally, she reviewed the places the team had seen on the hunt so far. The caves of Rouffignac. The Tomb of Charles in the Basilica of Saint Servatius in Maastricht. The Pazzi Chapel. And where she stupidly ditched Maddy: Capitoline Hill in Rome.

Where would the old prophet hide something in this cave? Time was running out.

The medallion could be buried in the floor, under a rock. But none of the clues lent itself to that, except maybe the sarcophagus. She sensed the French caves were part of the thread that led them here, but was there anything in them that might be a clue? Her mind raced back over the train ride with Will and Doyle. Nothing stood out.

What about the tomb? It had been a king's body buried in a lead casket with an inscription above. She looked around for any sort of rock casket. No stone formations looked like a box.

Capitoline Hill, then. That quatrain had been about the founder of Rome. It directed them to a square, with a statue in the center. Hopeful, she led the men back to the firepit in the middle of the cavern. She scuffed the dirt with her toe. No, that would be too obvious.

That left Florence. The zodiac clue at Pazzi Chapel had been on the ceiling of the dome. Hmm, the ceiling, or maybe the upper walls. That held promise in a cave like this.

She turned, searching the walls. Seymore caught her gaze with his single good eye.

"Direct your flashlights to the top of the walls," he ordered. "The ceiling, too."

She saw it first, and hesitated.

"What?" Seymore asked, grabbing her arm in a vise-like grip.

Sighing at the inevitability of death, she pointed with her head. "Look over there."

Light plastered the left wall. Near the ceiling, a large round rock stood on a ledge. Below it, a series of boulders led up, forming a crude staircase.

"Let's go," Seymore barked.

One man went ahead.

Roughly, Seymore pulled her up the stairs. Their pace was slow as they sought out safe havens for their feet, and she was hampered by the inability to use her hands. Twice, she stumbled, falling once to her knees and skinning them.

The two men left at the foot of the staircase trained their lights on the round rock.

Grunting with the effort, Seymore and his man pushed the rock aside. It crunched bits of sand beneath it as it rolled.

Light played on the inside of a closet-sized geode. Deep-purple amethyst sparkled amidst snowy crystal. It was like the ice cave in her dream.

But that wasn't why she gasped. Thrown over a jagged piece of quartz, a bronze medallion hung at eye level from a thick gold chain.

CHAPTER 84

Seymore gaped in admiration as light flashed off the bronze of the medallion. He took a deep, satisfied breath and rushed into the geode, barely noticing the surrounding purple crystal.

Reaching out, he plucked the hanging prize from the piece of quartz and cradled it in his palm. It took up about half the meat of his hand.

On one side, zodiac symbols were carved into the spokes of a circle. A bearded face stared out from the disk's center.

Words in old French were etched on the opposite side. Across the top: *Know Thyself.* Across the bottom: *Know Others.*

In random places on both sides, other esoteric symbols and Latin words were interspersed.

Ah. The formula—revealed at last.

He traced the words with his index finger. *The future rests in the palm of my hand!* He shuddered as a tingle of pleasure rose up his spine.

His smile was wide as the gulf of years that defined his quest. It was the find of a lifetime. There was no way he could turn the medallion over to the general; an unplanned jump out of the helo was in the future for the old man.

It might take a little time for Seymore to decipher the formula, but it rightfully belonged to him.

He caught the girl looking over his shoulder and instinctively tucked the medallion into his pocket. The thick gold chain brushed against his thigh on the outside of his pants.

Avril's eyes were wide. "What does it say?"

"That doesn't concern you. Like your grandmother decades ago, your time is done."

She shrunk back from him. "What do you mean? I thought she drowned. You killed her?"

"That was a cover story. She fled back to the States and died in an icy accident. Brakes don't work well without fluid."

Shock caused her eyes to widen further. "And now you're going to slay me?"

"I knew you were smart." He pulled a knife from his pocket and grabbed her wrists. "Yes, it's your turn to die."

CHAPTER 85

8:05 P.M.

A shout came from inside the cave.

A minute earlier, Maddy and Bear had swooshed down to the snowmobiles as Doyle and Will finished subduing the two beefy guards.

She'd willed her heart rate to slow as she stepped out of her skis and set them aside. Now that the action was underway, the pregame jitters had given way to an adrenaline-fueled focus. She *listened* to get out of her head and into instinct. As always, her senses sharpened, and she noted the hot gasoline smell of the machines, the distinctive sound of wind blowing through tree branches, and the sensation of blood hammering through her veins.

They crouched behind the machines to give them cover from bullets that might come flying out of the cave like tiny, deadly bats. As part of Bear's plan, they'd combined their hydro supplies—two water bottles each—and given them all to her and Bear. Going to the first green snowmobile in the back row, Maddy popped open the gas tank lid and poured water into the tank before refastening the cap. Nearby, Bear repeated the sabotage on a black machine.

While she'd worked on the middle vehicle, she kept one eye on the cave mouth. The sloped opening was wide as a garage and towered over her brother's tall frame. Once, she saw a flashlight beam skitter about in the depths.

She'd finished hamstringing her third iron horse when Will joined them, appearing unharmed from his attack on the guard. She hoped he'd not had to kill the man.

Just as she and Will made eye contact, a ruckus sounded from inside the depths of the cavern. Had they noticed their guards had gone silent?

"Move, move!" Bear subvocalized.

She dropped the water bottles and ran for the cave mouth in her clunky, ill-fitting ski boots. She and Bear veered right, Will and Doyle left.

As they'd planned, Bear entered first, Glock drawn, a wraith in the darkness. She followed by feel, one hand on the wall, one on Bear's back, wishing for night-vision goggles they didn't have. Her part of the plan revolved around the enemy's similar inability to see in the dark. The inky black depths of the cave would be their salvation or damnation.

Excited voices echoed toward them. The words sounded French. Why the excitement? Had they found the medallion? Or was the enemy onto them?

After scraping along the downhill wall for several minutes, Bear stopped. Far ahead and to the left, two men in black tactical suits had their flashlights fixed on an opening on the wall near the ceiling. Another man stood near a large rock that must have once blocked it. Light emanated from up there, refracted into brilliant shards, as if a giant diamond glittered inside. Maddy caught a glimpse of Seymore's bald pate. Avril's voice, brittle and scared, came from within, but Maddy couldn't see her or make out her words.

She wanted to rush up and rescue the girl, but that was not the plan. Clenching her jaw, Maddy crouched down, still as death.

Four other men were moving about the monstrous cavern, one near the middle, exploring what looked like an ancient fire pit. Bear had been right about the cave's size. Even with only the faint light of the men's flashlights, it was obvious the space was humongous, at least a hundred feet wide. No claustrophobic feelings here. The top arched up like a cathedral.

Her target was the second man on this side of the cave. Will would get the man in the center and Doyle the one furthest away. As Bear slipped off to neutralize the first fellow, she focused on her goal, naming him Stocky, because his build came from the same muscled mold as the guards outside. He wore no headgear or goggles and moved slowly among the rocks and stalagmites, as if biding his time. His posture and movements were loose and when he swung his light, she caught glimpses of a short-cropped dark beard on a square, flat face. Maybe he'd been a boxer and taken one too many hits to the nose.

She stalked him like a panther, knowing her teammates were doing the same with their own prey.

Suddenly, Avril yelled. The men by the wall shone their lights to the top, where Seymore was holding a half-dollar-sized item aloft. As the men cheered, Maddy saw a glint of bronze.

The medallion!

Seymore and one of his men rolled a large rock in front of the hole, shutting Avril, and her screams, inside. Frustrated, Maddy bit her lip to keep from reassuring the girl. She had no choice but to stay focused.

Stocky swung his light her way and she flattened herself to the wall behind a boulder, praying his light would move on. It did.

She crawled forward. This needed to happen now. They were out of time!

In her ear she heard Bear's southern drawl. "In position?"

Only six feet from her quarry, she breathed into her mic. "Yes."

Will and Doyle likewise affirmed they were ready.

"Go," Bear whispered.

They'd argued over the next step. As an aikido practitioner, she shouldn't respond until attacked—that was the aikido way of peaceful resolution. But Bear reasoned they'd been assaulted back in France and their opponents had Avril, so force was appropriate. His marine training called for a knife across the neck to ensure silence; she'd tried to convince him a kick in the knee would suffice.

Using the compromise commando move they'd agreed upon, she slid up behind her bearded opponent and palm-slapped him on both temples.

It worked. He dropped to the floor without a sound. Those pressure points were sensitive and she prayed she'd not just killed him.

Before she could check his breathing, stuff a glove in his mouth, hogtie him, or grab his gun, yelling and gunshots erupted in the middle of the cave.

Someone else's attack had not gone according to plan.

CHAPTER 86

Will swore.

As he'd jumped for his quarry, his foot had caught a rock near the edge of the fire pit. The movement made just enough sound that the man he'd been stalking had spun to face him while bringing the rifle to bear. The man had fired his semiautomatic, but by that point, Will was pressed up against the guard's chest.

The gun fired wildly and Will had no choice but to use his knife to slash under the ribcage and into the gunman's heart.

Will grabbed the automatic weapon from the fingers of the dead man and ran for the cover that had been illuminated by the man's flashlight. He figured Bear, Maddy, and Doyle had done their jobs better than he had, but that still left the two men near the wall. Plus Seymore and his helper, who had closed Avril inside the upper cave less than a minute before. Will needed to keep Seymore from using Avril as a shield.

Lights strobed the wall. His teammates must've recovered flashlights and were smartly using them to highlight the location of the attackers.

From behind the tapering column of a stalagmite, Will aimed his rifle and fired a quick burst at the four men. Seymore started to turn back toward the upper cave, but Will's bullets deterred him and he dove behind rocks. *There must be a rough stone staircase back there*, Will realized.

Three of Seymore's goons returned fire, and the stalagmite began to crumble. It was not made of stone, Will knew, but probably calcium carbonate. Definitely not on the same level as granite.

A bullet ripped across the side of his thigh. He fell to the floor, grasping his leg in pain.

Bear and Doyle released bursts of rounds toward the enemy. And Maddy? Will couldn't tell.

Suddenly, three men, with Seymore following, emerged from behind the rocks and made a push for the front of the cave.

Maddy shrieked. Had she been hit, too?

Feeling like an army grunt in the trenches, Will flattened onto his belly, ignoring the hot agony in his leg, and fired on the fleeing group. One man twisted and fell, bullets from his gun shredding the ceiling. Chunks fell like brimstone. Will ran out of ammunition and swore again, slamming his hand on the ground.

Seymore and two remaining enemy combatants disappeared. A second later, snowmobiles revved, and then the sound fell away.

His teammates rushed toward the entrance, guns continuing to blaze. Will tried to join them, but his leg hurt too much. He could barely put weight on it, but crawled as fast as he could to ensure the enemy he'd knifed was dead. There was no pulse. Will retrieved his sharp weapon of choice and stood, using the empty rifle as a crutch.

As he limped up the rough stone staircase, anxious to get to Avril, Doyle reappeared.

Alone.

Will panted, "Where are Maddy and Bear?"

CHAPTER 87

Breathless, Maddy rushed out of the cave just in time to see Seymore and a short attacker on one of the two front machines they'd had no time to sabotage.

She swore out loud and tried to strafe him with bullets from the stolen rifle, but it jammed. Throwing the useless metal aside, she prepared to fire a burst of lightning at him with her rings, but had to hit the ground when the minion on the other working snowmobile fired a volley of submachine gun bullets at her. She swore again as the impact jarred her injured shoulder. In the firefight inside the cave, a bullet had grazed her left deltoid, slightly behind and above her bicep. It hurt like the devil.

Seymore gunned his engine and the snowmobile disappeared over the cliff. Snow fountained into the air.

She clenched her fist and howled in frustration. He'd gotten away!

His minion followed, spraying bullets as he left.

It was either dumb luck the three men had chosen the working machines, or they'd had time to try them all while she was running for the entrance.

Bear arrived, pulling her up by the elbow. "C'mon!"

"What?"

"The skis!"

Could they catch Seymore on skis? Then what? But what the hell. Not only did Seymore have the medallion, she wanted to look him in the eyes and ask him about her mother.

She ran over to their discarded skis and shoved her boots' toes into the locking mechanisms, wishing again for proper downhill equipment. This would have to do. At her side, Bear did the same.

They grabbed the poles and shoved off.

The cliff was deep and steep, but no match for her experience with vertical runs, even with the stabbing pain in her left upper arm.

A full moon showed its silver face between two sets of moving clouds, briefly lighting up the landscape. Down the hill, on the far side of a row of houses, the helicopter's blades were beginning to turn.

There! She spotted the two snowmobiles, which had gotten stuck in the branches of a tree. Although the men were struggling to unhook the sled's front skis from the tangle, they were still too far away.

The man on the left looked up the hill and elbowed his teammate.

She and Bear had been seen!

The three jumped back on the machines and tore off.

The single-rider snowmobile made a beeline for the side of the mountain, where it was even steeper than the section she and Bear were skiing. That slope had to be at least forty-five degrees.

Why isn't he heading for the helicopter?

The machine skyrocketed up the steep cliff while she and Bear zoomed by. Their enemy was taking his snowmobile to the top side of the sheer face.

What's he doing?

A monstrous crack broke the night and, in horror, she understood. He'd started an avalanche. On purpose.

Maddy risked a glance behind her. One of her worst fears was coming true. The mountain was coming down on top of them.

Ahead, the remaining men—one had to be Seymore—zipped between the houses built into the hillside and drove his machine into the waiting maw of the helicopter. Seconds later, it slowly began to rise, like a fledgling getting its wings.

Bear subvocalized, "Crap, crap, crap!"

"No, the roof!"

He risked a glance at her and saw she was serious.

Behind them, the rumble of the avalanche was gaining in volume. She'd seen way too many good skiers perish in the kind of rolling, massive land tidal wave that was about to hit them. It was eating up trees and picking up steam as gravity took hold. She grimaced. The ground shook.

The helicopter rose higher.

Tucked into the mountain was a house whose roof seamlessly connected to the snowy hill. She aimed for the rooftop, which to her, had transformed into a ski ramp. Next to her, Bear hit it at the same time. They both launched into the air and, after hanging a long two beats, caught the helicopter's skids, one on each side of the flying beast.

Her shoulder screamed in protest. She ignored the pain and swung her good arm up and over the skid for a better grip.

The roaring avalanche was nearly on top of them.

CHAPTER 88

Avril shrieked Will's name from inside the pitch-black geode. She couldn't see her arms, but she knew they were bleeding. In the end, Seymore had taken no pleasure in killing her. With something akin to sadness in his good eye, he'd pushed the sleeves of her jacket up to her elbows and sliced the flesh on the outside of both her arms, saying orders were orders and she'd bleed out soon if she didn't run out of oxygen first.

Yet, she'd heard gunshots, and hope swelled in her chest. Was Will out there to rescue her?

She was already dizzy. With her hands tied, the only way to apply pressure to the wounds was to put her arms between her legs, but there was no good place to sit. Tears rolled down her cheeks as she slipped to an uncomfortable seated position and tried to staunch the bleeding.

"I am up here!"

"Avril! Hold on!"

Her heart did double flips. It *was* Will! Relief rolled over her like a wave. She closed her eyes and exhaled.

Boots scraped on rocks outside, and then the large round rock was rolled aside. Light from Will's flashlight burst into the geode, setting the cavern alight like it was covered in purple sparklers.

She pushed herself up and into Will's arms. She sobbed like a child, not worried what he thought of her tears. He stroked her hair and told her it would all be okay now. She wished it were true, but at least she'd live long enough to go to an orphanage. *Just stay in the present for now. At the moment I'm safe.*

He broke the spell, pushing her away and grabbing her arms. "You're bleeding!"

She ignored the comment, focusing on the bigger threat. "Are they gone?"

Will cut the ties on her hands, took off his jacket and shirt, ripped his top in half, and began to wrap her arms with the rags. "Mostly. Dead or tied up."

She looked into his green eyes. "Mostly?"

"Seymore and one of his team are trying to get away in a helicopter. Maddy and Bear went after them. Doyle is stalking one other."

She took a deep breath. Having overheard a few of the twins' conversations, this was going to be difficult for him. "She should know—you should both know—what he told me."

He finished wrapping the makeshift bandages. "What did he say?"

A loud crack came from outside the cave.

"That one crazy eye of his rolled around in his head." She paused. The rest was hard to say, but she spit it out. "He said he killed my grandmother in that icy accident. 'Brakes don't work well without fluid.'"

Will took a step back as if he'd been struck. Color drained from his face. "You're right. I need to radio Maddy."

"Will, wait. I also saw the formula on the medallion before he tucked it into his pocket. Maybe it will help her bring him down."

CHAPTER 89

8:22 P.M.

Inside the helicopter, Seymore jumped off the snowmobile; his minion did the same. He yelled to the pilot, "Go! Go!"

The avalanche that his other henchman had started was bearing down on them, along with two stubborn members of the VanOps team.

The helicopter's rotors roared as the bird rose slowly in preparation for takeoff.

Wong held his hand out. "What did you find up there?"

Seymore panted. "Nothing."

Wong pointed to the gold chain dangling out of Seymore's pocket. "Oh? What's that?"

Seymore whipped his gun out and shot Wong twice before his pistol clicked empty.

The bullets flew into the general's chest and pushed him backward, into the side of the helo. But Wong bounced off the wall, reaching for a weapon.

How is that possible? Seymore thought. *Is he wearing body armor?*

Before Seymore could react, Raphael ran forward and drove his head into Wong's gut. Wong grunted, hammering the other man in the neck. They collapsed to the floor, fists flying.

Seymore ran over to join the fight. The old dog needed to be put down.

As he arrived, Wong kneed his other attacker in the groin. Raphael fell backward, screaming and clutching his privates.

Seymore aimed a kick at the general's face.

Wong twisted his head at the last possible instant. Quick as a snake, he reached out and grabbed Seymore's ankle, yanking hard. The younger man fell to the floor and rolled, feeling the tug on his pants as the general snared the medallion from his pocket.

Tumbling toward the snowmobile, Seymore tried to stop his momentum by throwing his arms out to the sides. The sharp tip of the snowmachine's ski caught him in the diaphragm and the breath left his body in a whoosh.

His gut lurched as the helicopter launched into the sky.

CHAPTER 90

T he roar of the rising helicopter combined with the sound of the approaching avalanche stopped Maddy from hearing the rest of Will's radio transmission.

An icy accident was her last thought before the slide shuddered beneath the helo. The force of the snow-tsunami ripped the skis right off her toes as she clung to the rising metal bird.

That was close. Another two feet and the avalanche would have grabbed her legs and tossed her into the whirling maelstrom. Good thing they hadn't had actual downhill skis with locking boots after all.

As the helicopter rose further into the night, Bear wrapped his de-skied legs around the skid and pushed himself up, preparing to attack the cabin.

Maddy wanted to follow suit, but her arms trembled with the exertion of simply holding on. Her left index finger twitched aggressively and her wounded left shoulder screamed its displeasure as wind buffeted her body.

And she was in shock, trying to figure things out.

Will had said the formula on the medallion was *Know Thyself. Know Others.* What the hell did that mean?

An icy accident was familiar to her, but not to Avril. Yet . . . Seymore had mentioned it to her, saying her grandmother had been involved. What were the odds?

What if Avril's necklace from her grandmother was not a tiger, but a lion, just as the old acupuncturist had claimed? A lion from a French operative named Leo.

The icy accident that happened to Avril's grandmother had also happened to someone Maddy loved.

It didn't take a genius.

Avril's grandmother was Maddy's mom. Wow. *Holy of all holies.*

Maddy's mother had left a child behind, the report had spelled that out, and Maddy had never considered that haunted love child might be Avril's mother.

Which meant Avril was Maddy's niece.

It was a lot to take in. She shook her head. Her trembling arms felt like gelatin. She had to get into that helicopter. Bear's boots disappeared inside.

Somehow, she managed to wrap her legs around the skid.

However, that was as far as she got. She was stuck. A memory came to her. She was hanging on a jungle gym like she was now, her arms aching, the blue water of Lake Tahoe in the near distance behind the park. Her mom was on a bench, watching her play. Maddy tried to pull herself up and fell, landing on her backside in the sand. She'd cried. Mom came over and kissed her on the forehead. "It's okay. If at first you don't succeed, try, try again."

Maddy had smiled through her tears at her mom, her heart full of golden light, and jumped back up and tried again. It had taken three tries, but she'd succeeded and her mom had clapped, cheering her on.

Where was her mom now?

Maddy looked down. The helicopter was over the ocean, increasing in altitude. There was no soft sand below. That water would feel like concrete if she fell. Was it her day to die?

She closed her eyes, holding onto the feeling in her heart as tightly as she gripped the helicopter skid. That golden feeling that everything was right with the world. It had been so long since she'd felt it. Felt like her mom loved her.

A tear fell from her eye and was ripped away by the wind. All that love had been taken away in an icy crime, thanks to the men who sat in the helicopter above her at this very moment.

She'd been right all along. It had been murder. Anger surged through her veins.

Sounds of a struggle drifted out the open doors. Bear had found Seymore.

She ached to help him, but still, she could not will her arms to push her up. Her mind spun on the medallion's message. The formula. *Know thyself. Know others.* Knowing the future wouldn't do her any good if she perished in the ocean below. However, if Maddy died today, she had no doubt her mom's spirit would greet her like Bear's father had greeted him.

In a heartbeat, everything flipped.

Know thyself.

The flash of understanding nearly blinded her. Nostradamus had indeed been talking about souls. She didn't *have* a soul. She *was* one. She'd always thought she was her body, but if she was killed today, the essence of who she was would survive. She was a timeless soul.

The insight made her head spin.

Know others. Everyone was a soul, not just her. Bear. His father. Her mother. They were each drops of water in an ocean of bliss. A sea of infinite knowledge. Knowledge of the future even.

A vision came to her. If she failed in this mission, China would attack Taiwan. She could see the beachhead landing and the bloody fighting in the streets. Russia would stand by China with their warplanes and battleships, while the US and her allies fought to protect their foothold in the South China Sea. Battles begun on land and sea would end in a blinding flash and a mushroom cloud. She wouldn't allow that. Not out of responsibility, but because it was her honor to serve the greater good.

Maddy's eyes flew open, staring through the underbelly of the helo. Her breath quickened.

The strength of that interconnected web of souls washed through her. It was time to try again.

With a martial arts shout from deep in her belly, Maddy ground her teeth against the pain, pulled herself up, twisted around, and got a hand on the floor of the helicopter's cabin. She struggled into the section behind the cockpit and crouched there, gasping for air.

To her left, the pilot operated the controls, an aluminum board on his knee. In front of her, Bear fought Seymore, taking a punch to the gut before returning the jab with a hook to the face. Another man lay nearby, unconscious.

To her right, about ten feet back, a man wearing a creepy theater mask sat in a jump seat along the wall. In one hand, he twirled a palm-sized bronze medallion on a gold chain. In the other, he held a semiautomatic, trained on her chest.

The gun was problematic, but Maddy was far more concerned about what the formula would accomplish in the wrong hands. In *his* hands, doomsday would fall upon the planet in a matter of days.

"Who are you?" she yelled, over the wind.

"I'm the master behind the puppets," he answered with an Asian accent.

Hot anger spread like lava across her face. "You ordered my mom's death."

In response, he aimed his weapon at her chest.

She took a deep breath, *listened*, and focused her power in her heart, ready to use her hands. Time slowed down. The whir of the helicopter rotors was deafening. His finger tugged at the trigger. Pointing her hands like imaginary guns, she sent energy out through the lorandite rings, letting loose a stream of light aimed at his pistol. There was a brief flash as the lightning struck the metal. The gun jerked up, fired into the ceiling, and fell to the floor with a clatter.

He stood, drew a silver blade from a jeweled sheath at his belt, and assumed a fighting stance.

By the way he moved, she could tell he also had martial arts training, and in that moment, she remembered he was like her on some level. Her anger fled. She didn't want to kill him. But he had to be stopped.

He came in high with the blade, but she pushed up and halted his right elbow with a *tanto-tori*, knife-taking move. Continuing the motion, she grabbed his elbow and wrist, and stepped aside, attempting to throw his body to the floor and pin his arm. He was too clever, though, and rolled forward, breaking her grasp. He came up in a crouch and threw off his tricolored mask.

She got the impression of baggy eyes, large ears, white, combed-back hair, and a flabby, clean-shaven face. There was no time to get a better look at him because he shifted the knife to his left hand, whipped the medallion in his right, and came at her with a snarl.

Blue lightning flared from her outstretched fingers. She intended it as a warning shot: a jolt equivalent to sticking a finger in an electrical socket. However, her index finger chose that moment to twitch and her volley went wide, instead hitting the side of the helicopter. She swore under her breath.

He shook his head, lowered his shoulder, and charged.

She entered his space from the left, turning. Immediately, she struck his front knife hand with her handblade, then grabbed his palm, and continued to pivot. The movement forced his wrist around, pushing the silver dagger into the air. The medallion in his other hand stopped spinning. She went for a *hiji-shime* elbow lock but he pulled away, knocking the blade against the ceiling and dropping the knife in the process. She kicked the antique dagger through the open door, getting a glimpse of the black ocean far below.

Fury filled his eyes. "That was mine."

She saw his lunge a split second before it happened, giving her time to evade. He thrust his entire body toward her. Stepping aside, she sprang for the cockpit, and shot a beam of lightning at his torso to immobilize him. Frozen for an instant, his eyes flashed wide and his impotent hands grasped only empty air. His momentum caused him to fly through the door like a baseball player going for home plate. In what seemed to be slow motion, he twisted to look back at her and a film-worthy Wilhelm scream escaped his lips.

In a last act of defiance, he threw the medallion into the tail rotor. The helo immediately began to wobble.

Bear threw a knockout punch to Seymore, who fell to all fours next to his follower.

The helicopter dipped to the side. Maddy grabbed the back of the copilot's seat as Seymore and his minion slid toward the open door. She reached for them, but they plummeted over the edge. The pilot's silver kneeboard clattered to the floor and swooshed out, following her mother's killer and rocketing into the damaged tail rotor.

The helicopter's wobble turned into a slow spin that picked up speed by the second. Bear pulled the pilot out of his seat and tossed him toward the back.

Grabbing the parachute from the copilot's seat, Bear threw it at her, and grabbed one for himself. "Put it on!"

She thrust her arms into the straps, clipped it on, and leaped headfirst away from the dying bird, Bear at her side.

While they were still diving toward the water far below, the helo exploded. A thunderous boom crashed through the air, and searing gold and crimson fireworks lit the night sky.

CHAPTER 91

Watching the fiery explosion over the Gulf of Corinth, Will sucked in his breath. Had Maddy and Bear just been blown to bits?

Avril stood between Will and Doyle, holding each of their hands with her roughly bandaged forearms. Will squeezed her fingers before dropping them. He needed both hands to steady his binoculars because his own digits were trembling.

Doyle asked, "What do you see, Will?"

"It's dark as sin except for the exploding helicopter."

"Oh no!" Avril said. "Are you sure they were on it?"

"Unfortunately, pretty sure," Will answered.

Earlier, there'd been the telltale thump of chopper blades bleeding into the connection when he'd radioed Maddy. Every attempt after had brought only radio silence. He patted the radio, unsure if the information had done his sister any good, but he'd known it was essential that she hear what Avril revealed.

Avril's grandmother, Sébastien's wife, hadn't drowned. Like many good operatives, Mary Louise Marshall had pretended to die, eventually relocating to Lake Tahoe.

Taking his grip off the thermal-imaging binocs for a second, Will put his hand on Avril's shoulder. She was his niece. The thought pleased him, and his jaded heart. When he'd seen that she was alive, relief had washed over him like a warm blanket. The feeling was short-lived, however, once he realized that Maddy and Bear were still in harm's way.

At least Will's party was under no further threat. The man who had caused the avalanche had been swept up in the slide, and all the attackers in the cave were dead. But he wouldn't relax until he knew what had become of his sister and Bear.

Will muttered, "Where are they?"

He tapped his foot, and then stopped when the movement caused his thigh to burn like the sun. Instead, he tapped his fingers on the binocs. It had been too long. The odds of them surviving without a chute were one in a million. Or less.

Just as he started to move the binoculars from his eyes, he caught movement near the water. Two puffs of white fluttered toward the sea and splashed down.

"Yes!" he yelled, pumping his fist. "It has to be them."

Doyle burst his balloon. "What if it's Seymore? Even if it is them, that water must be ice cold. How long will they last before hypothermia sets in?"

"Guess Jags had better get the Greek Coast Guard out there to see. Pronto."

CHAPTER 92

Two days after the water rescue, Maddy and Bear nestled under the covers in their bedroom back home, the bandage on her arm as white as the sheets. In the predawn light, a gas fireplace gave the room a warm ambience.

Bear, however, was giving her a cold shoulder, lying on his side and facing the window. Wide awake due to the time change, she could tell from his breathing that he was done sleeping, too.

She poked him in the ribs. "Hey."

"Umm."

"What's going on? It's a happy day. Mission accomplished. We're home safe with a new member of the family."

He rolled onto his back. "That's just it."

"What?"

"I'd really like a new family member. Or two. I love AJ, don't get me wrong."

"But . . ."

"I want little ones running around. I'd like to make children with you, and I worry . . ."

Was he really going to say he wanted her safe? Nevertheless, she asked, "About what?"

He looked away. "That you don't really love me."

Her heart melted. She put a hand on his chest. "It's not that at all. I'm just not ready."

His blue eyes connected with hers in the firelight. "Are you sure?"

"Yes," she said softly. "I adore you."

"Good. So, what's the 'not ready' part?"

"I'm really enjoying our work with VanOps. And don't think I could raise an infant and be an effective operative at the same time."

His face fell. "I see."

"But our missions take a physical toll. VanOps won't last forever."

He raised an eyebrow, an impish look returning. "What's it look like inside your crystal ball?"

"We tromp around the world, saving it, for a few years. *Then* we make babies."

"Really?" His squeak sounded as high-pitched as AJ's.

"Yes."

He blew out a big puff of air. "Okay. Okay, that's good. I can live with that."

He threw his arms around her and kissed her with a passion that soon had her melting.

For a moment, she flashed on the image of her mom's skeletal postcard and its injunction to remember death. The next mission would be here soon enough, and might take their lives. Even though she could see the most likely future, there were an infinite number of possible outcomes.

In the meantime, living in the present moment was *far* more satisfying.

Later, after breakfast, they all moved into the living room to be near the woodstove, and gathered on the couches and chairs around it. It was a sunny but cold California morning and the heat drew them in. Except AJ and Avril, who were impervious to the chill as they played with Damien in the yard.

Maddy, Bear, and Will sat on the couch. Deana had just flown back to DC so Jags was sipping coffee in a rocker alone. Doyle was looking at his phone in the leather arm chair. Will was focused on his harmonica, puffing random notes as if he were testing to see if it were in tune.

After a minute, her brother put the harmonica aside and looked at Maddy. "What do you make of the formula on the medallion?"

"I think we were both wrong all along."

"Oh?"

"Although either might help with a trance state, it wasn't solely about herbs, or meditation."

"What do you think then?"

"Well, the Oracle proclaimed it on a temple, and Nostradamus figured out the rest. *Know Thyself. Know Others.* It's about identity."

Will sat back in the couch and crossed his arms. "I don't get it."

"We're not just our physical forms. We are souls who have bodies, not the other way around."

His eyes narrowed. "How is that a formula?"

"It's a method. A signpost. Instructions. By knowing our true nature, and seeing the spark inside everyone else, we can realize that we're part of the Absolute, as the CIA called it."

Bear's eyes lit up. "I get it. All the world's souls are like tiny points of interconnected light—a golden web shining as bright as the sun."

She smiled at him. "Exactly. And those connections allow for information sharing. Information such as likely future scenarios. We just need to quiet our minds and take the time to connect."

Will's expression still held a note of the skeptical, but that was his nature. He'd figure it out someday.

A text came into Maddy's phone. She glanced at it.

"Sorry to interrupt, but it's official." She glanced at her twin. "Will, you and I both lost out in the bid for Aunt Carole. She wants to spend time with Bella and her kids."

Will uncrossed his arms, stretched out his long legs, and put his feet on the coffee table. "I suppose it's for the best."

Maddy agreed. It seemed Will was wanting a truce, and so was she. Maybe now he'd stop bugging her about controlling her dreams and they could finally lay the ghost of their mother to rest.

Her phone pinged again. Bella had sent a photo of an envelope, along with a short burst of text.

"What the hell?"

"Now what?" Will asked.

Bear peered over her shoulder. "What is it, darlin'?"

"Aunt Carole was going through some papers, getting ready to move, and found a sealed envelope from Mom to be given to us when Aunt Carole died. Bella said it feels like there's something heavy inside, and she also got an envelope holding a safety-deposit box key."

Will thrummed his fingers on the side of the couch. "Aunt Carole isn't dead yet."

Maddy waved him off. "She decided with her stroke she was close enough to dead that it was time we had it."

"Tell Bella to open it."

Maddy relayed the message and held her breath until the next text came through. "It's a key. Fremont Savings and Trust. Bella's key has a different box number."

Will looked at his Rolex. "It'll have to wait until tomorrow."

Maddy groaned. She wanted to know now.

Doyle interrupted her train of thought. "Speaking of family, I got this great video from my grandparents last night. Want to see it?"

They all nodded.

Doyle pulled the armchair close as they all gathered around. He swiped the screen on his smartphone. "I've got the volume turned down, as I'm guessing none of you speak Taiwanese."

Doyle's grandfather waved the front page of a newspaper at the screen. Maddy figured the large headlines were about the Chinese withdrawal from the Pratas Islands. Their wide grins and happy eyes spoke volumes, but Maddy still wanted to know what his grandparents were saying. "Will you translate?"

"Of course. My grandmother says that today is a special day. She has put away her sharpest knife and hopes to never have to pull it from the kitchen again. She says it's for carving chickens, not people, and is very happy to not have had to take out many Chinese soldiers."

Doyle chuckled and they all laughed with him.

Will flicked his wrist and a blade appeared in his hands. "I wouldn't want to take her on." He sheathed the knife.

"Nor would I," Jags said. "You're lucky to have her, Doyle."

He put the phone away. "I am indeed."

Jags looked at her watch. "Seems the director is calling. Shall we head downstairs?"

As they headed for Control Room West, Maddy asked, "Think he's going to interrupt another celebration with a new mission?"

Jags turned on the lights. "Hard to say."

Once they were sitting around the large monitors, the director's image appeared on the center screen. He looked relaxed in an eggplant-colored cashmere sweater.

"Another VanOps mission is in the books. Avril is safe and China has backed off Pratas Island." Bowman smiled. "Based on the enemy knowing our moves after I met you in Maastricht, we identified an audio bug on my jacket, and are using it to feed disinformation back to the Chinese."

Maddy and Will exchanged a glance. There was no other mole. She took a deep breath and relaxed.

Bowman continued. "Between that, not knowing how'd we respond to their invasion, and without General Wong, who died over the Mediterranean in a helicopter accident, they lacked the fortitude to invade Taiwan. Congratulations."

They gave each other high fives.

"Actually, I take that back," the director continued. "You've wrapped up two missions: Codename Hourglass is laid to rest as well." He looked at Will and Maddy. "I hope your mother can rest in peace now."

"Thank you," Will said. "Her legacy lives on in Avril. It turned out we're related. Maddy and I are her aunt and uncle."

The director nodded slowly. "I wondered what became of the French love child. She had a daughter. Did you ever find out how Avril was able to prophesize that invasion?"

"Not yet. I plan to ask her about it when we're done here."

"Keep me posted. Perhaps you can visit her now and again," Bowman said. "Nice to know you are family. I do wish you'd brought back that medallion, though. Bear, what happened?"

"Wong threw it into the rotor, sir. That's why we ended up in the Med, dripping wet."

"It's too bad. I'd love to know what our enemies will be up to next."

Maddy thought again about the formula Nostradamus had spelled out on the medallion. The CIA had figured it out once before. Although infinite knowledge was there for everyone, she wasn't sure the government needed a reminder.

Instead, she replied to the director's unspoken question. "I can tell you our enemies' plans."

"Oh?"

"They'll be vying for world domination, trying to destroy democracy, and using every tool at their disposal to sow discord at home and abroad."

"You're a smartass." He chuckled. "But I think you're right. And no oracle required. Now go have a proper celebration."

Upstairs, they interrupted AJ and Avril playing a video game.

"Hey," Maddy called. "Why don't you guys join us?"

The kids frowned at each other and reluctantly put the game to sleep. Avril pounced on the couch next to Bear, and AJ sat at Maddy's feet, leaning back into the sofa.

Will stood next to the woodstove. "Avril, I think now is a good time to tell you about your grandmother and our mother."

Now that she knew they were related, Maddy saw the resemblance between the three of them. She and Avril had full lips. Will and Avril shared their mom's aristocratic nose.

As Will summarized what they'd figured out, Avril's fingers found her necklace, and twisted the lion's head round and round. Her grandmother had been an operative codenamed Leo, hunted by Seymore at the request of General Wong. Leo had fallen in love with Avril's grandfather, and accidentally had a baby, Avril's mom. When the mission had been exposed, there'd been no choice but to leave the child, but Leo kept an eye out as best she could, as evidenced by the postcard and testimony Bella had recently dragged out of Aunt Carole. Once back in the States, Leo, their mother, had married the twins' father, and been killed eight years later when Seymore had tampered with the brakes on an ice-cold Tahoe day.

AJ looked between the members of the gathered group. "We're related?"

"That's right, AJ," Will replied. "You're cousins."

AJ gave Avril a huge grin. "Right on!"

Will looked at Avril through his long lashes. "On your dad's side, though, is the blood of Nostradamus. Why don't you finally tell us how you foretold the Chinese invasion of Taiwan?"

Avril pulled her legs up to her chest. "Do I have to?" She suddenly looked younger than her sixteen years.

"Yes," Will replied. "It was part of the deal to let you come with us."

Avril looked at each adult in turn, as if hoping for a pass.

None came.

She bit her fingernail.

AJ reached over and tugged her toe. "C'mon. How'd you do it?"

"Fine," Avril said. "I had a dream about the ice cave where purple ice surrounded a dying world, which nearly came true, at least for my world." She chewed her lower lip, then blurted, "But for the invasion, I used an AI program, all right?"

The sudden silence in the living room left Maddy feeling like she'd been slapped by a wet towel. "AI? You used artificial intelligence to predict that invasion?"

Avril hung her head. "I did. I wanted the kids at my new school to like me, and decided to pretend to be a seer, like Nostradamus."

The silence continued.

"One of the cute boys was from Taiwan. And I saw a headline . . ." She trailed off.

It seemed everyone took a deep breath. They'd probably all done something foolish for love.

"Anyway"—Avril picked her head up and jutted her chin out—"there are some very cool AI programs out there. I just cross-referenced ten of them."

Maddy raised an eyebrow. "I know of a few. Still, that's impressive."

Avril hugged her knees tight. Her voice started to tremble. "I suppose this means I will be sent back to France. To an orphanage."

Before Maddy could get around Bear to comfort Avril, Will sat down next to the girl on the arm of the couch. He put a hand on her slender shoulder. "Whoa. Actually, I've got a surprise. We're your kin, but I found someone closer to you. How would you like to live with your mom?"

Another thunderclap of silence ensued.

Avril jerked away. "What do you mean? She is dead."

He nodded. "When your grandfather told us your mother was lost, I also assumed she had died. But when we met your grandfather, Maddy found a sample of hair in your room and we sent it off to the lab. I looked at the DNA results and had the team run a report for relatives." His eyes lit up. "Your mom, Caroline Durand, is alive. We spoke earlier today. After the fire happened, she was brokenhearted and horribly guilt-stricken. She disappeared, and lived on the streets in Spain for a time, drinking too much. There was a brush with the law, which is why her DNA was on file, but a few years ago she got sober."

Maddy's eyes got misty, realizing she was about to gain a half sister and, even better, Avril was getting her mom back.

Avril looked at Will intently, her accent thick with emotion. "You are not jesting? This is for real?"

"Yes, it's real."

Avril stood up and threw her arms around Will's neck, crying. Clearly the two had bonded. Maddy hadn't thought Will had a fatherly bone in his body, but she was obviously wrong.

After a minute, Avril peeled herself away and sat down. A cloud passed over her eyes. "I am excited, but I don't know. I might be a little mad at her too."

Will patted Avril on the knee. "That's understandable. And you can stay with us while you get to know her if you want."

The worry left Avril's expression. "Thanks. It will probably be fine. I just don't know her at all."

"I learned she's been working as a teacher in Lyon. Maybe we even saw her in the library. She said she'd thought constantly about reaching out to you but couldn't bring herself to do it. She feared you wouldn't want to know her. When I told her your father and grandfather were dead, she immediately said she hoped you'd forgive her and would come live with her."

Avril's smile was as wide as the moon. "Wow. She wants me?"

"She does," Will replied, whipping out his harmonica and playing a quick happy jig. He put it away and added, "And as your favorite uncle, I'll pay for that surgery you want. You can start over."

She put a hand to her neck. "I realized in the cave, when I thought I was going to die, that it's okay. At the time, I realized the scars were all I had left of her. I am more than this body anyway. Anyone who doesn't see that can go to hell."

Will's eyes rose in surprise, but he soon smiled. "As you like. Instead, how about we get your gecko back and buy him a girlfriend?"

Avril's face lit up. "That would be fantastic."

"Great. We'll fly to meet your mom next week. In the meantime, you can spend time here with your cousin."

"Really?" AJ squeaked.

Will ruffled AJ's red mop. "That's right, little man."

Everyone chuckled, but Maddy could see they all had tears in their eyes. She wiped one away with a thumb. Two ends of time, frayed and separated by decades, were now neatly tied. Somewhere, her mom's heart, like hers, was bursting with joy.

EPILOGUE

Maddy, Bear, and Will walked into the stark lobby of the bank the instant it opened. While her stomach performed anxious flip-flops, she went through the solemn ritual of handing the key to the manager with her noninjured right arm, watching while he inspected it, and then followed him through an electronically sealed door and into the vault. The storeroom was lined with look-alike bronze safety-deposit boxes.

The manager, a youngish but chinless man with gold-rimmed glasses and a paunch, put his master key into the lock on box 369, and Maddy inserted her key into the other keyhole. The lock released with a click. He removed a narrow metal box and laid it on a stainless-steel table in the center of the room.

Manager Brown nodded his head deferentially. "I'll give you some privacy."

They waited until he was out of sight.

Maddy said, "I'm nervous."

Will stroked the scar on his chin. "Just open it."

She pulled open the long lid. Inside was an electronic contraption. It took her a second to recognize it. "Is that what I think it is?"

Will picked it up and examined it. "I think it's a Walkman."

Bear laughed. "I remember my mom listening to music on one of those."

Will flipped open the battery compartment. "She was smart. Didn't leave batteries inside. They'd have corroded by now."

Bear peered over Will's shoulder. "What's it take?"

"Looks like two AA batteries."

Maddy put her hands on her hips. "We don't have any."

Will pulled the flashlight off his belt. "Oh yes we do."

Her Boy Scout brother proceeded to remove the batteries from one device and install them in the other. He handed her the unit. "Play it."

"But we can't all hear it."

"It won't self-destruct. I can check it out later. For now, you listen and tell us what it says."

After Bear nodded his agreement, Maddy put the old-style wired headphones over the top of her head and, with her heart beating like hooves pounding across a great prairie, pressed the play button.

Her mom's voice came through clearly. "My dearest Will and Maddy . . ."

Maddy stopped the cassette, her eyes welling with tears, and she turned away to take a moment to collect herself. She dabbed the moisture from her eyes, and took a deep breath before turning and pressing play once more.

"I hesitate to commit these words to tape," her mother said, "but I have seen the future. Much frightens me, but I suspect the world has escaped an apocalypse thanks to your bravery. I have reason to believe my time in this body is limited, so I've asked your aunt to hide the key to this box for me. Just in case.

"Please do not share this message with Bella. Her path in this lifetime is different than yours, and I've left her with a worldlier heirloom, one she will appreciate.

"You probably know this, but perhaps my confession will fill in some blanks. Before you were born, I was involved in covert operations work in France. There, I had an unplanned child, your half sister, who I was forced to leave behind for her safety when I returned to the States. She knows nothing of you. Her name is Caroline. I hope you'll find and embrace her as part of our family.

"When I got pregnant, I married Sébastien Chirac, the baby's father. I always believed he tipped me off to the enemy, so didn't feel bad convincing him I drowned myself. Your father was the true love of my life.

"The reason I was in France is classified, but you may be able to learn more through a Freedom of Information Act request. Ask about Codename Hourglass.

"Suffice it to say that I found what I was seeking, but felt our government would not have used the information for a worthy purpose. I've seen too much of what blue-suited men will do for power, or money. Stopping hearts at a distance was only the beginning. The two of you, my bright and shiny children, *will* use the secrets wisely, and for the good of mankind. This I know in the deepest part of my heart.

"The family of Nostradamus, in Saint-Rémy, France, possesses a medieval walnut box passed down through generations in the seer's family. I made friends with them during my time there. I learned everything I could of the seer, including his handwriting and the type of paper available to him during his life. Inside the box's hidden compartments, I left clues that appear to come from the prophet while they let me study it."

Maddy's eyes grew wide at her mom's trickery and she made a shocked face at Will and Bear. They motioned for her to finish listening.

"I believe you have solved, or will solve, the riddle to learn the most powerful secret of the ages. It is your true inheritance. The mysteries you'll find do not belong to me or to Nostradamus. He discovered them on his journeys, and I uncovered them while walking in his footsteps. They are as old as mankind, and are woven in plain sight through the threads of all religions and spiritual paths.

"Yet, even with the knowledge of eternity, the ties of the world remain strong. I wept when I wrote this and my voice breaks now while I read it. It's hard to leave you behind. Never doubt that I love you dearly."

At those words, Maddy's heart burst open.

"Finally, I must beg you to be wary. Do not repeat my mistakes. Whatever career you choose, please do not work for the government in a covert capacity. I trust your lionhearted courage will make you want to continue listening as I explain why . . ."

AUTHOR'S NOTE

Dear reader,

First let's separate fact from fiction.

The quatrain about the French Revolution and the prediction Nostradamus made of his own death are rendered accurately.

As described by Henri Seymore, Nostradamus's predictions of the death of Henry II, the Great Fire of London, Napoleon's conquest, the discoveries of Louis Pasteur, Hitler's rule, and Charles de Gaulle's reign were called out as "shockingly accurate" in a *Business Insider* article from 2014. That article included a quatrain that had de Gaulle's name in it.

The five quatrains in this novel, although similar in style to what Nostradamus wrote, are fictional.

This quote from 1555's *The Treatise of Cosmetics and Jams* is real: *After my having spent the greater part of my youthful years . . . in pharmacy, and in the knowledge and understanding of medicinal herbs, I moved through a number of lands and countries from 1521 to 1529, constantly in search of the understanding and knowledge of the sources and origins of plants and other medicinal herbs—(exploring) medicine's very frontiers.*

It's true that the last fifty-eight quatrains of the seventh "century" have not survived in any known edition.

The part about Nostradamus studying in Moldova is fictional.

The Orus Apollo, French manuscript No. 2594, does exist in the Lyon library and is a translation about hieroglyphs by Nostradamus in his own hand.

He did devise a method of hiding his meanings by using word games like anagrams, and a mix of other languages, such as Italian, Greek, Latin, and Provençal.

It's also true that the seer had a walnut box that he passed on to his daughter. No one knew what was inside.

STARGATE and the psychic programs the CIA ran in the seventies are well documented, including the CIA's Gateway report on astral projection that was declassified in 1983, but without page 25. They were studying and practicing remote viewing, remote killing, and experimental drugs like LSD, while trying to weaponize parapsychology. The lost plane found in Central America is factual. The Monroe Institute still offers the Gateway program, similar to the modules the CIA operatives studied, to achieve out-of-body experiences on demand. The much-speculated-about page 25 from that report was made public by the Monroe Institute in the spring of 2021 and was published by Vice.com on April 8. Their take on the Absolute is fascinating reading and inspired parts of this novel. My fictional organization, VanOps, was born out of my interest in these types of programs where east meets west and science meets spirituality. Project Hourglass is a fabrication.

Although Alpine Meadows has a double-black-diamond run named Keyhole, I made up some of the details to fit the story.

According to Olive-Drab.com, an online resource for all things military, the C-23A Sherpa entered service with the United States Air Force in Europe in 1985 and was based at Zweibrücken Air Base. It remained in use until November 1990. At that time, all the Sherpas returned to the United States, meaning the one in Chapter 7 would probably not be found in present-day France.

Bear spoke the truth about ancient locks. The Romans had combination versions, and there are a couple that Muhammad al-Astrulabi made around AD 1200 in museums in Copenhagen and Boston.

The information presented regarding the past conflicts in the Chinese Civil War is as accurate as I can make it. According to the People's Liberation Army Press, the Communist military forces lost 1.3 million in the 1945–1949 phase of the war alone, but that number discounted irregulars. Nationalist casualties during the same time period were recorded after the war by the People's Republic of China at 5,452,700 regulars and 2,258,800 irregulars.

The tidbits about the peregrine falcons at the cathedral in Brussels are accurate.

The tomb of Charles, Duke of Lorraine, does exist in a crypt below the basilica, and the inscription above it is rendered accurately. The access to the crypt is from my imagination.

The superyacht taken from Italy to Greece was inspired by the *Miami*, built by designer Kurt Strand. He designed the ship after Hurricane Dorian's destruction of the Bahamas.

Acupuncture is a popular career for the blind in Japan.

If you're wondering about the veracity of parachuting from a helicopter, defense24.com reported that Poland recently ordered ten rescue parachutes for a series of helicopters, including the Mi-14 helo.

Sadly, in September of 2020, CNN reported that Chinese warplanes crossed the median line that separates the mainland and Taiwan almost forty times. Much conflict remains in the region at the time of publication, and my fervent hope is that this novel's description of the Chinese/Taiwanese conflict does not become prophetic.

Thanks for reading *The Doomsday Medallion*.

Lastly, are you curious about Maddy, Bear, and Will's next mission? To stay informed about my new releases, and get a behind-the-scenes look at my writing process, email me at Avanti@VanOps.net.

I have several other books available, two are earlier books in this series, and there's a forthcoming standalone novel that I hope you'll enjoy. All can be read separately, and are written in a similar way, with short chapters, global threats, and award-winning style.

Thank you for your kind reviews.

Avanti

ACKNOWLEDGMENTS

This book wouldn't have been possible without Aunt Kate's encouragement and support over the years. My mom's twin, and my "other mother," she's been an inspiration to me throughout my life and I'm pleased to dedicate this book to her.

As always, Michelle Ocken helped shape the earliest outline, brainstormed along the way, and is the unwavering president of my fan club. She deserves boatloads of appreciation.

The fingerprints of world-class editor Andrea Robinson are all over this book; she took the rough story and spun it into gold. Marianne Fox provided top-notch copyediting, polishing the manuscript to a fine sheen. Talented cover artist David Ter-Avanesyan patiently illustrated the story with a beautiful cover. My publishing house, Thunder Creek Press, does a fantastic job with formatting and distribution.

A special shout-out to Valérie Jacquot, who confirmed the first quatrain was correctly translated into French. No editor is perfect, and I'm ever grateful for the continuing contributions of my fantastic beta readers. Margaret Cambridge found several inconsistent plot points. John Bernstein filled me in on the interiors of C-17 cargo planes. Richard Davis made excellent suggestions about the thriller elements of the story. Ruth Thompson provided details about how to raise Fleck and Alexis Martin-Vegue suggested he be a leopard gecko. Kenneth Mitchell was helpful with the prose, especially Avril's French to English word choices. Joseph Harrison urged me to add background on the lorandite. Silvia Pascale provided a European point of view. Melissa, Brooke and Julie, made good suggestions and found some lingering typos. I wish I had space to name all my other friends, family, and readers who helped polish the book or get the word out.

The generosity of my fellow authors amazes me, and I'm deeply grateful for their kindness and support.

Finally, thanks to all the fans who encourage me to shoot for the moon. You're the best!

ABOUT THE AUTHOR

International multi-award–winning author who blends intrigue, history, science, and mystery into nonstop action thrillers

Avanti Centrae is honored to have won eight literary awards.

She finds inspiration from her father, who served as a US marine corporal in Okinawa, gathering military intelligence. Avanti graduated from Purdue University and has spent time in a spectrum of professions, from raft guide to Silicon Valley IT executive. When not traveling the world or hiking in the Sierra mountains, she's writing her next thriller in Northern California, helped by her family and distracted by her German shepherds.

If you'd like to hear about specials for her fans, such as giveaways and deleted scenes, you can visit her web page (http://www.avanticentrae.com). Drop her a line, or sign up for her quarterly-ish newsletter.

For more frequent updates, follow her on Facebook (www.facebook.com/avanticentrae), Twitter (@avanticentrae), or Instagram (www.instagram.com/avanti.centrae.author). Either way, let her know what you loved about *The Doomsday Medallion* and what you want more of in the series to come.